WILD ANIMUS

Rich Shapero

Outside
Reading

San Mateo, California

Outside Reading
P.O. Box 1565
San Mateo, CA 94401

Library of Congress Cataloging-in-Publication Data is available.

ISBN: 0-9718801-0-7

Cover art: François Burland
Cover design: Adde Russell

Printed in the United States of America

12 11 10 09 08   2 3 4 5 6

WILD
ANIMUS

Prologue

The Alaskan forest rose steadily, patched with muskegs and trenched by rivers. Ridges and crags broke through, and at the heads of valleys, glaciers appeared. Out of this confusion, Mt. Wrangell's giant white dome towered into the midday sky, icy curve glinting, a thousand blue hatches splitting its flanks as if something were stirring within. A storm was sweeping from the south, and in that quarter gray clouds cloaked the lowlands. The mountain's summit seemed smooth from a distance, broken only by a few points of rock. Closer, the rocks became the rims of three craters, and from the northernmost coils of steam rose. In human terms, the crater was huge—three-quarters of a mile across—dwarfing the yellow helicopter that circled above it.

The chopper tossed in the high winds. The rotor faltered and a downdraft sent it careening to the right, banking around a fumarole rising from the crater floor. Billows blew past the cockpit's curved glass. Inside, the engine's pulse was thunderous. A state trooper with a headset was speaking over the intercom to the pilot beside him.

"There's blood on his chest—"

The trooper choked as sulphur fumes invaded the cabin and the windows turned white. The intercom silence was broken by the sobs of a young woman behind them. Raising his arm to breathe through his coat sleeve, the trooper watched the pilot's hand tremble the collective. The pilot's feet were pedaling, fighting for control as they circled the steam. Again the rotor hesitated, the helicopter's nose dipped. When the pilot tried to master it, the machine bucked, instrument needles quivering. He glanced to the south. The tide of gray storm clouds was moving swiftly, obscuring forests and rocky spurs.

"Only a few minutes left," the pilot warned.

The trooper nodded. To remain longer would be fatal. The storm would seal over the lowlands, cutting off their retreat, and they'd be stranded on this white island, circling above it until their fuel ran out. "Miss?" He turned with a regretful expression.

Lindy Altman regarded him mutely, her cheeks washed with tears. Beneath the band of her headset, a star-shaped scar flamed from her hairline. Rescue paraphernalia was piled beside her. The windshield cleared as the chopper came around the fumarole. Her fingers found the pendant on her sternum, lifting it to her lips. She kissed it as she peered down. The crater's broken rim rose to rocky peaks in places, the snowy interior tumbled with ice and crossed by blue rifts. Seething solfatara rose from caves and pits, staining the snow lemon, and in a dozen places the crater's bowl was streaked with rusty ash. At the base of an obelisk of ice, on a steep white slope gleaming with refrozen meltwater, a figure lay twisted. His head was dark and strangely enlarged, and his chest was splashed with blood. One leg verged the funnel of a steam vent, and the white tatters of his legging, eaten by volcanic acids, were flapping in the winds.

Lindy stared through the glass, unprepared despite everything that had happened. The memories she had let crowd her mind vanished, and the last embers of hope in her eyes blinked out. The chopper lurched and her shoulders came forward, making a hollow of her chest. Her gaze was fixed on him, trying to say goodbye. Then a veil of mist intervened and all she could see was the point of the obelisk, shining and corniced with rime.

The pilot clenched his jaw and budged the collective, and the chopper lifted its nose to clear the crater rim. A sudden downdraft threatened to dash them against the rock. At the last moment, they were boosted on an upswell and passed over. Lindy could see the trail of prints leading to the cauldron, and she craned to keep his track in view until the waves of loose snow racing across the dome's summit obscured it.

In the buffets, she heard his voice—a frightening remembrance —his invocations heartfelt and frenzied with emotion.

They banked to the west and fell down the side of the dome, racing the advancing storm clouds. Crevasses glided beneath them, swathes of mist shearing past.

"Hang on," the pilot muttered. The intercom crackled like a foretoken of atmospherics to come. They hit a bump, rolled into a roil of gray cloud, then plunged through a tear and the vista blew open. "There's the Chetaslina," the trooper said with relief.

To Lindy, the dark spurs and rolling lowlands waiting below were like a world in ruins at the bottom of the sea.

The Ram

One

A canister hit the asphalt thirty feet from Sam Altman, and white smoke coiled from its top. Waking from his reverie, he came to a halt—a six-foot statue with shoulder-length hair, his oversized shirt billowing out of burgundy bell bottoms. He watched the smoke spread, face expressionless beneath a three-day stubble, listening, his gray-green eyes sharp and intense. The air was pulsing violently around him. Sam lifted his head and saw a drab helicopter hovering toward him like a giant insect, spotting him through the trees with glass eyes. The helicopter tipped its aureole and drummed over him, unknotting a scarf of white fog from its side. Sam turned to follow it, hearing the cries of alarm and seeing the panic behind him.

Hundreds of students were racing from all directions, converging on Sather Gate, trying to leave the Berkeley campus. In the courtyard below the Student Union, they were scattering toward the stores on Bancroft Way. On his right, they poured into Sproul Plaza, shouting and shielding their faces as they hurried past. Sam's eyes stung, his lids slitting reflexively. He drew a disbelieving breath and choked on it. Tear gas.

A month before, radicals had squatted on a university parking lot, laying sod and planting trees. They called it "People's Park." When the National Guard arrived to evict the squatters, demonstrations started. Now the government was retaliating. Facing forward, Sam joined the crowd leaving campus, laughing at the absurdity of his circumstance. He cared nothing for the Park or the radicals, or the belligerent reactions of California's governor. They were turning the university into a war zone, and somehow he'd landed in the middle of it.

His eyes seared suddenly. His lips scorched, and the air was like fire in his throat, as if he'd thrust his head in a furnace. The way forward blurred. He could discern moving bodies, bright areas, pools of shadow. Instinctively, he reached his hand out.

Another hand appeared, brushing his own. It hung before him like a flesh-colored bird lost in a cloud. Then it was sinking. He clasped it, feeling thin fingers, soft and feminine, tense with fear. It was a girl, gasping for breath. Sam continued forward, his purpose sharpening, taking her with him.

The smoke thinned. Through his smeared vision, Sam saw a line of soldiers standing shoulder to shoulder in the street. Their eyes were goggled beneath olive crowns, the black snouts of their gas masks protruding, long hoses coiling down. Each held a rifle with a bayonet pointed, while behind them, a convoy of trucks and jeeps stood ready. Sam was stunned. Beyond the cordon, the streets were crowded with troops and vehicles. He felt his female companion hesitate, fearful, but he held her hand tightly, continuing toward the line.

As they approached the gap between two Guardsmen, one turned. His bayonet shifted, its blade two feet from the girl's chest. Sam jerked her behind him, facing the soldier with an angry look. The soldier mumbled an apology, turned his rifle aside, and shuffled his boots to let them pass.

She cried out as they reached the sidewalk. Through his burning squint, Sam saw her vaguely—blonde, trim, maybe five-six, wearing a brown leather vest and a green skirt. She made a sound of gratitude, then grew unsure, pulling her hand away.

"I can't see," she said, rubbing her eyes.

"We need to wash them out." Sam started down the block.

She followed.

He wove through the crowd, coughing as he went, wondering what she looked like. As he turned down a walkway, he felt her hand again, taking his lightly. He led her around a corner into a burger joint and stumbled among the tables, nearly turning one over. She laughed through her gasps. Then he was fumbling for the men's room door, opening it and pulling her in behind him.

Sam turned on the tap and splashed water in his face. She drew beside him and did the same. The stinging subsided. He straightened and pulled paper towels from the dispenser. He passed a wad to her, then held a handful over his eyes, hearing her muffled breath beside him. It was a fantasy from his childhood—in the bathroom with a girl, and the adults didn't know.

He drew the towels away. Through the resolving blur, he saw hair divided in the middle of her crown, a pyramid of high forehead, and cheeks bounded by sickle-shaped locks that pricked her chin. Her eyes were blue, fixed on him with the gravest stare he'd ever seen. He waited for her to bow her head, to turn, to laugh—but she didn't flinch. What made those great gulfs of eyes? And how could she invite a stranger to fathom them? Sam gazed deeper, imagining he saw the bottoms of rugged canyons in her eyes, the dark foundation of a different world. A hidden joy flickered in their depths, burning amid a consuming sorrow, and as he focused on that brightness, it blazed up, hopeful. Without thinking, his heart went out to her. There was no foundation here, only the desperate longing for one, more solid and lasting than the world she knew.

"Are you a part of…" Sam gestured toward the bathroom door. He meant to ask whether she was a protester, but before he could re-phrase the question, she shook her head.

"I feel like I know you," he said slowly.

"I understand your sadness," she replied.

"Sadness?" He gave her a puzzled look, then realized the cause of her confusion, and laughed. He'd made the same mistake, reading a chasm of grief into her red eyes and wet cheeks.

She smiled, willing to give the riot gas credit. But her look left open the possibility that through their tears something had been shared. "You'll find your way," she said.

Sam struggled to meet her gaze, discomposed by the thought that the sorrow he'd imagined in her was nothing but a mirror of his own troubled state.

She turned to put the towel in the trash, and he saw the under-side of her breast through the armhole of her vest. Then she swung the door open and strode out.

He followed. She moved through the burger joint with a jaunty stride, confidence mixed with sexual posturing. But it was the buoy-ancy of childhood in her gait that spoke loudest to him. He felt boyish himself.

She paused on the sidewalk, gazing across the street as if un-aware he was behind her. He saw her frame clearly now, narrow-waisted and curvy, her sleek calves and thighs cased in chocolate tights. The traffic was frozen, drivers watching the students collect on Telegraph Avenue. She left the curb, threading between the cars. He followed, coming up to her on the far side.

As she glanced at him, her words echoed in his head. *You'll find your way.* Did he seem lost? It was true, Sam thought. He was at the brink, and it was visible to a total stranger. But the moment they'd shared—there was more to it than that. They had some kind of understanding. He couldn't name it, or divine its source, but he could feel it. She was watching him out of the corner of her eye.

"Can I call you?" He turned and regarded her directly.

She recoiled as if his eyes were flames that might burn her. Then she drew her breath, and nodded.

They reached the corner. The crowd was thick with red-eyed, coughing students. Demonstrators with black armbands were arguing with Alameda deputies in blue jump suits. Sam felt in his pocket and found a pen. "I don't have anything to write on," he muttered.

She shook her head. Neither did she.

A group of protesters suddenly barged up Telegraph, shouting and forcing people off the curb. She was sideswiped and elbowed into the crowd. Sam lunged, circled her with his arm and pulled her across the sidewalk into the corner smoke shop.

He reached for a magazine with a white shape on the cover, put a dollar on the counter and turned back, handing the pen and magazine over without looking at her. She wrote her name in the white space and was halfway through her number when she glanced up with a covert expression, as if to sneak a look at him and make sure what she imagined was really there. He gazed at her full in the face, and the power that leaped between them made the pen point tear the cover. She tightened her grip and completed the number.

He pushed the door open and they stepped back into the crowd. She handed him the magazine and pen.

"I'm Sam," he said.

"Hello Sam." She smiled, fear edging her eyes. Then she turned and started across Telegraph.

Sam stood watching. At the peak of her stride, she seemed to glide, as if gravity had lost control of her. His heart was beating furiously. He glanced at the magazine. *Alaska Sportsman.* The white shape on its cover was a ram with golden horns standing on a mountain precipice. "Lindy" and a phone number were written across the animal's chest. Sam's finger felt where the pen had cut, imagining the tension in her hand.

When he looked up, he saw Josh Shuman moving toward him, quivering with emotion and shaking his head, a black armband around his sleeve. In the wake of the attack on the campus and his unexpected encounter, Sam was glad to see a familiar face. He and Josh had been friends since childhood. Even so, as Josh wrestled his way forward, Sam hesitated, coiling the magazine.

Josh jabbed Sam's shoulder with rough affection, snarling at the Guards. "Pigs!"

Sam smiled, knowing Josh's anger was for show. As soon as Josh saw his expression, his rancor vanished and he was laughing like a five-year-old, bangs jumping on his forehead, intelligent eyes trapped between.

"You got gassed." Josh noticed Sam's swollen lids.

Sam nodded, wide-eyed, suggesting something other-worldly.

"What was it like?" Josh said excitedly, playing along.

Sam made a blissful face. "Incredible."

Josh saw the glow in Sam's eyes. "What happened?"

"I vuz in dee cloud," Sam spoke a nonsense dialect and beamed like a yogi. "I reach vit my hand," he raised his right arm. "Dee angel come down."

"Just now?"

"Jess," Sam nodded. "Returning to oort from dee long journey. Sad, but vize." He brought his hands together, fingertips touching. "She vill stay vit me."

Josh saw Sam's longing. "Some chick," he guessed.

"Jess," Sam sighed, remembering. "She has dee legs and dee tits."

Josh laughed and touched his forefinger to Sam's chest. "It's about time."

Across the street, two policemen were cuffing a demonstrator over the hood of a car.

"Come on," Josh said. He forced his way through the corner crowd and started down Telegraph, away from campus. Sam followed. They skirted a group of students huddled around a self-assigned street medic with a water pail and sponge. A pair of jeeps drove past with Guardsmen in masks.

"What's going on?" Sam wondered.

"It's war," Josh replied, "and we're the enemy. Reagan's cruising around like a general in his limo. They've got a tank down at the marina."

"Wow," Sam muttered. "What's with the armband?"

"Vigil for James Rector." Josh gave him a critical look. "We marched to the chancellor's house."

"Rector?"

Josh rolled his eyes. "The guy who was killed?"

Sam nodded, recalling.

"It's murder," Josh said. "We've got to do something."

Sam watched a girl in tie-dye pinning notices to the plywood boarded over a store's broken windows. "I don't care about any of this."

The comment pained Josh. "It's your world, too."

"I'm not taking credit." Sam let his disillusionment surface. "Look at this." He glanced at a pair of teenage panhandlers across the street. "What are they doing here?"

"Helping the cause," Josh replied.

"It's a carnival for them," Sam said. "Throwing firecrackers at daddy."

"Don't be an elitist. We're all looking for the same things."

Sam shook his head. "There's no 'we' anymore. The higher view is gone. The flower children are making yogurt, the bikers are shooting smack, and the lowbrows are sniffing glue. Fifty years from now, people will look back and say, 'What a bunch of idiots.'"

"Everything's a downer these days." Josh's upset was aimed at Sam, but his sigh betrayed his own disheartenment.

"Four years of this," Sam gestured wearily toward campus. "We learned more on LSD." In high school, they had imagined classes with some modern-day Aristotle, trading ideas with Walter Pater or Henri Bergson. There had been little of that at Berkeley.

Josh took a breath. "Any news on grad school?"

"Not yet," Sam replied. "You?"

Josh nodded. "Got my acceptance letter yesterday. Another five years and I'm a professor."

Sam stared at him. "Going to do it?"

"Probably." Josh made a resigned face, knowing Sam would see this as a defeat.

Sam looked away. "I need the fellowship."

"That's a given, with your fans."

"We'll see."

"You give great lectures on Blake," Josh told him. "Might as well get paid for them."

"So kind of you, Professor Shuman." Sam laughed. "The nearer it looms, the odder it seems. Deep down, I've always thought of school as a warm-up. The rehearsal, not the main event."

"There's the corporate world." Josh made a wry face.

"It's climbing the human pyramid, either way."

Josh nodded. "That's what grownups do. Theo signed his recording contract last week."

Sam didn't react.

"Maybe you should have stuck with him," Josh said.

"*The Future,*" Sam muttered, remembering the long nights they had wrestled with the alternatives together. Sam was still wrestling. His gaze drifted eastward, into the Berkeley hills.

"It was easier a few centuries ago," Josh said. "You could just look at your last name. Cutler? I'll make knives."

Sam's concentration narrowed, his expression growing perplexed, as if he was trying to recall where he'd left something.

"Carter?" Josh went on. "I'll make carts."

Sam's introspection affected his carriage strangely—his neck and shoulders stiffened, like someone headed for judgment, unjustly accused of a crime he didn't commit.

"Shuman? I'll make shoes." Josh laughed. "Sam?"

"I'm thinking."

"You're not here, man. I'm looking at you, I'm talking to you, but you're not here."

"I'm wondering."

"About what?"

Sam frowned. "There's something beyond all this." He spoke of the waking world as if it was a wrapper. "We see hints in books and music. We feel it when we're coming or when we're high, when the things that don't matter are stripped away. We can't just pick up our diplomas and forget."

Josh laughed. "You're a drug, all your own." He sounded wistful. "My favorite, I think."

"You're the only real friend I have," Sam said.

"That's not true."

"Tell me, Josh. Your honest opinion. Is there any greatness in me?" Sam was painfully conscious of how this sounded, but with his voice lilting with doubt, he chose to speak it out.

"You know the answer to that," Josh said.

"'In his heart there was something that glowed like a gypsy's fire seen across the hills and mists of night, burning in a wild land.'" Sam's voice brimmed with feeling. "'These are the gems of the human soul, the rubies and pearls of a lovesick eye, the countless gold of the aching heart, the martyr's groan, and the lover's sigh.'" The corners of his mouth drew down and a softness circled his cheeks. "I want to reach for something precious, to make whatever sacrifice that requires. It's all so vague and grandiose. Purity of heart. Poetry and daydreams." He gave Josh a helpless look. "Nothing like a career or a job."

"Some people do that," Josh said tentatively.

"What?"

"Follow a dream."

Sam saw the desire in Josh's eyes.

"Not a corporal dream," Josh said softly, "of deeds or position or possessions. But a dream of the soul. Of the spirit."

Sam nodded sadly. Josh yearned for some home for the aspirations he was about to set aside. "Growing up means letting go of those, doesn't it."

"Not for everyone."

Sam shrugged. "I don't have a dream worth devoting my life to."

"You might find one." Josh smiled. "'No bird soars too high, if he soars with his own wings.'"

Sam laughed. "You're supposed to talk me down."

Josh shook his head. "Remember that night in Marquez Canyon?"

Sam took a deep breath. The experience in the gorge behind their grade school, where Los Angeles crumbled into the sea, was one he'd never forget.

"Pouring rain," Josh painted the picture. "The earth getting softer, we're walking along the edge of that cliff."

Sam could feel the bluff collapsing. They fell a long way, tumbling in an avalanche of earth and weeds.

"You saved us," Josh said. "Carrying Freddie and his broken leg all the way back— I couldn't have done that."

"We got into trouble because we were acting out one of my fantasies."

Josh smiled, remembering. " 'Sip Dawn from the thimble of San Grudolce, or Night will swallow the world.' We never found our sacred stream." The thimble belonged to Freddie's grandmother. "I really thought Night had brought the bluff down to destroy us. Lucky you found that paddock and the old sheep."

Sam could see the white creature ambling toward him, one horn broken off, molting fur hanging from his sides, ominous at a distance. "It was he who saved us." They had huddled around the animal. Sam could smell the ram's wet wool and the heat pulsing beneath his chest as he clung to his neck.

Shouts came from a rooftop lined with students. A dozen Berkeley policemen hurried down the street, clubs in their fists. From the crowded sidewalk, hisses rose.

"I peed in my pants all the way up that cliff," Josh said. "You weren't afraid. You knew what to do."

"I was terrified."

"But you knew what to do." Josh gave him a sober look. "You're at home in the void."

Sam frowned.

"That's why you never freak out," Josh said. "Too bad acid won't ever be legal. You'd have it made as a guide."

"I don't want the void," Sam replied. "I don't want fantasies. I want something real, not another fragment of truth to puzzle over, the morning after an acid trip. I want to live in a new world, a true one of my own devising." Sam's features quickened, gaze turning inward, pondering the domain he imagined lay hidden there. "Inexhaustible desire, at the service of a unique perception. That's what life should be. A journey of the mind and heart that gives birth to something like Hopkins' inscape or Machen's hieroglyphics. Germinating an idea like that, tending it, urging it to grow until it roots itself in you and takes you over, and your life becomes the proof of it." He raised the coiled magazine, extending his forefinger to touch the air. "Something so concrete, you can feel its edges a century later—"

Sam's expression froze, and he halted mid-stride. He stared at the magazine and unrolled it.

Josh glanced over his shoulder at the white ram with golden horns. "Where did that come from?"

"The ram who saved us," Sam mused. "It's his wild brother."

"Were you thinking about—"

"No, I just grabbed—" Sam stopped, wondering. He'd seen the animal out of the corner of his eye. Had it been unconscious? "Maybe *he* found *me*." He imagined the wild creature leaping from mountain to mountain, headed for the corner smoke shop, just as the old ram had crossed his paddock to meet him that night in the canyon.

"Looks a lot smarter than the old ram," Josh said.

"He's free." The glossy rectangle of the magazine cover was a window to a distant realm, and Sam imagined he had stepped through it and was with the animal, standing on that small shelf, a scrap of green carpet without tree or brush at an unbelievable height surrounded by rugged peaks. Pure white with black hooves, the ram bore a striking nobility, his golden horns curled nearly full around. "Look how high he is." Sam could feel the ram's exhilaration, his love of precarious altitude, the command of vast terrain, the clarity of vast space.

"There's great wisdom in his eyes," Josh said.

His friend's voice drew Sam back. Josh knew he was seeing in the ram qualities he wished for himself.

Josh grinned. "He got some ewe to write her number on his chest."

Sam nodded. "He lives on love. For him, sex is like rocket fuel."

They laughed. Sam coiled the magazine and slid his free hand into his pant pocket. As they continued down the street, he drew his hand out and extended it to Josh. A pair of pink capsules rolled into Josh's palm.

"Ho!" Josh examined the caps. "Christopher?"

"Who else. Had a grocery bag full of them."

Ahead, the crowds were thicker, students milling, indignant and contentious.

Josh put the caps in his pocket. "He's going off the deep end." He gave Sam a warning look. "Keep your distance."

"No kidding."

"Big-time dealer," Josh said wryly, shaking his head. "What is he thinking? A friend of Theo's just got shipped to Lompoc. No future in that. Locked in a cage with psychopaths for fifteen years. Speaking of which—" His expression was apologetic.

"What?"

"Julia called."

Sam exhaled with frustration. When his sister couldn't reach him, she would phone Josh.

"She said—"

"I don't want to know." Sam's gaze returned to the crestline of the Berkeley hills. "Their hearts are dead."

"This acid would do the trick," Josh patted his pocket. "Hey Mom, hey Dad— 'Afraid to leave your life behind? Swallow this—'"

Sam faced him.

"'It'll change your mind,'" they said in unison. The ditty was Sam's version of "bottoms up."

Sam nodded. "It might." He glanced at Josh's pocket. "It might change yours, too."

The comment hurt Josh. "I wouldn't want that."

Sam regretted his words. "You'll be a great teacher. The kind we hoped we'd find."

Josh shrugged off the compliment.

"I mean it," Sam said.

Josh gave him a sidelong look. "Been a while since we got high together. We had some good times."

"We'll have more," Sam said, unnerved by Josh's implication.

"Still taking acid alone?"

Sam nodded.

The corner ahead was crowded. A girl naked to the waist was handing flowers to the soldiers posted there.

Josh pursed his lips and peered at Sam. "Think our friendship's going to survive *The Future?*"

Sam laughed. "Of course."

"Just checking."

They reached the corner and gazed east, up Haste. There were Guardsmen flanking the street entrance. Beyond, People's Park was visible, surrounded by the chain link fence the military had erected five days earlier. They were using it as their headquarters, and there were tents and trucks, and soldiers bivouacked inside.

Josh glanced at the magazine in Sam's hand. "Who's Lindy?"

Two

The following day, the sun was declining over Berkeley's Elmwood district. The aging two-story houses shadowed each other, but their western windows shone golden. A tree with leaves like colored glass reached toward the face of Sam's rental cottage, set back from the noise of College Avenue. Glowing gnats wove arabesques before the door.

Inside, Sam braved the mirror. His eyes were mostly pupil. "I'm coming on."

Lindy stood across the room, beside his desk, watching him. They had taken the pink capsules forty minutes before, and the acid trip was starting.

"I'm counting on you," she murmured. She'd only been high on LSD a few times before.

"Don't worry," Sam said. "I get confused and frightened, but—" He smiled. "There's always a happy ending."

She lifted his key chain from the desktop and toyed with it. Her hand was trembling. She was nineteen, two years younger than he, and the self-assurance she'd shown the day before had vanished. Her small features looked delicate and vulnerable inside the crescents of blond hair. She had changed her skirt, but the leather vest remained. "What's this?" She waggled a brass disk attached to the key chain.

"Track medal. Broad jump."

She watched him step closer, seeing the agility in his wiry frame.

"Jumping was a way to escape," Sam said.

She considered his words, examining the figure embossed on the medal. "A torch."

"The Greeks ran races with them," he said. "They carried fire between their temples." The inadvertent wordplay struck him, and he saw it register in her face at the same moment. The magazine with the ram on its cover lay in a pool of sunlight beside the phone. "Like him," he said, pointing at the ram's golden eyes.

"What made you pick this from the stand?" Lindy eyed the mountains behind the ram. "Have you ever been to Alaska?"

Sam shook his head. "I thought he'd be easy for you to write on." The words seemed absurdly loaded. His tether to the world was unraveling. He watched Lindy touch the ram with her fingertip. The ram seemed to shift, shanks quivering.

"You'll laugh, but—"

She smiled at his shyness. "What?"

"All I've been doing since yesterday afternoon is thinking of you. And staring at him."

The gulfs in her eyes opened.

"Dall sheep," Sam thumbed the pages. "They live five or six thousand feet up. Most of the year, the mountains are covered with snow. That's why they're white."

Lindy watched him.

"It's like I stumbled over directions to a buried treasure." He regarded the ram.

"When you look at him, what do you see?"

"Inspiration," he replied. "Passion. A wisdom that comes from gazing at immensities."

"He's vulnerable."

"It's an exposed place," he agreed. "He could fall a long way."

Lindy considered the ram. "He looks nervous to me. Fearful."

Sam studied the animal's face. "Yes, I can see that now."

Lindy turned and stepped away. To Sam, the room was like a green aquarium in which her hips made waves. A hundred dark parentheses rippled toward him. She stopped in front of his guitar, propped against the dresser.

"Play something."

"It would be a disappointment," he said quietly.

"To whom?"

He laughed. "Me."

She sensed there was more and waited.

"Have you heard of Volt Vogel?"

Lindy nodded. "The band? I've seen them."

"I wrote most of their stuff."

Her gaze narrowed.

Lindy's reaction wasn't positive, and Sam wasn't surprised. "That's why I quit." He realized how sour he sounded. "The singer's Theo Vogel. It's his band. He acts like a half-wit on stage, but he's a bright guy and he works hard. He just doesn't have any integrity. That's what brought us together. That's what I admired."

She frowned. "That he lacks integrity?"

"That it doesn't get in his way," Sam said. "I was afraid that if I required every word and action to be a true expression, I'd never do anything."

"And now?"

"It's the truth or nothing."

Lindy smiled. His confession didn't disturb her. She was energized by it.

"Unfortunately," Sam laughed, "nothing's come to mind."

"Forget your mind," she said. "Let your heart speak its own music."

Her injunction was so simple and reflexive, it startled him. She felt what she said deeply, he could see that in her eyes. Her intuitions weren't guesses, they were convictions, rooted in an animal wisdom.

She picked up the guitar and passed it to him.

Sam dropped the *Alaska Sportsman* onto the bedstand, sat on the mattress, and rested the instrument on his knee. She retrieved her water glass and drank, watching him over the rim.

He lifted his left hand to the guitar's neck, the pearl dots dancing between the frets. He imagined a power welling inside him, set loose from his center—his heart's music. But his fingers were still. "I don't know what that would be."

He laid the guitar aside. As he rose, Lindy put the glass down on the magazine.

"You will," she said. Her eyes met his, glowing as if she saw that power surging before her.

Sam smiled at her blessing, then saw there was more. Quick as a child, she embraced him and kissed him. He felt the warmth of her mouth, then a floodgate opened and a torrent of tenderness bore him up. His lips were tentative, struggling with her gift.

She put her hand over his heart. "Hear it?"

His pulse was pounding. Her eyes seemed bottomless. Whether it was real or a confusion of the drug, the yearning he saw was unlike anything he'd experienced.

Lindy reached up and touched his hairline.

Without knowing why, Sam drew back. Her wonder dissolved,

replaced by sorrow. It struck him wrong, and the irritation must have shown in his face, because her gaze turned inward. She seemed dangerously poised, a collection of unstable pieces, ready to fall to tears or despair.

He was the cause, Sam thought. Why had he pulled away? That's what he was doing these days. Pulling away. He had his reasons, the ones he admitted to himself—he was getting serious about his life. But there were other reasons for him to shy from sorrow and need. He sensed that the unusual blessing Lindy offered came with an unusual obligation.

"Let's go outside," he said gently.

She seemed not to hear, but when he opened the door, she followed.

The sun blared in their faces and the drug played havoc with their senses. The runners of fence ivy were swollen with light, sparks flying from the leaves. Sam stepped into a scroll of energy, the glittering gnats whirling around him. He saw Lindy turn in his slipstream with her eyes closed. Then she stopped, sniffed the breeze and moved down the drive.

When he reached the street, she was stooped over a burst of nasturtiums, smiling and restored. They started north along College together and she took his hand.

"I love these big old houses." She scanned the fading grace of the neighborhood. Ornate balustrades and classical colonnades bespoke the nouveau riche pride of the original owners, but the fences were leaning and the paint was peeling. Across the street, someone had taped a picture of Che Guevara in a gable window.

"There used to be families in them."

"Families," she nodded.

"How was yours?"

Lindy gazed at a blackened shingle two-story on their left. Its uncurtained panes were small and sooty. "As dark as that one." She let go of his hand.

He watched her lips part, then close again. "I had some dark moments," he said.

"For me, there were a lot of them."

Sam let a few strides pass in silence.

"I never knew my mother," Lindy said. "She died in a car accident when I was a child. My father's sister and her two kids, my cousins, came to live with us in Fresno. Usually it started at night. They cocktailed. By eight they were drunk." She might have been talking about something that happened long ago to someone else. "I felt sorry for my father. My stepmother—that's what she became—would goad him till he got his gun out. Then she'd call the police and they'd haul him away."

Sam stared at her. Her face had aged.

"When he was gone, she'd break things. Glasses, plates, mirrors, windows—" Lindy laughed. "Then she'd get on me."

He saw the ferment in her eyes. "How bad was it?"

She raised her hand to her face and he thought she was combing her fingers through her hair. Instead, she held the locks back with a smirk. At the corner of her forehead, below the hairline, was a star-shaped scar with bright scarlet arms.

"She did that with the fireplace poker."

Sam was stunned. Lindy's skin had shattered around the blow like crusted coals, the glowing interior visible through the cracks. Her fingers were trembling.

She let her hair fall back. As her arm returned to her side, her mouth went slack and the life drained from her eyes. It was as if she had departed and Sam was gazing at a mask. Her vulnerability, the violation of her beauty and innocence brought him toward her powerfully. "You're shaking," he said, and he took her hand.

"Nice, huh?" Her blue eyes blinked.

Sam felt her humiliation. In her smirk, he'd sensed a veiled rage. Now her face was creased with self-pity. She was born for joy, he thought. A world that could do this, didn't deserve her.

The traffic on College halted, and a car honked. Sam surfaced from his brewing emotions and looked around.

"This way," he said, stepping off the curb.

He led her across College and they started up a side street, away from the bustle.

"What about you?" she mumbled, her eyes dark with misgivings.

"Nothing like that." Too late, Sam saw how his words stung her. He tried to give her a reassuring look, but she had turned to face the houses.

Like those on College, they had been divided into student quarters, but the quiet made them seem less violated than abandoned. A tangled garden hose lay buried in foot-high grass. Shrubs had invaded a veranda, smothering the threshold. Eaves were cracked, rain gutters hanging.

Sam felt Lindy squeeze his hand. Her cheer had returned. Her rage and self-pity were joined, as he watched, by a childlike hope that rose to brighten her features.

"Come on," she said. "Tell me."

"Just another broken family in the city of the stars." Sam heard the bitterness in his voice. "My mother thought she was one. She never let go of it, and she took her failure out on my father. He was a machinist, an emotional dwarf. She tied him in knots."

Lindy's gaze was clear. She seemed to understand.

"They'd fight," he said. "She'd leave him crying in the bedroom.

I'd try to comfort him. It got worse and worse. Then she caught him with some woman and he left."

"Left?"

Sam nodded. "They were divorced when I was nine. Eventually he remarried, but it didn't last. Now he has cancer. He's dying. Mother sues him every couple of years. There's nothing to get, but she can't forgive him."

"Can you?"

Sam shook his head. "I despise him." The truth was hard to utter. "All he wanted to do was crawl away to his shop. Julia and I didn't exist."

"Your sister?"

"Yes," Sam said softly. "My sister."

Lindy could see that a wound was opening.

"She couldn't separate herself from it," he said. "She cracked up, and no one cared. She wouldn't eat unless I fed her. She couldn't sleep unless she was with me."

"Didn't your mother—"

Sam shook his head. "She was oblivious. I'd help her out of bed and dress her, while she told me about how happy a family we were before she got pregnant with Julia. When she was still getting parts." He blanched. Pity for his mother made him physically ill. "I still love her," he confessed, "or what I remember of her. She gave me my imagination."

He sighed. "They aren't bad people. They took a wrong turn and never found their way back. I couldn't help them. I tried, but I couldn't." He glanced ahead. The sidewalk was spidered and buckled. His back stiffened, his features went slack, and again his face took on the look of someone unjustly accused.

"You were alone."

He nodded. "I still am."

28

Lindy's gaze wandered from Sam to the houses on their right, windows crowded by creepers, balconies drizzling with vines. "I forged my father's signature on my college application. The day after graduation, I hitchhiked here from Fresno. I've been living off student loans."

"Do you talk to them?" Sam asked.

She shook her head blithely. "It was public knowledge when I was in grammar school. Neighbors, teachers, everyone knew." Her tone was almost whimsical. "One of my cousins is in remedial classes, the other is in a foster home. You try to ignore it, pretend it isn't happening."

The look in her eyes startled Sam. It was mystical, fixed on some distant joy.

"A nervous disease. That's what the school nurse thought." Lindy laughed. "I'm in a frenzy. People call, but I don't come." She cocked her head. "Didn't I hear them? I'm not sure. Their voices are a long way off. Maybe I'm pretending I don't hear." Her eyes glinted as if sharing a prank. "The only sensation I feel, really feel, is speed. Running, flying, never coming back. That's happiness—speed that carries you away from everything."

Sam felt her yearning, her loneliness and despair, and all the hope and energy seething around it. The throbbing in his chest made it impossible to speak.

"Am I fast to you?" She laughed and looked away. "I'm still frenzied, aren't I? Still breathless, still crazy to leave."

The root of an elm had raised the sidewalk and her toe caught the concrete.

Sam dove to save her. He teetered for a moment, his arm curled around her, seeing relief in her face, then surprise as he let them both fall. A gentle bank met them. He embraced her, feeling her quiver against him, lips finding hers.

Her heart roared at him like fire from an opened furnace, and the world around him dissolved. All he could feel was the welling in his chest, a bulb of heat mounting, chugging his pulse and stopping his breath. His center seemed to burst and he was giving himself over, his pain, his loneliness, everything. The miracle was that she was there to receive him. Her innocence welcomed him, her wisdom understood him, and her longing engulfed him. Their hearts, so hot and so close, melted and flowed together, surging with an impossible power.

The bliss Sam felt was suddenly familiar. He was a little boy spinning in circles with his arms raised to the trees. Memories of childhood joy blossomed inside him, as if they had been waiting for this moment. He sensed a similar remembrance in Lindy. This was what she had dreamed of and prayed for when she was running and flying and never coming back: love rising like a fountain inside her, vanquishing the doom. She would risk anything for that, Sam knew. It was all that mattered. In this clarity, they hovered for what seemed a long time.

As they drew apart, Sam saw the star-shaped scar flaming on her brow. Her eyes spoke to him—her love had come, and all the frenzied pieces of her shattered spirit were calm and united. Her strength and purity rang inside him. She knew who she was. The center hadn't been lost. Then, as he watched, her expression grew secretive, doubtful. He felt her fragility, and wondered at how little it took to tip the balance.

"Where are we?" she murmured.

Sam looked around, seeing a derelict garden, gently sloped. A hedge separated it from a white clapboard house. "Someone's front yard," he said. Fuchsia bells and glowing pomegranates grew on either side, and spikes of digitalis tipped creamy urns over them. A plant part rested on the lapel of Lindy's vest.

He picked it up. It was a nodule the size of the end of his finger, with appendages crankling from its top, all finely fashioned. Maybe a root, maybe a fruit. The wind and sun had polished it amber and it had a magical translucency, esses and crescents swirling within, as if it had once been fluid.

"A heart," Sam showed her. "A molten one."

Lindy saw the meaning in his eyes. "Is the music reaching you?"

At first, he didn't understand. Then she put her hand on his chest, and turned her ear, as if listening. He narrowed his gaze and listened with her, thinking of the nodule as the impulse to surrender, love in its yearning state.

"It's us," he said, turning the nodule like a precious stone.

Lindy's eyes welled with feeling, urging him to continue.

"The molten heart," he said, "shot into us at our creation." The image was suddenly vivid for him. "It's hardened into something with boundaries, discrete and alone. But it longs to rejoin its source." Did she understand what he was trying to express? Yes, he could see the joy in her eyes.

"That's the sweetest song—" She could barely speak.

"There isn't another human on earth I could sing it to." Sam felt something precious taking root inside him. His eyes narrowed. He rose onto one knee.

Lindy frowned, but he didn't see her.

He was standing, glancing down the street. "I want to be physically high."

"Right now?" Lindy rose beside him.

"Yes, now. Come on."

A minute later, they were at the corner of Piedmont and Ashby. Sam faced the oncoming traffic and stuck out his thumb.

A camper van braked to a halt on Grizzly Peak Road. The door opened and Sam and Lindy jumped out. As the van pulled away, they crossed the road and started along a trail leading into the forest. Twenty minutes later, Lindy was sitting beneath a knobcone pine on a knoll overlooking San Francisco Bay. A thick bough twisted like a sheltering arm above her head.

"Put your shoulders down," she said. "Okay. Head up—"

Sam stood hunched at the edge of a steep drop, trying to imitate the bearing of the ram. The dark pines formed an amphitheater behind him.

"Now the lofty look," Lindy said.

Sam flared his nostrils and gazed wide-eyed at the buzzing gridwork of civilization below. He held the regal pose for a moment, then glanced back at her, wondering how he was doing. When she giggled, he staggered toward her and collapsed beneath the bough. "How do sheep screw?" he wondered.

She gave him a sly look. "Like dogs, I bet."

He saw the gulfs in her eyes open again, brimming with tenderness. He kissed her. Then he sighed and drew away.

"What is it?" she asked.

"I'm not enough for someone like you."

"Let me decide that." She turned the amber nodule between her thumb and forefinger.

"You will," he eyed her with discouragement.

She shook her head, confused and disturbed.

"Hear that?" Sam gazed over the drop. Down in the urban hive, campanile bells were tolling. "Mankind's sleeping heart." He glanced at the nodule. "It sits in its prison, dreaming." He gave her a bleak look and gestured at the world below. "I want more than that, but I don't have anything to offer."

Lindy put her hand on his arm.

"I'm saying goodbye," he muttered. "Not just to my family, but my friends, the professors who've helped me—everyone. Making myself an outcast."

Lindy watched him.

"It's envy," he shook his head. "I hate the home I never had." The accused was confessing.

"Sam—" Her eyes were full of promise. "Look where we are." She gazed around them as if the web of giant pines was a nest out of which a new life might spring.

On the strength of her hope, he let his doubts go. They were borne away like leaves on a breeze. The knoll was more than an over-look, he realized. It was the boundary between two worlds. The line of tree crowns rising from the ridge below was the capstone of a wall, and only wild things were on their side. He had joked at playing the ram, but now he felt the sensations he had come here to feel—the ram's exhilaration, the mystery of remote peaks, the thrill of being free to climb them.

Then all at once, a great idea, the kind of truth he'd dreamt of, was before him—as tangible as the amber heart nodule between Lindy's fingertips. The joy he'd felt in the derelict garden, and was feeling now, was the most sacred power of creation. In the west, the sun was tangled in pine boughs, and as he turned to face it, he imag-ined he was gazing at a cosmic font, great limbs of flame welling from the scarlet trunk, molten rivers branching out. If, at his birth, a dollop of some universal heart was splashed into him, perhaps that same heartbeat enlivened everything. No sooner had the thought formed itself, then a veil seemed to fall. The knoll was thumping beneath him. The pine needles were quivering. The arcs of the dragonflies followed that duple, and so did the songs of the birds in the brush.

"Lindy—" Was it his own pulse, or had a stray frequency reached his receiver?

She could see his excitement.

"I can hear the molten heart," Sam said, his gaze wandering the overlook. From who and where was this great gift bestowed? He imagined what it might take to answer that question, what a great distance it might lead him, and what sacrifices he might make. He felt Lindy circle his waist with her arm. When he glanced at her, she was listening along, her eyes gleaming like a conspirator's.

"Look," she whispered, directing his gaze toward San Francisco. "It's just floating there. Like a piece of drift."

Sam put his cheek to hers and touched the Bay Bridge with his finger. "Held in place by a rope." The bridge piers hung like trailing algae. "If you cut it," he snipped his fingers, "they would all wash out to sea."

Before she could respond, Sam turned on himself. His attitude toward the world repulsed him.

"You're the one," Lindy whispered.

He saw the adoration in her eyes. Was she waiting for him to speak? No, she closed her eyes and put her lips to his. The knoll seemed to drop from beneath him. Only her kiss kept him suspended. Where had her confidence come from? They barely knew each other. Her commitment seemed absolute.

As they drew apart, all Lindy's yearning was before him, naked and vulnerable. This was the start of their journey, and he was supposed to proclaim it.

Instead, he turned away.

Standing, Sam gave a low laugh, doubt invading his overactive mind from every direction. He wasn't ready for this. He didn't have enough resolve to inspire belief in her, or anyone else. He took a breath and looked around the knoll, still sensing the beat, but knowing his perception was fleeting. It was the drug. Tomorrow the molten heart would be inaudible, and everything would be as bleak as before.

Lindy rose and moved toward him.

"It's getting dark," he said. "We'd better start back."

She nodded, accepting his disengagement. Was he mistaken? No. At a word, she would have cast her fate with his. Pinpricks of light twinkled below, the false stars of the human grid. She had invited him to jump off the world and he was clinging to its edge.

"I never imagined I would meet someone like you," Sam said.

Three

A week after the military action on campus, the troops were withdrawing. The demonstrations had subsided, and the curfew had been lifted. It was evening, and Josh Shuman and Theo Vogel were walking along College Avenue, on the way to Sam's cottage.

"I know the producer I want." Theo's long straight locks swung beneath his flat-brimmed cordoba, opening and closing his aquiline face. "But I'll listen to Sam's opinion."

Josh, nearly a foot shorter than Theo, gazed up at him with a wary look. "I wouldn't launch into that right away."

"Course not," Theo agreed, putting his fists in his pockets. "Asshole," he muttered.

Josh slowed. "Maybe this is a bad idea."

"Okay, okay. I love Sam, you know that." Theo's voice grew plaintive. "We're brothers, we belong together. Fuck—I'm going into the studio in sixty days." His aggravation resurfaced. "You're his friend—do something."

Theo's self-interest was so blatant that Josh laughed. Theo laughed too, irony darting from his nervous eyes.

"That first night," Theo remembered, "he was bringing over some dope for Frank. He just starts making verses up, and the next thing you know, it's four in the morning and we're a whole new band."

"Sam told me," Josh said. "He was pretty excited."

"I thought, 'Shit, this is what Elvis felt like when he met Otis Blackwell.'" Theo made an incredulous face. "If someone had showed up that night and handed us a recording contract, Sam would have been hysterical. He's sure changed."

Josh's boyish face grew thoughtful. "He has, and he hasn't."

Beneath the streetlights, cars sped past. The sweet scent of jasmine drifted over them from a nearby hedge.

"Sam's a seer," Josh said. "He was that way when he was five. He'd dream up adventures with long journeys and trials, and heroic conquests, and we'd act them out." He scowled. "It was competitive. There were fights for the best parts. Grade school's a blur, but I'll never forget being the Prince of Catumbria." Magic echoed in Josh's voice. "I loved the Prince. No one understood him the way I did. But when Sam was done with him, he put him to sleep. And no matter how much I badgered him, he never woke the Prince up."

"What are you telling me?" Theo said with irritation.

"Don't count on Sam." Josh could see how this agitated Theo. "Volt Vogel is pretty far from his thoughts."

"What about this new chick of his?" Theo countered. "She might be crazy about us. That would change things."

Josh shook his head. "I've been so close to Sam for so long—" He struggled with his thoughts. "I'm finally realizing how different he is. It's hard to imagine myself as an adult, but with Sam, it's impossible. He lives in his dreams, and the larger the real world looms, the bigger and bolder his dreams have to be to overshadow it. Knights and castles won't cut it," he glanced at Theo, "and neither will songs about love and war. He needs the Unified Field Theory of fantasies right now. And if he finds it—"

"What?"

Josh shrugged. "It might not include us."

Theo rolled his eyes. "What the hell are you talking about?"

Beneath his dark bangs, Josh's gaze sharpened, reaching a conclusion that had been months coming. "Sam's getting ready to leave."

Surprise lined Theo's face. "Where's he going?"

Josh raised his brows. "I don't know," he said weakly. For a moment, he was lost in thought, then he spoke again, looking straight ahead. "There's a piece of Sam's history you haven't heard. He won't talk about it now, even to me. It happened when we were eight. He and his mother and Julia, his sister, were at the beach. Julia was in the water, hanging onto one of those inflatable toys, and Sam had gone to the hot dog stand to get his mother something to eat. His father showed up, and he and his mother got into a fight. Mom picks up her things and stomps off in a rage. I guess she thought Dad would stick around and take care of the kids. Then Dad takes off. He said later he didn't see Sam and Julia and figured they'd walked home. Sam's watching all this from the hot dog stand. Julia's doing the same, sitting on her toy while it's drifting beyond the breakers. By the time Sam returned, she was halfway out to sea. Julia waved her arms at him, then she panicked, let go of the toy, and started dog-paddling back. Sam tore his clothes off and swam out to get her. He saw her go under and come up quite a few times." Josh shuddered. "I don't know how he did it. Both of them nearly drowned. Julia swallowed a lot of water, and he was fighting a strong current. The next day, he told me that the whole time, he was wondering what he was swimming back to."

"Parents are fucked," Theo said, waiting for Josh's point.

Josh exhaled. "He dragged Julia up onto the beach. Then he carried her to the pier. He begged some change and called me. Dad and I picked them up." Josh shook his head. "I'll never forget the look in his eyes. He acted calm. He had to control his fear to save Julia, and he was still controlling it. 'Yes,' he told Dad. 'I'm by myself.' But he was fine—that's what his eyes said. There wasn't any cause for concern. It was simple—his parents and his home had disappeared while he was at the hot dog stand, and he was going to move on."

They turned down the drive toward Sam's cottage. Night was thick beneath the trees.

"That's the same look I've been seeing these past few months," Josh said. "It's just like it was then—he doesn't think he has any choice. He's written everything off. He doesn't know where he's going, but he's not staying here."

Theo turned his head. A spare guitar line throbbed against the cottage window, a tightrope of minors and sevenths, far from the home key.

Theo smiled. "There's one thing he hasn't written off." He knocked on the door.

Josh noticed letters in the mailbox and retrieved them.

The door opened a few inches and stopped. Lindy peered at them in the light from the cottage's interior. She recognized the singer and waited for him to speak.

"Where is he?" Theo said impatiently, gazing past her.

Lindy didn't move. "Sam," she called out.

Sam came to the door, greeting them with half a smile.

"Can we come in?" Josh asked.

Sam glanced at Lindy, nodded and stepped back.

Theo passed over the threshold and pivoted on his boot heels. He hadn't been in the cottage since Sam's departure from the band, but everything was as it had been. He shook his finger at the guitar, beaming.

Josh handed Sam his mail and nodded to Lindy. "My name's Josh."

"Sorry," Sam said. He faced Lindy. "My friend from the Palisades," he explained.

"Good to hear you play," Theo said, giving Sam a selfless look. "A new style," he grinned. "*Perilous.* I like it."

"Thanks." Sam turned away. "What do you want?"

"Just business," Theo passed the interaction to Josh with a wave of his hand. He gazed around the cottage as if considering the place for his own use, picked up the guitar, and collapsed in Sam's chair with it.

"Those pink caps were crazy," Josh said by way of thanks. He sat on the sofa. "Can we score a couple dozen more?"

Sam shook his head. "Gone. I've got white tabs. Five bucks a hit."

"Good?"

"Christopher says they're the strongest he's ever had." Sam looked at the clock, then at Lindy.

"We'll take twenty." Josh glanced at Theo, who was fingering chords silently.

Theo smiled at Lindy. "Has Sam played any Volt for you?"

She smiled back.

Sam was thumbing through his mail. He frowned at one of the letters, and sat on the bed to open it. Josh saw Theo's agitation mounting. He pulled a wad from his pocket and counted the money out.

Sam scanned the letter and passed it to Josh.

Josh read it and laughed. "Congratulations."

His response seemed to disturb Sam.

"You have a decision to make," Josh hurried to correct himself.

Sam took a breath, picked up the bills, and stepped into the hallway.

Lindy watched Josh return the letter to the pile. A slapping came from Sam's chair. Theo was staring at her, his hand beating time on the arm. He craned his neck and stooped his head, mouthing silent lyrics. Lindy looked away.

Sam returned and tossed a baggie to Josh. He remained standing, silently inviting them to leave.

Josh rose. "It was good to meet you." He glanced at Lindy.

She stood and so did Theo.

"Gotta try this." Theo slid his hand beneath his hair and pulled a joint from behind his ear.

"No thanks," Sam said.

"Be cool." Theo struck a match and lit it. "To celebrate." He inhaled and blew the smoke toward Sam. "The pigs are gone," he grinned. "The people overcame." He handed the marijuana to Lindy.

She did her best to be polite, but shook her head. Josh signaled Theo with a glance, but he acted oblivious.

"We pulled them together," Theo told her. "Sam and I." He passed the joint to Josh. "Volt played 'Dream of Love' last night," he smiled at Sam. "The crowd went wild."

Lindy watched Sam for his reaction. He was eyeing Theo wryly, falling into an attitude from their past.

"*Away crawls hate,*" Theo moaned. "*I'm standing straight.*" He jiggered his wrist. "I put my hand in my pants and jerked off like Jim Morrison."

Josh burst out laughing. Sam was amused despite himself.

Josh gave Lindy an abashed look. "He needs to learn an instrument."

"Come on," Theo urged Sam, gesturing at the marijuana.

Sam's eyes glittered, admiring his old partner's panache. If nothing else, Theo could loosen things up. He glanced at Lindy, took the joint from Josh and drew on it.

Theo was in his triumph, his nervous eyes struggling to absorb Sam's attention, a childish glee gurgling in his throat. "We were good together," he told Lindy. She was still tense, and by facing her, he drew attention to that.

"I've heard," she said, with an edge of disdain.

Theo ignored her. "Hey," he thrust his face close to Sam's, "You gotta take a look at this song I wrote." He shrugged. "The guys think it's good, but—" His expression sobered. "It's the big time now."

Sam leaned away, but Lindy saw him nod. Either he was fending Theo off, or weakening to pressure. Theo caught her tic of irritation, and his attention shifted, recognizing an enemy.

"Are all these about Alaska?" Josh turned from the bookshelf, a green volume in his hand. "Who's Charles Sheldon?" He opened the book to a photo of a white ram lying dead on a slope beside snowshoes and rifle.

"Friend of Teddy Roosevelt's," Sam replied. "He fell in love with Dall sheep." He noticed Lindy's sullenness, and broke off.

Theo was regarding her critically, as if struggling to understand what attracted Sam. Lindy ignored him, her upset mounting, her hands clasped tightly over her middle.

Josh read Sam's expression and set the book down. "We'd better go."

In the few days he'd known Lindy, Sam hadn't seen her like this. She averted her face, pained and fearful, unwilling to allow any of them a deeper view of her turmoil.

"Is she living here?" Theo gave Sam a puzzled look.

Sam put his hand on Josh's shoulder, nodding to him. Josh

grabbed Theo's coat sleeve and sidled toward the door. Lindy exhaled, a smile flickering over her lips.

"Look at that," Theo shook his head at her, amazed. "She's fucking laughing. Sam's turning on his friends," he mimicked Lindy's expression. "Bitch."

Lindy recoiled as if she'd been struck. Sam saw the helplessness in her eyes, and the shame, Theo's attack instantly aligned with those she'd endured as a child. He wheeled and slammed his fist into Theo's face, cracking bone. Theo staggered, grabbing his jaw and eyeing Sam like an ingrate, as if his sole intent was to protect Sam.

Sam watched a red trickle fall from Theo's ear. "Why did you bring him here?" he demanded of Josh.

Josh was speechless, seeing a chasm open between them. Lindy had turned her shoulder to the fray.

"He's scared and he wants my words," Sam lashed out at Josh. "He's hollow without them. I'm fed up with Volt, and it has nothing to do with her."

"Tell *him*," Josh glared at Theo.

But Sam didn't have to say another word. Theo had heard. He wiped the blood from his chin, his coat streaked with it. "What are *you* afraid of?" he growled. "What do *you* want?"

"Will you get him out of here?" Sam fumed at Josh.

Josh threw the door open.

"Fuck the world," Theo told Sam. "Lock yourself in your ivory tower with some poison cunt."

"You moron." Josh turned, swung his arm around Theo's middle, and dragged him through the doorway.

"Want to be left alone?" Theo raged. "You will be. Dead alone. That's where you're headed," he sneered at Lindy. "That's Sam's new music—bones rattling in a box."

"I'll call—" Josh shouted.

Sam slammed the door. He took a breath and turned. "I'm really sorry." Lindy was looking askance at him, one eye narrowed, as if still cringing from Theo's epithet. The matting by her foot was dribbled with blood.

"I shouldn't have let them in," Sam said.

"Nice friends," she lashed out at him.

Her viciousness took him by surprise. He accepted the punishment, understanding that this was what she needed.

"I'm sorry—" Lindy was suddenly regretful, castigating herself. "That was hateful—" Her eyes pleaded with him. Abuse had turned her into an abuser, leaving her doubly shamed. "I know it wasn't your fault. I didn't mean that."

Sam's face clouded. "It's alright."

Lindy realized her contrition had overshot the offense. "Oh Sam," she murmured.

The phone rang.

Sam ignored it, embracing her. "It's over," he said. "I don't think I'll be seeing Theo again."

She nodded, but there was the shadow of a question in her eyes. The phone continued to ring. She saw Sam wasn't going to answer it, gave him a dutiful look, and picked up the receiver. After a moment, she glanced at him and mouthed "Julia."

Sam made a weary face and shook his head.

"He's not here," Lindy told the caller. She listened to a long response. "Really, he's not here. I'll take a message—" Lindy gave Sam a helpless look. "Yes, I can tell you're upset. I'll let him know it's an emergency—"

Sam sighed and held out his hand. Lindy saw the remorse in his eyes, mixed with fondness. She passed him the receiver.

"Hello?" he said hesitantly.

"Sambo?" The high-pitched voice on the other end gasped with relief.

"I'm here, I'm here," he reassured Julia.

"No you're not!" She laughed, overjoyed at the sound of his voice. "You're *there*! If you had any idea what's going on— I've been trying to reach you—"

"I just walked through the door."

"I mean this week. I called twenty-two times. I make a mark each time."

"I'm staying with a friend." Sam gave Lindy a pained look.

Julia giggled. "The one who answered the phone?"

"What is it, Julia?" Sam asked, his voice somber.

"She's frozen his bank account."

Sam was surprised. "How did she do that?"

"The lawyer got a court order. It's terrible. He doesn't have enough money for his treatments. She's killing him—"

"Hold on," Sam shook his head. "He was going to the county hospital, last time I heard. The care's free."

"They cut him off or something, I don't know." Julia sounded confused. "He's desperate. I've been taking things to school and selling them for whatever I can get. It's not much. I'm afraid Mom's found out." Her voice trailed to a whimper. "She checks my things. You know how she is."

Sam was stunned. No matter how he braced himself, it was always worse than he imagined.

"If you were here—" Julia sounded hopeful.

"Be serious," Sam sighed.

Julia whimpered. "If you had a job here—"

"Is that why you called?" Sam closed his eyes. The family alarms were always false. His mother wanted companionship. His father never had enough money—his pride was gone, and he'd take whatever Sam would give him.

"If you don't come back," Julia was saying, "I'm leaving school." She was indignant. "I'm old enough. Mom thinks it's a good idea. There's a job at a donut shop in Santa Monica, but I'd have to show up at three in the morning." Her voice grew tentative. "They'll just fight over who gets the money." She started to cry. "I don't know what to do."

Sam moved the receiver an inch from his ear. His sister's voice reached him like an insect's—a little cricket, caught in a web.

"What's happened to you, Sambo?" the tiny voice said. "Don't you care about us? You still have a family."

"I'm trying to forget," he said softly. The only sound on the other end was her sobbing. It was more than he could stand. "Julia, please—"

Lindy watched him with dismay.

"You know I want to help," Sam said, putting the receiver back to his ear. "Maybe—"

The sobbing ceased.

"Maybe there's something we can figure out," Sam said. "The two of us."

Lindy sighed and Sam met her gaze. His struggle to remain aloof was failing.

"Not right now," Sam told his sister. "I'll call you tomorrow. No, Julia. It has to be tomorrow. Alright. You'll be fine. Pretend Sambo's tucked you in. That's a good girl. I love you, more than anything."

He hung up and stood staring at the phone.

"She won't let go," Lindy muttered.

"She's not strong enough," Sam said.

"She wants you to save them."

Sam looked beaten. "Everyone's upset with me."

"You've given them a lot," Lindy said. "They can see that's going to end."

He met her gaze. "The ram follows his heart."

"He climbs," Lindy nodded. "He doesn't look back. He leaves the lowlands behind." She smiled. There was humor in this for them, but only a little. "His heart is pledged," Lindy said, love burning in her eyes. The Dall had become a presence in their lives. They talked in code, using his world to describe their own.

"They can see the ram inside me," Sam said, "and they know what that means."

Lindy's eyes left him. "Do you?"

Sam felt her agitation. His interactions with his friends and sister threatened her, and he knew that was his doing. He was still vacillating, still uncommitted. Lindy was braver. She wasn't confused. She'd crossed the threshold, and stood facing love's wilderness, eager and restless. She was gambling her heart on him.

"I wish I wasn't so—" Sam wanted to reassure her.

"What?"

"Twenty-one," Sam laughed. "I've never been like this," he touched the air between them, "with anybody."

"Neither have I," Lindy murmured. "What's in the letter?" She eyed the envelope Sam had opened.

"A fellowship," he said.

"Josh was right," she mused. "You've got a decision to make."

Sam opened and closed his hands. She was holding up a mirror to him, challenging him. "My fingers are numb," he said. He wasn't sure what he really wanted from life, and the burden of others' needs discouraged him. "This should be a great trip," he said sourly. They had taken the white acid just before Josh and Theo arrived.

Lindy shuddered, the first chills of the drug spasming her jaw and shortening her breath. Sam watched her retrieve the letters from the bed, slide them under a notepad, and wave away the phone. "None of that happened," she said, giving him a daring look and pulling her sweater over her head.

Sam stared. Breasts drew the senses, even unpleasing ones, but for him Lindy's were the breasts of fantasy. She drew her skirt down, and the sight of her nudity turned his emotions inside out. In an instant, the drug wiped his memory clean. There was nothing but her flesh glowing in the yellow lamplight. It appeared like a halcyon landscape, all ocher and peach—promised, through some mistake, to him alone.

Sam unbuckled his belt with trembling hands and stepped out of his pants, conscious of his nakedness in a way that she was not. He faced her, his body narrow and sinewy, muscles barely contouring his thin limbs, as if planed by a stern carpenter.

Lindy closed the distance and embraced him. He felt his heart pounding in his chest, and then the future was crashing toward him, time accelerating suddenly, thoughts and feelings he'd just experienced disappearing behind. The room seemed to pivot around him. He could feel the drug's strength.

In an hour, Sam would know this was the most powerful drug he'd ever taken. In ten hours, his quandaries would be behind him. The next day's dawn would find him gathering himself back from an earthshaking experience, utterly changed, his ties to Lindy and the world clearly defined. He would know who he was and where his destiny lay. What he sensed as he stood in her embrace, feeling the onset of the drug, was the beginning of something momentous for both of them.

"Are you ready for this?" he murmured.

She seemed as quickened as he. "I think so. Wait a moment."

She drew away and his life's page seemed to turn. The room

held nothing familiar. It was part of the past, and he was moving too rapidly into the future to recognize it. He stood on a strange floor, peering at strange furniture, a sofa he'd never sat on, a bed he'd never slept in. On a desk, clock hands mocked him, frozen on their numbers, pretending to mark time. He heard water running in the kitchen, and the cottage came back. Lindy was getting something to drink.

Sam stepped over to the bed, observing his legs from what seemed a great height. His hand clutched the covers and turned them back. The frontier of the fitted sheet stretched fresh and white, smooth as a fall of snow. His gaze fell on the *Alaska Sportsman* magazine atop the nightstand. The ram had entered his life with Lindy, and he was living with them now, an icon of freedom and independence, judge of things large or small. "It's too slow," Sam would say of a guitar phrase. "He wants to lope." Lindy would shake her head and say, "The broken pace gives him time to think."

He picked the magazine up. Lindy had set her glass down on the ram's chest, always in the same spot, adding something magical. The air was fluid, and the beating of the ram's heart sent out rings as in a pool. Sam saw a great desire glowing in the animal's eyes, welling golden from his molten heart. And with his desire there was pain— perhaps, Sam thought, from the cut in his soft front that the pen point had made. He laughed.

As he sat on the bed, the light from the nightstand flashed over the ram's eyes, and they seemed to shift. Sam gave his hallucination free rein. The ram was watching him, muzzle lifted. He'd stood motionless, letting them guess who he was and what he intended. Now the moment was right, the glaze had broken, he was about to declare himself.

Sam heard the kitchen faucet turn off. The ram tensed, listening. It was Lindy's dare that had brought him to life, Sam realized. Her challenge. It was his own willingness to accept it, to venture into their personal unknowns together, that had worked this magic in his mind. Sam felt his pulse pounding, gripped by the illusion, wondering where it would lead. Fear flashed in the ram's eyes. He was nosing the winds for danger, expecting it any moment. Lindy's footsteps approached, and as Sam set the magazine back on the nightstand, the ram's eyes shifted to follow her, muscles swelling in his shoulder, hooves treadling the grass.

Sam felt the bed squeal and slope beside him. Lindy's body was near, warm but not touching his. Without knowing why, he kept his distance. Perhaps he sensed the part of her that was waiting for his commitment, threatened by the other forces pulling at him. Like the ram, he felt vulnerable and was wary. He saw her glass descend toward the magazine, landing on the rumpled circle with the predictability of ritual. Lindy's hand touched his shoulder. It was trembling.

His trepidation abated. He turned and her features loomed large before him, her eyes troubled. He could see all her pent-up fear, how she struggled to master it, and his heart went out to her. She smiled, innocent as a child, and brought her face closer, seeking a kiss. He responded, lips touching, tongue razing hers, the budded surface like gravel.

"How do you feel?" Sam's voice sounded loud and foreign.

"A little cold." Shivers ran down her arm. "I survived the torrent," she said, as if recalling a recent ordeal.

He couldn't make sense of her words.

"Coming out of the tap." She glanced nervously toward the kitchen. "Is something wrong?"

He shook his head, watching the afterimages proliferate till there were half a dozen of her, cheek to cheek, all regarding him strangely. "I'm hallucinating."

"Hold me," Lindy said.

"Did I hurt you last night?" He'd been afraid to ask.

"What do you mean?"

"You groaned. At the end."

"No," she laughed. "It was the weirdest thing—what I was thinking." She gave him a bewildered look. "I was taking your sperm, and it was you. I could feel you in my womb, like a child. A new Sam."

"Wow."

Her face grew adoring and sank from view. He felt her tongue trail down his neck. Her thighs clasped his leg, squirming for contact. A soft undercurrent rose from the sheets, shadowy folds slewing around him. The drug was coming on powerfully, images firing in his head—worshipful hands, insinuating caresses.

He rolled on his hip, tipping her. The room rocked around him and her thighs parted. He lowered himself into the splay, touching stiffly against her. She flinched. He made a humorous face, but it faded straightaway. Then he strained forward and she spread around him.

Sam felt her emotions in a vibrant cascade: her wonder, her joy, her longing. She tendered him what was innermost—her hunger, her sadness, her desperate hope. And then she was asking, reaching for his heart. He hesitated at her insistence. She met his fear as she had before, elation vanishing, risking abandonment, summoning her courage and asking again, showing him how to surrender. His resistance dissolved and he let himself go, heart molten and flowing to meet her. He felt himself at her center, warm and joined, her soft moan in his ear. It was as if she'd been searching for her real self her whole life, and now she had found it. They rode the moment together.

Then, strangely, Sam felt her ask again. Had he only imagined her peace? How could it fade so quickly? Her body strained violently, ignoring the pain of a still tighter coupling, or seeking it, as if what had just passed was nothing, and there was something deeper and more meaningful to feel. He hesitated as a sigh hissed from her throat, and her teeth raked his neck. It was as if she was seeking some kind of weakness in him, delving for flaws, or stirring herself to create them. Lindy appeared to sense his alarm, but instead of calming him, she grew bolder. *This body isn't my real one,* she seemed to say. *Watch me shred this soft skin and pull my sweet face off.* The hidden Lindy filled Sam with fear, revealing a hunger, and a willingness to do violence to herself, beyond anything he'd imagined. And she seemed bent on working a similar change in him, as if, inside his human wrapper, a wilder self was lurking. He felt a terrible danger in her desire. She was breaching something that should remain inviolable.

But he'd opened himself, and he had no defense. The physical world had dissolved. Only the moorings between them held him to the earth. Mercilessly, she cut them and his frail ego collapsed like an empty sack. All that was left wafted up like a wraith, a twist of white smoke, coils lifting from its top. Euphoria infused him, the glory of letting go. He was dying, wasn't he?

The walls of the room blew away, the dim air of the cottage flattened beneath him and slid into the abyss. He was rising into a realm of peaks and cliffs, that window on the magazine cover through which he'd peered. The ruggedness was real, and the vastness and breezes in this high place. The ram had stood here waiting, a patient spirit. He knew Sam's essence even as he absorbed it—a creature intimate with great heights and great danger. Sam felt his hooves in the soil. The throbs in his chest rippled outward like rings in a pool, his heart forever molten. He breathed fear and desire as a birthright, the way men breathe air.

"Lindy," Sam murmured blindly. "What's going on?"

"I'm raw," she was clutching him. "Bloody, in pieces."

"My body is gone."

"Don't leave me," she begged.

But in the new world they inhabited, her sudden movement

spooked the ram. He sprang from the shelf, bounding toward the cliffs, and she had no choice but to follow quickly. Sam felt himself thrusting, vaulting, his pulse like hooves in his ears. He heard her in stride just behind, scattered faculties packing, in desperate pursuit. Two strange animals racing in a boundless wild.

His ardor mounted, his fores reached out, his native power churning inside him, making his chest swell and his mind glow, turning his eyes golden. In that frenzied state, he felt at last the liberation he'd dreamt of. He glanced back mid-leap. Within a furring of darkness, her eyes glowed too, but with craving, and his golden glance spurred her, whetting a different kind of power, violent and vicious. She hated him for trying to escape, and if she caught him, she would devour him. Her womb dreamed of him reduced to sperm, ductile and white, living a new life inside her.

They climbed for a long time, mounting steep inclines into the clouds, at odds but panting close, and then at a dip between high peaks, she caught him. He felt her lunge, he struggled to free himself, and she slashed at his front and tore him open. Sam felt an enormous welling, and a great golden river flowed out of his chest. This time, he gave not some, but all. And in the moment of his destruction, as the molten heart left him and he yielded to those feasting eyes, he felt himself joined with something infinitely larger and finer than himself, even the glorious glowing self he'd become. He surrendered everything, and finally, truly, he was not alone.

Lindy, too, found the peace she had sought. In that great flood of love from Sam's heart, she was recognized and knew who she was. In a moment, all her fears and sadness collapsed—the running and flying and endless hoping were over. Sweet tears burst from her, tears of welcome. It was a wandering orphan, returning after an absence of so many years—her lost self. What a wonderful girl she was: full of love, wise and fearless, with a child's joy and a child's trust. Sam had found her. Only Sam could have done it, and Sam was finally hers. With all the bliss within her, Lindy knew that. He had left the world that had abandoned them, and he would never return.

Four

The summer was a perfect one. The trees along College Avenue turned amber and carmine slowly, unhurried by frost or bad weather, their sprays floating on the breeze beneath a gentle blue sky. Sam crossed the street, books under his arm, his appearance as changed as the foliage. His hair was short, and instead of boots and bell-bottoms, he wore jeans and tennis shoes. During the four months he and Lindy had lived together, he'd been reaching back. It pleased him to dress like a boy, and the spirit of a child showed in his quick stride and his sparkling eyes. The random music of wind chimes sounded from a neighbor's porch.

He turned down the drive leading to his cottage, stepping among shriveled leaves and coins of light. Josh Shuman was leaning against a tree, waiting. When he saw Sam, he came forward, his expression uncharacteristically grave.

"Hey," Sam nodded, trying to smile. "Where have you been?"

Josh laughed, following him toward the entrance. "I've come here a dozen times." He gave the cottage a mystified look. "Nobody answers the door."

Sam took a breath, but didn't respond.

"What is that?" Josh peered at an index card taped to the door. It read, *Opposition is true friendship.* "You're cutting yourself off?" Josh asked.

"Concentrating," Sam said, shifting his books.

"You look like you're joining the marines." Josh glanced at the spines: Apuleius, *The Bacchae*, and a book with *Shamanic Ritual* in the title. "You can't turn your back on the world."

Sam made a puzzled face, but he could see Josh wasn't fooled. "Why not?" he muttered, letting Josh see the joy in his eyes.

"That's crazy."

"The more Lindy loves me, the crazier I get."

Josh gazed at him with his jaw set, as if an expected sadness had come to pass.

"You won't believe this," Sam whispered, his eyes glowing. It was only right Josh should know. "I have my great idea. The start of it, anyway."

Josh regarded him.

"Behind these cold bars," Sam put his hand over his heart, "lies an ocean of bliss."

Josh laughed at Sam's grandeur, and Sam joined in.

"Being with Lindy has changed everything," Sam told him. "I've never felt such hope, never imagined there could be so much light in my life." His voice softened. "The greatest thing I could wish for you, is that you will find someone like her."

"Whew." Josh's eyes widened. He was happy for him, but disturbed. "Would it turn me into a recluse?" He peered anxiously down the drive.

"There are things I have to be cautious about," Sam replied with irritation. "I can't look back." He was speaking half to himself, warding off doubt. "I don't expect you to understand."

Josh saw the regret in Sam's eyes. "Before you make any irreversible decisions—"

"You're the best friend I could have had," Sam said. "But—" He sighed. "This story only has two players."

"I hate to—"

"You're not going to change my mind about grad school," Sam said.

"That's not why I'm here," Josh shook his head. "Christopher got busted yesterday. He called his parents and they called me. So I could warn you. Narcs have been watching him for weeks. They're probably onto you."

Sam stared at him.

Josh glanced down the drive. "Some guy in a Tempest is parked across the street."

"What?" Sam's eyes darkened with fear.

Josh exhaled. "Maybe he's doing repo." His expression was grim. "They could put you away for a long time."

Sam nodded.

"What are you holding?" Josh asked.

"Not much."

"I parked on Benvenue," Josh nodded at the back fence, pulling a key from his pocket. He held it toward Sam.

Sam considered the offer. He was near the edge, deciding whether to leap, and now fate was hurling him over the brink. He opened his hand and the key dropped into it. When he raised his eyes, Josh's face was swept with sorrow. He realized the risk Josh had run.

"A little help from your friend," Josh said.

Sam saw the deep affection in Josh's eyes, and he embraced him. Their first adventure was together—climbing onto the roof of Josh's garage when they were four. They'd reached manhood together, they'd left home together. It was a long hug, but it couldn't express all the things they'd shared. As they drew apart, Josh's mouth twisted into a wry smile. "Peace." He held his hand up, making a vee with his first two fingers.

Sam sighed and returned the gesture. "Peace."

His friend turned and strode back down the drive.

Sam lowered his hand, the key in his palm, two fingers still extended, gazing at them as he turned to the cottage door, imagining a creature with two toes moving quietly away, barely crunching the gravel.

He knocked twice and twice again. Lindy opened the door.

She was wearing his tee shirt. Her smile was intimate, and as he crossed the threshold, she stroked his arm and kissed his shoulder. Parting a stand of reeds, Sam stepped before a table covered with jars and peered down. Lindy took the books from him, setting them on an upright log between buckets of earth and sand. The cottage was crammed with wild things they had collected on their forays, and rich odors wafted around them. A white sheep pelt was tacked to the wall, along with skins from local roadkill. Skulls peered from a dozen angles through plants pulled from Berkeley hills and gardens.

Lindy reached for a cassette recorder on the desk. "Listen," she gave him a secret look, and depressed one of the recorder's keys. A shrill chrew-chrew-chrew filled the cottage.

"What is it?"

"A rosy finch," she said. They lived in the cliffs with the Dalls.

"Neat." Sam removed a pill container from his shirt pocket and upended it. A beetle fell, landing in a jar. He watched it scuttle under a rock, wondering what he was going to do.

"Josh was here again," Lindy said. "I didn't answer."

Sam nodded. "He waited for me."

"I know," she said quietly. "I could hear you outside."

Sam could see how troubled she was. Her blue eyes, which trust had made so bright, were clouded. The shadows below them, left by sleepless nights, gave her a worn look.

"Why won't he leave us alone?" she wondered.

Sam was silent, weighing the alternatives.

She sensed his distraction and moved closer.

He put his left hand on her back, Josh's car key in his right. "As long as we're in Berkeley, the past will hound us." He turned aside, sliding the key into his pocket.

Lindy kissed him. "We don't belong here."

Sam nodded. They had talked about leaving, but it had always seemed fanciful.

"North and west," she muttered. The phrase had become part of their lexicon.

"You'd have to quit school," Sam frowned.

"I don't care—" Lindy sensed something was wrong. "What is it?"

Sam sighed and raised his brows. He was suddenly a criminal. Was he going to ask her to flee the law with him?

"Talk to me," Lindy pressed him.

He put his hands on her waist. "You're everything to me. All my dreams are with you." Even as he said it, he felt those dreams evaporating. He had to leave, and quickly.

She was peering at him, waiting.

"I've got to run to the city," he said.

His words confused her. "You want me to come?"

"No," he said. "It's a drug deal I did last year. The guy finally came up with the money." He avoided her gaze.

"When will you be back?" Lindy could tell something was wrong.

"Tonight probably." Sam headed across the room. "I might have to stay over."

She followed him. "How will you get there?"

Sam halted before the closet. "I'll hitch a ride." He regarded his hanging clothes, reached his hand out and stopped. What could he take without being obvious?

"Sam?" She edged in front of him.

"I'll just take a coat," he muttered, pulling it off the hanger. Her face was desperate, gaze bewildered, mouth trying to smile but failing miserably. She could read his mind. All the hopes she'd nursed were groundless, and all her fears were coming true. He was abandoning her.

Sam froze with the coat in his hand. Lindy was his inspiration, the beginning of his journey. What was he thinking?

"Sam—" She spoke softly, like a young girl.

All at once, fleeing with her seemed to Sam the greater act of courage, and the greater devotion to them both. He clasped her and kissed her deeply, then drew back to look in her eyes. "Let's go." He grabbed his duffel bag from the closet and threw it on the bed.

She smiled tentatively, uncertain what he meant. He pulled the dresser drawers open and they dipped in, loading the duffel.

"Are we coming back?" she wondered.

"No." He grabbed a wad of currency from the bottom drawer.

"Where are we going?"

"North and west." He straightened himself and untacked the *Alaska Sportsman* magazine from above the bed, eyeing the ram. "When he's threatened, he seeks higher ground."

"Instep a shank, toe a hoof," she said, using their secret language.

"Unguligrade," Sam completed the phrase. He stuffed the magazine in the duffel.

Lindy laughed like a child. It was running, flying, never coming back. But this time she was with someone, going hand in hand.

"I've got a car. That's why Josh was here." Sam unclipped the broad jump medal from his door key, set the key on the table, and nodded at his guitar. "Grab that."

"There wasn't any drug deal." Lindy scooped a handful of bird feathers and threw them at him.

He hushed her. "We need to be quiet." He put his hand on the doorknob. "We're going over the back fence."

Her eyes widened. "Somebody's after us," she said playfully.

"Exactly." Sam eased the door open.

They stepped quietly across the drive, scaled the fence, and disappeared over it.

They followed the interstate north through Redding and Weed. After eating at a roadside truck stop, they crossed the California-Oregon border, and around midnight, just outside Portland, they exited onto a quiet farm road. Sam pulled over, they laughed at their escape, made love, and slept in the car.

The next morning, they woke to a gray haze and continued north. They were in the land of the giants, the road signs pointing the way to Mount Hood, and then Mount St. Helens as they crossed into Washington. When they reached the cutoff to Mount Rainier, the car was filled with their shouts and screams, and Sam headed east.

After two hours of winding through forests, steadily ascending, they crossed a bridge over a river flowing off the great mountain, and realized they were on its flank. Giant steeps of rock on their left led into the clouds. A few minutes later, the road ended in a parking lot, five thousand feet up, and as the car turned into it, they saw an enormous white mass hovering before them, veiled in mist. As high as they were, Rainier seemed to float in a different dimension. Its cracked and buckled ice was visible through gaps in the veil. The sign said *Paradise*.

Mountain climbers were gathered by a trailhead. Sam parked, glanced at Lindy and opened the car door. As they approached, the climbers fussed with clothing and equipment, too solemn for chatter. Sam could see another team far up the trail, drawing near the snows. The mist was dissolving, revealing the dome's lines. He stopped a dozen feet from a gangly man in tan knickers.

"Going up?"

The climber eyed him through glare glasses and nodded.

"Done this before?"

"Tried," the climber answered. "Got blown off last time."

Sam could feel the man's fear. What a great thing, he thought— to stand here facing this mountain with your pack piled high, nerving yourself, resolved to be bold. "What are those?" He touched the spiked metal objects lashed to the pack.

"Crampons. You use them to walk on the ice."

Sam pictured them attached to his boot soles. Two metal prongs extended from the toes, like hooves. He glanced at Lindy. She was beaming, sharing his fascination and excitement. He stepped closer. "What about that?"

"Sleeping pad," the climber said. "If we make it to the top, we're going to spend the night in the steam caves."

"Steam?"

"It's a volcano."

"Really?" Sam smiled, confessing his ignorance.

"It was built up, one eruption after another. See those terraces?"

Sam looked up. The climber was pointing at a headwall below the summit.

"Each one is a lava flow."

Sam gazed at the top of Mount Rainier, imagining.

"It's still hot," the climber said.

"Ready?" One of his companions gestured toward the trail head.

The climber nodded to Sam, hefted his pack and moved away.

"Of course." Sam turned to Lindy with a stunned expression. "The earth's heart is molten. You learn that in grammar school." He scanned the crags around them. "All of this was fire, hot and flowing."

"It's incredible," she agreed.

" 'Hard as rock.' Our idea of permanence. 'Rock solid.' " Sam's gaze wandered inward. "We're born from the earth and we're just like it, molten in our depths." He turned back to the mountain.

Lindy moved around his elbow, staying in the corner of his eye. "I can feel the heat." She grabbed his arm, shivering against him.

Sam saw the tenderness and devotion in her eyes.

"It's wonderful," she whispered, kissing him.

As their lips parted, he smiled broadly, settled on something. "Let's see how close we can get." He nodded at the trail. "We'll need warmer clothes." He stepped toward the car.

He opened the trunk and removed a couple of sweaters from the duffel. Then he drew a dark blue jar out and unscrewed the lid.

"What's that?" Lindy peered inside. It was full of green tablets.

"Acid," Sam said. "Got them from Christopher last week. For us."

"I thought you'd decided—"

Sam nodded. "I'll never take a full dose again. Too disruptive. I might lose the thread." He smiled. "Just a quarter tab, now and then. To unhinge myself."

"Now and then?"

He glanced at the trail and gave her an inviting look. She laughed, and he took a tab from the jar and broke it for them.

A half hour later, they were ascending a steep slope bordered by dark conifers, breathing hard. As they crested a rise, the trees thinned, giving onto rolling meadows studded with rocks. The sun was behind them, shining directly on the mountain. Two rugged headwalls were visible near the summit, and below, two enormous glaciers merged into one.

Lindy pointed. On a large boulder, a pair of marmots crouched, watching them.

Sam gazed at her, wiping his brow with his sleeve. "Alright?"

She nodded.

"Let's find our own way from here." He took her hand and they left the trail, climbing the grassy swells.

A few moments passed, then Sam glanced at her. The time seemed right. "I want us to change our names," he said.

She gave him a curious look. "To what?"

"Ransom and Lindy Altman."

Her eyes flared with surprise.

"I've been thinking about it for a while," he said softly.

A gentle wind blew sidewise, from him to her.

"I want to be surrender's ransom," Sam said, "with the vaulting ram as my emblem: the leap of white love, the lost heart's return." He spoke it like a vow of undying love.

Lindy bit her lip.

"You're everything to me now." Sam's voice was meek as a child's. "I want our love to be my religion." His smile shone with a new purity. He had found a devotion equal to hers.

"Oh Sam—" Her eyes brimmed.

"We'll cut loose of everything. Leave that world and enter this one." His eyes climbed the vast ice fields, swept up by an imagined labor of love, long and arduous, requiring a fierce dedication. "Where the molten heart is always flowing."

Ahead, the slope leveled off.

"I'm going to tell our story," Sam said. "As a fur-covered shaman, a wild ram-man, chanting the liturgy of surrender." He flexed his knees and stooped his shoulders, using his forefingers to draw the horns curling out of his brow.

Lindy peered at him. "A shaman?"

Her incredulity made Sam laugh. For a moment, she thought he was kidding, then Sam nodded.

"I wrote the first chant last night," he said as they stepped onto a high meadow. The chill emanation of the mountain struck them, like a giant freezer door opening. It rose unobstructed, dazzlingly complex, all its myriad cliffs and fissures of ice close enough to touch. "So I could sing it to you," he explained. "Here."

Her heart melted. He kissed her tenderly. It wasn't an illusion—the mountain was theirs, born not in ages past, but hours before, still steaming from the outpourings that morning. They sank into the meadow's warmth, lush with ankle-high lupine and maroon huckleberry, the redolent grasses ringed by pasqueflower seedheads on tall stalks, big and round and luminescent against the sun.

"Don't let this fire go out," Sam whispered, a pledge for them both.

She waited, eyes wide.

"Be with me always," he implored her.

Between them, a hidden hopper twitched the grass.

"I want to," Lindy whispered. "More than anything." She put her fingertips to his heart.

Sam drew his hand from his pocket. In his palm was a little silver cage with a leather thong through its top. He hinged it open and placed inside the amber nodule from the derelict garden, then snapped it shut. "To wear."

A tear tracked down Lindy's cheek. He reached around her neck and tied the thong.

"Always," she said, touching the pendant.

He kissed her lips and her eyes and the star on her forehead, and her tears kept coming. "Its heart is welling inside it," Sam whispered, gazing at the great mountain looming over them. His own breathless anticipation seemed part of that enormous power, white and blinding and limitless.

He pulled her sweater over her head, his blood boiling, and as he undid the buttons of her blouse and lay back with her, he imagined his heart had burst into flames. He fanned it, concentrating, nursing the fire as she unbuckled his belt, feeding it with his longing. The flames spread, his belly ignited, then his back, bright tapers worming through his flesh. Tremors shook him, his breath like a bellows, crackling the blaze, smoke twisting up.

"Ransom," Lindy sighed.

She was with him, thighs opening, dreaming the same dream, reaching through the heat for that wondrous self she'd lost. He pressed his lips to her ear, feeling his heart about to pour out, the pasqueflower batons beating feverishly on the billowing skins of smoke. Everything between them glowed and seethed, and then a voice rose in his throat, lower than his own, someone older singing passionately, with confidence and command.

> *The flesh is sizzling,*
> *Limb muscles twitching,*
> *Deep tissues pulling where the boiling blood anoints.*

Lances wriggled into his shoulders, glowing thorns sputtered along his nerves, following them like fuses to the tips of his fingers and toes.

> *The bones are cracking.*
> *The cracks leak marrow,*
> *Bubbling as the firebarbs pry the joints.*

Bowing spars, taut sinews.
The homes you had, forever lose.

His belly blistered and popped, flames tonguing and forking over his groin and thighs. The thickening smoke wavered, and he glimpsed himself hunched and writhing, swarms of orange arrows emerging from his chest. Then the billows folded over him, blotting everything.

——◆——

Struggling for air, breathing fire, I force my shoulders up. The flesh splits across my front. I raise my arms to save them—flaming torches, fingers charred, thumbs burnt to knobs. The fire won't let go. It curls me forward, bones bending, ligatures ravelling and popping. A pressure bursts behind my nose and my face pushes out, eyes bugged to the sides, neck swooning unsupported, nosing helplessly back into the blaze.

Gradually the hot tools leave off. The fire shrinks to a core. Through the ruin of my senses, I feel the bent spars stiffen. Sinews contract as the cool air fans them, flesh freezing over gashes. My trunk tips, and I rock onto my belly, a film of smoke over my eyes. Teek-teek—embers cooling.

I tense my limbs, digging in. My shoulders lift, and as I strain to raise my head, a weight descends on it, above my eyes. My legs wobble. I try to straighten my spine, but there's a binding in my back. I reach my arm out, seeing a wild sight—a thin white stick with two black toes, shining and deeply cleft.

My shoulder is covered with white fur. A white muzzle starts out from my face. I run my tongue over my teeth and my jaw joggles. I turn my head and golden cusps turn with me, one in each eye's outside corner. I lower my head and lift my right fore, my hoof pad riding up the horn, bumping over the ridges. Up, back, around, and down.

Ram. I try to speak the word, but only a grunt sounds in the stillness.

The last traces of smoke are dissipating. I'm standing on a bluff, in a bed of ash. The slopes are covered with tussocks of pale straw. Below is a whispering stream. I feel a thrill of spaciousness—the world seems to have opened around me. Then I realize it's my eyes—I can see halfway behind me without shifting my head. There's a rich picture in the wind. Scents crowd beneath the arches of my nostrils, and when I suck them into my muzzle they burst into images: fanning sprigs, soaked moss, brown middens piled by small burrowers. My own smell mixes with them, sweet and pungent, woolly and wild. The freedom I've sought is finally mine.

I search for memories of this land, but there are none. This creature I am—has the senses of a ram and the thoughts of a man.

I lift my right foreleg and bring it forward. My body sways, the weight over my shoulder funneling down. My limbs are spindly but there are four. I bring my left hind up, whisking it through the grass, feeling the braided muscles woven into my will. Where am I bound? My legs seem to know—they want to gain height. I'm headed upstream, wading through brush, cages opening before me and closing behind. It's spring in this land, bird smell on the boughs and birdsong in the air, the earth covered with unburst buds. Amid all of this energy about to let loose, I feel an uncomfortable solitude. This too is an instinct of the ram. To be low is to be exposed, vulnerable to uncertain threats.

I reach the edge of a narrow ravine, and as I look for a way across, a power cocks in my hinds, hams quivering, hocks trembling down. Without a thought, the tension releases and I'm rearing, fores reaching, sailing over the ravine and coming down on the far side fores first, hinds reaching under to do it again. Leaping, cocking and springing, down and then up again, down and then up. I'm calmer, much calmer. What can't I escape, vaulting over this wild terrain?

Five

*I*t was mid-August, high on a dark face in the Cascade Mountains north of Seattle, almost a year after Ransom and Lindy first arrived in Washington. A red rope hung down to a narrow shelf where Erik Mortensen stood on belay, paying the rope through his hands and peering up. His pale features were framed with curly blonde hair and a bristly beard. He licked his lower lip, watched a loop spring from the coil by his boot, checked the drag through his fist, then looked back up the wall. Ransom was balanced there, nerving for his next move.

"Use both toes," Erik advised him.

Ransom clung to the rock, his brow creased and strained as if he'd absorbed some of its age. He committed to the move and his trunk rose slowly, the small pack on his back shifting, weight poised over his straightening leg. He wore specially made shoes with toes cloven like hooves. The right lifted, black points scratching at a nub.

"I'm gonna get a job in Alaska," Erik mused, "belaying real sheep."

Ransom's toes held. He turned to scan the rock above, sorting the choices. To the right, the way grooved and angled. To the left, a dark spine arched out of the face. "Hopscotch for a Dall," he muttered, goading himself. He swung out of the groove, eyes dark with dread, hands crawling up the rocky spine.

Below, Erik froze.

Ransom's arms were fully extended. His left leg abandoned its hold, flexing, feeling up the spine with two black toes.

"What're you doing?" Erik laughed.

Ransom's toes settled and he shifted his weight, giving up his safety, calm as the creature he mimicked, creeping higher, a dozen feet above the point where the belay was anchored.

Erik shuttled the rope in. "Back off!"

The red cord tugged at Ransom's hips. He seemed not to feel it. His eyes glazed ahead and his lips mouthed silently. He reached to complete the move.

"You're stoned," Erik exhaled, disbelieving. "Goddam it—"

Ransom seemed not to hear. The tension on the rope threatened his balance, so Erik gave out a few inches, praying he'd ease down.

But Ransom was rapt. "Huffing, heart-flooded," he sang to himself, making his move.

"Dickhead," Erik raged, trying to brace his shaking legs. He held the rope by his hip, fist quivering. "This won't happen again."

Ransom's hand left the rock, sliding to his groin. Without looking, his thumb tripped the carabiner gate. He unhooked the lifeline and cast it aside. "Huffing, heart-flooded, headlong—"

Erik watched as Ransom rose beyond the limp rope, climbing with nothing to protect him if he should fall.

Mumbling the chant beneath his breath, eyes bright, Ransom moved with an animal grace, confident and agile as a ram, picking his holds like one, feeling the exhilaration a ram feels—

His right hoof slid off a nub. His chest swung out and his hand brought him back just in time. He clung, foot scraping desperately till a toe caught.

"I'll just sit here and watch you kill yourself," Erik called out. He coiled the rope in.

Ransom stared at the rock, shaken. The top of the spine was six feet above. His were human legs, not ram's. The agility was in his head. He found fresh holds, trying to think past his weakness, rising slowly, one careful move after another. His arms ached terribly, his knees were quivering. The rock felt hot. It seethed beneath his fingers, speaking to him in an ancient voice, lifting him. He gripped the ledge and clambered up onto it, gasping.

For a moment, he knelt there, staring into space, listening. He could hear a throbbing deep in the mountain. Gradually it subsided.

Ransom crawled to where the ledge widened, out of Erik's sight, and removed his pack. As he pulled off his shirt and pants, the gleam returned to his eyes. He drew a bundle of white fur out of his pack, lips moving as he unrolled it. Fur vest, fur leggings, fur cuffs. They were silky soft to touch, the sweet wool odor wafting up. He pulled on the leggings, remembering the hours spent sewing the skins, every stitch bringing him closer to the ram. The leggings made him feel lighter, and as he buttoned the vest over his front, his trance returned powerfully. He slid his feet back into the cloven shoes, and fitted the cuffs on his wrists. Then he crept to the brink of the ledge, and stood there with his legs flexed, gazing across the rocky canyon.

He imagined a stream valley with sere grass. He lowered himself into a half-crouch, and then began to dip his body, back straight, head high, knees hingeing rhythmically. He was vaulting across the distant slopes, feeling the boundless joy of the leaper, a deep voice chanting through him.

Poise tripped, lunging into a cock and spring assault.
Huffing, heart-flooded, headlong over a flashing flush I vault.
Yes, I hear you chattering.
No, I will not halt.

At 5 p.m. that day, the shift was ending at an Italian eatery in the Seattle university district. In the back room, two waitresses in their mid-twenties were hanging up their aprons. The shorter, a brunette with a pug nose and ponytail, wore a name tag with *Jean* on it. She nodded to the other as Lindy stepped toward them, counting her tip money. Lindy's delicate features were hard-set, her blue eyes tired.

"Better?" Jean wondered.

"Not bad." Lindy sighed and untied her apron.

The taller waitress, Eva, smiled. "It takes a while to put any money away. How old are you?"

Lindy saw the solicitude in Eva's face. "Twenty," she said.

"Why don't you come over for lunch this Saturday?" Eva asked.

Lindy was surprised. Her gaze shifted, then she smiled and seemed about to accept.

"We're going to plan Solveig's baby shower," Jean explained.

Lindy's eyes went cold, and she looked away.

Eva sensed her discomfort. "We're getting together at noon," she said tentatively.

"Thanks," Lindy nodded. "It was a nice thought, but I'm busy."

Jean and Eva traded glances. There seemed nothing more to say. Lindy was making ready to leave when she recalled something.

"I'm sorry," she turned, fixing Jean. "Did you—"

Jean frowned.

Lindy made a pained face.

"Oh, I nearly forgot," Jean laughed. She fished in her purse, glanced around to make sure they weren't being watched, and passed

Lindy a baggie of yellow capsules. "Have you been to the Arboretum?" she muttered. "Great place to be high."

Lindy gave her a thankful look. "They're not for me."

Eva raised her brows. "The mystery man."

"When do we get to meet him?" Jean asked.

"Don't hold your breath," Lindy said wryly. She was thinking of how Ransom would respond to a baby shower invitation, but when she closed her handbag and looked up, she realized they had taken her comment the wrong way.

"Relax," Jean said with irritation. "We've got our own."

Eva shook her head.

Lindy watched them leave. A minute later, she exited alone, stepping quickly toward her beat-up Dodge, digging in her handbag for her keys. By the time she reached the car, she was in tears.

It was dusk when Lindy reached the small house they were renting on Sunset Hill. It clung to the edge of a cliff overlooking Puget Sound. Erik's van was in the drive, so she parked the Dodge on the street, descended the walkway, and climbed the short stair to the front door. Across the Sound, a hundred bright torches flared on the peaks of the Olympic Mountains. She paused to admire them, fit the key in the lock, swung the door open and stepped inside.

The walls of the front room were a patchwork of maps and mountain scenes. Books and climbing gear were piled on the furniture and strewn across the floor. From a re-creation of the wilds, their living space had been transformed into a base camp. Ransom stood beside the bookcase, reading. Erik was across the room, loading his carryall with the street clothes he'd stowed there that morning.

As Lindy set her handbag down, she sensed the tension between the two men.

Erik retrieved his jacket from a chair, combed his hand through his curly blonde hair, and gave Lindy a sullen look. "Why do you put up with it?"

She glanced at Ransom. He made a cautionary face, and she remained silent.

"We played 'lamb chop in outer space' again," Erik said accusingly. "He went straight up an overhang. The rope was in his way, so he unclipped."

Lindy didn't respond, but her gaze grew dark.

"Then he put on his duds and yowled the afternoon away," Erik said. "Quite a climb." He stepped toward the door, and as he passed, he touched her shoulder.

She recoiled, saw his gallant look and laughed. "Are you leaving?"

Erik exhaled with disgust, eyeing them as if they were deranged. "You deserve each other."

As the door closed behind him, Ransom moved to embrace her.

"What happened?" she wondered.

He shook his head, dismissing Erik. "How was work?" He saw trouble in her eyes.

She sagged in his arms. "Not so good."

"Tell me." His tone was protective, edged with guilt.

She shrugged it off. "*You* tell *me,*" her face creased, "about the climb."

He beamed. "It was incredible."

Lindy laughed, livened by his passion.

"I was at the top of this peak," he said excitedly. "I could hear my echo from across the canyon. It was like the ram had leaped out of me and was springing across the slopes."

The glow in his eyes nourished her. These past months, his monomania had conjured a potent magic, and she was the only person he shared it with.

"That piece I wrote after our trip on Mt. Rainier—about the birth of the ram?" He was joyful with some discovery. "He has a story. If I follow him," he glanced beyond her, tracking the ram's progress, "he'll reveal it. And I'll write it down. Through the chants and this manuscript, he'll relate his quest, in his own voice."

"What happens to him?" she wondered.

Ransom gave her a mystified look, acknowledging his challenge. His gaze turned inward. "Don't you have a clue?" he muttered, chiding himself. "I brought a little of the mountain back." He stooped over his pack and rose with a rock fragment in his hand.

Lindy fingered the rock's dark grain, imagining his cloven shoes planted on it, feeling some of the exhilaration he must have felt.

"I wouldn't be doing this without you," he said, his eyes deep with devotion. He raised the rock to kiss her fingers.

Lindy saw him sniff and frown, and she jerked her hand away, gazing at it as if she wanted to cut it off. "I wiped out the ashtrays before I left," she said, wounded and self-pitying.

"I'm sorry."

Her eye caught something behind him. "What's that?" she glowered. A new spotting scope stood on a tripod beside the sofa.

He gave her a confused look. "We talked about—"

"Look at this!" Lindy's gesture took in all the gear in the room.

Ransom turned aside. "I can't pump gas and be a shaman in my spare time."

"No," she said bitingly, "I'm the one who gets the dead-end job."

"Lindy—" He frowned.

"I want you to realize your dream, but—"

"*My* dream?" Ransom stared at her.

Her eyes were resentful. "I have some dreams of my own."

"Such as?"

One eye narrowed on him. "A man who provides. A family."

Ransom was stunned.

"Does that mean anything to you?" Lindy wondered.

"A family?" He laughed and gave her a helpless look.

Lindy flushed with rage. A hundred smothered pangs rose at once. She hooked her fingers on the thong around her neck and tugged at it, the red star flaring on her brow. "I hate you."

Her words stabbed him to the quick. Anger had always seemed part of her courage, directed outward, keeping them close. "Hate?" He eyed her despairingly, feeling shame descending on him. He had to believe in the nobility of his quest.

"All you care about is your ram," she said bitterly. "I buy you drugs and you get high by yourself." She gave him a grieving look.

"I always imagine you're with me." Ransom shook his head, realizing how foolish that sounded. Their great journey was ending, he thought. He wasn't equal to it.

The sight of his devastation jolted her. She twisted about. "I've infected you," she said mournfully. "You've got the fleeing disease."

Ransom was inconsolable. She needed him, and he had forgotten how much. The doubts that plagued him—they plagued her too. What was he doing to them? "The disease comes from me," he said. "My obsession."

She grew still.

"We're cut off from everyone," he lamented. "I don't have a job, a future— Just this idea. The shred of a story, a few songs—"

She regarded him somberly.

He shook his head. "I'm going back to school." At his words, he saw that terrible longing for escape well in her eyes, and he knew he'd failed her.

"Ransom—" She hugged him. He was the only real happiness she'd known.

"I'm Sam," he said with defeat.

"No," she sobbed into his chest, embracing him desperately. "You're Ransom. I don't want kids or a man with a job. That's someone else's life."

He felt her heartbreak, even as she voiced it.

"I just want you back," Lindy sobbed. "When we're apart, I can't bear it. What I said—" She couldn't repeat the words. "I didn't mean it. You know that, don't you?" She shuddered. "It's my aunt, inside me."

He shut his eyes, seeking that place beyond doubt for both of them, feeling its strength infuse him. His lips moved, singing softly.

> *At the edge of the world, over the grass I fly.*
> *Knowing this gait is right, without knowing why.*
> *A feather-thin fate glowing*
> *In a golden eye.*

"I try to hide her from you," Lindy mourned. "But when I'm afraid, she comes out. I'll never be rid of her."

Ransom stroked her temple as he sang.

> *The doubts chatter louder, into my ears and through.*
> *Where are you headed so fast? Don't you have a clue?*
> *This mounting dread, what does it mean?*
> *Don't you wish you knew?*

The melody soothed her, and the feelings he voiced—the hopes and fears of a traveler in a strange wilderness—brought her back. "Forgive me," Lindy said, lifting her head.

He put his arm around her. "I love you," he said. "All of you. Even when you hate me. When I was fearful, that was the part of you that opened me up."

Her eyes were dark. "I won't let you go," she whispered.

"It's just like then," Ransom said. "I was pulling away. You've brought me back."

She kissed him, and all her hunger and longing reached through. His confidence returned, and as their lips parted, he glanced at the spotting scope.

"Don't be angry with me, but—" He looked abashed.

"What?"

He eyed her uncertainly. "It would break the bank—"

She laughed at his resilience. "Let me guess." They had talked about a trip to Alaska since arriving in Washington.

"The two of us," he said tenderly.

She smiled at the devotion in his eyes, finding her hope again. "When?"

"Next week, if you can get the time off." He coaxed her toward the spotting scope. "The optics are unbelievable. You can see McKinley Park from here." He trained it to one side of the window and adjusted the focusing ring. "Hold your breath—"

She squinted one eye and peered through the ocular at a picture tacked to the wall.

"That's Cathedral Mountain," he said. "See the sheep?"

Through the scope, a half-dozen Dall rams were visible, poised on the crest of a rugged peak. The rock around them glittered and the sun was golden on their horns.

A week later they were in a jetliner headed for Fairbanks. They crouched together before the oval window, watching the rugged mountains and ice fields of the Alaskan coast, Lindy hugging Ransom's arm, full of wonder. Ransom was like someone waking on the far side of sleep, the world of his dreams before him.

In Fairbanks, they rented a car and drove south to Paxson. A hundred miles of gravel highway threaded forests of stunted spruce, leading them to a lodge outside McKinley Park. The next morning dawned clear, and they followed the road in. The foothills were dark, the intervening slopes tinged pink by the northern autumn. As they rose above treeline, the vistas that Ransom had imagined from photographs and descriptions appeared. A great valley opened before him, and beyond, a rugged upland, ridge on ridge—a place where neither heart nor mind could feel confinement. Lindy grabbed his sleeve. A herd of caribou ambled across a green slope, and below on the gravel bar, a grizzly bear was digging. The sight of large animals roaming free surprised them both. They looked for the giant white peak, but it was shrouded in clouds.

When they reached Cathedral Mountain, Ransom pulled over, glancing at Lindy as if he expected that the sheep in the picture back in Seattle might still be holding their pose. And there they were—a different band, in a different spot—but the white dots on the steep rock could only be Dalls. He set up the spotting scope with trembling hands. When he focused, he was looking at the real thing—a dozen ewes grazing the tundra while their lambs leaped in the rocks.

The road continued into the park, across a bridge spanning the east fork of the Toklat River, and up into the Polychrome Cliffs, a place that rang through the writings of Charles Sheldon and other early seekers of rams. With reverence, Ransom parked the car on the roadside and stepped out. They packed the scope and some warm clothing, and started through the willows, heading for a high ridge.

Above the brush, the tundra blazed scarlet. As they angled around the slope, cliffs came into view, deeply grooved, gleaming ocher and orange. A breeze was blowing, but the air was warm and everything was touched by sun. They climbed in silence. To draw close to wild sheep, Ransom had read, you had to stalk them as a hunter would: get up high without being seen, stay in the lee of crests, and look over and see. Unlike the sheep men bred, the wild Dalls had keen senses. They were smart and wary. As the slopes grew steeper, and rock replaced foliage, his own senses sharpened. Every sight reached him, every sound.

A hundred feet below the ridge, he glanced over his shoulder and sank to his knees, his heart pounding in his ears. There were sheep on the opposite side of the stream valley. He pulled the scope from his pack and focused it while Lindy huddled beside him. Three rams sprang across the eyepiece, horns half-curl, full-curl, and three-quarter. White as winter snow, necks stiff, balancing the golden coils as they leaped, they were every bit the archetype of purity and command that Ransom had imagined. What a blessing to the earth, he thought, that creatures like this moved upon it. They slowed as they reached the divide, and one turned his head to regard them. "Look." He ducked aside to give Lindy room. A few moments later the rams were gone.

Ransom groaned, hooking Lindy with his arm and rolling over her. "The way they spring—" He kissed her, full of wonder. "They keep their hinds together. A unified thrust." He arched against her, demonstrating. "That's why people think sheep and goats are creatures of lust."

She laughed, embracing him with her legs, gazing adoringly in his eyes. They were running, flying, in their own world again, just the two of them, as he'd promised.

He unbuttoned his shirt. The hunger it triggered in her surprised him. She stripped his pants down, biting his left pectoral, rolling the muscle between her teeth. They tore their boots and underclothes off.

"Like they do," he said. Without a word, she rose onto her hands and knees. Trembling all over, he mounted her, her warmth like a current flowing to meet him. His loins fired, and he was suddenly the creature he'd dreamed of, head high, hunched and thrusting between earth and sky.

A hundred feet up, on the crest of the ridge, a curl of gold rose. It hovered there, rugose and glittering like a comber thrown up by an unknown sea brimming on the far side. Steadily, a great ram bore it up, standing on the ridge with his head turned away. Ransom froze. The horns were beyond full curl, tips rising to his crown and flaring out. Lindy glanced back, and as she turned to follow Ransom's gaze, the patriarch faced him.

The wisdom in those features stunned Ransom. He drank in the sight—the ram's sensing nostrils, the calm in his golden eyes—expecting the animal to flee. But the patriarch stood motionless, regarding them both.

Ransom raised himself, heart racing. The ram could smell their lust, and Ransom thought he saw an indulgence in his eyes. Lindy was on her feet now, arms around her middle, looking bewildered and vulnerable, wondering what Ransom was going to do.

Naked and trembling, Ransom stepped forward. The patriarch lowered his head and lifted his fore, doing the same. Ransom stopped. The ram did the same. Again Ransom came forward, heels lifted half-consciously, walking on the balls of his feet. The patriarch descended to meet him, hooves crunching the amber gravel, staring straight at him. His fearlessness was unsettling. Ransom expected him to spook and wheel. Fifty feet. Forty. For a moment, Ransom wondered if he was in danger. The ram was his size, emanating power, male confidence and command. These were the ram's peaks, his swards, his cliffs. His neck was thick and stiff, bearing the golden coils high. *You seek,* the ram's eyes said. *I've found. You aspire. I am.*

A strange thought came to Ransom—he needed horns. He raised his hands on either side of his head and flexed his wrists. He felt foolish, and worried he'd scare the ram. Then he saw with astonishment the ram's eyes were smiling. The ram knew him without horns. Who he really was. A leaper, one of the white band, born for high places.

They were a dozen feet apart now. The patriarch stopped. So did Ransom. The power in those golden eyes seemed to open up, as if the ram understood his quest and had been expecting him. It was an arduous journey, but a treasure lay at its end, more precious than Ransom had ever imagined, and the old ram knew the way. The molten heart was secreted in these heights, and all the years of the ram's life, his fibers had drawn power from it. Not through his mind, but through his hooves and his stride.

Ransom saw the ram's white chest quiver, felt the throb in his own chest beating the same time. The ancient face softened and the patriarch reached out, flowing his heart to him through his glowing eyes. The ram was showing him— Ransom let go, surrendering as Lindy had taught him, feeling himself borne toward the mysterious current, wild and roaring with lives unhuman, so much more powerful—

It was too intense. He turned aside, half-ashamed, glancing at Lindy as he backed away. She was standing there naked, watching. The patriarch turned toward her, suddenly fearful. His shoulder rose, he pivoted to flee. Perhaps he finally recognized them for who they were, or saw something threatening in Lindy's face. With a series of vaults, he regained the crest and passed over, coils held high.

Ransom wobbled down, the broken rock needling his feet. Lindy stooped to gather their clothes. When he reached her, they embraced. He was in shock.

Neither spoke till they had descended the slope and were approaching a small stream.

"I've always been a leaper," Ransom muttered. "That's what broad jumping in high school was about." The sensation of thrusting himself from the earth, hurling himself into the air, came back to him. "He saw that in me." He shook his head. "Is that crazy?"

"You communicated with him," she said softly. A strange calm possessed her. Her gaze brimmed understanding, as if something obscure had been finally revealed.

"He was frightened at the end."

"Not until you looked away."

Her confidence braced him. "I could see the molten heart in his eyes," Ransom said. The encounter felt more and more like a meeting with destiny. "And the wrinkles in his horns—" He gave her a musing look. "A record of the wild thoughts emerging from his head, year by year."

She nodded. They descended in silence.

"You're as rare a creature as that ram," Ransom said softly.

Lindy turned to him, the sweetness of their first week together shining in her eyes.

"There's no one else in the world," he said, "who would understand this."

They reached the stream. Lindy took her pack off.

"How old do they get?" She knelt to fill her water bottle.

"Fourteen or fifteen. He has another summer or two. This might be his last."

Lindy motioned excitedly.

"What?" Ransom crouched beside her.

"Something was here." She pointed.

Inside a crescent of gravel, there were prints in the sand. Each had a deltoid palm with four toe pads and sharp holes where claws had sunk in.

He eyed them with amazement. "Wolves."

She stepped forward, following the tracks to where they disappeared beneath the flow. "When do you think they were here?"

Ransom didn't reply.

She glanced back, seeing his absorption. "What's wrong?"

He gave her a solemn look. "They're death to sheep." He'd read many accounts of packs running Dalls down. "They were looking for our patriarch."

Lindy smiled. "They didn't find him."

"Creatures of nightmare." Ransom conjured the wolves from their prints, imagining the terror a ram would feel. "Coursing the hills, hoping to catch you at a weak moment."

"They have to eat," Lindy said.

"Whose side are you on?" Ransom laughed. Then something strange happened, one of those moments when the fabric of reality thins and a deeper truth surfaces through it. The sun was low, and as Lindy's face turned, the star on her hairline caught the light. It was like a prism, refracting the fragments of her personality from between its arms. The overpowering need, the unforgiven abuse, the wisdom, the child's joy struggling to be heard. Traveling together like a pack.

"Yours," she said playfully. "I'm on your side."

Ransom gazed at her. "I'm the ram and you're the wolves."

Her lips parted, stunned. "How can you say that?"

"It's the miracle of my life," he shook his head, seeing the pain clouding her blue eyes. "You wouldn't let me retreat, you wouldn't let me escape."

Her gaze shifted, wandering some dark byway. "I'm not your enemy," she said, half to herself.

"Of course not—" He embraced her, lifting her face up to his. "Forget that they're predators. I was fearful. You opened me. You bared my heart and taught me surrender." He caressed her temple, gazing at her with great tenderness. "This ram cherishes his wound."

"Wound?" Her laugh was strained and she frowned. But she knew what he meant.

Ransom kissed her lips. "The blood *my* pack thirsts for is the molten heart, the power of love." He kissed her nape, and pressed himself against her.

She sighed into his shoulder, disturbed but still glad to have him close.

"We're born with joy," Ransom said. "The self grows like a husk around that fruit. Surrender—giving the self up—takes us back." He sank into the grasses, pulling her with him. She murmured as he unclothed her. When he drew her pants down, she tried to squirm away, but when he wrestled her back, her naked thighs clutched him. "Finding our hearts," he whispered, "is the greatest thing we've ever done. The greatest thing we'll ever do."

He entered her, and she was warm and welcoming, eager to have him. As their desire mounted, the notion that she was wolfish tickled her. She sniffed his collarbone, growling and clawing his ribs. But as the strokes deepened, her resentment grew, the rage inside her twisted her closer, insistent, making angry demands. Ransom, as always, was fearful. But he surmounted his fears and let himself go, gasping desperately in her ear, and as his heart opened to her, Lindy's resentment died, the seething in her belly ceased and the spasms started, and there was only her need mixed with his own. In the commingling, their hearts, it seemed to Ransom, melted. And in that flood of love, Lindy felt the sweet child inside her returning, whole and safe once again.

They held each other for a long time. The true Lindy, innocent and cherished, cried with blissful disbelief in the outpouring of Ransom's heart, feeling perfect peace, sealing the devotion that made it possible. Nothing had to be spoken. They were closer than they'd ever been—because, for the first time, they understood how fragile their love was, and because in this vast land they felt themselves finally in a world of their own, ascendant over the one they'd fled. There was something, as well, in the relation of wolves and ram that shed a more poignant light on their intimacy. At the moment of their most passionate feelings, both were awake to it, and as they listened to their sighs merging with the burble of the stream, along with their gratitude and reassurance was a sense that some secret compact of their natures was running its course.

An hour later, they reached the park road. A truck approached, raising a train of dust. They waved, the truck stopped, and a park ranger rolled down his window. He spoke, they climbed in, and the truck started up a grade.

The ranger glanced at Ransom, impressed by his story. "It happens, but not often. They crave salt. A biologist brought them clay from a lick a few years ago—maybe you smelled like him." His eyes twinkled. "Maybe you've got Dall karma."

"You noticed," Ransom smiled.

"The cliffs are beautiful," Lindy said.

The ranger nodded. "They're volcanic."

Ransom imagined the peaks erupting. "Must have been exciting for the sheep."

"All that happened before the sheep," the ranger said. "A hundred million years before." As they rounded a bend, the sun flared through the windshield. "The Dalls in the Wrangells—they've seen eruptions."

"The Wrangells?"

"Southeast of here. All the record rams come from there. That your car?"

"Yes," Lindy said, glancing at Ransom. He was lost in thought.

The truck halted. Lindy shook Ransom's arm and he opened the door. Outside, he turned again to the ranger. "It's a park? The Wrangells?"

The ranger shook his head. "Just a giant wilderness with four volcanoes. No people and no roads. Mt. Wrangell is active."

"Active?"

"Technically," the ranger nodded.

"How do you get in?"

"Fly."

They thanked the ranger for the lift. As his truck disappeared around the bend, Lindy started toward their car. Ransom went the other way, wandering onto the tundra. She came after him.

"Ransom—"

He stopped, his eyes roaming the distant ridges.

"Are you alright?"

"I'm on fire." He turned, eyes glazed with awe. "There's a mountain where wild rams live and the rock erupts molten from the earth's heart."

She smiled, watching him, wondering where this would lead.

"Imagine," he said. "A fountain of glowing fire. The white leaper in the cliffs and the wolves below." He gave her a marveling look. "That's it."

"What?"

"The story. A ram pursued by a pack of wolves up Mt. Wrangell—the headwaters of the molten heart. Love through surrender—a drama enacted in the wilderness by a man who's a ram and a woman who's a pack." He looked for her reaction.

She nodded, understanding the idea and troubled by it.

"That was a big leap," he admitted.

"It really was." In their intimacy, she'd felt her powers restored. She clung to that calm now.

"It would express our love," Ransom said. "What you've taught me about surrender." He embraced her, reassuring her, and himself as well.

She closed her eyes. "The love is more important than the expression."

"Of course it is. The story wouldn't mean anything if I lost you." He gazed at her, seeing her retreat. In a heartbeat, the foundation of his vision crumbled. "What was I thinking?" he mumbled darkly. "What's the matter with me?"

Lindy heard his despair, and when she opened her eyes it was as if she was seeing him for the first time. Ransom was plagued by self-doubt. Her devotion alleviated it, allowing his spirit to soar.

"I'll never turn my ideas into anything." Ransom saw the perception in her face, and his shame at having his incapacity recognized overwhelmed him. "Those golden eyes— I imagine I have that kind of power, but I don't. I never will—" The glory of the fateful encounter faded, and all he could see was the great gulf that lay between himself and the ram.

Lindy hugged him. She cherished the dreaming child inside him, as she cherished her own, and she wished it freedom with all her heart. "Ransom," she looked at him. "Think what's just happened to us. This is one of the most wonderful days of my life."

He seemed not to hear.

"The wolves and the ram," she nodded, giving him a wry smile. "Head for the clouds," she made a threatening face, "if you know what's good for you."

He regarded her gravely. "If I keep on with this, I'll risk what we have."

"Not if we stay close."

"We need to rejoin the human race," he said. "Before it's too late."

Lindy's eyes grew dark, seeing the death of his joy, and of her own. "You can't give up."

He struggled with his humiliation. "You want a man who provides, and you deserve one."

She shook her head, summoning her strength. "When I'm lonely, I get frightened." She put her hand on his thigh, recalling their lovemaking. "I long for a family and the home I never had." She spoke wistfully, realizing their path led a wilder way. "Ransom—" She turned his face toward her.

Her eyes said she was strong enough for both of them. Ransom sighed. She kissed him. "I'm weak," Lindy said. "You have to help me."

He took a breath. "If it wasn't so vague and confused—" His gaze drifted over her shoulder. "The story, the chants—" His goal seemed impossibly distant.

"You're trying to express the mystery of our hearts," she said. "You can do it. But it won't all be leaping. Some of it has to be deliberate, a step at a time."

Ransom frowned. Her words were sobering him to his tasks. "The next hurdle—" He glanced at her and saw such confidence and calm, it made him laugh. "I need to learn a lot more about wolves."

The Wolves

Six

***U**pon their return to Seattle, Ransom applied himself with fresh determination. He started one draft after another of his story, writing during the day and doing research at night and on weekends with Lindy's assistance. All winter, they commuted between Sunset Hill and the University of Washington, in the libraries till closing time poring over books and scientific articles, learning everything they could about wolves, volcanoes, and the Wrangell Mountains. They had adventured together, and lived together, but this was the first time they'd worked together. And it went well—so well, in fact, that when spring came and Ransom proposed that he was going to make a quick trip to Alaska on his own, neither saw anything amiss.

Ransom's intent was to fill in some gaps at the University of Alaska, and he expected his stay in Fairbanks to last a week or two. To his surprise, one opportunity after another presented itself, and before he realized it, two months had passed and June had arrived. They missed each other terribly, but Ransom and Lindy were too strapped financially for him to return to Seattle even for a few days. Out of his discussions with field researchers in Fairbanks, a trip to the

Wrangells materialized, and he proposed that he would remain in Alaska another month, through early July. Lindy was upset, but she couldn't leave her job for more than a week or two, and they could see no other alternatives.

It was June 4, Friday, in a birch forest on the outskirts of Fairbanks. The tree crowns were bright green and quivered with light. At seven in the evening, the sun was still high enough to make the white trunks glow on either side of a weathered shed.

Inside the shed, Ransom turned the cock on a water jug and filled a cup. He glanced over his shoulder, drew his hand out of his parka, eyed the quarter tab and put it on his tongue. He grabbed a fresh syringe from the bench and stepped out of the shed, crossing the tramped ground, his boots rustling the leaf litter.

On the ground beside a chain link fence, a man with khaki pants and a chamois shirt stooped over a large gray wolf. As Ransom approached, he drew a needle out of the wolf's haunch and raised his face, smiling gravely. Calvin Bauer, University of Alaska professor of biology, passed the scarlet cylinder to Ransom and received the fresh syringe in exchange.

Ransom watched Calvin jab the comatose wolf. The animal's hazel eye blinked, a long tongue hanging from its muzzle. Calvin gave a tired sigh, as if he too was sedated. Except for his eyes, which darted keenly from the wolf's face to the syringe filling with blood, his movements were dulled by an exhaustion no sleep could erase. Like most of the faculty members Ransom had met, love of the wilds had brought Calvin to Alaska, but somewhere along the way his passions had mired. There were times when not even his beloved wolves could lift his spirits. As he removed the needle, breezes swayed the trees.

"Done." Calvin rose and touched his palm to the holstered pistol on his hip. Then he dug in his pants pocket and tossed Ransom his keys.

Ransom opened the padlock and swung the gate back. Together they carried the wolf into the enclosure, moving slowly and cautiously, setting it down ten feet from the den. On the far side of a hillock, the other pack members were watching.

"I'll chill them," Calvin muttered at the blood samples, "and we'll get dinner."

They exited the enclosure and Calvin headed toward the shed. As Calvin ducked inside, Ransom pulled a second padlock from his parka and swapped it with the one hanging open on the gate latch. Then he strode to the end of the rutted drive where a road-killed moose calf lay huddled, its fores and hinds bound with twine. He slid a pole beneath its limbs and lifted. Calvin met him on the other side and heaved his end up, balancing the load over his shoulders. They carried the dead animal through the gate, taking small unhurried steps. As they set it down, the wolves crept forward, eyes intent, snouts aimed. Packs in the wild didn't attack humans, but approaching them in an enclosure could be dangerous—especially when meat was near. The two men moved back through the gate.

Calvin secured the padlock. "Thanks." He gave Ransom an earnest look.

Ransom smiled. "It's been a great couple of months."

"I've enjoyed your company," Calvin said, sitting on an observation bench facing the enclosure. He watched the wolf pack surround the calf. "Got what you wanted?"

Ransom nodded. "There's one thing—more a subjective question, not something you can measure."

Calvin was listening.

"What's their psychological state during the hunt?"

Calvin glanced at his hands and brushed them together, making a considered face, as if about to read from one of his papers. "Eager. Playful. The dominance hierarchy is preserved—"

"I mean when they're running down prey." Ransom saw reticence draw over the professor's face. "Come on, Cal. What's going on inside them?"

Calvin laughed, a childish sound. "They're crazed."

"Tell me."

"Ever see a falcon stoop? Hear it screaming?"

Inside the enclosure, the pack was pulling the moose calf apart.

"You've seen them up close?"

"Once," Calvin said.

Ransom paused before Calvin's reserve. The professor was secretive about his wolves, didn't talk to the press about them or allow them to be photographed. Calvin said he was fearful of wolf politics, but Ransom discerned another reason for his guardedness. "Tell me about it."

"We were on a tributary of the Koyukuk. It was twilight, we were eating. A pack charged into the middle of our camp, nine of them chasing a young caribou. They'd already hobbled him and they knew he was theirs."

Ransom saw the glint in Calvin's eyes.

"They brought that caribou down right in front of my tent. I was standing ten feet away, but they didn't see me. They were raving mad. Bloodlust is the only word for it. One of them had his hind legs in the campfire. I could smell his fur burning."

Ransom was transfixed. The scientist was gone, and the man in his place shared his turbulent emotions as he'd felt them.

"They tore his hams apart and ate his intestines. They were deep inside him. He was still grunting and struggling. It went on for twenty minutes. Finally, when the caribou was dead and they'd eaten half his carcass, they woke up and realized where they were."

Ransom shuddered, envisioning a ram in the caribou's place.

"To say they take pleasure in it—that doesn't come close. Killing is like sex for them, a state of rapture. We're omnivores, we have a little of that in us, but—" Calvin shook his head. "'The wolf's role in the ecology of ungulate prey populations,'" he mimicked his lexicon, "doesn't quite capture it."

"No, it doesn't."

Calvin gave him a thoughtful look. "There's something special about you. You're invigorating to be around." He laughed. "Like dawn in the woods, when it's freezing and all your senses are alert. You feel a little more alive." He rose. "By the way, I'd be happy to review your book for technical accuracy, if you'd like."

Ransom nodded. "Thanks. And thanks for hosting the dinner."

"We're looking forward to it." Calvin started down the drive toward his car, expecting Ransom to follow.

"I wonder, would you mind if I howled with them one last time?"

Calvin smiled. "Go right ahead. See you Sunday."

Ransom returned to the enclosure and peered through the fence. The calf was in pieces now, the wolves calmer, chewing on their chosen parts. Ransom waited for Calvin's car to disappear, then went to the gate, found the key in his pocket and opened the padlock.

When he entered the enclosure, the pack was instantly aware. The omega wolf, curled to the side, having lost its fight to join the feast, raised its harried face and stared. A pale female drew her snout from the split belly, legs tense and quivering. A yearling whimpered. As he drew closer, Ransom could smell the calf's insides. One by one, the wolves met him with their eyes. The lead, a male weighing a hundred and twenty pounds, challenged him, standing his ground, hackles bristling through his gray fur, his muzzle shiny to the eyes with blood. Ransom avoided his gaze, feeling the courage and calm of the patriarch guiding him step by step. The other wolves moved quietly to either side, circling.

Ransom stopped and took a breath, imagining he was a ram in

their midst. The wolf musk sickened him. They were lunging, sinking their fangs into him, bringing him down. He could feel their hunger, their mad craving. This was what it was like to be prey. He lowered his vision slowly till he was staring the alpha in the face. The power in those eyes couldn't be denied. Ransom's heart throbbed like a frightened rabbit's, but he let his arms go limp and offered it to them, and a beatific sensation welled inside him—the treasure of martyrs, an ecstasy only the hopeless know.

The alpha growled deep in his throat, tensing toward him, and terror exploded in Ransom's brain. But before he lunged, another wolf shouldered into him and the alpha backed away, licking his jaws. Ransom's rescuer peered up at him with a strange knowing, the same care and wisdom he found in Lindy's eyes. They weren't going to attack. The alpha sat on his haunches and the others followed his example.

Ransom craned his head back and raised a high-pitched moan. The knowing wolf responded, low and mournful, then the two yearlings joined in, one squealing, one yapping. And then they were all howling in chorus.

They were death and he was among them, but Ransom felt the soul in their voices, and the love. They sang to each other's hearts, and to his own, and to the source of all hearts who had fashioned life and death and built a beautiful river of blood between. It was desire for their prey that drew the pack together, just as love for him made a shattered Lindy whole.

The birches were weaving and turning, their tops opening and closing, fountains bursting with glowing leaves, sprays of flame scattering from the flashing boughs. Through this dizzying spatter, Ransom imagined himself rising. Beyond the trees, a blinding sun shone: the source of everything molten. He was headed toward it, high above wolves and forest, rushing to meet that living fire.

The Bauer residence was close to its neighbors. The Alaska Range spread out on either side as far as the eye could see, the endless forest lapping against its small green lawn. At eight in the evening it was still daylight. The windows were lit and there were cars on the gravel drive. Two children on bicycles turned onto it, hollering.

Inside, Ransom and four professors from the University of Alaska were gathered around a dining room table cluttered with pictures and papers. Calvin Bauer was on his left. Sid Yasuda, a geologist at the university's Geophysical Institute, was on his right. Yasuda was slight of build with short-clipped hair, about forty, and overdressed as always, in a gray sport coat with a white shirt and a thin black tie. Across the table was Katherine Getz, professor of ornithology, and Hank Papadakis, professor of botany. Ransom's relationships with them had come quickly, assisted by the fact that the academics had their own curiosities about the Wrangells, nearly unknown to science.

"I added three species," Hank Papadakis said. He smiled at the list of plants through his trimmed beard and passed it to Ransom. He was youthfully dressed, a necklace of beads looped across the front of his turtleneck sweater. "He's collated Scott's work in Chitistone Pass with Murray's collection from the Skolai, adding and dropping using Hultén's range maps." Hank's voice was eager as a teenager's. "What's the total?"

"A hundred and sixty," Ransom said.

Katherine Getz smiled crisply. She was perusing the field guide Ransom had assembled, eyeing the pictures cut and pasted from books and journal articles. One hand turned the pages, while the other tucked her short brown curls behind her ear. Her small frame was stiff and professional, commanding its share of respect at the table. "Lichens too?"

Ransom nodded. "I'll collect anything I can't identify."

"Isn't this wonderful?" Hank shared his admiration with Calvin and Yasuda. "Like a Victorian naturalist."

Ransom smiled. Calvin gave him a private wink.

"There's no information on the birds of Mt. Wrangell," Katherine told the group. Her eyes were sharp and her lip curled into a smirk. "Don't forget to ID my gulls," she reminded Ransom, then swallowed what was left in her wine glass.

"Probably pipits up high," Hank said, glancing at her.

Katherine ignored him. "You'll see pipits." She spoke curtly, as if scolding Hank. Then to Ransom, "A special bird."

"What makes them special?" Ransom asked, sensing Katherine's hostility. Hank was frowning at her.

"They're small and brown," Katherine said, "not much larger than a house sparrow." Her features softened. "But there's no bird as brave." She spoke to Ransom alone, avoiding Hank's gaze. "They're so curious, so free and full of heart."

Ransom saw the longing in her eyes, and when she smiled, instead of seeing cheer in her face, he saw the lines crossing it. It was like a broken windshield on the verge of collapsing.

"The bird world is full of obnoxious males," Katherine said. "Strutting and cheeping, gaudily dressed. Pipits are the real thing. True romantics."

Her colleagues laughed at her invective, accustomed to it. Ransom saw her sadness.

"Calvin and I were talking about magpies," he said. "How they follow wolf packs."

Katherine nodded. "For scraps."

"Or to help them hunt." Ransom watched her.

"There are reports of magpies spotting injured prey," Calvin said, "and calling wolves to the kill."

"It's possible," Katherine allowed. "In England, they thought they could smell sickness. 'By the window a magpie flies. By the midnight chimes someone dies.'"

"There'll be none of that once the food's served," Mrs. Bauer warned them. She circled the table, refilling glasses from a dark bottle with an air of tolerance. Short and simple, she was a woman who had resigned herself to the respect and attention of her children, and who, as a consequence, now treated all adults like toddlers. "Are you sure you won't have a little wine?" she asked Ransom in a chiding tone.

Calvin scowled and glanced impatiently at his wife.

Ransom, conscious of her discomfort, smiled and shook his head. She gazed around the table for other takers. Just then, the front door slammed, and her two children pounded across the living room.

"Guess what we found!" a towheaded boy exulted to the group. His shirt and trousers were caked with dirt.

"Upstairs and wash yourselves," Mrs. Bauer barked. "Now!"

The boy turned, pouting, and his sister skulked after him.

"Aren't you the least bit interested?" Calvin glared at his wife.

The dinner party was instantly silent. Katherine stared at her wine. Hank raised his brows. Ransom watched Mrs. Bauer turn crimson. She seemed to be waiting for Calvin to recant, but he just waved her away with irritation. She gave him a wounded look, but returned to the kitchen.

Hank took a breath. He pointed at one of Ransom's maps. "There have to be wolves in the area." He glanced at Calvin.

Calvin nodded. "It's unlikely he'll see them."

"Who do you think's been through here?" Hank's finger traversed Mt. Wrangell's southern spurs.

"Indians and prospectors," Yasuda replied. "Hunters more recently." His answer was precise and formal. Behind his narrow glasses, his dark eyes shifted. "Oscar Rohn crossed the range on horseback in 1899."

Hank passed the map to Katherine.

"Is Burt Conklin coming?" Ransom wondered. He'd asked Yasuda to invite the head of the Geophysical Institute, the world's expert on Mt. Wrangell.

Yasuda made a regretful face. "Burt's a busy man."

"How long will you be out there?" Katherine asked.

"A month," Ransom replied.

"Alone?" Yasuda frowned.

Ransom nodded.

"You have an understanding wife," Katherine observed with her characteristic smirk.

Ransom nodded. "There's no one like her," he said softly.

Katherine's smirk faded. She peered at him with a quizzical expression, as if she'd stumbled over an unusual bird and was struggling to identify it. Ransom eyed her directly, inviting her scrutiny, and her features grew sober and intent.

"All this information you're gathering—" Yasuda seemed troubled. "You're not getting a degree or collecting for a museum."

"No."

"What's the purpose?" Yasuda's brow furrowed.

"Sid." Katherine gave him a disparaging look.

Hank chimed in. "Does everything have to be in the name of science?"

"I'm just curious." Yasuda's manner was deferential, but his hand moved with insinuating intent, floating palm-down toward Ransom's, settling on his wrist.

"He's writing a novel," Calvin said.

Yasuda made an impressed expression. "What about?"

"Wolves and sheep," Ransom said.

"Who wins?"

"They both do," Ransom said. "It's a love story."

"That's idealistic," Yasuda smiled.

"It's a time for idealism." Hank gave Yasuda a patient look. "He was at Berkeley. If I'd been there," he confided to Ransom, "I'd have been marching with you."

Ransom was gazing at an aerial photo of Mt. Wrangell's North Crater. "This is where I want to be." He slid the photo toward Yasuda.

"Not a friendly place." Yasuda's smile was humoring. "We put in survey stakes a few years ago. Solid steel, three inches thick. When we came back they were bent at right angles."

Ransom frowned at the research papers before him. "What does Burt Conklin really think?" He'd read the material carefully, but a key question remained unanswered. "Is it going to erupt?"

Yasuda shrugged. "The summit's getting hotter," his gaze circled the table, sharing a scientist's frustration with the lay world. "That's all we know."

"According to the local paper—" Ransom raised a copy of a news headline reading *Mount Wrangell Now in Active Eruption.* "On April 14, 1911, 'an immense volume of fire swept up into the sky.'"

Yasuda made a patient face.

Ransom saw the hint of a sneer in the professor's thin smile. "You don't believe it."

"The most recent lava flows scientifically confirmed," Yasuda replied, "are fifty thousand years old."

"Do they look like these?" Ransom pulled some photos from the pile and handed them to the geologist, his eyes flashing.

Yasuda nodded, uncertain what the point was. "Those are common flow structures."

"It looks like medieval armor, doesn't it?" Ransom glanced at

Hank and Calvin, passing one of the photos around. "You think of shields, bucklers, hip and shoulder coverings." He raised his brows at Sid.

Yasuda frowned. "Fracture planes."

"Look at these cliffs." Ransom passed another photo around. "The rock is like masonry. The walls of a fortress, with castellations and keyholes." He handed a picture to Katherine.

She gazed from the photo back to Ransom. He was obviously building to something.

"These squared-off structures," Ransom went on, "this columnar jointing—" Another photo. "Merlons and turrets— There's a lot of this in the Cascades."

"Typical of basalt flows." Yasuda eyed him suspiciously.

"Amazing, isn't it," Ransom continued. "That this seething effusion from the earth's core, so free and glowing, could cool into a landscape of defense." He watched their faces. "That's what my story's about."

Mrs. Bauer returned from the kitchen with salads.

Ransom gazed around the table. "How hearts that are guarded and protected can find their way back."

"Back?" Yasuda smiled, brow wrinkling.

"To the molten state." Ransom's voice rang with daring.

Hank looked delighted, but he didn't speak. Mrs. Bauer set the salads down, her attention over their heads, avoiding eye contact and further humiliation.

"A mountain explodes and magma fountains from it," Ransom said. "Can you remember when you felt like that? When your heart was welling inside you?"

"That's not geology," Yasuda laughed.

"It's more important than geology," Ransom said quietly.

Calvin eyed him with surprise. Mrs. Bauer scowled to herself. Katherine Getz tucked her curls behind her ear and peered down.

Ransom turned to her. "Katherine?"

At first, she didn't respond. She seemed to sense what an act of courage it was for him to share these ideas. Normally she would have remained aloof, but she wasn't her normal self that night. She was at a crossroads.

"I'm a woman fighting for a place in a man's world," she said, looking up, speaking stiffly to the group. "I've battled in the field and in faculty committees, and proven I'm man enough for both." She faced Ransom, regret softening her defiance. "I thought that was what I wanted, but it's not."

Hank sighed.

"I'm unmarried and childless," Katherine said. "Not even the birds give me joy." She gazed before her, at no one. "Their freedom reminds me of what I hoped for and how short I've fallen."

The tenor of the dinner party changed dramatically. Ransom gazed around the table.

Hank was regarding Katherine sadly. Calvin was riveted, his keen eyes taking it all in. Mrs. Bauer looked from her husband to Katherine, appalled.

Katherine faced her. "How does a woman stay young at heart?" she wondered softly. "Maybe she has to sit on a nest."

Yasuda unfolded his napkin quietly.

"We all have problems of the heart," Hank said with an understanding face.

"What are yours?" Ransom asked.

"That's a very personal question," Mrs. Bauer objected, defending the group, as if they all had a right to be as shut-in as she. Calvin ignored her. Yasuda laughed and shook his head.

Hank held his hand up. "Getting too easily attached," he said, answering Ransom's question. His expression brimmed with bravado. "Like Katherine, I've never married. I love women," he shook his head. "Too much, really." He combed his eyebrow with his finger.

"Hank—" Katherine rolled her eyes at him, as if she knew better.

"They're all still friends," Hank protested. It was obvious Katherine was one of them.

"What does that tell you?" She cocked her head at him. Then some buried resentment got the best of her. "Hank's a warbler," she laughed, speaking to the group. "Bright, cheery, and gone for the winter."

Hank stared at her, his face crimson. For a moment, he looked as if he might burst into a rage. Then he sat back, laughed, and stroked his thin beard.

Katherine lightened, sighing at Hank to ask his forgiveness for the remark. Ransom glanced at Calvin. He was rapt, watching Katherine the way he watched his wolves. Hank turned to Calvin, as if it was the host's turn. Calvin's eyes widened, mulling his response.

His wife was distraught. "Can I get you anything, Sid?" When Yasuda declined, she hurried into the kitchen.

"These are great questions," Calvin said, "for someone with his life before him." He scratched his graying head and frowned, as if to show how weary he was. Then he regarded Ransom with tenderness. "If I was twenty years younger—" Calvin left his words hanging.

In the silence, Hank gave Ransom a knowing look. When it came to the affairs of youth, Hank thought of himself as the adult who understood. He turned to Yasuda. "What do you think, Sid?"

The geologist considered the question. "I think," he turned politely to Ransom, "you've wasted a lot of our time."

"Come on," Hank glared.

"I don't feel that way," Katherine said.

"On false pretenses," Yasuda added, compounding Ransom's offense.

"I'll admit," Calvin mused, "I didn't know till tonight what this book was about." He gave Ransom a thoughtful look. "I'm surprised, but I'm not upset. I hope something good comes of the questions he's asking."

"Absolutely," Hank agreed, eyeing Yasuda harshly. "The rest of us stuck our necks out," he laughed. "You never answered the question."

Yasuda made a conciliatory face. "The heart beats without love," he said simply. "It has to. We're all alone in this world."

Ransom saw Yasuda's dark eyes glinting at him through the narrow lenses. Yasuda, recognizing what was politic, made a show of leniency and lowered his hand to his wrist again. Ransom felt a strange electricity.

Mrs. Bauer returned from the kitchen with two platters. She put one down and started around the table with the other. "Some pot roast, young man?" She regarded Ransom dubiously, raising her fork.

He smiled, declining with a humble face, apologizing for unsettling her. "My wife's the meat eater. The vegetables look good."

At ten-thirty that evening, the sun was still above the horizon and the sky was blue. Outside a diner near the entrance to the university, the traffic was as busy as midday. Inside, Ransom stood at the back, talking on a pay phone. His expression was strained and apologetic.

"I tried again yesterday morning."

"It's been five days," Lindy complained. "You told me you were going to call Friday. I sat here by the phone all night." She was on the verge of tears.

"I'm sorry." He chastised himself. "I was with the pack. It's no excuse, but I came up with a title."

In the silence, she seemed to collect herself. "What is it?"

"I keep screwing up—" Guilt was swallowing him. "I know how much trouble it is to arrange your shifts around—"

"Tell me," she insisted.

He smiled into the receiver. "It came to me when the wolves were howling." He realized a burly man was standing beside him, glaring impatiently, waiting for the call to end.

"Ransom?"

"*Wild Animus,*" he said, turning the other way.

"That's the title?"

"Yes. An animus is a spirit, an animating passion. But it's also the will to destroy, as in 'animosity.'" The characterization of Lindy as a wolf pack still stung her at times, and this was one of them. He could feel her recoil across the line. "*Wild Animus,*" he repeated. "The passion within us that attacks to possess, and surrenders for love."

"I miss you." Her voice trailed with self-pity.

Ransom took a breath. "I miss you, too." He could feel their bond unraveling.

"You're starving me again," she said miserably. "I should never have agreed to this. I want to go with you. I'm fit enough—"

"You can't quit," he reminded her. The Wrangell trip would be financed by her earnings. He sighed, feeling the burden she was carrying. "Are things any better at work?"

"A little." She sounded unconvincing. "I told them why I need the tip money, and the girls understand. Dave's agreed not to put me back on the day shift."

"This was all a mistake," he said sadly. "It's not fair to you. I should have come back."

"I love you," she said. "But—"

Her anguish raised all of his fears.

She sobbed. "I won't be able to talk to you for a month—" She swallowed her tears, trying to calm herself. "I'll be alright."

"Lindy—"

"When do you leave?"

"Tomorrow morning—" He shook his head, now very unsure.

Hearing his doubt, Lindy made as if she had none. "Did your skins and headdress arrive?"

"Yesterday."

"I'll be there on July fifth," she assured him. "I've got my tickets, and the directions from Anchorage."

Ransom stared at the dial. "Lindy—"

"Do you care?" she raged suddenly. "No! You don't give a damn about me, do you?"

She was shrieking so loudly, he had to pull the receiver away from his ear. Then she was sobbing, not just blurts, but a continuous toll of injury and pain.

"That's it," he said. "I'm coming back."

"Forgive me," she cried, realizing how far she'd gone. "Oh Ransom, I'm so sad without you. So terribly sad. You understand. Don't you? Please, tell me you understand."

"I understand," he said sorrowfully. "I'm coming back."

"I won't let you," she laughed. "After all this preparation? That was so peevish of me, so selfish— It's that bitch again," she said angrily, collecting herself. "I'm fine."

Ransom wondered. He could hear her wiping her tears. "Are you sure?"

"Yes," she sighed, feeling his care. "I'm fine." Through her sorrow and her rage, she'd found her hope again, and she clung to it. "How was your dinner?"

He wasn't sure how to respond.

"Ransom?"

"Revealing," he said, the dinner far from his thoughts. "I think Yasuda's a queer."

She laughed. "Is everything ready?"

"I think so."

Ransom glanced around. The burly man had gone. The crowd in the diner was thinning. Behind the broiler, a cook was telling a joke to a busboy. The wilderness of the Wrangells seemed very distant.

"You're nervous," she said, feeling it over the line.

"Yes." He had a hundred fears. "The rock is dangerous," he said. "Everyone keeps warning me about it."

"Don't do anything crazy."

"If you're going to think like a ram, you have to climb like one." He sighed. "The wolves are gnawing at me, too."

She laughed. "You said you understood."

"I mean the real wolves." His Friday night encounter with Calvin's pack was indelible. "I don't think I'd want to run into them alone in the mountains."

"Should you take a gun?" she wondered.

"They're shy," he parroted what he'd been told. "I'll be lucky to see any. They don't attack humans."

"Go light with the acid." Her voice was grave. "Please."

"Don't worry." The conversation seemed to be drawing to a close. He was realizing how much being out of communication with her would affect him.

"I love you," Lindy said, sensing his hesitation. "What you're doing is so important—" Her commitment to the quest affirmed their devotion to each other.

"I love you, too," he said. "It will be hard—" His voice choked.

"I'll be with you, Ransom."

He heard her wisdom across the wire. His aspirations were

sacred to her. It was her belief, as much as his own, that nerved him for what was to come. "I know you will," he said.

Tolsona Lake was Ransom's destination, forty miles by air from the westernmost Wrangells. He could have rented a car and driven there, but a mail plane ran twice a week to a small public airport fifteen minutes from the lake, and the seats were cheap, so he booked one. He was the only passenger that morning. He hugged the window, but the approach to the Wrangells was confused by fog. The lowlands were vague and gray-green, the mountains dark hulks lobed with snow. Now and then, a crag would surface, wrapped in scarves of cloud.

They landed at the airport, taxied over the blacktop past a couple of hangars, and stopped. Ransom stepped out and looked around. There were a few parked planes, a small outbuilding, and a station wagon with a boy leaning against it. He was short with tousled hair and wore a down vest. It was chilly. The boy came toward him.

"Ransom Altman?" the boy asked. The top of one of his ears was nicked. His manner was cocky, but his expression was open and clear-eyed.

"I spoke with a man named Skinner," Ransom said.

"Skimmer," the boy replied in a gravelly baritone. He laughed, noticing the boxes being unloaded. "That yours?"

Ransom nodded. Skimmer took one. Ransom grabbed another and followed him toward the wagon. They slid them in the back.

"Are those the Wrangells?" Ransom glanced to the east.

"Yep."

The clouds were like gray soil and the rain like black roots raying down. The dark flanks of a mountain were visible, pleated with snow.

"What am I looking at?"

"Mt. Drum." Skimmer eyed him curiously.

A short while later, the station wagon was turning off the Glenn Highway, headed toward Tolsona Lake.

"You'd have plenty to eat," Skimmer was saying, "if you shot a moose."

"I'm packing my food," Ransom said.

"Cover more ground," Skimmer nodded. "That's the way."

The lake spread to the left, edged with brush.

"When can I leave?" Ransom asked.

"You need to talk to my dad." Skimmer's tone was reserved.

Ransom glanced at him. The boy seemed uncertain how his father would react.

Above the lake, dark lanes of cloud rolled from the west, knotted in places and streaked with silver. Along the shore, willow and poplar were bursting bud, raising candelabra with small green flames. The drive split and Skimmer turned down an incline. A white building appeared beside the water, next to a float plane moored to a crude dock. A sign read *Hurley's Flying Service.* The car came to a halt.

Skimmer nodded and exited the car. Ransom followed him down the path. On one side, a large pelt was draped over a sawhorse. On the other was a cairn of antlers and bleached skulls. As they reached the door, a gunshot sounded. Skimmer raised his brows, then opened the door.

The office was small. On the left, two old sofas with blankets covering tired upholstery were cornered around a rickety coffee table. A man sat on one of them, pulling on rubber boots. To the right, boxes of motor oil were piled shoulder high. A woman stood behind a battered wooden desk, talking on the phone, her eyes bright, with a shadow of sadness. On the wall was a photo of a plane crushed to shrapnel below a sheer cliff.

"I think so. I'll check with him," the woman said. She closed a file folder. "Certainly." Her voice was warm, her skin pale, her hair dark brown streaked with gray. "Alright, Burt. We'll be expecting you."

She hung up and reached for a coffee cup. Ransom saw a strand of rosary beads beside it. Another gunshot sounded.

"Mom—"

"Yes?" The woman turned, glancing from her son to Ransom.

"Ransom Altman," he introduced himself. He saw from her expression that she had no idea why he was there. "That wasn't Burt Conklin by any chance?"

She smiled and nodded. "I'm Ida Hurley. Can I help you?"

"He wants to be dropped off on Mt. Wrangell," Skimmer said.

She gave Ransom an apologetic look. "How many in your party?"

"Just him," Skimmer said.

Ida looked Ransom over, seeing someone not much older than her son. "Hunting?"

Ransom shook his head. "Just wandering around."

She sensed his shyness. "Where are you from?"

"Seattle," Ransom answered. Ida's eyes glittered like candles behind a screen. They struck him as saintly, pledged to some abiding faith amid a world heedless and profane.

"The Wrangells are dangerous," she said.

Skimmer exhaled with irritation.

The man on the sofa watched this interaction with amusement. He was big-chested and muscular. His glossy black hair billowed over his forehead.

Ida swallowed her coffee. "Do you have experience with—"

"Mom—" Skimmer rolled his eyes.

Ida ignored him. "You should talk to Doug."

"Come on," Skimmer motioned, heading for the back door.

Ransom followed him into a gravel yard. The little office was attached to the hangar which accounted for most of the building's space. Its large doors were open and the skeleton of a wing lay on benches. By the lake's edge, a small red prop plane with large balloon tires was parked. Another shot fired.

Ahead, Ransom saw a man facing into a patch of aspens, lowering his rifle. He turned, gray with humiliation, speaking angrily to a shorter man behind him.

The shorter man, Doug Hurley, was rigid and expressionless. "I warned you," he said.

In front of the aspens, three log sections were standing on end, a tin can perched on each.

"I'm rusty." The shooter gave a helpless laugh and raised his left arm. It ended at the elbow.

Hurley had a squarish head on a thick neck. His ball cap was down to his brows and his eyes were shelled over by mirror sunglasses. "You're not going to maim my animals," he said lowly.

The hunter stared at him, stunned. He glanced into the hangar, eyeing the mounted bear's head on one of the walls. "I saved three years for this. It's a big deal to me."

Hurley's expression was hard and impenetrable, his lips motionless beneath a carefully trimmed mustache.

The hunter heaved an aggravated sigh, turned and strode away.

Doug glanced at his son. Skimmer scowled at the hunter.

Ransom watched the mirror lenses turn to him.

"What kind of head suits you?" Doug's tone was wry, but not unfriendly.

"One with golden horns," Ransom smiled.

"Flightseeing?" Doug glanced at Skimmer.

Skimmer shook his head.

"I'd like you to drop me off on Mt. Wrangell," Ransom said.

The corner of Doug's mouth twitched.

"And pick me up," Ransom said to fill the quiet.

"How long?"

"A month."

Doug gazed at Skimmer. It was impossible to tell what was going on behind the mirror glasses. Without a word, he turned and stepped across the yard. Ransom and Skimmer followed.

By the time they reached the office, Doug seemed to have forgotten Ransom. "How's the north?" he muttered, moving behind the desk to examine a calendar.

"Low ceiling," Ida replied.

"What happened to Stahl's fishing trip?"

"Canceled."

Doug stared at her. The man on the sofa lowered his gaze, tucking his pants into his boots. Skimmer looked out the window, as if noticing something on the lake.

Ida was suddenly indignant. "He didn't like being bawled out for tracking mud into the Cessna."

Ransom watched her small mouth glower. Its seams were deep.

"Someone should have told him not to," Doug said coldly.

Ida turned aside. There was no escape in the tiny office. Her kindliness looked gnawed and abandoned. Skimmer picked his nails as if this bickering had been going on for years.

Doug faced Ransom, his attitude speaking through the silence. This is my world, he seemed to say. My wife, my son, my planes, my mountains. Mine to love or curse, depending on my mood.

"What do you know about spending a month on Mt. Wrangell?" Doug made it sound like a ridiculous idea.

Skimmer's expression turned doubtful. The man with black hair grinned and settled back to enjoy the exchange.

"I've done a lot of climbing in the Cascades."

"We dropped off a guy like you," Skimmer said, "year before last. Wasn't there for his pickup."

"We never found him," Doug added.

Ransom nodded. Ida was regarding him with concern.

"Going to live on berries?" Doug asked drily.

Ransom laughed. "I've got a stove and freeze-dried food. Warm clothes and rain gear. A good sleeping bag—" He glanced at the man with black hair, and the man gave him a humoring nod. "I'm not going higher than five or six thousand feet. It won't be cold."

The room was silent.

Ransom stared into Doug's mirrors. "I know what I'm doing."

The pilot's condescension seemed to abate.

Ransom turned to the wall map. "Somewhere in this area." He pointed at the volcano's southern flank. Below the white of the dome's glacial mass, brown contour lines defined a half-dozen spurs radiating into the solid green of the surrounding forest.

Skimmer smiled, back on Ransom's side.

Doug considered him for a long moment, then shrugged as if foreswearing responsibility for him. "There's a strip on the Dadina River. Chichokna's rutted out." He approached the map. "I could get you in here. Or here." His stubby fingers caressed the ridges like an old lover.

"What about the Cheshnina?"

Doug pointed at the snout of the Cheshnina Glacier, following the watercourse that flowed from it, to a spot five miles downriver. "There's a strip here. Wasilla Bill's got a cabin. Uses it once or twice a year. Probably wouldn't mind if you slept there."

"I'm going to keep moving," Ransom said.

"Can't carry a month's provisions." Doug frowned at him.

"I can go for two weeks. I'll need an air drop."

Doug nodded slowly. "We'll take the Super Cub. Won't be today. I'm counting caribou with Vince. When it clears," he added with irritation.

The man on the sofa raised his brows to Ransom. "Vince Sil-

vano," he introduced himself. Ransom saw the patch on his sleeve—
Alaska Fish & Game.

"What about our hunter?" Ida wondered.

"Flunked his ordination," Skimmer said.

Ransom smiled. Inside, he was ebullient. "Can we fly the area before you put me down?"

Doug nodded.

"Alright if I pitch my tent beside the lake tonight?"

Doug nodded. "Bring a firearm?"

Ransom shook his head.

Doug gave him a stony look. Ida and Skimmer were alarmed.

"There are bears out there, you know," Doug said.

Ransom smiled at Ida to thank her for her concern. "I'm not figuring bears into this." He gazed at Vince. "What about wolves?"

"Plenty," Vince replied. "Buzzed a pack on the Cheshnina last fall."

Ransom's heart stopped. "How many?"

"Seven. Three blacks."

"What were they doing?"

Vince laughed. "Looking for something to kill."

Seven

The little red Super Cub seated two, front and back, and the fit was tight. Ransom kept his knees together and made sure, as ordered, that his boots weren't on the elevator cables. During takeoff Doug was motionless, welded to the plane. At five hundred feet, he settled back, shifting the stick between his legs, watching the spruce and muskeg pass as he felt his way through the sky. Without radar or radio, the Cub was self-sufficient and pugnacious. When Ransom's elbows touched the fuselage, he could feel it growling. When the wind struck, it bucked.

Mt. Wrangell was obscured by a cloud ceiling at seven thousand feet, but the spurs building up to it were visible, lit by beams raying through, like knees and thighs stirring beneath a green sheet. As they headed up a river valley, Doug turned. "The Dadina," he said over the engine's drone. Ransom saw the tail of Doug's eye glittering behind the mirrored sunglasses. Doug's ire had dissolved.

Checking the topo in his lap, Ransom watched the ridges rise on either side. Steep slopes emerged from the forest, smooth with tundra, and the first crags appeared. Then they were in it—the world of rock, peaks and cliffs spewed out of the invisible mountain. The Cub banked beside a line of gray columns that looked like guard towers. Ransom clutched Doug's shoulder and shouted over the drone, pointing, his face glued to the window. Through a break in the ridge, a sweep of triangular scarps caught the sun. Doug's head cocked. He read Ransom's excitement and wristed the stick, sending the Cub wheeling through the break. Black colonnades sped by on the left, pink turrets on the right. Then the Cub's right wing dropped and Ransom was staring at a giant amphitheater terraced by thick flows, the highest frontwork with slides breaking through, the triangular scarps sheer and gleaming before him. He shouted and the window flew open.

Ransom gripped his seat. Doug's arm lifted, hingeing the clamshell door up and latching it to the wing's underside. The bottom hung down. Doug's head cocked again, inviting. They rose over the amphitheater's shoulder, touched the cloud ceiling and fell down the far side, descending toward the Chetaslina, past cliffs grooved with dark galleries and armored with shingled plates, the vacant battlements of a dead castle tipping below, carpeted with snow. With the plane's side open and the wind blasting through, Ransom pointed at a sheer cliff. The Cub tilted and careened toward it, and Ransom unclasped his seat belt and pushed his head and shoulders out. The gray slab swung giantly before him, undercut by red caves, eroded maws with red tongues sticking out. Then Doug was diving by scalloped arcades, past merlons rising from crimson slides. Ransom set his right boot on the Cub's tire and hung in midair, his heart racing, surfing a red wave through the frozen flows, his streaming eyes imagining the original outpourings.

Freezing and wiping his cheeks, he fell back in his seat. Doug was quiet, but Ransom could feel the excitement burning inside the man.

When they crossed the East Fork River, Ransom leaned out

again, scanning the terrain, looking for the level place he'd marked on his map—a boulder bed beside a terraced stronghold. He pointed. "There."

"Edge of those boulders?"

"Yes."

The reconnaissance completed, the Cub crossed to the Cheshnina Glacier, skated over its falls and descended into its rumbling gorge. At the bend, a peak rose mid river. A half-dozen Dall rams stood among the dark buttresses below the summit. Unlike Polychrome Pass, the rock was damp and mossy, and roofed into caves and cells. The rams were rigid with alarm. Ransom saw fear in their faces.

Then they were arrowing down the Cheshnina. Doug throttled back the engine. They dipped and the river came charging up, trees hurtling past. Ransom couldn't see where they could land. The river canted, gravels blurring, then the wings evened and the wheels touched down. The plane bounced and settled, slopes shuddering and freezing as it taxied to a halt.

Doug opened the cab and Ransom stepped out into the stillness. While the pilot unloaded his backpack, Ransom made a wide circle around the plane. The landing strip was a narrow path cut through the willows. A loose woodland surrounded it, climbing halfway up the peaks. Above treeline, the slopes were brown and straw, and streaked with snow. Ransom was breathless—an émigré landed on a deserted shore. His fear of being alone in this vastness was suddenly real.

"Back in two weeks," Doug said.

Ransom turned, nodding, trying to smile.

"That's Friday. Edge of the boulder bed." Doug spoke in a low voice, as if the wild place and their business there required it. "Put your tent up and lay out your sleeping bag so I can see you. Pickup's two weeks after that, Friday again. Here." He pointed at a trail through the brush. "If you get back early, Bill's cabin is over there. Just leave him some firewood."

Ransom knelt beside his pack. His parka was lashed to the top. He freed it and put it on.

"What's that?" Doug frowned at the horns emerging from the pack's top, curling to either side.

"Dall."

Doug laughed. "Usually we fly them *out*."

Ransom saw the mirrors staring at him, the hint of a sneer beneath Doug's perfect mustache. He was being dismissed and it shook him to the core. Doug was his lifeline. He took a breath. "Where are you from?"

Doug read his distress and softened. "Nebraska."

"Why here?"

Doug seemed to consider his answer. His tongue appeared and licked his upper lip. "Alaska was my dream," he said evenly.

There it was, Ransom thought. The signature of the heart. "Mine too," he said simply. He gazed at the mist drifting through the spruce, up where the treeline ended. "You've been in these mountains."

Seconds passed without a response. When Ransom looked back, Doug was a couple of feet closer to him, peering at the same veiled slopes.

"Fifteen years ago," Doug said, "I swam horses across the Copper River." He pointed. "We rode that ridge, Ida and I."

"You sound like someone who's lost something he treasured."

Doug regarded him stonily. He glanced at the horns coiling out of the pack. "What are you doing here?" His voice was grave.

"You know the sheep," Ransom said, as if making sure.

Doug nodded. "As well as anyone."

Ransom eyed him with silent intent, thinking his wild thoughts. I'll tell you, his eyes promised. Come closer. Take off those glasses.

What are you afraid of? Come closer and see who you've transported to these mountains of yours.

Doug saw the invitation and resisted. He'd agreed to fly Ransom, and that was the extent of it. He had work to do. But Ransom caught Doug wavering. Curiosity? Or something deeper? We have a connection, Ransom thought.

The pilot took the few steps toward the Cub, then stopped and turned, giving him one last chance. All Doug did was stare, but Ransom read his mind. Was he sure he wanted to do this?

"Two weeks," Ransom nodded. "The boulder bed."

Doug smiled a real smile, shrugged to himself, then climbed into the plane and started the engine. A minute later, he was bumping down the strip and lifting into the sky.

Ransom boosted the pack onto his shoulders, turned his back to the river and set off through the forest.

The brush was leafless, gray twigs clicking, admitting him without a struggle. Just their tips were green. But around his boots, the colors were lush, ruffles of bright lime *Peltigera* lichen woven through beds of apricot moss. Was something moving in the undergrowth? He stopped, and so did the sounds. It was the willows whisking against his parka.

The way grew mucky and he heard the stream. His readings said it would be greenstone, and green it was—ocean green above the flow and pale jade beneath, colors that seemed to him as pure and clear as the water itself. He followed the stream, the air thick and humid, banks oozing mosses and purple blooms. Noiselessly, two white butterflies—pierids, to be exact, for Ransom was identifying everything—chased each other out of one willow cage and back into another, vanishing as quickly as they'd appeared. The mysterious land was playing with him, revealing and concealing itself, enticing him.

At 3,500 feet, the brush thinned and he began to wander the

slopes hunched over, muttering into his cassette recorder and clicking his camera. He'd see something and throw off his pack, scrambling around on hands and knees, checking his field guide to identify everything in sight. It was late afternoon when he saw it.

Where the last brush met sere grass, the slope blazed orange. He hurried up the incline and the closer he got, the brighter the bushes blazed. They were waist high. He went down on his knees beside one, hearing it hiss and rustle, seeing its glossy tapers writhing and flickering in the breeze like a field of flames. It was diamondleaf willow, according to his guide, and the flames were last year's leaves. He curled beneath them and blurred his gaze, imagining himself at the center of the bush with the flames flashing over him.

He glanced down and saw ash. It crumbled beneath his fingers. And there were wisps of smoke rising from it, frozen threads white as chalk. He thumbed through his guide, the shadows of the flames dancing over the pages. They were ground lichens, *Stereocaulon* and *Thamnolia*. The embers were crackling. Teek, teek. A small bird hopped through the bush. It had a finch's bill and a golden stripe on its crown. Ransom turned on his recorder to capture the sound. The land he'd dreamt of was rising around him. And the ram was rising with it, real and alive.

He continued up the slope, angling toward the crest, logging impressions as he went. The earth was scattered with tussocks, potentilla mounds budded with yellow-starred eyes, tangles of crowberry tassels. Sights for the ram to see, odors for him to smell. Windflowers were everywhere, tilting on thin stems, like white bubbles bursting above the straw. It was a favorite Dall food, so he ate a few. Where the soil grew hard, magenta rhododendron burst like inch-high fireworks among the stones. He heard a scolding noise and saw a small figure on a rock standing and whipping its tail. Then others, calling to each other with indignation and alarm. They were ground squirrels, and like Ransom's detractors they scampered at the threshold, calling him foolhardy or crazy, jabbering to turn him back.

At 5,000 feet, the cassiope took over, dark green beds winding between the hummocks. He crossed a snow flush and the ground lichens changed, *Cladonia* clumped like cauliflower, emerald *Alectoria* like branching hair among the rocks. His energy seemed inexhaustible, as it was on those acid nights when he and Lindy first met and all that power was released. It was 2 a.m. when he reached the crest. He trudged through ankle-deep snow and mounted a prominence hoping to see Mt. Wrangell, but the vista was obscured by haze. He pitched his tent and collapsed on his sleeping bag.

The next morning he was awakened by a rusking sound. He sat up, squinting at the filtered sun. Birds were strafing his tent, brushing the nylon with their wings. Sensing he'd roused, they fluttered around the entrance. He opened the flap and they settled in a half circle, eight or nine of them, small and brown, peeping as if they wanted him to come out and play. Ransom grabbed his guide. Pipits. He crawled out of the tent and they rose and hovered around him excitedly. Then he turned.

An enormous island floated before him. A white dome, like Rainier but so unlike it—larger, broader and smoother—and so much more ethereal, utterly removed from mankind and the world he'd known. Its curves glowed, the snowy skin distended, swollen to bursting with what he was sure was the selfsame desire that filled his heart. It had stood here alone all these years, giant glaciers pouring down it, fires burning within, its great power mounting and subsiding—with hardly a human on earth aware it existed. In the sky above, a giant spine of cloud was arched, like the spirit of the ram leaping across the firmament. He found his notebook and began jotting impressions while the pipits did acrobatics around him.

Later, after he'd examined glaciers and flow structures carefully through his scope, and glassed one of the pools at the valley's head, he made himself breakfast and explored the crest. Then he opened his pack and removed the headdress.

It was a wild visage, wilder when he raised it before the white dome. The eye orbits were shielded with black metal screens. The face was twined and beaded, extending to the cheekbones, the nose covered, the mouth unobstructed. Dall horns curled golden from its brow, and between them his high school torch medal had been woven into the ropy skin. From the hairline back, the headdress was covered with white fur. Locks of beaded twine hung to waist level on either side. It had taken Ransom all winter to assemble it, modeling the frame with plumber's tape, then getting a metal sculptor at the university to weld him the real thing. Horns were illegal to buy or sell, but he found an abandoned pair at a Portland taxidermist. They were three-quarter curl, an uninteresting trophy, but just what he wanted—a ram in the prime of life. The taxidermist had mounted the horns on his frame, and a Seattle macramé artist wove the face and locks.

After sharing the headdress with the dome, Ransom rested it on a boulder facing the pool and sat beneath it. With his back to the rock and a fantasy world of ground lichens around him, he began to write in earnest, pausing to glance at the pool or refresh himself with a handful of Wrangell snow. It had a sweet taste. The pipits returned that afternoon to see how he was doing.

———◆———

The wind darts my flanks, the ground yanks beneath me. I'm following the stream, hinds cocking and springing, fores rustling down. Windflowers festoon the slopes like a tidemark of froth, flaring and shaking, mouthing bravely at the wind. A ground squirrel chatters, raising the alarm. I watch my hooves swish through the tussocks, marveling at the miracle of four legs. This body knows this land, these mountains at the edge of the world, and this heart yearns for the unseen, opening ahead with every thrust. I feel myself more and more a ram.

To be a leaper. To live life on my toes, letting what greets me sharpen my eye an instant before. Fores reaching, spindly but assured. Hinds powering, wired with muscle and nerve. The golden-crowned sparrows sing a five-note song, simple but stirring. My leaping flushes them. They skim the willows and drop back down, my fate like theirs, glowing and hopeful but hinged on the moment, feather-thin. Forward, a saddle rises at the valley's head. Beyond that, peaks are dimly visible behind a veil of cloud. The doubts chatter louder—squirrels calling from swell to swell. Where are you headed so fast? Don't you have a clue? This mounting dread, what does it mean? I wish I knew.

My pace is quick, the way untraveled— I cross a hillock matted with cranberry, the tiny leaves meshed like overlapping tongues. "Your dream, your dream," they stutter stiffly. Keep in stride, trust this heading. The ground is changing, rocks punching through. My hooves clack down, magenta blooms bursting as I land, willow flounces hissing, pebbled by nets of nerves. The stream skeins to strands trickling down a knoll.

I head for a bright slash of orange moss, vaulting wet gravel and then up, mounting the embankment, toes sinking in, pads cooled by wet velvet. The rill tacks among the rocks, and then the slope lays back. Set in the saddle is a scoop of green.

I rise on the rim, eager for a better view. Between the valley's thighs, a river and a low spur are visible. The sun casts longing looks across the land—a special light, meant to surface things precious. Ripples are traveling the river's back. A lake glitters like a jewel rising out of the earth. Along the stream's banks, wickerworks of willow glow like filaments of gold. The wind is in my face, and I inhale, savoring the rich scents as I pull them apart: ledum turps, alder balsam, the ginger of arctic willow, and over it all potentilla's heavenly rose.

I draw back from the lookout and face the green—a bed of cassiope, and in its center, a blue pool, rock-ringed, fringed with sedge.

Up to the liquid mirror I step. A white face glides over the reflected sky, curious, ears perked, jaw firmly set, golden horns coiled. I lower my head and the image rises to meet me, its long muzzle drawing closer, parted lips black, nostrils flaring rhythmically as I breathe. Golden eyes peer up into mine, and as the reflected head tilts, the eyes brindle gray-green. My eyes—the recognition is instantaneous. I see my thought train, the concealed remnant of my human self.

What have I become? My frame and my senses are animal. My voice is shrunk to an inner whisper. Behind my eyes, a kernel of cognition survives, surprised on all sides by wild instincts and emotions. I have no ram memories, only impulses. That's troubling, frightening. They clamor inside me, speaking their powerful sufficiency, urging me to yield to them.

I curl my lips and sip, and the pool awakes. My image wavers. Across the water, an oblong rock washed by the ripples gives back a fateful drip, as if something has been set in motion and can't be stopped. On the pool's bottom, luminous scallops appear, along with a strange thought—my presence here is known. The scallops are a golden net cast at me. The scallops flicker—there's an uncertainty in the light. I raise my head.

Thin lanes of cloud are gliding over the western hills, putting bars across the sun. The earth is stalked with shadow. My ram senses tense with dread. The lances of cloud merge at their rear in a broad caul, and as I watch, the last rays of the sun are clipped by its embrasures and the bright peaks and valleys sink into its pall. Is dusk so fearful? Below, the shadows of two cloud prongs glide along the ground. They reach the backlit willows, cross the stream and climb the incline, headed toward my lookout.

A jeering caw, above me. I lift my head. At the tip of each of the two tapers, a magpie flies command. Black claws hooked in the cloud, thrashing tattered wings, they drag the shade across the land. The forked shadow reaches the green now, a prong on either side, swallowing the far rim, tarnishing the pool, lapping over my hooves, sliding up my legs onto my chest.

I'm shivering. My pulse is skipping. My breath flutters in my nostrils. The dimness is like an affliction, fears of darkness leading my thoughts into cramped channels. Shapes are stirring there, in the depths of my brain, curling and turning, spectral and amorphous, gaining substance in the gloom. Shapes of nightmare. My breath stops, my limbs stiffen. I shake my head to clear it, but the vague impressions grow distinct. I see the mouths of tunnels, and creatures shifting within. A snout appears, pushing out. A beast with dark fur, then others, pointed faces raised, eyes glittering, jaws gaping. Up from their netherworld they come, milling in the ghostly haze and stealing through it.

133

The wind has dropped to nothing. The valley is still. A squirrel yips from a distant slope. The crests have fused with the ceiling of cloud, seamless except for the threads of snow strung like nerves down the gullies. Then I hear it.

A cry, faint and muted, like a star flickering in the depths of the sky. It reaches out and dies away. I stand rigid, listening. Again it comes, louder, long and rising, fervently sustained. A second joins in, deep and guttural with a downward slur, black with craving. And a third, shrill and tremulous. The first quavers, dwelling on some desolating sorrow while the second mounts, modulating its plaint with a horrible intimation. Then a fourth starts up, and a fifth. The howls gather and roll, woeful and wooing. Then the perverse entreaty fades, arching and dying across the gulf of space. Silence returns, leaving me alone with my fear.

I listen, waiting. Turning my head, holding my breath, stretching my senses. But all I can hear is that there is nothing to hear.

———◆———

Two days later, the phone in the office of Hurley's Flying Service rang. Ida picked it up, exchanged greetings with the caller and held out the receiver to Doug. He'd just come from the hangar and was wiping grease off his hands, mirror glasses in his shirt pocket.

"It's Ransom's wife," Ida said, braced for a grumble of irritation. But Doug just nodded and took the receiver.

"Hello." He gazed through the window, in the direction of Mt. Wrangell.

"I'm sorry to bother you," Lindy said. "I wanted to find out if—"

"I dropped him on the Cheshnina River," Doug told her. "Weath-

134

er's good, and the mountain's in clear view. He should be having the time of his life."

There was nothing dour about Doug's smile, and that surprised Ida. He noticed her staring at him and laughed, as if he'd been caught in some mischief.

"Can you check on him?" Lindy asked.

"That's the plan," Doug nodded. "We have a date set to drop him provisions, twelve days from now. Give Ida your number, and we'll call and let you know if he's still alive."

"Doug—" Ida scolded him.

"I'm sure he's fine," Doug said into the receiver.

Lindy sighed. "You don't know how much I'd appreciate that."

Doug glanced at Ida with a tenderness she hadn't seen in a long time. "Oh, I think I do," he said gently.

"Can I write to him?" Lindy wondered.

"Sure. We'll drop whatever you send us along with his food."

"Well, I guess—" Lindy wasn't sure what else to say.

"You know," Doug spoke off-handedly, "I'm curious as can be about those horns he's packing with him."

Lindy was silent for a long moment. "He showed you the head-dress?"

"I got a peek," Doug said.

There was another pause as Lindy tried to decide how much to share. "That's my greatest fear," she said finally. "That he'll get so caught up in playing the ram, he'll do something dangerous."

Doug's brows lifted. "I guess we'll just have to hope for the best." He faced Ida with a look of astonishment. "Hang on, I want you to give my wife your number."

Ida took the receiver and jotted down the information. When she hung up, Doug was back at the window, gazing toward the dome.

"What was that about?" she wondered. "Horns?"

Doug nodded. "Ransom's a lunatic." The harshness had returned to his voice, but as he faced Ida, a reckless emotion broke through—the exhilaration a young man might feel, high on those ridges, pretending to be a ram. "We're all a little crazy when we're young."

Ida was startled, more by the look in Doug's eyes than by his words. She saw longing, something he dared to ask her for, without any expectation of receiving. "Yes," she said softly. As distant as they'd been all these years, her own longing lay just below the surface. "I remember."

Back in Seattle, Lindy stirred herself from beside the bedroom phone. She was still in her work clothes, having called the moment she arrived home. The comfort of Doug's words was already fading. As much as she tried, she couldn't calm herself. She unbuttoned her blouse and removed her brassiere, regarding herself in the mirror. Her features looked drawn, her body slack and unattractive. Where was the joyful child? She peered into her eyes. Her hope was gone. Without Ransom, she was a ghost in a world of shadow. He had found her real self, and now it was bound to him. When he left, he took it with him.

That same evening, at the head of a valley on the southern flank of Mt. Wrangell, Ransom stood naked as well, regarding his reflection in a pool. It was not unlike the one he'd described in his story. Its water had green esses and blue eyes, the colors swirling and recombining as the breeze crossed it. A crescent of snow was banked against the far rim. To the west, golden beams fanned down through tears in the clouds. His clothing lay on the straw by the pool's edge. As he undressed, he'd thought of Lindy. He missed her, but it was strange—as distant as she was, he felt her with him, close to his heart, ready to accompany him on his journey.

Like the ram, he held his breath, not a muscle moving, listening to the quiet on the land. The only sound was the murmur of the stream in the valley below. His exhilaration was mingled with unease. The drug was coming on.

He tossed a pebble across the pool and watched the concentric arcs bow toward him, imagining the wolves had sipped the water there. Then he tilted his head back and howled from deep in his chest, imagining it was the pack he was hearing—the hungering moan, the soaring cry, the yapping and looping—roving across the land, echoing among invisible ridges, beating back and forth, searching with fierce intent. Fear took hold of him, left him and took hold again, moving through him in waves. The pack was hurrying toward him. What fearsome things might their hungerings inspire? How close was the danger now?

Ransom turned. His regalia was on the green behind him. He pulled on his fur leggings and cloven shoes. He buttoned his fur vest and slid the cuffs with fringes of knotted twine onto his wrists. Kneeling before the headdress, he raised it by its horns, faced it toward the lowlands to hear the echo of the howls, then turned it toward the refuge of the rocky heights. Then he lifted it over his head.

"Golden eyes, know," he pronounced. "Golden horns, grow." He lowered the headdress, hinged the facepiece close and fastened the latches on either side, feeling the padded frame lock itself to his skull. He tried the weight, moving his neck stiffly, flexing his legs as he turned from the lowlands to the invisible heights behind. Then he began to chant, his voice hushed and tremulous with dread.

> *Listen—*
> *The very quiet is alive and pumping.*
> *Pulsing pouts in the cooling umbra thumping.*
> *Muffled throbs, measured beats*
> *Of an unseen rigadoon,*

A nimble padding on my reason,
Palpable and importune.

Was he imagining it? No, the sounds were sharper, borne from a greater distance. Through his eye screens, Ransom saw a different vista, broader, deeper. The trembling in his limbs, the leaping of his heart— His thoughts were still human, but the rest was ram. He shuddered at the thrill of it.

Pierce, pierce, eyes, pierce the thickening shade and see
The dread pad-padding approaching me.

Shafts of sun struggled to cross the western ridge. The clouds strangled the last of the light, and dark fur covered the slopes.

Essence of fear, herald of pain—
Striking through my nostrils into my brain.

The odor invaded his muzzle with a terrible familiarity—earthy, musky with a sour tang, frighteningly intimate. The ram took a step back. Ransom gave his sheep instincts their head, letting them turn him toward the land behind. As in his story, the incline blocked the view. He reined the animal in, continuing to chant.

Legs moving in place,
Pad-pad-pad, wanting to go, pad-pad.
The germ of panic sprouting
In my chest, don't let it grow.

The ram rebelled with the force of instinct. His heart throbbed madly, bones thrumming, breath chugging, and the more firmly Ransom held him, the more wildly his heart beat. The view quaked as if suspended in gel, as if the land itself was stretched over that pulsing heart. Fear flooded his brain—the thudding had a life of its own. Something black in his bloodstream had been set loose. Even as he listened, the throbs grew louder, sensing his infirmity.

Pad-pad, pad-pad. He could hear their paws on the slope below. Wolves, striding toward him. He tried to pierce the shadows, desperate to see the danger, cocking his head to fix the sound. Pad-pad, pad-pad. A noise like panting, the clink of gravel, the rustle of tundra. Ransom was exultant. The ram was wild to flee.

Suddenly the padding stopped. At the edge of the shelf, he saw an odd-looking prominence—a head-shaped rock. It rose as he watched. A large face pointed at him, eyes glaring as a black wolf stepped onto the green. At its rear two more appeared shoulder to shoulder, dark gray, moving on lanky legs. Then another, smaller with a jouncy stride, and three more behind it. The others spread out to either side of the Lead, lining the crescent of snow.

Seven of them, tense with excitement, their faces looming across the pool in a gloating arc. On the left, a large wolf bobbed its blunt muzzle, huffing and craning toward him, its curious features surrounded by a fanning gray ruff. The fur of the wolf's underside was spiked with water and his male genitals were dripping. Beside the Ruff were the pair with lanky legs, wowing to each other, the tail of one draped over the other's back. Their odor was female and they studied him, one knowingly, eyes looking up from her downturned head.

The ram quaked with fear. Ransom struggled to calm himself, capturing the images for his story as he edged around the rim, trying to buy a little more distance, wondering how much of this was illusion. His steps were awkward. He glanced down, realizing he was on his toes in a half-crouch with his knees bent. The wolves could smell his fur. They could see his horns. They thought he was a ram. On the far right, the smallest jounced in place, fur black, eyes bronze—a yearling female, bucking her chin and dancing her paws with the eagerness of a child. Beside the Younger, another female skulked in the sedge, nearly prone, harried and haunted, her features trenched, eyes regarding him through her woeful mask.

A squat wolf grumbled, shoving the Ruff aside, lugging against the Lead's shoulder, winded and panting—a female, much older, grizzled and paunchy with a sour stench, her belly stuck with dead leaves. She grappled her jaws at Ransom, fangs clicking viciously, tail snapping from side to side. One eye menaced him, the other was scarred into a permanent squint.

Ransom's composure cracked. He stepped back, feet hissing through the sedge. The lanky pair shifted instantly, snouts pointing at his cloven toes. *I'm not a ram,* he thought, hands going to his headdress. He fumbled with the latches, desperate to shed his disguise. One popped open, but the other was jammed. He struggled with it, then reached into his pocket for his folding knife. The Younger stooped with her fores splayed, tail wagging, enjoying the game. The Hangbelly's lips drew back, a dollop of drool stringing from her chin. Ransom opened the knife and pried at the latch, hand trembling. The blade snapped off. The knife fell from his grasp as the Lead put his fores on the bank of snow and leaned over the water, huge and male with his tail up. His white-rimmed lips twitched, baring wicked fangs, nostrils flaring with a frightening ardor.

Ransom's senses reeled. Amid his confusion, the Lead's sulphur eye drew him. Its bright iris seethed, smooth-sheened with concentration, then wheeled with knobby spokes. Ransom felt the wolf's mad desire: to tear him open and lap his blood, to bolt his innards, engulf his eyes and swallow his tongue, to gnaw to slivers the bones that upheld him. In the center of the wheel, the black pupil pulsed hypnotically, porthole to the void, and into it Ransom fell, feeling a gulf deeper than the animal, a hunger no flesh could sate. Ransom turned his head with a snap, wrenching away, staggering back.

He glanced for his footing and saw thin white shanks, a white chest and a white muzzle starting out from his face. He could feel his corded muscles and recumbent spine. He was the ram. Along with his human shape, his dizziness dissolved, sobering him into a new reality. The Lead was still fixed on him, the Hangbelly grumbling, worried he might escape. He shifted his left hind. Back and back again, trying to mask his motion, fighting panic, resisting headlong flight. The Hangbelly's rancor swelled to a growl. Back, back, lifting his hooves through the cassiope. The Lead's snout swung from side to side, cueing the others as he slipped off the snow bank and started around the pool at a trot.

The ram reached the back of the shelf, still facing the wolves, hooves prancing, tossing his head toward what lay behind, hoping for higher ground. The Lead slowed to gather the pack in a single body, tensing for the rush. The ram turned his shoulder, heart hitching crazily, and the Lead lunged, thrusting and gulping, the others following in a bounding charge. Shying wildly, the ram bucked up the cassiope, blasts of breath and the pound of paws right behind. He vaulted a snow flush, measured the height of a ragged wall jutting through the tundra, and sprang with all his might. Over the top he passed, forelegs reaching and coming down. His heart sank. A gray tableland stretched before him.

I must cross. I'm plunging headlong down the bank, hoarding the momentum to keep my lead. Over my shoulder, the wolves hurtle the bank, headed straight for me.

Faster, flee, flee!

I'm galloping on the flat, nothing but matted leaves and gravel between me and the ramparts beyond. They follow fast over the open ground, Lead in front, the others bunched, the bleak-face falling to the rear. The Younger slips and rolls, vaulting back up without losing a stride.

Faster, faster! High rock is my only hope. Over dry grass, diapensia, azalea, quilts of willow spread over the grit, thinking I must be pulling away. But the huffing mounts at my rear—how can that be? I glance back and see them closer still, strung out in a line: the Lead, the lanky pair, the Younger, the Ruff, the squint-eyed Hangbelly and the Dangler. You are mine, their paws chant. You are mine.

At the head of the tableland, beyond a tangle of branching ridges, a bulwark of rock rises, castellated and squared off where it meets the pall's underside. An unbreachable stronghold, but I'll never reach it. I break off from my course, feint to the left, veer to the right, switching and swerving to cut clear. The huffing fades, then the pack recoups its loss, eating up the spread, the Lead striding powerfully four lengths behind, face looming large, ears pricked, eyes sizzling. My hope dies, replaced by panic. Safety's too far, I'm losing ground too fast.

To the left, the tableland abuts a confusion of slopes—my only chance. I wheel at full tilt, aiming for a blind alley, a draw between low ridges that bends as it ascends. The pack pivots like a blade on its point, swinging around the Lead, the lanky pair running right behind. The knowing one, the Wise, is in front, seeing my fright. The other, the Scout, is at her sister's tail, following my every motion with shallow eyes. The grass is suddenly cool to my hooves, ground soggy, snow flushes everywhere. My fores punch holes, hinds slipping and sliding.

Gray shoulders, pumping by my haunch! The Scout, even with the Lead, readies to strike. I'm galloping up the narrow

142

alley, feeling the earth quaking beneath their paws, ground changing, turning stony. My wind is going, breath coming hard, chugging the last ounce of flight from my frame. The bend comes and I take it in stride, musk billowing as I turn, the Scout lunging, snapping at my ham, snagging my shank. I go down and the Lead hurtles over me, tugging at my chest. A sharp pain—a tuft of my fur is caught on his fangs. I roll, shuddering with terror, hinds digging and springing, bolting on up the ride.

A wall bulges out where the spurs come together, an incline of broken plates descending from its base. The grade steepens, my muscles at their limits, fear whipping my body on. The musk billows and the Lead lunges, snapping at my thigh, the void so close it blackens my mind. He misses and I'm onto a loose shuffle of rock, bounding up the stacks from scrap to scrap, frantic but exact, using my last reserve. At the wall's base, I stop and glance back.

The pack is still on the ride, except for the Younger who stands on the breakings, looking up at me, wagging her tail and whining. The Dangler is at the bend, sitting on her haunches with a troubled look. The others are knotted together in united menace, watching to see what I will do. I'm breathless, heart beating madly, in their sights but out of their reach.

Above, the convex slab rises smooth and sheer, like the back of a giant beetle emerging from the foliated rock on either side. My instincts say climb and my legs agree, moving me up onto the offset tops of the shingled rock as I scan the heights. The slab is striated in the vertical, cracked into long sections. I cross a rift, following a thin curb. A scurf of lichen angles up the rock, roughing its smooth surface. I see a hoofhold in the gangway and reach

143

for it. Then others—a dimple for the hind, a ready pock. I edge up to a kerf, plant the tip of my toe and reach for a stirrup, slowly shifting weight.

A clatter of rock below. The Younger is scrambling among the breaks, imagining she's following me. The Scout scans the slab, guessing where I will head while the Wise watches my hooves tremble, plotting the trajectory of my confidence. The Hangbelly grumbles to the Lead, nuzzling him without taking her eye from me, galled by my escape. He pays her no mind, staring hungrily, licking the blood from his chops. There's a dull pain in my chest and a creeping warmth. I glance down. To the left of my midline, the fur is torn away, leaving a bald and bloody oval. Below, the Lead's muzzle drinks the scent off the wind.

Heart, stop your quaking! You'll jar me from my holds! I tense my chest and continue up, fore on a fragile flake, hind in a niche—a hard move, no room for a mistake. I cross to a loose stub, steady, then stretch over a blank space, ascending onto a small ledge. Below, the wolves huddle, the Scout wowing, the Lead with his back to me, the strength of his gaze evident in their averted faces. He touches the Hangbelly's nose and starts back down the ride at a trot, tail straight out. She follows and so do the Younger and the Ruff. At the bend, the Lead nips the Dangler who rises and takes her place at the back of the line. The five are loping back down the ride. The Scout and the Wise remain below, watching me, preventing my descent.

Keep on moving, up a short scotch onto a nub. Is the Lead projecting my course? The slab's base is invisible now—all I can see is the rock bowing darkly out. The exposure is severe, but I'm feeling my powers, the perilous holds keyed into my nerves. My pulse has calmed. I'll find some high crossing at the top, a route that will keep me out of their reach. The growing chill invigorates me. The heights are my home.

The slab breaks into setbacks. I step onto loose shingles, sampling the air. The cold wind makes me shiver. To the left, ridges lift, so riffled with peaks that I'm unable to tell which lies beyond which. Behind me, the tableland stretches away. Ahead, a slender bridge of rock extends itself between this high point and the next, bristling with spines and descending in steep slides. A saddle dips down to it.

I make my way cautiously, scanning for signs of the pack. Nothing on the inclines to the right, or below the bridge. Nothing in the breeze. The far side of the bridge moors on the nape of a rounded peak streaked with pale slides. Or there's another route—through the half-light, I see a stair of ledges leading from the bridge's end into the trough below.

I step out onto the splintered strip, stumpy pickets leaning this way and that. Some are loose, shifting dangerously. Pads of desiccated moss are lodged in the crotches. I put my hoof on one and it comes away. If a spine breaks out— If I slip—

I skirt a broken lance and squeeze through the vee in an expanding fork. They came upon me by accident. They chased me and I escaped. They're far away by now, finding other victims to slake their thirst. A spike grates, shifting against me. I'm nearly across, but the hedge is thick, forcing me out where the exposure is greatest. There's no reason to remain high. I'll take the route down and find my way back.

Suddenly, the dark file appears from behind a spur, coursing into the valley below, the Lead's snout aimed, eyes upon me. The

Ruff breaks off, ascending a rocky slope at my rear, angling toward the saddle and the start of the bridge. The lanky pair continues, the Scout running half a length in front of the Wise, heading farther into the mountains. The others slow and stop directly below. The Lead rivets me with his sulphur eyes. The Hangbelly stumbles against the Younger, badly winded, but at the sight of me, her ears perk and her jaw gapes. My heart jumps at those upturned faces.

There was nothing accidental about our encounter at the pool. They found me then, and they've found me again. It's me they want, not just any prey.

The thicket at the start of the bridge has parried the Ruff. He stands before the bristling thorns, cutting off my retreat but unable to proceed. The Hangbelly grumbles, nuzzling the Lead's throat, her evil eye glaring up at me. The Younger jounces excitedly, prancing her fores and wagging her tail. I face forward, hooves raised, shoulders shifting, balancing over the void, their eyes following every move. My steps are awkward and tremulous. The Lead's ears tic, hearing my breath sounds, my hoof sounds, seeing it all—

The rock teeters! I feel myself floating. I bunch my legs, striving against confusion, bobbing and bending, searching for an out, fores beginning to slide. Below, the Lead's snout shoots up a column of steam. My head tosses, eyes fixed on the rounded peak as I come off, springing wildly from the hocks—a rearing leap over the deep drop. Landing on a corbel where the bridge meets the slope, I bound forward without looking back.

Safe, safe—I leave the deadly trough behind, heading across the flanks of the rounded peak at a lope, taking the high route, staying high. My breath escapes in snorts. I'm out of their sight. The peak's slides are ocher, soft and powdery, my hooves barely audible. To the right, as I round its flank, another mountain swings into view. Its face is blotted by darkness, but its silhouette is massive and rimmed with battlements. A moat of boulders fills the space between.

Where are they now? The quiet can't be trusted. I start an angling descent toward the boulder bed, headed for the sanctuary of higher rock, hoping I've lost them.

The next morning dawned cold with a high overcast. Ransom woke, uncurling slowly, his limbs stiff and his feet like ice. He was still wearing his furs. His headdress was on and he was feverish inside it. His face felt like melting wax. He rose, sluggish and ungainly, balancing on his cloven shoes, trying to remove the headdress. One of the latches was loose, but the other was jammed with fur, bent badly enough that he had to bang it with a rock to open it.

He set the headdress on the ground where he'd slept—a flat spot pawed out of the sod, littered with white hair and dark pellets. A sheep's bed. He gazed around, recognizing the rounded peak, seeing the slides, amber in the daylight. He was high on its flank. How had he gotten there? He remembered his transformation, and he shuddered and turned, seeing the bridge of spines.

Then he looked down. His vest was streaked with blood. He drew a breath and parted the fur carefully. It stuck at first, he felt a little pain. Then the oval was visible, raw and abraded. He touched it, his eyes glittering, a bewildered smile forming on his lips as if he'd passed some kind of test. He retrieved a pinch of sheep fur from the bed and put it in his pocket. Then he started back across the rounded peak, carrying his headdress by one horn, following the cuneate prints.

When he reached the bridge of spines, he scanned it with disbelief. Every detail was familiar—the corbel, the section where he'd been forced out, the trough below. He couldn't have crossed it, he wasn't capable. But he saw Dall prints by the corbel. They lacked heels. Had he stood on his toes? No, the prints were made by a real sheep. His shoes were larger than that. Weren't they? He measured and fretted without any conclusion.

He made his way down the stair of ledges into the valley, threaded a maze of low hills and came out onto the tableland. When he'd moved far enough up the bended ride to see the beetle-backed slab, he stood staring at it, terrified by the thought that he'd climbed it. The convex was gray basalt, fragile and untrustworthy. Crossing the tableland, he found where he'd slipped, and not long after, a flock of pipits appeared. The birds followed him for quite a ways, peeping and circling. One faced into the wind, holding himself stationary and turning his head to peer at him. Are you alright? the bird seemed to ask.

When he arrived at the pool, reality pushed his confusion aside. There were his discarded clothes and his pack where he'd left them. He set the headdress down and retrieved his pants with a nervous laugh. He changed quickly, finding himself in small things, buttoning his shirt, lacing his boots, taking comfort in reminders of his humanity. His thoughts turned to Lindy, and he felt a great relief, imagining her beside him. He loaded his regalia into his backpack, while she whispered in his ear, soothing him, knowing what he'd been through. Then she was before him, the wind lifting her hair from her brow.

Ransom froze. Her face was fractured. He saw it unpuzzling— not one nature, but seven, loose around the scarlet star: hungering for love, understanding his actions and what they meant, playful as a child, caring, but hateful she'd been left behind, fearing no good would come. The Lead, the Scout, the Wise, the Younger, the Ruff, the squint-eyed Hangbelly, and the Dangler. The pack that had chased him through the night was Lindy.

It was an impossible thought. He pulled the drawstrings, closing his backpack over the furs and headdress, wondering if the wolves were imaginary. Had he crossed the tableland in a panic, unhinged by the drug, fleeing for his life with nothing behind him? He gazed at the pool, then stepped slowly through the grasses, approaching its edge. On a bald spot, he saw his boot prints, and beside them the impression of his cloven hooves. A couple of feet farther, the soil was covered with wolf prints. He stared at the largest, the center pad and the four satellites aligned before it, each with a protruding stem where the claw sank in. *I'll be with you.* Lindy's parting words echoed in his ear.

Ransom drew back, shaken, his eyes on the grass. He saw the folding knife and something glinting beside it. A green caterpillar was crawling on the broken blade, and as he picked it up, the larva fell, coiling to protect itself, making the sign of the ram on the rays of straw. His fingers touched the wound beneath his shirt. Breezes from different quarters were crossing the pool, and where they met, the water was a lattice, countless diamonds shimmering hypnotically. What had happened here?

Then quickly he put the question aside and hefted his backpack, reminding himself of his suggestibility and his regimen of acid. For a few hours, reality had been reshaped by the ideas in his head. It had passed, and he had another twenty-eight days alone in these mountains. As he skirted the pool and descended from the green, he vowed to abstain from LSD and focus on his story. Preserve his sanity, and just write.

Eight

is tent was pitched next to a stream on the far side of the boulder bed, with the mountain fortress at its rear. Eleven days had passed, and in that time Ransom had moved his camp to follow his story, writing scenes as he went. He sat hunched over his notebook now, in the midst of a devastating solitude, his pressed plants and rock samples around him, his sleeping bag spread out on the tundra. He'd kept his vow to abstain from drugs and the ram's progress to the fortress was complete. Despite bad weather, he'd found locations for the scenes to come, and they were labeled on the map beside him, with a route traced between.

He stopped to sharpen his pencil with a handmade tool—the blade broken from his folding knife bound with twine to a haft of willow. His whittling ceased and he lifted his head. A drone echoed from the corners of the sky. He spotted the red Cub and a sob blurted from his throat as he rose and waved. It circled and came in low. Ida was in the back seat, and as the plane skimmed toward him, she leaned out of the open clamshells with a bulging pillowcase in her hand. The Cub banked and her hair blew wild, and as the pillowcase fell she regarded him with a curious expression, like an astronomer's wife who, being told of a new constellation, has come to the observatory and put her eye to the telescope to see for herself. Doug stared through his silver glasses.

Then the moment had passed. Ida sank inside. The Cub's wings wagged and it droned away.

Ransom hurried to the drop, opened the pillowcase and saw the freeze-dried food and gas, along with a gift—a head of lettuce. He smiled, glancing again at the plane, tiny now against the mountains. As he walked back to his camp site, he felt like he was coming back to himself after a long absence. Strange, what a little human contact could do.

He knelt and unloaded the pillowcase, finding an envelope at the bottom. "Ransom" was written on it in Lindy's script. It seemed a miracle the letter had found its way to him. He held it to his lips and kissed it, imagining the message inside. Then he opened it.

"My Ram— If you're reading this, all is well," the letter began. "You made it to your rendezvous and received your air drop. Doug and his wife have been wonderful. We speak every few days by phone. I'm frightened, I admit. But they know where you are, and they care, and that has made it easier. The time alone has made me realize how selfish I've been. Does that sound strange, coming from me? Whenever I'm lonely, my vicious side strikes out at you, right off. It just happened again, but I tore that letter up, and started fresh!

"All I want to say is that I love you very much. I know what is in your heart, and I believe in you. That's the real Lindy. Who but you could conceive of *Wild Animus*, and pursue it as you have? Whatever risks you take, whatever dangers you encounter, I understand. I will share the uncertainty, the doubt, and the fear while we're apart. And when you're back, I will take you inside me, and tell you again and again—you are everything to me. Lindy."

Ransom raised his head. A cloud was scrolled above the rounded peak, like a white iris in the blue. He began to cry. It was a lucky mistake. What had he done to deserve this kind of devotion? He held the letter to his heart, knowing it was the Wise who had written it. Then he stood, feeling a great welling of confidence. He strode along the stream bench till he reached a pile of dark boulders, where he stooped and gazed into a shadowed crevice. He saw a silken web, the wheel of threads glittering with rain, and there was a spider at its center, legs banded black and white. Laughing, he swept the web away, and pulled his headdress and bundled furs from the crevice. As he stood, a pika squeaked. "Don't worry," he murmured.

On the way back to his tent, a rockslide let loose from the fortress. They were frequent this time of day, following the afternoon heat. At first it sounded like something was turning inside the mountain, shoveling insistently. A billow of smoke rose from the terraced cliffs and a load of rock cascaded out, crashing onto the talus. Blocks left white puffs as they bounded down.

He set the headdress and furs beside his tent, kissed Lindy's letter again, and folded it inside his field guide, remembering her words. She had pledged her love, and now he would do the same. Devotion to *Wild Animus* was his pledge. Not just its relics—the manuscript and chants. But the incarnation of its deepest truths. The miracle of his heart's surrender must live and breathe.

He raised the map and gazed from its penciled route to the sheer cliffs of the fortress, weighing the risks. Then he unrolled his furs, removed the blue jar and arranged his costume on the tundra: headdress among the fireweed fountains, vest on a mat of diapensia, leggings on moss campion, shoes and cuffs among the draba. He raised the blue jar before him and faced a dwarf blueberry. Its leaves hung like eager tongues, each holding a single pill of water. He saw this every time it rained. At first it was a temptation, later an invitation he deferred. Now it was a sign that the time had arrived. He opened the jar, put a quarter tab on his tongue and swallowed.

It was early evening and the sky was blue. The giant mountain fortress rose from a pediment of tailings, its stepped cliffs burnished by the sun. Ransom was high on one of the slopes, approaching the lowest bulwark in a crouching gait, dressed in headdress and furs, chanting beneath his breath. He made treadling motions with his arms, the willow knife tied to his wrist with a thong, while his cloven shoes struggled in the scree, imitating a cautious jog as the ram approached the refuge, eager to put himself above the wolves.

The surface changed. He clambered over broken flags, turning his head to quarter the terrain, playing at a ram's fear, imagining the pack coursing through the mountains trying to find him. He was headed for a break in the cliff—a greenstone cove thick with shadows. By the entrance, two pale poppies floated above the flags. The dark vault swung over him and he fell to a walk. The air was cold and still, the scuffle of his shoes echoing in the quiet space. The details of the rear wall grew clearer as he approached—a broad chimney split the massive riser. He studied the neck of rock as a ram would, lifting his muzzle, checking his nerve.

Stepping into the chimney, he lifted his right leg and boosted himself onto an edge. He pushed his imagined fore into a niche, his hind found an indent, he shifted his weight gingerly, testing and choosing and glancing above. He felt the stony chill enter his chest with each breath, bracing him for his task. Hind on a tilted prop, fore on the sill of a block—everywhere he looked, holds offered themselves. It was as if some invisible presence was speaking to him, encouraging him in a soft voice.

He angled onto the flue's rear wall, looking up as he came

around. The blue was gone, replaced by a low roof of cloud. The pall. Ransom's chest shook, his heart pounding suddenly louder. He drew himself out of his fiction, regarding the cloud with fear. How had it eclipsed the sky so quickly? Below, the dark chamber gaped. He pored over the stonework with renewed concentration. Don't linger. Look and choose and move.

There were strange growths—paper thin *Umbilicaria* lichens, black and crinkled like dead leaves. Each had a pale spot at its center where it attached to the rock. He set his shoes between them. A drop fell, landing with a tap. He peered up. More drops. The sky was dripping, playing over his back like the pat of paws. He imagined the wolves drawing closer, loping across a rocky slope, sniffing the air for the sweet wool scent, so much stronger when it's wet. Pleased and frightened by the vivid images, he tried to ignore his increasing exposure.

As he approached the chimney's mouth, the rain suddenly came harder, drumming his withers. Rills ran between outcrops, collected on edges, washing over in thin sheets. A peculiar sight—the rock beneath his left hand was moving, twitching and writhing like something alive. The lichens were going wild, flexing beneath the film of rain. He fingered one. It was rubbery and slimy, like pliant skin. Move!

Ransom's fingers struggled for friction. His awkward shoes scraped, but the disks slipped beneath, swiveling on their navels. The choice of holds was narrowing every moment. He planted his right leg, straightening it slowly as he rose, hands feeling above, moving his left foot carefully, gaining a few inches, trying to be bold. His hand slipped. He groped blindly, foot skating, horn clattering against the rock, left shoulder catching—giving him time to jam his calf in a notch.

He hung there, drawing a tremulous breath, legs quivering, realizing he couldn't climb on the frictionless rubber and he couldn't

155

descend. The downpour continued, the shelves rilling with rain. He rocked the brow of his headdress against a jut, knowing he couldn't cling there for long, mourning his weakness, wishing he was a ram. He was cold to the bone. His hands were shaking, his fingers were stiff and numb. What had happened to the willow knife tied to his wrist? It was gone. The chimney's cold frosted the hair of his forearm.

And then, as he watched, his arm narrowed and his fingers retracted. The fourth and fifth digits disappeared. His thumb dwindled to a knob and rode up his wrist. The fore and middle fingers thickened to stiff black toes.

Ransom shuddered with terror, regretting the drug, regretting the chimney, regretting Alaska and his crazy quest. His legs were changing, turning spindly. The left slipped out of its notch and his body dropped, chest sliding onto a fang of rock. He peered through golden eyes, feeling the sharp edge speaking strangely to him—a voice without and a voice within, waking from his flesh, encouraging him, calling him.

———◆———

The fang has found the naked oval, pressing against my unprotected flesh. A current of ice sucks the warmth from my trunk. I still my fores and get one back on the rock, but the other gropes uselessly in midair. Move! I heave myself up, making a long reach, but my grip goes, hinds jabbing wildly, fores tearing out lichen. My neck twists, horn grinding over an edge, chest landing hard on the fang of rock. Steam rises beneath my chin, a rusty odor, salty and tartly sweet. There's a rhythm to the pain—my heart is pounding against my chest, threatening to take the fang deeper. I blink the rain from my eyes and turn my face up, steadying my nerves. Putting the weight back on my limbs, I rise slowly, chest coming off the fang, higher, higher.

Above, the chimney's mouth is opening. My legs are trembling. Closer, right fore feeling and finding, strength going, left fore on the lip. Up and over.

A ledge leads to the right. I start along it, shivering, taking the rain. Down the center of the oval is an ugly gash. As the ledge turns a corner, the length of the fortress comes into view. No sign of motion on the inclines below. Up canyon there's a breach where slides tumble from the frontworks, but there too, I see nothing. Close up, the fortress is a stepwork of broken walls, slopes of sand and scree, benches slumping and cut by talus. I trace the lines of the three risers above me, connecting benches and low-angle inclines, matching them to the shelves in the distance. Shall I risk my life to gain height? As if to answer, the rain stops. The air is suddenly calm. If I continue on the level, I can descend—

The Wise and the Scout appear at the canyon mouth. A dull crack jars my hooves. I leap to the side, shuffling in scree, watching craze lines ray along the ledge. A large fragment drops from sight, banging onto the slope below, chattering out my place. The two wolves slow. Their pointed heads lift, going back and forth, searching the face. I try to slot myself between two outcrops, but their muzzles aim knowingly. One breaks the silence with a howl to summon the others.

I scan the rock above, pick a route and leap, springing to the top of a fan, pumice clinking beneath my hooves. I continue on the level, skirt a gouge and glance back. The others are loping up to join the two. They drink my scent from the breeze, then put

157

their heads together, touching noses with the Lead. Wind whis-
pers along the cliff. The Lead bolts from the huddle and the
others follow. The wolf line crosses the canyon floor, fords the
stream, and starts up the fortress.

Heart leaping, I pitch forward, hooves clacking through
loose shards into a blind ditch. The fragments catch at my legs,
trying to shear through a shank. Behind me, the wolves are
bounding, following patches of sod. The next riser looms ahead.
I hurtle toward it, seeing a giant cleaver through the murk. I
swerve just in time, chest quaking, pangs shooting through my
open wound. The way darkens suddenly, everything a pulsing
blur.

A great rumbling! The mountain kicks beneath me. Ahead,
an enormous span of rock is keeling out of the cliff! It lands and
the slopes explode, bastions tumbling. Canopies of fragments
open over me, the air hissing and humming. Then the drumfire
dims, and through gaps in the smoke, I see a hole in the bulwark.
Over the last purr of talus comes a sharper sound—the scrab-
bling of paws. I glance back and see them lunging from a narrow
ravine just below.

I buck furiously among spindles and snags. The broken slope
is spotted with pyres. I'm choking on the sulphurous reek. The
wolf line cleaves the smudge only six lengths behind. My heart
raps at my ribs—rap, rap! I gag and stumble, hooves unbalanc-
ing a barrow of warm rock, something dozing beneath. A terri-
ble face rises from my tread, its horns coiled to either side, skull
staring with eyeless sockets, mandible detached, a black beetle
crawling from the crack in its brow. My heart goes wild, I'm
gasping for air, hooves jabbing madly. The death rattle is right

behind me, Lead's eyes seething, the Wise peering into my brain. My heart booms and I'm blind again, lost in darkness. Breathe, breathe! My limbs flail the scree, my sight comes back and I'm bounding out of the cut in a panic rush, leaping banks of scree. Behind me, the pack has paused to nose the dead ram.

Above, the final riser of the fortress shows, badly fractured, leaning and weaving across the slope. I angle through sinks of snow, over a slab spidered with cracks, racing toward its base. I leap onto a steep stair, bunching and springing, defying the drop, landing and swinging over the hump. Strength drained, my pace slackens. A few strides more and I'm onto the top.

Flanks steaming, breathless, I turn along the broken back of the fortress and kick into a lope, praying I'm out of reach, hoping they aren't running on a parallel just below. Strange pillars guard the battlements, statues molded of crust and stones. The sentinels crouch and totter among the beds of snow, sleepless and careworn, frozen at their patrols. What travail follows this traverse! On either side, cliffs drop at a steep decline. I turn and sweep the ridge—safe for a time.

A statue's head bursts in two—a pair of magpies, flapping toward me with ragged wings. One sails low to the ground and lands a few lengths ahead. The other circles and alights on my withers, stitching me with its claws. I buck, but the bird refuses to let go, flopping from side to side, whistling insistently. Wings slap my cheeks and there's a stab at my front as the other magpie pecks my wound and flaps away with a piece of my chest in its bill. The birds settle together on a debris heap and bolt the morsel. Then they're flapping toward me, returning for more. I rear, whacking them with my horns, flinging them like torn rags.

Their screeches destroy the quiet, hectoring me and alerting the pack as they wheel and flap away. You will see, they cry. You will see.

I scan the fortress. Vertical slabs protect my flank. The draggled ridge narrows to a giant keel. As I ascend, the wind comes against my front, pushing the cold down through my skin. From this lofty height, the truth of my whereabouts comes suddenly—behind, the peaks descend, but ahead, they continue to climb, reaching into the clouds. The mountain beyond towers into sight, its face hollow and confused by shadow—a dark and cheerless place, higher and colder, and still more barren.

The cloud cover has parted. To the right of the peak, through a narrow tear, a lens of blue sky appears with a silver crescent lighting the way ahead and down. The ridge drops steeply, bottoms at a saddle, and climbs into the cliffs of the hollow peak. My hooves shift nervously, fearful of a trap. At the low point is a large block. I can't see behind it.

I scuffle forward, descending the prow of the keel while I test the air, drawing scents into my forehead—damp rock, old snow, nested straw, and a faint musk. Heart, hold your beating! I clench my pectoral, but it's no use. Moonstruck, it's surging, shaking its cage. My limbs jerk forward in fits and starts. I can't put fear aside. They are down there, waiting.

With a lurch, my legs escape me. I burst into a lope, shooting down the ridge, crouched low. A rosy finch crosses the saddle, calling chrew-chrew-chrew like a blade sharpening on a stone. From the block's blind corner, the Lead lunges as I pass, jaws gaping, death upon me, white foam around his mouth. I vault, but he follows, ears flattened, jaws closing on my shoulder,

160

The Wolves

crushing nerves and flesh. A gripping and wrenching, and a deep shooting pain. The Lead's nose snuffles hungrily and I jerk free, whirling. The Wise looms before me, fangs twitched apart, reaching and clamping, skewering through my right fore.

The craving faces hover. The Lead waves his muzzle, Scout beside him, Hangbelly approaching my flank, Dangler circling my rear. Snared by the pack. The long jaws of the Wise tighten, tugging me to the right, while the Scout lunges at my left fore, spongy nose puckering, fangs gripping my shank. I buck and plunge, both fores shackled, their musk pouring over me, a sour fetor stopping my breath. I stagger, kicking blindly, something scrabbling above. I glance up as the Ruff springs from the block's top, his weight coming full on my loins, buckling my hocks, forcing me down.

Their gaunt faces jerking, the Scout and the Wise wow and growl and pull me to my knees. I struggle to rise, squirming wildly. The wolves crowd close, nostrils steaming, then the jostle grows still. The Ruff slides to the side and the snare opens toward the front, the Wise and the Scout swinging apart, relaxing the shackles on my fores. I rise, seeing the Hangbelly facing me in the gap, moving toward me, tail whipping, lips peeled back, her one eye fixed on my chest.

I'm rocking forward, leaping with all my strength as the Hangbelly lunges. Her fangs slash out and one hooks my wound. I feel a loosening and her snout sinking into me. I vault forward and she falls beneath, her fang still buried, extending the rip under my left fore, stopping me cold as it catches on a rib. Her wicked eye gleams, her muzzle wrenches. A dull snap, bones grating, and her muzzle drives deeper, her eye slitted, brow knot-

161

ting as she invades the cage, needling my core. Time stops. I feel myself pounding against the cusp, nothing between death and the heart. A terrible pang and the deep pulse wells, aching with tenderness, rushing up.

I lurch forward, dragging the wolf with me, straddling her body. The Hangbelly rolls, the sour stench suddenly strong. She is on her back beneath me, dugs slewing as she roots in my chest. With a furious twist, I come free and spring through a gap between the Ruff and the Younger. The Scout lunges and misses. The Lead is right behind me, following fast. I'm leaping up the far side of the saddle, the mountains throbbing as if my pulse had passed into the scape. Just ahead, the saddle is cut by a gully of shattered rock. I measure the shrinking ground, shorten my stride and leap, arching over it, fores touching down. Then I'm vaulting toward the heights of the hollow peak, away from the pack.

The ridge turns and heaves skyward, and I rise with it, hocks hair-triggering, rock blurring and sluicing as I leap. I'm shuddering, still feeling the Hangbelly's snout, seeing her swollen dugs. Behind me, the pack descends the saddle, hurrying, intent. Ahead, the ridge breaks onto the hollow peak, heights illumined by the moon. It's an enormous amphitheater, a row of triangle scarps following its curve, intercut with deltas of snow. Like the ruins of a barbaric temple, its gleaming puddles blaze a route to the top. The light shining through the tear in the clouds throws my shadow among the scarps—a spirit leaping on ductile limbs, leaving the circling world.

At the top, the rock levels off and I drop to a trot. My limbs are quivering. I can feel the warmth creeping down my front. Something is broken, crackling. I slow to a walk, gasping, a weakness in me growing. I check my fores. My right shank has blood spots where the fangs were. The left is burled and gummy. A ragged trough angles down my chest. Blood wanders its ridges, the moonlight on it gleaming. Strangely, there is little pain.

To the left, I see a curtain of piers separated by cloisters. My heart leaves dark stars on the rock, the life flowing from me. As I wonder how to halt it, a murmur mounts like a chorus of hidden ministrants. The next cloister comes into view, its dark interior bisected by a white cascade. The wand of water bursts on the gravels, thumping and clashing in a cottony swab. I draw closer, waking to a remedy, taking a deep breath and reeling into the tumult. The cascade drops like a hammer on my neck, slamming me to the rock, freezing me and shocking me out of my stupor. I dig my limbs into the gravel, struggling to bring my front around. The pounding ablution comes onto my wound.

I let the torrent roll me to the side, then heave myself up and stagger forward. Up a stair of flags, shivering as the wind gusts against me, I reach the amphitheater's top and gaze at the rock between my fores. The dripping of my blood has stopped.

The way is dim again. I look behind me, seeing that the slit in the cloud has sealed over. Ahead, the murky crags are heaped like blackened armor. No sign of the pack in the canyon to the left or on the slopes below. A ridge connects the amphitheater to the next higher peak. My hooves are moving, but my mind withdraws, seeking a different kind of refuge, fancies forging perfect defenses—flawless cliffs, polished promontories, unreachable towers. A strange notion strikes me: that this linkage of peaks is my own imagining, mineralized by fear.

The ridge is before me. I'm moving up it, fooled by shadows, every stone a hole, every hole a stone. Are they near? I falter and the vista unhinges, its armor of mountains creaking around me, swinging on loose rivets. I right myself. The dizziness abates, but the creaking remains. The hectoring magpies are back, their long tails trailing and their wings thrashing like torn rags. Their cries announce my whereabouts, then they sail forward and settle on the crest ahead.

A rattle of rock. A trail of wolf musk through the gusts. I step behind an outcrop and look back, seeing their silhouettes moving along the ridge's twisting spine. My heart beats furiously, but the rest of me is inert. The thought approaches, not straightaway, but tatting like the pack along the ridge: the ram must die. The tireless pack passes behind a rise and reappears, Scout in front, muzzle low, the Lead right behind, head up, sulphur eyes searching. The magpies follow them, flapping from rock to rock.

I turn and scan the ridge. It continues at an easy angle. To the left is a narrow ravine, hemmed like a slaughter pen. To the right, a sheer cliff. Or I can do nothing at all. I glance at the wound in my chest, feeling the temptation to let the end come unresisted, imagining their jaws inside me, grinding my organs. Soon I'll be heave on the dirt of the den, disgorged for the newborn. Another rattle, very close. They see me and their strides quicken.

My pulse thrums fiercely. My hoof stamps. I draw a deep breath and lift my head. I can't just give myself to them, not yet. Moving to the right, I cross the crest, stepping down a sweep of scree toward the sheer wall. It's seamed with cracks and corded with moss. Nearby, a ledge runs on the level for a dozen lengths,

164

then narrows, dwindling and losing itself in the shadows. I hear the pack behind me. I step forward, knowing what I must do.

Feeling with the bottoms of my toes, I start along the ledge. It's sprinkled with grit. Wet seeps gutter the spalls. Below, the plunge ends on a broken slide. My eye shifts back—concentrating, I press my shoulder to the wall and lift my legs carefully, hooves shuttling ahead. Gradually the sill narrows. I'm breathing the damp rock, the moss cool and velvety against my flank, embedded in the crevices like green piping. A faint crushing sound, the hiss of gravel at my rear. I resist the urge to turn. The ledge is pinching toward the wall. I change to an edging step. Gaps appear ahead.

I reach my right fore to a sloping hold, bring my left hind forward slowly, trying my weight. Now the left fore, a long stretch, right hind suspended. The ledge is a crust, dwindled to nothing. Set the hind, extend the right fore, groping across the gap, toes rasping for a nub. I hesitate. The hoof slips, one toe going over. Behind, I hear a gasping.

I glance back, holding my breath. The Hangbelly is crouched where the ledge is widest, eye staring fixedly at me, tongue lolling, her cheeks matted with my blood. Why her, the most ungainly? Because she's blind to the danger. Viciousness draws her on.

I turn forward, facing my task. My fore finds the nub. I can see the continuation of the ledge ahead. Daring drowns my fear. Left fore to a wrinkle. A bold move. Bear down, lift the right hind, moving off three points to two, right fore reaching, balancing on one point and sending my fores to the far lip.

Safe. I pause and catch my breath, pulse pounding. Then I

165

continue forward. The wall relaxes, leaning back, and the ledge becomes a balcony with a broken parapet guarding its edge. Farther, a bartizan rises out of the cliff. Between my hoof sounds, I hear the Hangbelly's hoarse pants. I turn, feeling a fierce tenderness as my chest touches the wall. I peer back along it, over the network of green veins. The Hangbelly creeps toward me, her good eye harrowing me at close range, the other clearly visible for the first time. The scar is one leg of a bald star above her brow. Its other legs feed over the top of her head, thrusting their tendrils into her brain like the roots of a weed. She answers my scrutiny, wrinkling her muzzle and curling her lips, as if still in the agony of that shattering blow. She's far beyond her powers— the ledge isn't wide enough for her wobbling paws. But she advances anyway, seeing only me, grumbling and grappling her fangs, baring a fear as great as my own. The fear that I will escape.

Her hatred sends shivers through me. A rumbling sounds, like thunder before rain. The wall tilts strangely. She raises her head, glancing confusedly around. Her muzzle swings back, eye fixed on me, peering through a tunnel of concentration as she takes another step. The rumble breaks into fierce chucks, jolting me toward the parapet—the mountain is quaking! Across the canyon, peaks toss. The panels of the wall are shifting, green veins swelling in their crevices. The Hangbelly peers at me, vertigo rising in her black brain.

A roar breaks from the rock, an impossible wrath that convulses the peaks and depths, banging me against the parapet as the ledge-line ripples, the Hangbelly dancing on it like a spider on a thread. The cliff sinks suddenly and heaves, throwing her

off. Down she pitches, black limbs flailing. The roaring booms—
then, as quickly as it started, the jolts cease and the rumbling
fades. Hisses of sliding rock trail from the canyons. Across the
cliff, lengths of green cord hang from their chinks. On the slope
below, the Hangbelly's body lies sprawled, legs akimbo, her head
bent unnaturally on the stem of neck.

A nervous jubilation brews inside me, then drains away,
replaced by relief. I start up the shelves leading to the bartizan,
wondering at the power that rose to my aid. I turn back, peering
down. The pack is loping across the broken incline. The magpies
fly ahead. One swoops onto the Hangbelly's paunch, the other
settles on her brow. The Lead lunges furiously, driving the birds
into the air. Croaking spitefully, they rise and watch the other
wolves circle.

As I surmount the tower, a moan sounds below. The Lead
is beside the Hangbelly, grieving, pawing her shoulder to wake
her. The Scout sits close, stiff and solemn. The Ruff lies pros-
trate by the dam's head, ducking his muzzle to make amends.
The other three watch me, the Dangler with suspicion, her misgivings confirmed. The Younger is farther up the slope, legs
dancing in place, impatient to return to the chase. The Wise
regards me with her air of knowing, as though none of this was a
surprise. Without shifting her gaze, she wows to the Lead. He
looks up at me with his fierce sulphur eyes. Then the Scout
touches her nose to his, vying with her sister, turning the Lead's
attention from me, peering back across the slope in the direction
of the lowlands and the den.

I face forward, eager to be gone, taking short leaps. But my
limbs knot, and there's a bridling in my shoulders. I feel the pain

in my chest and hear the grating within. Below, the Wise is beside the Lead, nuzzling his neck, drawing him away from the corpse. Before they get far, the Scout jumps between them, gaping her jaws at the Wise, who responds in kind. The two growl and threaten each other, while the Lead slinks back to his fallen mate. I swing to the right, following the crest, breaking into a jangled trot. All they have to do is get back on the ridge and they would catch me in no time. My plight is no different than before. In the dimness, a mournful howl rises, giving vent to loss and a terrible yearning. Just the Lead at first, then the others join in.

<hr />

Two weeks later, the spurs verging the Cheshnina River were misty. All morning, the wind had chased clouds across the sky, shaking showers from them until they dissolved to fog. In the drenched spruce, a ghostly chant sounded while the suck of boots kept time.

> *Blood drips dark stars on the rock.*
> *Hope goes slowly as I plod.*

Ransom waved the birch whips aside and emerged, bearing his pack in an unhurried pace. His face was ruddy, burnt by the sun and chafed by the wind, and his hair was matted. The two days past had been hard. He'd torn through the mountains, sloshed across streams and bushwhacked through high brush with the rain pouring down, determined to make the pickup date, soaked and chilled the whole way. Lindy was often in his thoughts—the human, not the pack—but time and again his story swallowed him, and he would come back to himself an hour or two later, mumbling a fragment of chant or replaying some dark sequence through the maze of rock.

As he descended the last bench, a nimbus of mosquitoes rose

from the soaked moss and shrouded him, whining eagerly. A mob of siskins flushed, rasping their welcome. Through the green, cinquefoil blooms burst buttery, and a fresh breeze blew willow flock past his face. When the humping Cheshnina appeared, he remembered the day of his arrival and the world he'd left.

"Lindy," Ransom sobbed. He was aching to see her. So much had changed. With the Hangbelly dead, Lindy's rages were at an end. He was glad for her, and for himself. He laughed. What was he thinking? Lindy had no way of knowing what had happened with the wolves. He wasn't sure himself.

He made his way to the river bar and put his pack down, smiling at the short grass around the landing strip as if it was a forgotten friend. As he glanced down the strip, he saw a plane parked at the far end. A white Cub. From behind the brush, a twist of smoke rose. Someone was in the cabin.

Ransom turned and gazed upriver. The precipitation had been wintry around the dome. Wrangell was invisible now, but the peaks and cliffs at the head of the Cheshnina were covered with snow. The would-be sanctuary was freezing, and the ram was lost somewhere in it, fleeing from dreaded eyes and thoughts. As agitated as Ransom was by all that had happened to him, it was difficult to leave. Mt. Wrangell had become his world. He sighed, turned back to the strip, and started along the trail toward the cabin.

The frozen heights were quickly forgotten. Through a weakness in the mist, sun splashed warm and gold, and the summer danced into Ransom's senses. Lousewort pinwheels rose on his left, lemon and pink. Cotton grass bobbed on his right. Blackpolls twittered above the path, peavine tossed magenta bracelets across it, and lupine compasses edged it, a raindrop jewel in the center of each. A sulphur butterfly flung himself into the sky. Ransom smiled.

The trail turned and the cabin was before him, leaning against a tide of waist-high mertensia thick with blue bells. Its log walls and corrugated roof vanquished his delight. Ransom saw civilization and, for a moment, his dread of the creatures that had hunted him vanished, and all he recalled was the freedom of the wilds and the surge of energy a leaper feels. As he neared the cabin door, he heard the buzzing of flies. A quartered animal, skinned and bloody, hung from the rafters of an open shed. The sight repulsed him. Confusion crossed his face and he slid his hand beneath his vest, then thought better and drew the vest closed. He approached the door and rapped on it.

The door budged. Through the gap, Ransom saw a man's face and one bloodshot eye.

"What are you doing here?" the man asked.

Ransom gestured at the slope behind the cabin, struggling for words.

The door opened wider. With his gesture, Ransom's vest had parted and the man was staring at his shirt front. It was soaked with blood.

"Wasilla Bill?" Ransom asked.

The man nodded. He was in overalls, husky and paunchy with curly gray hair starting to bald. Ransom saw the shotgun under his arm and Bill's eyes met his, troubled. "Hurt yourself?"

Ransom drew the vest back over his pectoral.

"Better come in," Bill said. Inside, he tipped the firearm against the cabin wall. "Wouldn't you know," he muttered wryly. "Bear butchered that moose right by the door."

Ransom entered. Dirty pots rested on a woodpile, clothing hung from nails. The cabin reeked of wood smoke. There was a cot and a table with a bottle of whiskey on it, and along the wall, a cupboard and shelves with provisions. A box of pancake mix lay where voles had torn into it. Bill fed wood to an oil drum stove and played with the damper.

"You're drenched." He came up behind Ransom and pulled his parka and vest off.

Ransom stiffened, but he didn't resist.

Bill motioned him toward the stove, eyes soft and protective, as if comforting a frightened animal. With a shiver, Ransom stepped toward the warmth. "I've been out here for a month."

"By yourself?"

Ransom started to nod, then stopped. "I'm a little disoriented."

Bill's brows lifted. "Any fool could see that." He reached to remove Ransom's shirt.

Ransom drew away.

"Don't you want me to help you?"

Ransom felt the man's warmth, along with the stove's. In Bill's smile, he saw humanity's grandeur suddenly revealed. Where the molten heart flowed, no one was a stranger. He sighed and unbuttoned his shirt.

As he peeled the cloth back, Bill sucked his breath. "How did this happen?"

Ransom eyed the deep gash to the left of his sternum, unsure how much of what he remembered was real. "I was attacked by wolves," he said tentatively.

Astonishment froze Bill's face.

"They were waiting for me on this saddle, behind a rock."

Nodding for Ransom to continue, Bill stepped toward the cupboard. "How many?"

"Seven. Six now."

Bill returned with a jar, a rag, and dressings for the wound.

"One of them's dead," Ransom said.

"Let's sit over here." Bill led him to the cot. He opened the jar, wet the rag with a cloudy liquid, and daubed the gash. "Never heard of wolves stalking a man."

Ransom winced. "They thought I was a ram. What is that?"

"Wormwood. Indian medicine."

"I was dressed like one," Ransom explained. "I have Dall leggings and a headdress with ram's horns."

Bill peered at him.

"He's my true self," Ransom said. "That's why I'm here." He laughed. "The night they attacked me, I thought I'd turned into a ram."

The ministrations halted.

"That sounds crazy," Ransom muttered.

"I see the wildness of one in your eyes," Bill said.

Ransom searched him. "You have a wild heart," he said softly. His head sank and his shoulders slumped, exhausted, yielding himself to the older man's care.

Bill rocked back and glanced at the blood-covered rag. Then he stood, retrieved the whiskey from the table and took a slug. "Have some."

Ransom shook his head. Bill was smiling, but there was trouble beneath.

"We're fragile." Bill tore open a package of gauze. "Like that moose out there." He pulled a hide glove from his belt and set it on Ransom's leg. "My wife's."

The cuff had beadwork. The leather was stiff and the fingers inflated. There might have been a hand in it, patting Ransom's thigh.

"I was thinking about her when you knocked," Bill said. "Thinking and drinking."

Ransom saw the oblivion in his eyes.

"She loved these mountains," Bill said. "I built this cabin for her before she died." He pulled adhesive tape from a spool. "Tuberculosis. She was Indian, Ahtna. Had our child in her." He glanced over his shoulder. "Fathered it in the spruce out there." He held the gauze pads over Ransom's wound and secured them with tape. "She'd sit on a boulder beside the river and sing to it. That was sixteen years ago. A feeling comes over me this time of year and I have to come. I get sad, but I'm happy too, remembering."

Ransom imagined him drinking his whiskey, smelling the forest and the rain, listening to the voice beside the river. He thought of Lindy. Imperceptibly a drone grew out of the quiet.

"Your pickup?" Bill retrieved the glove.

Ransom nodded. "Doug Hurley." He reached for his shirt.

"You can't wear that." Bill took his Pendleton from the chair and held it while Ransom fed his arms through. "I'm coming out tomorrow." Bill stepped toward the door.

Ransom grabbed his vest and parka, following. The Cub was already upriver, circling above the snowline, red against the white slopes.

"After Doctor Jim's looked at that," Bill said, "I'll buy you a drink."

An hour later, Tolsona Lake was tipping below, flashing blue and gold as the Cub descended. Ransom saw the hangar and the roof of Doug's home. They wheeled, aligning with the lakefront, power leaking from the Cub's engine. Spruce spindles and parked cars raced past the windscreen, and their wheels touched down. The earth lurched, shimmied and froze. The engine gunned, the tail spun around, and the Cub went bumping back over the gravel toward the hangar.

As they came to a halt, Ransom saw a small group waiting for them. Doug killed the engine, opened the clamshell doors and climbed out. Ransom followed. Was it fatigue, excitement, or the plane's vibration that made his legs judder? The faces recognized him. They were smiling, relieved, curious. Lindy ran forward. He raised his arm toward her and she embraced him. He laughed, heedless, then recoiled, feeling pressure on his wound. Her eyes searched his, troubled.

"It hurts," he said, touching his chest.

She frowned at him, confused.

"Scrape with some wolves," Doug said, trying to help.

Her upset shifted to the pilot. "Wolves?"

The group drew closer, a tall man with a white crew cut and lively eyes among them.

"He was acting out his story," Doug explained, removing his glasses. "Probably the costume he was wearing, the smell of it. They thought he was prey."

Ransom saw Lindy's appalled expression. Ida was worried. Skimmer was beaming. Vince Silvano, the Fish and Game officer Ransom had met before departing, looked mystified.

"They followed him," Doug went on. "Thought he shook them, but then they'd find him again." He looked at Ida. "They ambushed him on a saddle. One of them got her fangs in his chest." Doug had been incredulous when Ransom related this an hour before, but something was happening in the retelling. His dourness battled with a boyish wonder and the wonder was winning. "He fought free. Made it into some cliffs. But they'd tasted blood. They caught up to him again, and the one that attacked him followed him out onto a cliff." He glanced at Ransom.

Ransom nodded, thankful he'd been relieved of the job of explaining. He saw Lindy's agitation, and he gave her a private look, wishing they could be alone.

"She fell," Doug concluded, turning back to Lindy. "That sidetracked them long enough for him to get away."

It was Lindy's moment and the group waited, but she could only eye Ransom with mute dread. The wind had died and the aspens were still.

"Wow," Skimmer said, bursting with admiration.

Ida was astonished by her husband's animation. Doug met her gaze, conscious of his state, but helpless to explain it.

Vince Silvano's rockabilly smile had faded. He looked from the Hurleys back to Ransom, unsure what to make of Ransom and his harrowing story.

The tall man with white hair stepped forward, his hand extended. "Burt Conklin," he said.

Ransom stared at him.

"I'm at the university, doing research on the Wrangell summit," Conklin said.

Ransom shook his hand. He'd been greatly disappointed when Conklin didn't show up for the dinner at Calvin Bauer's house. The head of the Geophysical Institute had an authoritative mien, but his eyes were kind and unpresuming.

"Those are dangerous cliffs," Conklin said.

"The rain helped," Ransom told him.

Conklin looked puzzled.

"Easier to climb. Rain fills the vesicles and weights the rock." Ransom scanned the group. "The talus is less likely to slide. It braces your mind, too. When the mist is swirling and the rain's pouring down—" He recaptured his state. "Keep going, don't get cold. You get a desperate feeling, an attitude toward things that threaten you." He saw suspicion in Lindy's eyes and drew a breath. It panged his chest and she flinched sympathetically, staring at his shirt as if she could see beneath the cloth.

"I'm going to call Doctor Jim," Ida said.

Lindy gave her a frightened nod, and Ida headed for the office.

"I feel fine," Ransom assured them. He smiled at Lindy, then turned to Conklin. "For the mind and body, it's a forbidding place. But for the heart, it's an inspiring one. Flows frozen in time. Creations of the moment, changing as the rock erodes, transforming from one fantastic shape to another." He shifted his gaze from face to face. "In a sense, the volcano is still pouring out."

"What's your purpose?" Conklin asked.

"To find the glowing magma in the heart of things," Ransom said.

Conklin gave him a bemused look. Doug exchanged glances with his son, then turned to unload Ransom's backpack from the Cub.

"How did you fight off the wolves?" Skimmer wondered.

Ida hurried back. "Jim can take us in an hour," she said.

Doug set the pack down and lifted his head, directing Ida's gaze to the horns and facepiece peering from its top. "Once you're patched up, maybe you'll tell us what the ram learned," he said.

Ida regarded the ropy visage with suspicion.

Ransom could see Lindy's distress was mounting. He glanced at Doug.

"You two need some time together." Doug motioned down the lakefront. "Use our guest house."

Ransom gave him a thankful look, nodded at the others and stepped toward Lindy.

They took the path along the shore. The lake was restive. The wind came up behind them, clapping the poplar leaves.

"Strange," Ransom muttered, "everyone making so much of a little cut."

Lindy was wearing her leather vest, but her appearance wasn't youthful. Her eyes were shadowed and her lips were straight.

"Talk to me," he said.

She sighed and gave him an abandoned look. "This is a lonely place."

Ransom saw the Dangler, worried and retreating. "Here?" He laughed, comparing the lake to where he'd been.

"It's grim, ferrying people to the end of the world." Above, the clouds were wispy and wattled, and the sun needled through. A ray touched her forehead, and her eyes flickered with light. "Oh, Ransom." She stopped.

He circled her with his arms and kissed her, feeling her hunger, glad with all his heart, loving her strength and determination. "You kept me going," he whispered, thinking of the Lead.

She bowed her head, touched her fingers to his wound and gazed up at him. "Well?"

He saw the Wise, grave and knowing, and the memory of that night rose before him—his panic flight, the fangs needling his core.

"What really happened?" she asked.

He swallowed, trying to collect his thoughts. She seemed to perceive his distress as surely as if she'd been there with him. "I don't know," he said finally.

She remained silent, waiting.

"I wasn't just wearing the skins," he said, his eyes flaring. "I was transformed."

"What are you talking about?" Her eyes searched him.

"I was high," Ransom explained, "but—" He sighed. "The places I went, the leaps I made, the things I felt— I was the ram." He saw her face cloud with fear, and he held her, hoping it would pass, hoping rage wasn't seething at the pack's center. The Hangbelly had died in his story, but she knew nothing of that. It was just his wish that peace would come to her.

"It's been too long," he murmured. He closed his eyes. Nearby, water sloshed beneath a dock, recalling that terrible moment on the saddle. His chest was torn open, he could feel the Hangbelly probing and hear her lapping.

She kissed his cheek. "All I care about is that you're back."

When he opened his eyes, Ransom saw the Younger, eyes glittering, joyful to be with him, and his anxiety vanished. The Hurley home lay ahead, warm and welcoming, sheltered in a cove of spruce. Beside the path, the fireweed quivered with bees. They stepped along it together, ignoring the dark discovery *Wild Animus* was waking within them, arms about each other's waists.

In the privacy of the guest house, their needy bodies spoke, clamoring till they were naked and flesh to flesh, excepting the bandage Wasilla Bill had applied to Ransom's wound. Then it was time, and Doug drove them to the doctor, who put a few stitches in, applied new bandages, and told them there was nothing to worry about. When they returned, Ida invited Ransom and Lindy for dinner. There were plenty of questions—first, about his climbing and camping, then about the molten heart in the abstract. Ransom explained his notion in a subdued voice, exchanging glances with Lindy. It wasn't until the meal ended, and Doug asked Ransom to help him move some cordwood to the guest house, that the conversation grew personal.

"So what's it like?" Doug added the last of the logs to the stack and removed his gloves.

Ransom cocked his head.

"Being a ram," Doug clarified.

"You're laughing at me," Ransom said softly.

Doug nodded. "A little. I don't want to feel like a fool for asking."

Ransom saw the vulnerability in Doug's eyes. "Different than I thought," he said. "Every moment is intense." He touched his wound. "The fear they live with is hard to imagine."

"But it's worth it?" Doug studied him. "To find what you're looking for?"

Ransom allowed some of his doubt to show. "I hope so."

"I hope so, too." Doug's face was wistful. "I used to have your kind of bravery. When I first came here. Now I've got six planes, and half the lake is mine." He smirked.

"And?"

Doug's gaze narrowed. "I like who I was," he said, "better than who I am." He put his gloves in his pocket, motioned toward the house, and started along the path. "Can your ram cure that?"

In the kitchen of the Hurley house, Ida was washing dishes. Lindy dried them and Skimmer put them away.

"Jesus was a sheep," Skimmer pointed out. "A lamb."

"That's true," Ida smiled at Lindy. Her reservations were dissolving. "I'm not sure why they gave the devil hooves and horns. All those kinds of animals eat grass."

Lindy laughed.

"What's important," Ida glanced at Skimmer, "is what's in your heart. I know Ransom means well." She turned off the tap and dried her hands. "We're done." She gave Lindy a satisfied look, conscious of the younger woman's insularity. "I'm happy we've had this chance to get to know you." She put her arm around Lindy's shoulder.

Lindy stiffened. "You've been kind." She tried to mask her discomfort at Ida's mothering.

"They're back." Ida raised her head, hearing Doug and Ransom on the porch.

"All I know," Ransom was saying, "is that my destiny lies with him."

Doug opened the door.

"Where he's headed," Ransom added, "I'm not yet sure."

The door closed, restoring the perfect silence outside. The water was smooth as glass. A Bonaparte's gull was beating across the lake. It fixed its wings and settled into its reflection.

Nine

It was ten at night, two months later, and Ransom and Lindy were back in Seattle. Darkness had gathered around the house on Sunset Hill, a downstairs window leaking light through parted drapes. Below, the mist was crawling through the grass toward the thistles and blackberry whips tangled at the edge of the cliff. In the space beyond, the air swirled strangely, illumined by the glow of the smothered marina. A foghorn droned, sounding deep and final, like a summons from the void.

Hands clutched the curtains and sealed the slit. Within, Ransom tried to regain his self-possession, returning to his desk. The room was white, the rug was white, the desk was a white door supported by cinder blocks. He wore a white shirt and pants, sat in a white chair, picked up a white pen and stooped over white paper like a monk shepherding a sacred manuscript. His attention burned on the words—only they were black—then strayed to the photos tacked on the wall. Pictures of Wrangell cliffs flanked a blow-up of a butterfly pupa girdled to a plant stem with a thread of silk. The pupa was still as rock, the creature within discernible, wings folded, legs and antennae welded to its cradle. He took a deep breath and focused on his words, but his distress returned suddenly, twisting him around in his seat, his hand clawing at his left pectoral as if something had coiled around his heart. Crying to himself, he rose, eyeing the creature in the photo as if he was trapped in a similar transformation, terrified of what he was about to become. Then he grabbed the sheaf and wheeled, fleeing from his cloister, stumbling up the stairs.

Lindy was in the kitchen, preparing dinner. She heard him coming and glanced over her shoulder. "Is the scene done?" She turned off the burners, swallowing her anxiety. "I can't wait—" His stricken look startled her. "What is it?" She embraced him with potholders in her hands.

Ransom didn't respond.

"Let me read you the letters," she offered.

He nodded absently, still clutching the sheaf to his chest.

She took his arm, led him into the living room, and sat him on the sofa. As always, the space looked like a whirlwind had struck it, but the subject had changed. Pictures scattered and tacked to every surface showed castles and armor, lava fountains and flows, all interlaced with photos of wolves. On the coffee table was a livestock manual, opened to a cutaway diagram of a sheep's chest.

Lindy took the manuscript and sat facing him, lifting the first letter. "This one's from Katherine Getz. Remember?"

He nodded.

"'Dear Ransom. Thank you so much for the write-up and the tape. It was good to hear how quickly you recovered from your injury. What an experience.'" Lindy looked up. He seemed to be listening. "'In response to your question about magpies: yes, we regularly find them at high elevations in the mountains. That's where they nest. Your tape has gotten a lot of listening, especially the golden-crown's five-note song. It's a new dialect, so it may be unique to the Wrangells.'"

Ransom smiled crookedly. "A new dialect?"

" 'Of course my favorite was your notes on the pipits. What an amazing courtship display. And to scramble all that way to recover one of his feathers. That's not something an ornithologist would do. Why did you send it to me? I can't express the joy I felt.' " Lindy creased her brow and wet her lips. " 'Whenever I look at it, I imagine the way you described his song—"hanging in the wake of his plunge like a string of red beads." A beautiful picture. It was, I'm sure, the purest trickling of the bird's heart.' "

Ransom looked thoughtful. He reached his hand out and Lindy passed him the first page.

" 'Hank is more excited than you can imagine about the dwarf sorrel. He says it's new to science. *Rumex altmanensis.* It will cost you ten grand to charter a chopper and bring a fresh sample back to Fairbanks so he can do a chromosome count. So much for immortality. Sid apologizes. He's been busy. The red cuts you photographed are erosional products and they have the color of blood because they have the same composition: iron. The amber sand is geothermally altered rock resulting from blowouts or the slow venting of gas. That's all for now. Please stay in touch. Sincerely, Katherine.' "

Ransom smiled. "The feather hit the mark."

Lindy peered at him, head downturned. "Obviously." Her tone was ironic, but her eyes were generous, without envy. "Ida's is stranger." She unfolded the second letter. " 'Dear Ransom. We're all relieved your cut's healed. I'm sure Lindy's taking good care of you. She's a darling.' " Lindy frowned. " 'How's the book coming? Summer's almost over. It's been a wild one. The day after you left, someone stole our truck. The troopers found it near Copper Center. It had been run off the road and was hanging over a ledge, front wheels in the air. The cab was facing Mt. Wrangell, so Skimmer said the ram hot-wired it. You made an impression on him. He's changed. The truth is that Doug's changed too, and so have I. The conversation you and I had on your last day here keeps coming back to me. I'm beginning to think your passion for the molten heart is the miracle I've been praying for. Doug is remembering. Last week, we landed at our old sheep camp above the Chichokna, and spent the whole day just wandering around, laughing and crying like children. He has always been a man of the spirit, I knew that when we met. I'd given up. Now I see what kind of help he needed. In a way, it's been my failing all these years, not his. This might surprise you, but I worship the heart too. Not the mortal heart, but the sacred heart we share in Him.'" Lindy glanced at Ransom.

"Capital *H*," he said.

She nodded. "'Please don't take this the wrong way. I know you aren't a Christian, but I don't think that matters. You touched the truth in us, and I want to let you know.'" Lindy took a breath and turned the page over. The serenity in Ransom's face surprised her. It was a moment of sweetness for him, just a moment. "'Now I'm off to get some moose hides scraped and buy groceries. If you're planning another trip to the Wrangells, you can save yourself the airfare from Anchorage or Fairbanks. Skimmer's happy to pick you up. We have relatives coming in May, but the guest house should be available most of next summer. There's often room for one or two more around the kitchen table.'" Lindy made her eyes wide. "'You know what I mean.'"

Ransom laughed. It was as if Ida was watching some animal from hiding, holding her breath and raising her sights, fearful it might flee.

"'Give my love to Lindy. God bless you. Ida.'" Lindy joined Ransom's laughter, relieved by his cheer. But even as she watched, it faded.

"They both mentioned the wound," he muttered, rising.

She flared her eyes, as if to ask "what did you expect?" Then she stood opposite, wary.

"That's what draws them. Don't you see?" He shook his head. "'Surrender for me. Die so I don't have to.' That's what everybody wants."

Lindy was appalled. "How can you say that?"

"That's what *I* want," he laughed. "A martyr—someone to take my place."

"Stop—" Lindy clasped her arms around him. He was shuddering. "No one wants you to sacrifice yourself." She tried to fix him with her eyes, but they wouldn't stop shifting. "What have you been doing down there?"

"Writing about terror," he said grimly. "Preparing to die."

"Two years of quarter tabs," she said accusingly.

Ransom didn't reply.

"Please," Lindy said. "Not at night."

He looked helpless. "That's where I am in the story."

"If we were like Ida and Doug—" Her voice was reedy. "If we had something to anchor us— A family—"

Ransom's eyes narrowed. "Thinking of your pups."

Her protest was choked. She was too distraught to speak.

Ransom looked bewildered. "You want to destroy me." He touched his left pectoral.

Lindy hunched and began to sob.

Her misery pierced him. The cruelty of what he'd said echoed in his ears. It was *he* who was destroying *her*, Ransom realized. He threw his arms around her. "Forgive me."

She hugged him desperately.

This is what *Wild Animus* had done to them, he thought. From a love so innocent, born from pure desire. He held her close, yielding to the guilt and shame that had been mounting inside him, wanting to confess. "I've been so afraid."

She caressed his cheek.

Ransom shuddered. "My heart—"

She stiffened and pulled away. "No." Lindy wiped her tears.

"There's something wrong with it."

"No!" She trembled with rage. "I'm not going to the hospital again." She shook her head at his shirt front. "It's healing, it's fine."

"I can feel the fangs—"

"How many times do the doctors have to tell you? The pains are normal."

"My ribs are moving."

"You didn't break any ribs."

"It's a clock that's only wound once," he murmured with remorse. "Everything depends on it—all these lofty thoughts and emotions." He eyed her despairingly. "It's damaged. It races, it freezes, then quickens to catch up. I was awake all night—"

"Stoned on acid!" Lindy was furious. "You don't care about your health. You spend it like there's no tomorrow. The only thing that matters is this pain in your chest."

Ransom sighed. "You've changed," he said sadly. "You don't know my inner state. You have to attack me to feel it."

Her rage burst and she flew at him, moaning and shrieking and raking his front, mocking his accusation. Ransom fought free.

"Your heart's withered." He scowled at the pendant.

"From you! Most girls get a ring."

Ransom waved his hands to erase her hatred, chanting beneath his breath.

My insides shiver and churn,
Trying to drive off the cold.

He grabbed her and pulled her against him. "The ram is in the rocks," he groaned, pleading with her to understand. "Threatened. Obsessed with self-defense. The outpourings of his heart are frozen into fieldworks. I want to leave the nightmare behind. But I can't escape."

She was limp, weeping against his chest, clinging to him like a beaten child. It had become terrible to her, but it was still love, and it was all she had.

"I found another today," he shuddered, glancing at a pile of copied journal articles. "A capitulation they can't explain. The pack attacked. The moose, with escape still possible, just offered himself." He drew a long breath. "Beneath the instinct to preserve the self, there is a darker one to give it up. A bliss beyond fear. That's the truth the molten heart knows." He regarded her with remorse. "When animals yield themselves for love, they draw pleasure from the river of surrender. When they're attacked, sometimes they submit to the killer as they would to a lover. It's a confusion. A mistake."

She gazed at him, eyes brimming, ready to heed any cause for hope.

Ransom saw the Lead, watchful and intent. Then the Ruff and the Scout emerged. Behind them, the Hangbelly was waiting. "A metaphor for our love," he said, "has turned into an enactment of my death." The Wise peered up from the bottom of Lindy's eyes. "Through the ram," he said, "I'm learning a surrender from which there is no return. Learning how those creatures feel as the river bears them away." He realized he was speaking to the pack.

Ransom froze. He swung around, grabbed the manuscript and hurled it into the fireplace. Then he was crouching before it, fumbling with a box of matches. Lindy gasped, spurring herself after him, kneeling to pry the box out of his hand. Matches spilled across the slate. Ransom thrust her away, struck one and began lighting page corners. "I'm Sam," he said. "I'm Sam, I'm Sam."

Her potholders were on the couch. She used them to bat the flames, but before she'd finished, Ransom had dashed her aside and was striking more matches. She grasped his wrists, struggling to stop him, feeling his determination and fearful of what it meant, shaking her head as if trying to take back something she'd done or said. Over his shoulder, she saw the flames spreading. She lunged, reaching to encircle the smoking mass, then turned and dished the sheaf across the living room floor, throwing herself on top of it to smother the flames. He wrestled briefly with her, trying to pull the pages from beneath her, then he broke down.

"I want it to end," he cried, "I want it to end."

She tried to comfort him, unsure what encouragement to give, fearful of her power, knowing only that she couldn't turn away and let his self-doubt dismantle him.

"I'm sorry," he said finally. He took a deep breath.

She hugged him, fearful for them both, feeling his weakness like never before.

Ransom wiped his tears. "It's time," he murmured, standing.

Lindy watched him, dazed. When he pulled her to her feet, she gave him an imploring look, but he averted his face. She stood there for a long moment, eyes searching and bewildered, realizing that there was no recourse, letting herself be calmed by his resolve. Then she moved away. She returned a moment later, holding a glass of water out to him in one hand and a quarter tab in the other.

A half hour later, Lindy was curled on the living room floor, asleep.

Ransom rose from beside her, feeling the effects of the drug, very much awake.

He opened the door and stepped out onto the balcony. The wind had been blowing, and while fog still blanketed Puget Sound, everything above was bright and clear. The bluff was steeped in starglow, grasses combed with it, vines pricked with it, leaves dripping it. A damp world, cradled in dreams. Overhead, the angled ceiling of night shifted, creasing from star to star, hints of a blinding cosmos winking through the joints of its flexing chrysalis.

I'm no longer fleeing. Just shambling slowly forward, toppling ricks of rock. I stir my limbs, kicking into a trot, but pain spears my chest and I fall back to a walk, strength gone. I turn to check behind me. No wolves that I can see. Forward, through the dimness, the ground is nearly level, cobbles banked in heaps, snow lobes everywhere. A misty shroud drifts past, the leaden cloud just above, thick and muffling.

My direction is doubtful. There's no uptrend, no higher place to head for. Are they below the cliff, mourning the Hangbelly? Perhaps they're returning the way they came. The Lead's face swims before me, sulphur eyes burning. They should have caught up to me by now.

A chill wind strafes my chest. My insides shiver and churn, trying to drive off the cold. The wound is sealed over with a wretched fancywork of grit and bits of moss embedded when it was pressed to the wall. Step by step, I'm making my peace with this barren place, crossing beds of lichen and puddled meltwater, barely caring what my hooves do. My dream of an exalted world is over. These shadows, this gloom—there's nothing more.

189

I recall the convex slab, the chimney, the amphitheater—seeing the labyrinth for what it is. An enormous prison. I've threaded its galleries, mounted its stairs, and now I'm secured in its frozen keep. Condemned.

Down a corridor, the tread of paws. I glance back, listening. The air seems to have changed, sounds sharper, scents more vivid. The padding follows an embankment. My heart stops. A crump of snow, a clink, and then through the mist, I see a dark shape approaching—the Ruff with his nose to the ground, feasting on my scent. I stumble forward, flight playing across my brain, searching for strength. The Ruff veers to the right, forcing me to turn. To the left, the Wise appears, head up, staring at my wound, knowing the time has come. The two wolves are guiding me around the base of a hillock.

Mist is everywhere, clinging to cobbles, winding over puddles of ice. Will it be painful? How long will it take? There they are, standing among the low boulders beyond a small plat of snow, the Dangler and Scout to the right, the Lead a few paces forward, Younger on the left. Strange, this absence of terror, this calm. Into the trap I step, feeling the magnification of this unremarkable ground—this gravel, these few blocks, the semicircle of snow before me looming larger and larger.

Waves of musk wash over me. The Lead gazes at the Wise. The Younger fidgets her fores. For a moment, the impulse to flee is overpowering. Then the impulse fades. The Lead inhales me greedily, ears perked, savoring the sounds of my hooves. Realizing I'm yielding, his jaws open and he embraces me with a ravening moan.

The plat of snow is suspended over the cobbles like a stage.

190

Here is my freedom. Six lengths to go. Five. Four. One more ordeal and then nothing to fear. The wolves close in, Scout wading through a pond of mist to the brink of the stage, the Dangler slinking around its edge, confident at the last. The Lead puts his large paws on the plat and swings his weight over his shoulders. Hold to the promise of calm. It won't take long.

Oblivion, I pray. Three lengths. Two. Finish me quickly. I set my right fore on the white scaffold and step onto it. No thought of escape, no defying fate.

I am yours.

My legs punch through, chest landing hard. The raw cold pierces my center. I hang on their lunges, waiting for the strike— The earth rumbles, shifting with that same power that hurled the Hangbelly from the ledge. The Dangler spooks and backs away. The Scout is frozen, gazing gravely at the Lead. He barely notices the tremor, his sulphur eyes flaring at the sight of me helpless. He takes a long step, getting all fours on the stage, the Younger's bronze eyes glittering right behind.

A fierce jolt wrenches me! The rumble turns furious, ice rasping my wound. A sharp bark—the Dangler cringes with alarm. The Lead raises his paw to take another step, and the quake mounts. The Scout jumps back, Younger mincing nervously, turning to the Wise. Her deep eyes sense the power ebbing and flowing around me, claiming me, threatening the wolves to keep away. The Lead gapes his jaws and takes another step.

A terrible roar! The Lead halts, hunger dying in his eyes. The others wheel in confusion, except the Wise who is staring across my front. I follow her gaze. The night has cracked open, the

cloud cover lifting above a nearby ridge like a giant carapace,
and through the gap I see day—blue sky above, and below, the
purest white. A world of snow and ice! The power warding off
the wolves has broken a way through with its furious shaking.

Who are you? Settling to a shiver, soft and intimate—you
might be my own breath, the tingling of my nerves, the throb-
bing of my flesh. You've saved me. Why?

I offered myself, and you saw. You. The god of surrender.

A confirming hum! You are the wildness I've felt, and the joy!
Animus, beloved of leapers! Revealed in the moment of blackest
despair.

I draw my fores up, plant them on the stage and rise, watch-
ing my chest lift from the snow. You rumble, protecting, ice
beads buzzing under my hooves. I see the spurs of torn flesh and
the imprint they made, connecting me to your power. The Wise
is gazing at my horns. The light has found them and the tips are
glowing. My limbs wobble. I'm weak, but no longer afraid. I
haven't come this far to feed the pack.

As I step off the stage, the lip breaks and the pack flinches,
the Lead freezing with one shoulder down. The Scout is poised
for flight, wowing lowly at the Lead. Only the Wise stands
straight, feeling the power beneath her paws, but unfrightened
by it. The light from the widening crack plays over her back,
turning it silver, and in the depths of her eyes, I see a dawning
like my own. The Lead faces her, seeing her confidence and calm.

My way lies between them, toward the world of white. I step
over the quivering gravel, Animus, in your care. The Lead is
ready to leave. His jaw hangs at the Wise and he shifts his paws.
But she remains planted, her muzzle toward the light. Yes, he can

see. The Scout wows louder, insistent. The Lead ignores her, watching the Wise turn and sniff me, ears trembling, reassuring him, saying they should follow.

The Lead lifts his fore and paws the air as if feeling my power, gazing warily at the Wise. Everything has changed, his eyes say. He's no longer ours to kill. The Wise puckers her snout and clicks her teeth, promising him my body as I pass, and the Lead's eyes reignite. But the rumble still threatens, keeping them at bay, and I continue, unmolested.

A dozen paces and I glance back. The Lead and the Wise are following me, the Younger jogging up behind them, the first to decide. Then the Dangler, whimpering, doubting the decision, but afraid to be left. The Ruff stays, comforting the Scout. Are you with me? Yes, the gravel still shifts beneath my hooves.

The crack of day is expanding. I'm stepping over boulders scratched like flattened grass. Ahead, tiny white blooms rise from chinks in the rock—far stars, winking out a course. Beyond, a slope rises from the level, the lid of cloud lifting from its crest. The wolves move in a line, six silhouettes in a shroud of fog.

A strange thought occurs to me—that they have been the agents of my ascent, that they too serve your desires and have ushered me here unwittingly. They forced me to cut short my course across the tableland and climb the convex slab. They drove me up the fortress when I would have descended at the canyon's head. They chased me across the saddle into the amphitheater. And now, a still stranger thought—that all my travail is a result of resisting. Of not being attuned to your sacred purpose. Rivulets gurgle to life, ribbons of silver bells threading beneath me.

Animus? The trembling is gone.

The gap of blue sky is growing. A white chute leads up to it, scoring the slope. I rouse myself to a trot, then kick into a lope, breaking up the rigor in my limbs. I was born limber, given life for the daring leap. The pain in my chest returns, but I pay it no mind. Just ahead lies the threshold of a new world. Is it an illusion, can I really be so near?

The incline rises steeply before me. A pika squeaks, juts its nose and dives beneath the rocks. I leap into the chute and bound up it, thrusts barely dinting the snow. Down the trough come cool drafts of mist and sky. The world beyond—I can smell it. I can hear it, clear as crystal, sharp as ice. There's a shelf of snow at the chute's top. I hurl myself onto it, cross a thick carpet, and stop with the wind in my face.

An enormous river of ice and cloud appears, beginning where the dark mountains end, tilting and rising into the sky. Its highest reaches are lost among icy ridges and distant fog, its lower invaded by waves of rolling vapor. Not made and complete, but a world being born, changing as I watch. I feel suddenly weak, stunned by the prospect before me and what I must dare. So high, so distant, so utterly unknown. To follow this path—that's the reason I'm here.

I ratchet my hocks and rear from the drift, plunging headlong for the tides of mist. A steep slope meets my hooves and the haze swallows me, cool and gray.

———•———

The stars glimmered over Seattle, alive with secret designs. On a bluff above the city, Harborview Hospital was settling into the night, only a few windows lit in its sheath of brick. Ambulances were parked on either side of the emergency room door.

In the reception area, Lindy stood with Erik Mortensen. "I don't know," she gave him a helpless look. Her hair was lopsided and her shift wrinkled. "All she said was that he was here and I could pick him up. And to bring some clothes."

Erik nodded, glancing around. There were people seated, but the quiet was oppressive, as if some invisible presence brooded over them, counting their chances.

"I can't thank you enough," Lindy said.

Erik gave her a sly look and was about to speak when the double doors to the emergency room swung open and a female med student stepped forward. "Altman?"

Lindy approached.

The med student smiled, her dark hair plaited flawlessly. "I think he's ready to go home."

"What's happened?"

"I'm sorry. He was brought in four hours ago. The police picked him up on Sunset Hill. He was wandering around naked on the bluffs, howling."

Lindy stared at her.

"And singing. He woke some of your neighbors. Has he had surgery recently?"

Lindy shook her head.

"He has a fresh scar on his chest—" She saw Lindy shiver and her voice trailed off. "He's communicating now." She cocked her head, recognizing her understatement. "Still a little high, but lucid." She regarded Lindy. "He was on LSD."

Lindy looked away.

195

"I'll bring him out," the med student said, and returned through the double doors.

"At least he's not hurt," Erik said.

Lindy sighed brokenly. "On the bluffs?"

"Must be crazy living with him." Erik gave her a sympathetic look.

"The storms break when you're least expecting."

Erik put his arm around her shoulder. "What's the scar about?"

Lindy shook her head.

"Come on," he wheedled.

She pulled away.

The double doors parted and Ransom stepped forward, barefoot and naked beneath a hospital gown. The med student was tying it behind him. He wasn't frenzied or raving, and he didn't appear to be hallucinating. His gaze was glassy and distant, his expression intense. As he drew closer, Lindy realized his arms and legs were netted with red lines.

"What have you done to him?" she demanded.

"The bushes were full of thorns," the med student explained. "He'll have a bruise around his ankle. We had to restrain him." She gave Ransom a chiding look.

Erik was astonished.

"He wasn't violent," the med student said, "just gregarious. Most of us were entertained. He's fine physically."

Lindy was little comforted. She could see Ransom's hands were trembling. His dilated eyes regarded her absently. She steeled herself and stepped toward him, reaching out to touch his cheek. He was sweating profusely and his skin was rosy. She could feel the heat.

"Ransom?"

He smiled. "Truly, I am. He sensed my willingness. Felt my longing." He spoke humbly, as if overwhelmed by another's love.

Lindy searched him. He barely saw her.

"He's taking me back." Ransom turned to Erik. "Strange, that he would care." His eyes found Lindy's again. "But—" He noticed the med student standing beside him. "He loves this little dollop." He put his hand over his heart with deep emotion. "I'm a part of him." He scanned the reception area. "We all are."

A seated woman regarded him over her raised coffee cup, haggard, her eyes sagging into their dark bags. An elderly Asian man pursed his lips and nudged the woman sleeping beside him.

"I'm sorry," Lindy stammered at the med student.

Erik was mightily amused.

"His name is Animus," Ransom proclaimed to the reception area. "And we're his outpourings."

Lindy was mortified. She held her face before his, then sheered away, eyes wide, her expression slack, putting her hand to her mouth to swallow her dread. Ransom was about to make a circuit of the room, but the med student grabbed his arm and held him. She'd been watching Lindy. "Animus is the god of molten hearts," the med student explained.

Ransom gave her a soulful look.

"Maybe we'll keep him till tomorrow," the med student said, seeing Lindy's distress.

"No," Lindy picked up the paper sack. "Where can he change?"

The med student motioned toward a restroom and pulled a form from her pocket. "He'll need to initial this."

Lindy took the pen. "Ransom."

Ransom signed and she handed him the sack of clothing. "Thanks," she gave the med student a cursory nod. "Put your clothes on," she said angrily and urged Ransom toward the restroom.

He did as she requested, closing the door behind him. The med student took the signed discharge and turned on her heel. Lindy watched her return into the bowels of the hospital.

"Flipped out," Erik muttered with finality.

"Stop it," she said.

The restroom door sprang open and before they realized what was happening, Ransom was striding through the reception area naked. Three seated men watched him halt before them, while a woman and the young girl with her rose and backed away.

"You have hearts!" He spread his arms. "Do you feel the wilderness of love inside you?" His eyes flashed and he sprang among the seats, fingers digging at the pink welt that scored his chest. "Throw yourselves open. Let it come gushing out!" The haggard woman rose, wide-eyed. The Asian couple and two college kids were herded by his gestures into a corner. Lindy rushed to intercept him, Erik right behind her. But Ransom was circling the other way.

"Surrender! The great secret! We're riding the sacred pulse. Our brains aren't smart enough, our senses aren't sharp enough. We can't see, we don't know." He grabbed the haggard woman by her shoulders. "Break open that chamber. The power of a god is hidden within you."

Lindy came up behind him and circled his waist with her arms, but he didn't stop.

"The world's a dream, poured out ages ago, and you're locked inside it—"

"Ransom!" Lindy hissed.

He heard her and turned, frowning. "It's fear. Leaping to escape. It's being caught." He recognized her, but he was speaking to the eons. "Letting go of everything. Life itself—"

"Your clothes," she said angrily.

Her words seemed to penetrate. He nodded, and when she urged him across the reception area, he made no effort to resist. Like a child heeding his mother's orders, he moved mechanically, his mind elsewhere, letting her escort him into the restroom.

Fifteen minutes later, the sky was graying. They were in the car, leaving the freeway, turning left onto 45th Street. Lindy checked the rearview mirror, insuring Erik was still behind her. The road was deserted. Night had passed, but the new day had not yet begun. Ransom was silent, staring through the passenger window.

"Are you alright?"

He nodded without turning. "It's over."

"What is?"

"The fear." His frenzy had subsided, and insights were rising from the ashes. "I feared my devotion to *Wild Animus* was a mistake. It's not." He remained facing the passenger window, speaking to his reflection. "Surrender to a lover is death's sister. The ultimate surrender, of life itself, is born from a deeper longing, in sorrow and despair." His voice was soft and low. "I've been seeking the foundation of love, and tonight I found him. Source of the molten heart. The great god Animus. The wolves are his instruments—a ministry of love, not death." He spoke this last with delicacy, as if the words would have special meaning for her.

"You saw God?"

"I felt him. He entered me. He embraced the part of me that's his." Ransom touched his left pectoral.

Overhead, a pair of power wires for city buses glinted in the street lights. For Ransom it was like a track of destiny revealed. A newspaper truck passed, then a bread truck. Sustenance for mankind. Thoughts and food for the coming day. Everything was an encouragement for him now, a love note from Animus. The evening had vaulted him into eternity.

"What about us?" Lindy wondered.

"His pulse beats in everyone," Ransom said. "What if I could open the floodgates to his power for all the world? Make the molten heart flow from every creature through every other and back to him? Turn the stony earth into an ocean of scarlet currents, weaving and seething and feeling each other and never slowing, never cooling, never freezing, never returning to that dark state, never knowing that terrible isolation again."

"Look at me," Lindy implored him.

He turned. "You've led me to this. The lesson of our surrender has made this possible. There's a wisdom inside you that's been guiding me, understanding that our struggle had a higher purpose without knowing what it was."

Lindy's dread mounted, wondering if the insanity of this evening was temporary. Ransom seemed to be reshaping their lives around it.

"Our love *has* been a struggle," he said. "That's the meaning of the chase. The wolves drive the ram through the rock world, ushering him, preparing him for the surrender Animus requires. And now—" His voice grew deeper, gentler. "The ram has reached the dome. He's poised to attain something unthinkable, undreamt of—a meeting with the source of the molten heart itself: the wild god Animus. And the pack will be with him. Just the two of us, Lindy. Together."

She regarded him fearfully, unable to ask what that meant.

"This life we've been leading—" Ransom shook his head. "People we know, material things. Jobs, school, a place called home—it's all in the past."

"Everyone needs a home."

"No home," Ransom said. "And no children. We will live the sacrament of Animus, we will be the ram and the pack. That's what is meant by the death of the Hangbelly. The mother is destroyed and the pack goes on without her."

They had entered a residential area. Lindy's gaze fixed on the road, seeing the pools of darkness cast by the trees, avoiding the houses, afraid to view the world Ransom wanted her to leave.

"The dome is a glorious place," Ransom said with emotion.

A car came toward them with its high beams on. Lindy gripped the wheel as the vehicle rumbled closer, something ominous bearing down. "I'm losing everything," she murmured.

Ransom didn't hear. He had rolled down the window to feel the breeze.

They descended toward Ballard, took Market Street west and headed north along the Sunset Hill bluff. Lindy turned down 71st and their house came into view.

"They're all sleeping," Ransom marveled at the quiet. "And here in their midst—" He indicated himself. "If they only knew."

"They have an idea," Lindy said, half to herself. "Those who heard you howling."

"That was the wolves." He scowled at the darkened dwellings. "Scared them, didn't they."

She thought he was serious, then she saw his wry look and laughed.

"They'll think I'm crazy," he nodded. "And that's only a small part of the price." He eyed her with regret, gazing again at the quiet houses. "What ransom must be paid," he wondered, "to make the blood frozen in people's hearts come crashing through their veins again?"

She pulled into the drive. Erik parked at the curb and went to meet her as she stepped from the car.

"How's he doing?"

"Coming back," she replied.

Ransom stood watching them.

Erik gave her a dubious look. "I should stick around."

"No, it's alright," Lindy said. "I'm very grateful to you."

Erik frowned, but she joined Ransom and they started down the drive. Erik headed back to his car.

As they approached the house, Ransom turned his head at the harbor sounds. A motor's groan. A gull's cry. A secret world spoke to him through the mundane one, and there was nothing he could ignore. Everything sought to glow and flow, everything was striving to regain that molten state, and he felt them all as if they were his own heart and his own striving. He felt Lindy too, how vulnerable she was.

At the top of the stair, he faced her. "I know how hard this is."

She embraced him, choking back her anguish.

"We can't hesitate," Ransom said. He saw the Wise nod. The Lead watched. The Scout suspected their fate was cast.

"I'm feeling hopeless," Lindy said.

"There's no turning back." Ransom spoke to the Dangler, caressing Lindy's temple, trying to smooth the creases raying from her eyes. It was a decision she had to make. "The cut is irreversible." He gazed over her shoulder at the bluff, remembering the moment his heart touched Animus and the god quaked inside him. "I'll never recover." His life had a purpose now—to enact the liturgy of the ram. Nothing else mattered.

She rocked her brow against his chest.

"Human love is so fragile," he said sadly, "so easily lost or destroyed. Unlike its source." He drew a breath, recalling his fleeting optimisms. In the midst of the greatest confidence he'd ever known, he could feel it waver. "I need you," he said. "I can't do this without you."

Lindy stifled a sob. She closed her eyes and held him tightly.

The fog had drifted back, covering the Sound with thin gauze. In the distance, a red light flared like an ember, died out and flared again. It was hard to tell whether it was stationary or moving—a beacon for lost ships headed home, or a running light on board some craft, signaling its passage from the harbor out onto the boundless sea.

By eight-thirty that morning, the air was sharp and clear. The bluff was vibrant, sparrows darting through the undergrowth, chipping excitedly, making the morning glories quiver. A hummingbird rose to watch a flicker call from a conifer, while towhees shot over the blackberry tangles to the cliff's edge.

In the house, Lindy lay sleeping. Ransom, upon their arrival, had descended to his white room and spent most of the dark hours writing feverishly. The result exceeded his expectations. Morning found him upstairs, pacing the living room with the manuscript in one hand and the telephone in the other, features animated, his lips moving silently. He set the phone and his papers down, and removed his clothing. Then he stepped into the bedroom and slid beneath the covers.

Lindy felt his nakedness and warmth, and reached for him. He stroked her brow and kissed her tenderly. She mumbled an unconscious plea, then love welled in her and she nuzzled his chest. He was charged with energy, and as he coaxed her thighs apart and entered her, her faculties stirred.

"I love you," he whispered.

Lindy's lids parted. She peered at him, shivered and drew away, recalling the events of the night past.

He respected her distance, understanding while his eyes beamed, opening his joy to her, letting her see all the gratitude in his heart. He'd been purposeless when he met her. The journey had been a trial for them both. She'd stuck with him through everything.

Lindy hesitated, then touched his waist, marveling at the innocence in his eyes. Unhinged, raving—it didn't matter. Nothing soiled that purity. His fantasies burned as brightly as the bars of the little silver cage on her sternum, and her heart was still inside it.

"Remember how we felt," Ransom whispered, "leaving Berkeley?"

She nodded. "Reckless." She tried to smile.

He saw the helplessness in her eyes and it pierced him. When she thought him distant, she was so terribly alone. "It was like flying off the edge of the world together," he said.

She regarded him tenderly. The memory was sweet. He kissed her neck, and she sighed, then stiffened, rolling onto her hip to glance at the bedstand. "I'm late for work."

"No you're not." Ransom smiled. "I just called—"

She saw the gleam in his eyes.

"—and resigned for you."

Lindy stared at him.

"We're moving to Anchorage." Ransom kissed her brow.

Lindy went limp, settling back on the mattress with a disbelieving face. He kissed her lips, then he kissed her neck and made her feel his excitement. Longing rose within her, his desire firing her as it always had. It couldn't be love, she thought. Her need was so merciless, so heedless of higher feelings. More and more, she resembled the wolves of *Wild Animus*. Or perhaps she'd always been this way, and was only now looking into the mirror Ransom held before her.

He sighed and slid deep. The sensations tore a sob from his chest. And then he was hunched and writhing, imagining himself in flames, assuming his real shape.

Lindy clung to that wildness, terrified by the power it had over her, but tasting the bliss to come. They were abandoned children, abandoning the world.

Ransom shuddered and the ram sprang forward, dreaming of the summit.

Outside, a train rumbled along the base of the cliff, headed north.

Animus

Ten

On my right, the glacier climbs through veils of mist, silvered by the moon. On my left, a giant cloud descends like a breaking wave, roiling furiously around me, turning everything gray. Ice spicules whisper against my horns. The cool crystals are coaxing me. Animus? I put the wind at my rear, stepping over the crusted surface.

The mist thickens as I move. A felt of frost mats my withers. Two cold disks expand from the roots of my horns. My toe-slots are clogged, crunches damped to thuds, legs tingling to the knees, like stiff clubs. I'm blind now. The glacier is nothing but the four points my hooves shift over, the guidance of the wind my only protection against a fall.

Are you with me? I take a deep breath and the mist prickles through my muzzle and down my throat. I feel it in my chest, freezing and burning—embers of Animus surrounding my heart. Asking. Asking. I'm afraid. I'm beleaguered, too numbed to pilot my own course. The chill works along my sides, traveling down my spine. Have faith. Trust and submit.

My skin feels fuzzy. The vapors are dissolving it. The wind brushes the tissues beneath, and my flesh lifts like a powdery wrapper. My hooves tell me little now—they're bulbs of mist, and then gone, sublimed into ether. I feel my knees working, then nothing at all, as if I'm floating, left to tread on spirit legs somewhere above the surface of the snows.

A gust peels muscle from my shoulders in thick scarves. My withers lift like a cape, lightening my frame. My flanks unfurl, hinged to my front like the wings of a butterfly, crumpled and damp, then spreading. Relief. A freedom I've never felt. What is happening? I know it's you, but this numbing cold— Your wind shudders through me, jarring my insides. I'm breathless. My center is rocking, deep tissues sliding on the bone, vitals churning. Enormous gasps shake me, a gulping and blowing that strains my unpleated self to its limits. My chest spasms and bursts, motes retching out from me in thick clouds—a shower of sparks, like Animus himself—giving up my core to something larger and unknown.

Weightless, free from drag, the wind lifts me from my clinging place: a spirit body with spirit senses, borne on soars and sways, riding the streaming fibers of the ether, alive to things hidden in the endless oceans of air. I'm wafting upward, twisted by interlocking gusts, feeling space as I rise. Hit by a blast, I careen suddenly, swooping and yawing, kiting crazily, the cosmos in my pores. Your wildness, your breath! Animus—this is you. These heaves, these heights, this imponderable vastness passing through me. Your oceans, your air! My stipples are quivering, the very jewels of life— I feel your purpose, I understand.

I'm not made of flesh, come not from mud or rock. But from this wild element, furious and free, born of passion and energy, big with air, feeling as I breathe. Let loose in a world beyond imagining, I'm expanding, and every moment there's more void between my sensitive specks. Life billows giantly, more and more tenuous, reaching out in all directions. Carry me, Animus. My faith is in these motes, and my courage. I am blooming, alive to the promise of this impalpable state, my instincts reaching back to a primordial past. A time of total outpouring, before vision had the eye's lens, before the boundaries of the body made living things distinct, before souls had flesh. When all was expanding, expanding, boundlessly confident.

Thick cords of fog snarled the Alaskan coastal peaks. To the west, Anchorage camped beneath a crowd of butted rooftops. Ransom and Lindy had moved there eight months before and spent a cold winter in a poorly heated apartment. Lindy worked two waitress jobs, while Ransom labored away at his manuscript and chants. In January, with a blizzard raging outside, he announced his intention to climb Mt. Wrangell, and before long, he was deep in preparations. He found a climber named Harvey Parrish, experienced with Alaskan peaks, to lead the expedition in exchange for a sizable guiding fee. All equipment and provision costs, along with the travel expenses of the climbers necessary to fill out the team, would be paid for out of Lindy's earnings. By the second week of May, details were being finalized. Ransom and Lindy were inside Harvey's garage near the edge of town.

"Biking's great exercise," Harvey nodded, eyes dancing. His light temperament was unusual for the northland. Unlike most of the Anchorage climbing community, he was clean-shaven.

"I'm doing four hours a day," Ransom said.

"Thunder thighs," Harvey smiled and clapped his hands. He was ten years older, shorter than Ransom and almost as wiry. "You'll wish you'd done more when you put your pack on." He meant to prepare Ransom for the shock. "Even with two carries and caches all the way, we'll still be hauling over a hundred pounds each." He glanced at the equipment and supplies arrayed in the cramped space. On the floor: tents, stoves, sleeping bags, and bundles of green bamboo garden stakes with red flags. On the plank wall behind: shovels, snowshoes, ice axes and saws hanging from nails in the studs. Lindy stood quietly, working a Jumar ascender with her hand, pale from the long winter.

"That's a lot," Ransom said, unintimidated.

Harvey smiled to himself. "On this kind of climb, you have to think about every ounce." He was leading up to something.

Ransom gave a perfunctory nod.

"You sure about the costume?" Harvey looked dubious. "Twelve pounds is a lot. That headdress will take up half your pack."

"I need it with me," Ransom said curtly.

Lindy watched his enthusiasm grow guarded. There were parts of his mission he hadn't disclosed.

"There won't be any room left for the group stuff." Harvey spoke matter-of-factly.

Lindy saw beneath the climber's easy manner, sensing he was concerned about more than the weight. "Maybe you could leave the headdress?" she offered. "Take the cuffs and leggings."

Ransom shook his head. "There are things I want to do at the crater."

Harvey looked stumped. "We'll have to divide all this," he motioned at the gear, "among the rest of us." There was a hint of warning, but Ransom ignored it. Harvey shrugged. "I lugged my niece's stuffed rabbit to the top of McKinley." He laughed at himself. "Alaska's full of odd people, isn't it? Bull's with us," Harvey went on, "and so is Gloster. Paying their expenses was great," he nodded. "But they still have to make the time. Yank's working on it. Be great to have a doctor. That's his nickname," he smiled at Lindy. "Obstetrician." He turned back to Ransom with a conciliating look. "Talked to Erik Mortensen by phone. Doesn't have expedition experience, but the climbing you two did in Seattle is great. Should be okay." He shook his head. "Not so sure about Skimmer. He's just a kid."

"He's very athletic," Ransom offered.

"He thinks Ransom walks on water," Lindy said.

"Calls me every day," Ransom admitted.

Harvey laughed. "He wants to drive to town to convince me."

"It means a lot to him," Ransom said, leaving the decision in Harvey's hands. "Any progress on the route?"

"Lots." Harvey turned to a pile of aerial photos and topo maps on a small table. "I think your idea makes sense." He pointed at one of the topos. "The Cheshnina Glacier doesn't look bad. The last group to go up Wrangell was in 1950, and that's how they did it. Start at that strip on the river. If we get some decent weather, we should be back in ten to twelve days."

"This area's interesting." Ransom touched a spot high on the dome. "Fumaroles. Like to get a look at those."

"Dangerous." Harvey made a wary face.

"I've heard that." Ransom's eyes sparkled with daring.

"Hot spots weaken the ice. You can go right through. We'll steer clear of any place steam's coming up."

"Except the North Crater." Ransom gave him a testing look.

Harvey raised his brows. "The climbers coming along with us want to reach the summit, not the North Crater."

"That *is* the summit."

"Not technically."

Ransom frowned. "There's no heat at the technical summit. It's dead. Just a jag of rock."

"It's still the top."

"Not for long. When Wrangell erupts, the crater will be higher."

Harvey laughed, conceding the point.

"That's why I'm doing this." Ransom's earnest look recalled their earlier discussions.

Harvey sighed. "Can't climb the mountain alone."

"I want to reach the North Crater," Ransom said firmly. "That's where we're going."

"We'll try to do both," Harvey said. "There's only a mile between them. If we get up on the summit snowfield in decent weather, it shouldn't be a problem."

"But we'll go to the crater first."

Harvey gave him a wry smile and saluted. "Maybe we'll run into some scientists," he raised his brows. "I hear Burt Conklin will be up there."

Ransom nodded. "You talked to Doug."

"Yesterday," Harvey replied. "He'll be great."

Doug Hurley would ferry the climbers one-by-one from Tolsona Lake to the Cheshnina River. It would take the better part of a day.

"He's flying us for free," Ransom muttered. Doug knew how stretched they were.

Harvey gazed at him. "Time for me to buy the food," he said gently.

Ransom glanced at Lindy.

She retrieved the checkbook from her purse. Ransom made the check out and passed it to Harvey.

"Good for now," Harvey said. "Stay on that bike."

Ransom thanked him, and he and Lindy stepped out of the garage.

"It's happening," Ransom said to her, full of energy. "I'm really going." He knew he'd be tested, but his fears were delicious. "The dome. Where the ram's spirit is set free."

"Maybe you should meet these climbers."

"Why?"

"They might not be as understanding as Harvey. They aren't getting paid like he is."

He waved the concern away, eyeing her with gratitude. "None of this would be possible without you."

She kissed him, then saw his gaze wander. His brow furrowed, he mumbled something and a smile played over his lips.

"Ransom—" Lindy waited for him to respond. His increasing distraction troubled her deeply. "Ransom!"

He saw the agitation in her face. "What's wrong?"

"People die on expeditions like this."

He laughed. The challenge was still before him, but he had already leapt over it. In his heart, he was approaching the rim of the North Crater.

"Are you sure about Erik?" Lindy wondered. "I don't trust him. The last time we saw him—"

"He's really charged up," Ransom told her. "If there's a problem, I can handle him." He shook his head. "You're always looking out for me." He eyed her fondly.

Lindy sighed as if inadequate to the task. "You've got to be alert. It's bad enough here in Anchorage."

He put his arm around her.

"You're disappearing into *Wild Animus*," Lindy's eyes searched him. "I'm going to fall asleep with Ransom one night, and wake up beside—"

"Who's Ransom?" he said gruffly.

They burst out laughing, halting and quaking against each other.

"That's better," he smiled.

"The money's a problem." Lindy's expression was pained.

Ransom's head bowed, his eyes hooded with shame. "I'm sorry."

"We're down to nothing," she said. "Every nickel we saved is gone. I can't write another check until payday."

Ransom sighed. "We were going to sell the stereo—"

"I did that last week."

"Maybe Katherine would pitch in the way Hank has."

Lindy glanced at her watch. "Want to ask her?"

"No," Ransom shook his head. "I know how hard this is."

"I'm late." Her second shift was starting. "Wolves are at the door."

He laughed. She kissed him and hurried off.

———•———

I've changed. My kiting motes glimmer. A glow permeates the ether, suffusing everything with a buttery warmth. I feel my specks reeling, caught by an undertow. Animus is taking my lightness away. I keel, rotating down. The brightness remains aloft, the gold drawing together, its border rounding, more and more dense. I'm diving through tiers of sky. Below, the mist swirls over smooth snow. Beneath my muzzle, two dark shapes keep pace with me—the Lead and the Wise, surfacing through the fog and disappearing back into it, trading bounds, one then the other. The dark shapes are my hooves.

I am a physical being, small, finite, with a test before me. But with Animus in my heart and my ministrants close, I feel the power in this body, and embrace the return. The mist is dissolving around me, clearing the air. The snow is firm. I hear my cadenced breath, my knees come up into sight and down. A jewel sparkles in the outside corner of each eye. Between the crusted horn tips, my muzzle is felted with frost. My front is padded with it, my fores are sleeved with it. I turn my head and the stiff thatch breaks.

A blowhole opens and a bright beam strikes my face, warming my cheeks. I shiver, lifting my head, bearing up my golden coils. Animus. I feel your abundance, your energy, your joy. More breaks—the fog is shredding, pastels pool the snows. My fores land among pinks and mauves and pale blues. Suddenly, the snows are dazzling. Over my shoulder, the sun seethes through a gap of blue sky. Ahead, a gigantic snowy mass appears, stark white through the parting clouds. Your home.

I kick into a lope, eyes trained on a world more tangible, more mystical than any I could have imagined. A jagged reef, gleaming blocks—openings give glimpses. High up, I can see where its curving white edge meets the sky. Broad portholes now: a shattered cliff, shelves tumbling. Then I burst free of the fog, and the enormous cupola of snow is revealed, full in the sun, the wildness of its broken ice compassed by a perfect arc.

Animus! I feel your welcome! My deepest yearnings— The promise of fulfillment— Did I imagine this was my destiny? What mad pride. I'm little, I'm nothing— That's why I'm crying inside—because I'm so blessed.

I'm warming, fur dripping, my movements smoother. At my side, pinpoints of light glitter—emerald, lapis, gold and vermilion—shifting as I lope. Behind me, a sea of cloud spreads to the horizon, lapping over the lowlands like a merciful amnesia. My track, a thin line of dots, is flanked by another that veers to the side and is lost behind a rise. The pack.

Ahead, a blue slot crosses the ice, bridged in spots by sags of snow. Shorten the stride, quicken my limbs. My fores should strike there, just shy of the edge. I'm into the air, above startling depths, angling chambers, grottoes draped with fresh velvet. Then I land, fores in, hinds under, and back into stride.

Where are you? I snort a banner of steam, my strength returning. Will I see you on this dazzling slope, under this blaring blue sky? My nostrils flare, chest expanding, imagining you secreted in your temple, my gaze drawn to the summit. Another rent. Fores to the edge, firing, flying, landing and bounding forward. The summit! My instinct for height stems from this! My gaze, my gait, the trend of my thoughts—higher, always higher. Why? The entrance to your temple is at the edge of the sky! I'm on my way to you. I've been on my way all this while. Pain in my chest. I glance down. The wound's ruby spurs are jagged and glistening. It's more than a badge of safe passage—my heart has been bared. I've come to be joined with you, to give your great heart this frail heart of mine, throbbing with longing, skipping with fear and hope.

Ahead, another crevasse. I leap it and land in a pool of light, the reflected sun bathing my belly. My front is steaming, wolf musk mingled with the sweet odor of wool. All I have to offer is this fervent flesh, my love and my leaping. If I give you this, will it be enough? My heart is racing as though you'd said yes.

The slope is steeper, etched with sastrugi that ripple toward me like lines of force. At the top of a rise, the far wall of a large

218

crevasse emerges from the glacier, ten lengths higher than the near, impossible to vault. Are you testing me? I angle to the left, hearing the hiss of something plowing through the drifts.

The pack is scoring the swells. The Lead lunges toward me, Wise following close behind, then the Ruff and the Younger, whining excitedly, the Scout and the Dangler at the rear. I keep my course, fighting fear, remembering they're my ministrants. The Lead's ragged breathing reaches me. He groans, and at his signal the pack splits, the Ruff and Scout veering to the right for the pinch. I'm yours, dear god. Aren't I?

I wheel and spring, putting the wolves at my rear, striking across the snow in a mad gallop, headed straight for the offset crevasse. Are you with me? Are you watching? The high wall looms. I hear the crush of paws and fast drafts, and glance back, seeing the sulphur eyes burning, the Lead's snout inhaling me greedily. I feel you watching, expectant. You're wondering if I know what to do.

I fold my fores, my shoulder hits and I roll. My wound touches the snow, crystals rasping the seal, cold shivering my core. My heart is yours! A thrumming—the glacier comes alive! Animus, directly beneath me, joyous, welcoming. A bark—the Dangler, alarmed. They've stopped. Animus rumbles, dismissive, testing, wanting to see. I spring with all my strength, hurling myself toward the chasm and the sheer wall.

The glacier heaves! Nothing frightens me now. Your power— show me. Louder! The ice hisses with your voice, a billion vibrating beads. I see the high wall through quivering lashes. Great strokes and poundings! My fores reach wildly, the chasm is here—

The wall emits a deafening crack. Fractures divide the blue surface with wild shrieks, icicles falling. The quaking mounts, panels shift like gilded doors. Then Animus roars and the ark explodes. Chips fly, fragments tumble and churn, panes of ice cartwheeling out, booming into the depths, others catching, wedged with fierce grindings. Large spans hiss to a halt, hanging precariously while the dome continues to shake.

A bridge. A way across! Fores to the edge, hinds digging. Will it hold? My heart believes.

I spring through the showering sparks onto the piled islet, up a linkage of edges—a white lintel, a sharp keel, a blue slab tipped up. The bridge jolts with quaking as I bunch and thrust. Below, from the bottomless moat, you're roaring up, your deep voice rising to surround me. The blue ice is spangled with bubbles, something jubilant breathing within, while the huge heart of Animus speaks to the little heart of the ram: "So fragile, so small, so dear. My love brought you here. Without it, you would never have dared."

Dear god, do you yearn too? Can that be? Have you been waiting all this while? All those lives you've flung molten to the world—now cold and lost. And you here, wishing one might find its way back? The god of surrender longs to surrender, too. But not here, not now. There's a place and a time that's set.

I reach the bridge's end and vault onto solid snow. The roar damps, wavering as I turn. I hear your urging: "The dome is for my ram to ascend." Your temple is just frozen water. Little you care whether it's altered, or how. It isn't the ice that makes this mountain sacred.

Animus sighs and fades. The bridge groans and collapses with a horrendous crash. My limbs are trembling, head quivering on my neck—a vestige of Animus himself. He inhabited this body. The molten heart's source flowed through my veins.

The Lead is watching me from across the gap. The Wise stands at the brink of the chasm, peering down. The Lead moans, doubtful, as the others rise from the snow. The Dangler whines and the Ruff quiets her while the Younger pedals nervously, unsettled by the Lead's agitation. The Wise turns to her mate, nuzzles him, glances at me, then bounds through the drifts, headed toward the tail of the crevasse. The Lead follows, then the others.

I face the dome's heights, understanding. The glacier steepens ahead, running into a serac field at the base of an icefall. Your power is mine to invoke. I can make miracles with this wound in my chest. The seal is broken, the blood is fresh. You flow through your temple, but you rise from its center. There's a wound on the summit, just like this. A sanctum with a ragged rim. The top of a well leading down. There you await me.

I spring forward, imagining that moment.

———•———

It was late afternoon and the sky was blue over Mt. Wrangell. From 11,000 feet on the Cheshnina Glacier, all of the great dome was visible except for its summit, which was obscured by a thin veil. The climbing team was traversing the edge of a serac field, winding among scattered blocks. All had red overboots, glacier goggles, white zinc on their noses and skirts hanging from their caps like French legionnaires. They moved painfully slowly, burdened by large packs.

Harvey Parrish stopped at the edge of a saddle between blocks and forced down a long aluminum rod to test the snow. Satisfied, he drew it out and marked the spot with wands. He glanced at Ted Gloster, a tall black man behind him on the first rope, and started forward. Gloster followed, then Skimmer, then a thin man with a beard, Dan Zweibach, the doctor called "Yank." Ransom was at the head of the second rope. A cassette recorder hung around his neck, and he was so immersed in mumbling his impressions into it, he failed to notice the march was resuming.

"Ransom." Bull Tompkins, a young man with a big middle and a nose to match, called to him from the end of the second rope. Erik stood watching impatiently between.

"Wait," Ransom shouted, waving his arm at the first team. "Hold up."

Harvey turned, hunched with discouragement. Gloster stared at Ransom. Yank scowled. Since they'd been on the glacier, Ransom had caused dozens of detours and delays.

"What?" Harvey yelled.

"That way," Ransom shouted, pointing at an icefall on the far side of the serac field. Harvey stared at him as if he didn't understand. Yank and Gloster regarded him with disbelief. Skimmer looked confused. "Huddle," Ransom shouted, starting forward.

Collapsing the rope teams was something Harvey disliked, but eight days of this had eroded his discipline. Ransom moved his team forward until he was a few yards from Harvey.

"Let's take the icefall." Ransom gazed up at the giant broken stairway, blocks inlaid like a blue mosaic. Harvey absorbed the request.

"That's crazy," Gloster responded, wiping his forehead with his bare arm. Even stripped to tee shirts, they were lathered with sweat.

Ransom ignored him.

"We don't have time," Harvey shook his head.

"Too dangerous," Gloster objected.

"We'll be fine," Ransom assured them. "It's a straight shot to the North Crater," he reminded Harvey.

Yank came up beside Gloster. "Bite your tongue," he muttered. "We're going to the summit." Erik made an indignant face, agreeing. A free ticket to Alaska had been hard to resist, but tolerating Ransom had been a high price to pay, and like the others, he was at his limit. Skimmer kicked the snow, upset on Ransom's behalf. They were turning against him. Bull looked to Harvey.

"It's not a matter of the crater or the summit," Harvey said. "We lost three days in the whiteout, and spent an afternoon playing around in that crevasse. We only have a couple days left before we have to start down."

"We'll make it," Ransom gazed knowingly at the icefall, "if we have the courage to take that route."

Harvey eyed Gloster wearily.

"We might as well head back now," Gloster growled.

"Let's get going," Yank said testily. "Harv's leading this climb."

"We're going up the icefall," Ransom gave him a cold stare. "If you want to do this some other way, come back on your own."

That left little room for discussion. Harvey raised his brows. Erik snickered. Skimmer bowed his head, ashamed at Ransom's heavy-handedness.

"Well—" Harvey glanced at the others. "We could give it a try." He turned and gazed over the serac field at the icefall. Then he started forward, drawing the rope out. Gloster was incredulous.

"I thought slavery was dead," Yank said.

Gloster laughed and followed Harvey's steps. Ransom pretended he didn't hear.

Ten minutes later, they were angling toward the center of the serac field, Harvey planting wands, Ransom mumbling into his recorder. A deep thud sounded and they turned to see a cloud of white powder billowing at their rear. Across what would have been their route, a swath of sagging snow had collapsed.

Bull's eyes twinkled at Ransom. "Good call."

A half hour after that, they were venturing over a snow bridge. Harvey probed and then crossed, and Gloster followed. But when Skimmer reached the gap, it gave way. He dropped without a sound.

"Harv!" Yank shouted as he fell to the snow, stabbing the spike of his axe for protection. Gloster felt the tug from behind, turned, realized what had happened and threw himself down, digging his axe in as well. A querulous sound echoed up from the crevasse.

Harvey spun around and worked his way toward the break, checking to make sure Gloster was secure.

Skimmer yelled, "Got me?"

"Sure," Harvey said, kneeling beside the hole. It was a couple of yards across. Harvey motioned and Bull hurried forward. "He's only a few feet over his head," Harvey said. "He's got his boot on a ledge."

Erik and Ransom watched from their rope positions. Ransom was stunned.

"There's a decent wall of ice," Harvey told the others. "If we can get his pack off, he can probably climb out."

Bull knelt opposite Harvey. When he peered down into the hole, his jaw dropped.

"Long way down," Harvey muttered. Then to Skimmer, "Stay calm."

Bull knotted a short length of rope around a carabiner.

"Can you get yourself upright?" Harvey asked Skimmer. "That's it. We're going to lift your pack out." Bull lowered the rope over the edge. Harvey got down on his belly and reached to help Skimmer clip the rope to his pack. "Okay now, ease it off."

Ransom's gaze was riveted, his expression intense. He watched them pull the pack out of the hole.

Harvey smiled with relief, but when he and Bull looked down, their faces fell. Skimmer was hanging over the bottomless abyss, unable to get his boot back on the shelf.

"Turn your leg," Harvey said. "Can you straighten it?" He glanced at Bull. "Lower your axe."

Bull reached his ice axe into the crevasse.

"Try and steady yourself," Harvey told Skimmer. A moment passed, then he scooted back out of the hole, shaking his head.

"What's wrong?" Yank asked.

Ransom saw Harvey's grave expression. Skimmer's voice sounded, muffled and distant.

"He's tangled in his Jumars," Harvey said. "And he's getting cold."

"What now?"

"Try to lift him out," Harvey muttered. Bull drew a pulley from his pack.

Erik flared his eyes at Ransom. That could take time.

Skimmer's voice wavered like someone talking in his sleep. Suddenly he cried out. It was more than Ransom could stand. "Come on," he said to Erik, and started forward.

Erik frowned and followed, unsure what Ransom intended. Fifty feet from the hole, Ransom turned and said, "Protect me." When Erik gave him a confused look, he pointed at Erik's ice axe. "Get down!" Erik obeyed, laying on the snow, in belay. Then before anyone realized what was happening, Ransom bounded toward the gap and threw himself over the edge, down into the hole. Fortunately, the rope stopped him before he fell much below Skimmer.

It was havoc above, Harvey frantic, crying, "Ransom!" and Bull appalled, muttering, "What the fuck—" Down in the crevasse, Skimmer was gasping with relief.

"You're going to be fine," Ransom said, kicking his crampons into the wall. He pulled his willow knife from his parka pocket. One of Skimmer's legs dangled free, the other was doubled and bound to his thigh.

"Hope so," Skimmer muttered, watching him cut the Jumar cords.

Ransom shivered. As he worked, Skimmer held his forearm in a trembling grasp, terrified, trying to be brave. The space was cold as a freezer. Beneath them yawned a giant abyss, crossed with drapes of white velvet. Thirty feet down, the tips of giant stalagmites glittered, rising from indigo cells far below.

The last cord gave way. Ransom straightened Skimmer's doubled leg, massaging it with both hands. "We're going to climb out of here." He glanced at the wall, grabbed Skimmer's boot and drove its toe into the ice. The crampons stuck. "Use your front points," he peered at Skimmer through his two raised fingers. "Like hooves." He clutched the rope and rose beside Skimmer, kicking the iron points in for a higher hold.

Skimmer did the same, hanging on the power in Ransom's eyes.

Another kick. They extended their legs, moving slowly up the turquoise wall together. Their heads emerged, then they were free to their chests. Harvey and Bull hugged them as one and dragged them out.

The two lay motionless and exhausted, like lovers heart to heart, Skimmer staring into the snow, breathing desperately, Ransom facing the sun, dazzled and thankful, smiling at something all the world was blind to but he.

They continued through the serac field the remainder of that day. It was slow going and by early evening, they were only halfway across. Harvey called a halt. He picked a camp site and probed it while still roped. After marking the site with wands, Ransom and Skimmer began shoveling, making the spot level and building a lee against the wind. Harvey and the other four started back through the seracs, returning for the cache of equipment and provisions they'd left a thousand feet below. The sun descended, turning the icefall into a golden stairway, and then it started to snow—not flakes, but tiny needles that glittered like clippings of white hair. Ransom and Skimmer were too cold to pause, but the magic surrounded them as they worked, needles whirling and catching fire in the last glow.

By the time the others returned, the light had been extinguished and the weather was threatening. As they made dinner, clouds swallowed the mountain. Now, an hour after, the camp was quiet. It was snowing in earnest and nothing was visible beyond the wanded area where the two tents were pitched. Packs and equipment were drifted over. The tents were already knee deep, and the flies had started to droop. All of the team had squeezed into the larger tent to eat. Dinner was finished, cups and spoons set aside, and they were sipping hot drinks in the light of a candle.

"Think we're close enough?" Gloster wondered.

Harvey regarded him through hanging socks and mitts. "Maybe. I'd rather be another thousand feet up."

"Depends on the weather," Yank said. "Man, what happened to your mouth?" He laughed at Gloster. Their faces were badly burnt.

Gloster pouted his swollen lips. "Shine, mistah?"

Yank and Harvey laughed. Skimmer and Bull wore blank looks, missing the joke. Ransom and Erik seemed not to hear, sunk in the blue shadow of the tent like wanderers from some other dimension. Between exhaustion and the altitude, they were all disoriented.

"Where did you get a name like Skimmer?" Yank said.

"We've got swallows around our place."

Yank waited. "Yeah?"

"When I was younger," Skimmer went on, "I'd run around with my arms out. That's what I was wishing in that crevasse. That I was a bird and could fly out of there."

"I fell through on St. Elias two years ago," Bull shivered. "Never forget it."

"When I was hanging there—" Skimmer's gaze narrowed. "Looking down— It was eerie. I couldn't see the bottom. But I could feel the air rising from down there. It was freezing. I thought the crevasse was breathing."

"Scary," Harvey said.

Skimmer seemed to see through him. "Beautiful, too."

"Like a cathedral," Ransom smiled.

Skimmer nodded. "I felt something." His eyes met Ransom's, sharing their new intimacy.

"You're a brave kid," Bull said.

"Kept your head," Yank agreed.

"Got out of there on your own steam," Harvey lauded him. "People turn to jelly in situations like that."

"It was my front points," Skimmer told Ransom. "They really worked."

"It was the spirit of the ram that saved you." Ransom spoke softly, only for him.

Skimmer regarded him seriously, wanting to understand.

Yank raised his brows and glanced around. Bull was blank.

Gloster gave Yank a mystified look and Erik rolled his eyes. When Yank looked in Harvey's direction, the climb leader turned his head down and fooled with his socks.

"What's the secret?" Yank asked with an amused face.

There was a long silence. Ransom seemed to ponder the question. Finally he turned to Yank with a solemn expression.

"There's a reason we're climbing this mountain." His gaze moved to Gloster. "It's time you knew." He included Bull and Harvey. "You're frustrated, upset with me. The delays, the crater—" He peered at Erik and settled on Skimmer. "There's a god in this mountain. I call him Animus, but his name doesn't matter."

Skimmer nodded reverently, seeing that power again in Ransom's eyes.

"He's given me the spirit of the ram." Ransom drew one of the ram cuffs from his pocket. "So that I could reach him." He held the cuff toward the candle flame. The white fur shone. "That's why I'm here."

The tension was palpable. There was a nervous silence during which no communication occurred, then Harvey nodded mechanically. Yank glanced at Gloster, Bull at Erik. A web of covert looks wove across the tent. Gloster's scorn was barely concealed. He wasn't going to say anything, but he considered Ransom's declaration ridiculous. Yank was more circumspect. Skimmer was transfixed by Ransom, oblivious.

"What are you thinking?" Ransom asked Yank in a low voice.

Yank took a breath and met his gaze. "I don't believe in spirits." He spoke with a surprising delicacy of feeling, unwilling to dissimulate, taking Ransom seriously.

"Creatures are born from the heart," Ransom told him, "as well as the belly."

Silence.

"What do the wolves have to do with this?" Skimmer wondered.

"They're the ram's ministrants," Ransom replied. "They're following me up the mountain."

Erik laughed and shook his head. "Come on."

Ransom regarded him with disappointment.

Erik's grin snagged. "Don't pull that holy man crap on me." He cocked his head with contempt. "A god in the mountain? A wolf pack following us? This isn't some day trip in the Cascades."

Gloster traded looks with Yank. There was a lot they hadn't been told.

"Who knows?" Harvey muttered. "There might be a god in this mountain. I don't think there is, but I can't prove there isn't." It was a feeble attempt to save Ransom from further humiliation. His gray eyes darted across the tent. Leave the poor guy alone, they said.

The appeal stunned Skimmer. Ransom was being dismissed as a nut case, and that pained him. There was something in what he was saying.

Ransom was quiet. A part of him was in their midst, wanting them to understand and hurt that they didn't.

"It's easy to feel spiritual things in a place like this," Bull said, trying to help Harvey calm the waters. "Like being high."

"Wouldn't surprise me," Erik returned to the attack. "He loves to climb stoned on acid." He eyed Ransom suspiciously. "The last sermon I heard him preach was at the hospital in Seattle. The cops caught him dancing outdoors naked, raving and ripped, like always." Erik eyed the cuff with disgust. "I'm amazed you brought all that garbage."

"All what garbage?" Gloster frowned.

"He's got a whole outfit. Head to toe."

Yank turned to Harvey. "*That's* what's in his pack?"

Harvey exhaled and bowed his head.

"It's important," Ransom tried to explain. "When we reach the crater."

Yank glanced at Gloster, then they both turned to Ransom. Yank's jaw hung open, his eyes deep with disbelief.

Ransom seemed about to speak. He wasn't surprised. They didn't understand. Would anyone? It didn't really matter at this point, did it? He put his cuff back in his pocket as if something weighing on him had been decided.

Skimmer was mortified, watching him retreat.

"Well," Ransom murmured, "I thought you would like to know."

The wind roared through the night. In his dream, Ransom imagined it had been unleashed not from the sky, but from the dome's depths. Raging from hidden caverns, it scoured the surface, seeking him out. Was it far, was it near, was it whispering close? The wind found the frail tent and engulfed it, shaking him as he slept, making the poles sing, stuttering the nylon, pulling at him. Was it time? He shook his head and turned away. But the raging mounted. Through his dream, he heard a pot clatter. Somebody thrashed in his sleeping bag and swore. The wind was a fluid now—water or blood, dashing against the tent. Pa-dup, pa-dup, pa-duppa, pa-dup. It beat like a pulse gone wild, the blood strokes of something inhuman. It was Animus, the first splashes of him. And then the torrent came, red and hot, descending on the tent and overwhelming it, bursting in on him. Ransom gasped and writhed as in a dream of lust, while Animus circled his poor heart, dissolved it to a thin liquid and bore it away. At the last, he felt sorrow, a wonderful sorrow. And peace.

The next morning dawned clear and calm. The dome had not a shred of mist or cloud over it, and mountains were visible all the way to Canada.

Ransom woke in the smaller tent to find Skimmer sitting up, watching him. Erik was dressing, silent and distant. Gloster was muttering outside. The occupants of the other tent were already stirring. Ransom laced his boots and crawled out. Harvey was putting zinc on, Gloster attaching his crampons. Bull stooped over the stove, making breakfast. At the edge of the camp, Yank was tromping the snow.

"Set up nicely," he said. There was rime on the wands. "Hard, but not too hard—" He turned back to the tents, saw Ransom, and went quiet.

Gloster nodded at Ransom. Harvey glanced in his direction, then turned and put his harness on without a word.

"Perfect," Ransom said, gazing around. His breath was steaming. The rising sun reflected off every edge and nick of the dome, as if the thousand eyes of Animus were watching.

Bull glanced at Harvey. So did Yank and Gloster. Erik emerged from the tent, realizing instantly something was up.

Harvey flinched. "Damn thing always pinches my nuts," he laughed, tugging at the harness. "Thought we'd run to the top."

Ransom nodded. "I'm for it."

"The group wants to go for the summit." Harvey gave him a regretful look.

"You mean the North Crater."

Harvey didn't respond directly. He glanced eastward, at a tangent to the icefall, to where the serac field gave onto smooth slopes. "We'll never get up the fall. We've got a chance of making it if we do what we originally planned."

Yank gave Gloster a look of triumph. Erik knelt beside them, watching.

"We could follow that alley," Ransom pointed. "Get through the rest of these seracs by noon." He stepped toward the icefall. "That alley there—"

Harvey dove for him, grabbed his parka, and pulled him back inside the safe area. Ransom had walked right between two wands. "There's not enough time," Harvey said, eyeing him sadly.

Bull turned to Ransom. "Even the direct way's a stretch."

Ransom saw the forces aligning against him. "Maybe we forget the icefall," he said, facing Harvey's route. "Take your way to the crater."

Harvey glanced at the others.

"Shit," Gloster said.

Erik made a disbelieving sound.

"Come on, Harv," Yank exploded angrily. "Show some spine."

Harvey grew morose, upset by the decision he was being forced to make. His instincts as a climber prevailed. "We're going for the summit," he said gently.

Gloster stiffened and rose, expecting a harangue from Ransom.

But Ransom just nodded. Was it the conversation of the night before, or his dream? Or something that occurred to him just then? "Alright," he said.

Harvey tried to smile. "You're coming."

"No."

Harvey gazed uncertainly at the others. Yank shrugged.

"Ransom—" Harvey's expression was troubled.

"Go ahead," Ransom said, understanding. "You've put up with a lot." He scanned their faces with sudden generosity. "It's the least I can do."

Harvey glanced at Bull.

"Maybe it's best," Bull murmured. The sentiment seemed to seal things.

Skimmer stepped out of the tent. "What's up?"

Harvey saw his duty. "We're going for the summit. Ransom's staying here. What do you want to do?"

Skimmer turned to Ransom, stunned.

"Go with them." Ransom's eyes were gentle and forgiving.

Skimmer was speechless.

"Maybe it's best," Ransom said, thanking Bull with a gracious smile.

Harvey lifted his pack. "Be back in eight to ten hours," he told Ransom, "assuming the weather holds. We'll start down tomorrow morning."

Fifteen minutes later, the climbing team was winding through the seracs beyond camp. From his position ahead of Bull near the rope's end, Skimmer glanced back one last time. Then they disappeared around a block. Ransom stood at the edge of the wanded area, watching. His set smile faded.

It had been a simple bit of duplicity, but now that he was really alone, the magnitude of the idea that had struck him fell heavily on him. He wasn't really sure he was going through with it. No, by dispatching the others, he'd only bought time to consider it. He turned and stepped back to the tent, drawing on his mitts. He found his pack and brushed the drifted snow off. Then, abruptly, he straightened. What was he thinking? It would be dangerous beyond anything he'd imagined. Insane, even for him.

He turned a half circle in a vague effort to ground himself. The snow beyond the wands glittered with prismatic sequins that shifted magically, winking out and springing to light no matter where he looked. The vacant camp seemed shabby and artificial—the stage set of a play, for which there was no further use. He gazed at the track of the departed climbers, then down the flank of the dome at the lowlands and the coast, realizing how far he'd come, how removed from humanity he was. Instead of giving him the courage to cut loose, it made him want to crawl back, to beg Lindy and everyone else to pardon his foolishness.

Then he saw the steam.

From a blue depression beside the icefall, a white gyre was rising into the sky. Heat! Animus was speaking to him from inside the dome. Calling him.

Ransom put his fingertips over his heart, remembering the dream—that moment of bliss when he was joined with his god and borne away. He didn't think of what he would or wouldn't do, only of how he felt and might soon feel. In this expectant state, he drew his willow knife solemnly from his parka pocket and set it on the snow. Then he turned to his pack and retrieved his regalia, placing his headdress to the left, his cuffs to the right, and the bundled furs before him. He unrolled the furs and the blue jar tumbled out.

Eleven

Three days after the summit attempt, the climbing team arrived at the Cheshnina River strip. The next morning, as planned, Doug Hurley began the job of shuttling them back to Tolsona Lake. Now, late in the day, the sun was muted by haze as it descended in the west. There was an unusually large number of people around the Hurley hangar. Harvey, Bull, Gloster and Yank were inside the hangar, packing up their gear. Burt Conklin, Sid Yasuda and the rest of their team were loading equipment and supplies into a van. Tolsona Lake was the base for their field research, and they had been ferried back from Mt. Wrangell's North Crater by a Valdez helicopter operator earlier that day. A third group had come from Fairbanks to see Ransom. University professors Calvin Bauer, Katherine Getz, and Hank Papadakis stood on the gravel, along with Alaska Fish and Game officer Vince Silvano. They were facing the eastern sky, watching the storm headed from the Wrangells. On a mount of gray showers, a cloudy black medusa rode, its arms swept back.

Calvin's watch read 8 p.m. He sighed and put his hands in his coat, hunching against the drizzle. "An hour late."

"Couldn't get off that strip," Hank Papadakis speculated.

Vince nodded. "They'll have to spend the night out."

Katherine Getz was silent, staring into the storm with a troubled face, as if she knew something worse was in the making.

Burt Conklin approached with Yasuda. "We'll be heading back to Fairbanks in a few minutes," Conklin told the group. He glanced toward the Wrangells. "I don't think Doug's going to make it through that."

"You got off the mountain just in time." Vince smiled at the scientist's good fortune.

Conklin nodded gravely. "It's a different world up there when it's blowing."

Hank gazed into the hangar. "The climbers don't seem to care if Ransom comes back."

"They're upset they didn't get to the top," Conklin said.

Yasuda raised his brows. "They said they didn't speak a word to him the whole way down."

Katherine glowered. "The goal was the crater. They betrayed him."

Yasuda looked unconvinced. "They say he's crazy."

"One of our grad students could see him through her binoculars," Burt Conklin said. "He was by himself, climbing an icefall, wearing this weird getup."

"With wolves following him." Yasuda grinned.

Hank and Katherine didn't smile.

Vince drew closer to Katherine. "It's a real pack," he told Yasuda. "I've seen them from the air. They're just as he describes."

Katherine gazed wide-eyed at Vince. He gave her a congenial nod.

A dozen feet away, Lindy turned, arms clasped around herself, worried and frail. Beside her, Ida Hurley stood with her hands in her jeans. "What now?" Lindy wondered.

238

Ida didn't respond. Whether she was immersed in her own thoughts or angry, Lindy couldn't tell. Ida remained square to the eastern sky and perfectly silent, her mouth firm and straight, counting the minutes like the beads of her rosary. Skimmer stood at his mother's hip, a new strength in his face, the remains of the Jumar rope tied around his thigh.

Lindy sagged, and Erik, who'd been waiting by her elbow, took the chance.

"The wind was incredible," he recounted. "The plane was shivering, the wings were flapping." His expression was cocky, as if his attitude had saved him.

Lindy shook her head.

"You look hungry." Erik leaned closer. "Let's get a burger."

"Drop dead."

Erik shrugged as if she was the butt of some practical joke and strode away.

"Jerk." Skimmer looked ready to spit. "When they turned on him, he stabbed Ransom in the back." He eyed Lindy with determination. "Dad will bring him through this."

Ida smiled at him and roughed his hair. "He'll find a way."

Lindy looked to Ida, but the older woman fixed on the storm again without a glance.

"It's the Cub." Skimmer angled his head.

All of those waiting grew silent to listen. Burt Conklin raised his brows at Yasuda. An organ note seemed to quaver in the distance. Was it the wind? The sound was obscured as Wasilla Bill's truck pulled up, but when he cut the engine, they heard it again. Yes, the Cub.

It appeared for a moment circling through smears of rain, then dove for the earth. They heard it touch down, roll along the gravel, then gun its prop to turn and come crunching toward them. It emerged through the mist, wet and glistening like something newborn. Hank shouted and a cheer went up. Ida smiled to herself. Lindy laughed with relief. The plane rolled down the slope and came to a halt. The prop chugged and stopped.

The clamshell doors sprang open and Doug Hurley climbed out. He was somber and distant behind his mirror glasses, as if he didn't see the group gathered there, intent on his passenger, turning to help him deplane. The wind dropped abruptly. Perhaps it was that, or Doug's strange solemnity, or the mystical lighting—one of those moments of perfect clarity, without sun or shade—but for whatever reason, absolute silence reigned as Ransom stepped down. He was in full regalia except for his headdress, but as his feet touched the gravel and he turned his face up, it wasn't the fur or the fringes of beaded twine that struck them. His eyes were like coals fresh from a brazier, burning with an unearthly intensity. His arms trembled, his legs dipped, and his back was hunched.

Lindy hurried forward, slowing as he turned and lifted his head-dress. Ransom seemed not to recognize her.

"Golden eyes, know," a deep voice rose from his chest. "Golden horns, grow." He peered beyond them at the horizon, as if this world was a byway, lowered the headdress onto his head, and fastened the latches. The beaded locks rattled as he turned, then his knees flexed and he moved in quick hops toward the hangar. He stopped beside a black oil drum and tilted his head at the climbers filing out of the dim interior, as if seeing them for the first time. Was he going to revile them? No. He put his hands on the drum and vaulted onto it.

Ida watched Doug move to within a dozen feet and post himself like an attendant to some dignitary. As she watched, he removed his glasses and stared straight at her, then at Skimmer. Then he glanced back at Ransom, and Ida saw in his solicitude how fragile Ransom was—dizzy, knees weak, his thin frame arched, arms angling to avoid a fall.

Ransom stamped and the gong of the oil drum filled the silence. Then his legs were bending, heels coming down rhythmically on the drum's top. His right arm scissored to his chest, touching his pectoral with his first two fingers, and he began to chant. It was an uncomfortable moment. The watchers turned to each other with strange faces, nervous, mystified, amused. Ransom was in a crouch, springing, head back, arms extended with the first two fingers of each hand pointed forward. Lindy gazed at the gravel. His madness was public. She could see their boots and shoes moving closer. And then the familiar voice sounded, intense, its precarious emotions following a jagged rhythm.

> *Ruptures, bursts of powder, giant holes.*
> *Invisible prints, pounding drum rolls.*
> *Your booming is tuned*
> *To the throbbing of my wound.*

Ransom quivered and jerked as if a current was passing through him. His hissing words seemed to pull invisible wires, stitching his legs, making his arms crimp spastically and his head buck. Murmurs brought Lindy's face up, and what she saw was so unlike anything she'd witnessed before, it terrified her. Doug was right with Ransom, following his every flex. Ida was repelled, but the pulse of the chant touched her. Skimmer was enthralled.

> *Gleaming spans lift with thunderous grinds,*
> *Crashing together. I rear on my hinds.*
> *Around me you've bent*
> *The blue ribs of a breathing tent.*

"The secret's out," Yasuda said, gazing wryly around. When Hank frowned at him, he grinned like someone who'd stumbled into a carnival and was happy to be entertained. Wasilla Bill was rocking from side to side, astonished, but joyful to see Ransom giving expres-

241

sion to whatever was in his heart. He realized he was still holding the whiskey bottle he'd been nursing in the truck, saluted Ransom with it, took a swig, and passed it to Calvin Bauer.

The Wise her snout aims.
The Lead his eye flames
At the trickle of my heart's blood.

Calvin listened carefully, his forehead furrowed. He took a slug and passed the bottle to Katherine. She held it before her, overcome by a sinking bewilderment. Hank took the whiskey and drank, squinting as if to see deeper into the disturbing tableau. But just as quickly, the bottle descended from his lips. He handed it to Harvey Parrish, who took a swallow, as did Bull. "Hey, he's good," Harvey laughed. Gloster made a disgusted face and waved the bottle away. Yank grabbed Harvey. "Let's get a beer." The climbers departed.

Surging through me, great strokes.
Giant cakes cracking, the icefall smokes.
Inside me, you roar.
Down the cataracts pour.

At the front, Vince stood beside Katherine. Her face showed her amazement. His was furrowed with intrigue for her benefit. Burt Conklin was mesmerized despite himself. The chant was loud and chopped, then softer as its violence subsided and the ram recognized what Animus had done.

Something was happening to the crowd. It wasn't Ransom's words, or his costume, or the image of him possessed like this on Mt. Wrangell. It was the rhythm of his clenching body, the choked explosions from his chest. A power barely modulated by the language of man emerged from that gaping jaw and those quivering lips, and it drove through them as surely as blood through the chambered heart.

Doug was shaken by it and so was Ida. Katherine heard it faintly. For Calvin it was fainter still. A wild stream, fearful but familiar, running fast and deep. Perhaps in Ransom, life was so threatened that the vital current rose to the surface to seek an outlet. The mind might not hear, but every heart was a drum for it to beat upon. It was as if a blade had cut through the gathering at the level of their shoulders. Above, each remained separate. Beneath, all were part of the same throbbing flesh.

Lindy saw Ransom was realizing his dream, but her pride was clouded by fear and shame. Hank caught her vagrant gaze and drew beside her, clasping her arm. "It's alright," he said. She smiled, binding him close with her dread.

The chant ended. The next began with the ram springing forward, but the oil drum lurched beneath Ransom's thrust. Doug and Calvin dove as the drum tipped over, and together they caught him. He lay motionless, limp and gasping for breath.

"Something's wrong with him," Calvin muttered. Doug saw red leaking through Ransom's shirt and pulled it open. The watchers froze. His chest was crusted with dried blood. A fresh cut followed the line of his scar, deep and bright scarlet.

Ida stifled a sob. "I'll get the doctor."

With Vince supporting his legs, Doug and Calvin carried Ransom into the dim interior of the hangar. A fluorescent tube flickered over a bench. Hank cleared it and they laid him down while the group gathered around. Skimmer helped his father remove the headdress. Ransom's face was gleaming and feverish. Doug pushed Ransom's matted hair aside and mopped his brow. Ransom murmured incoherently while the light blinked over him.

"The wound from last summer," Hank muttered.

"What's happened to him?" Katherine wondered.

"He cut himself," Hank said grimly.

Doug glanced toward the office, hoping Ida had reached the doctor.

Yasuda exhaled with finality, shaking his head. "Sick." The notion of self-mutilation was sufficiently repellent to turn Conklin away as well. Wasilla Bill was by the door and scowled as they passed.

"Why?" Calvin was stunned.

Lindy clung to Hank, trembling. She was too shocked to cry, or even speak. Her lips parted breath rapid and shallow, her gaze wandering Ransom's unconscious form.

"To wake his heart up," Wasilla Bill responded loudly through his drunkenness.

"It's his connection to Animus," Skimmer said. "His god who lives in the mountain. He told me about it on the way down."

Hank circled Lindy with his arm, and she hid her face in his shirt. Katherine's confusion dissolved. She stared at Ransom's ghostly features like an anthropologist observing some native initiation. Vince was behind her. He set his hands gently on her shoulders as if to steady her.

"When he puts the wound against the ice," Skimmer explained self-consciously, "and thinks certain things—" He glanced at his father.

Doug nodded. "The god rises to the surface." He met Vince's stare. "I heard the same thing. That's why we were late. I didn't realize—" He shook his head at the wound, and at his willingness to entertain Ransom's fantasies.

"He was trying to reach the North Crater," Skimmer told Vince. "Animus was with him. So were the wolves." He regarded the adult faces uncertainly. "He changed into a ram. He went as far as Animus would let him. Then the god 'drew a veil across the sanctum' and turned him back."

In the silence that followed, oil dripping from an engine was audible on the far side of the hangar, pinging the pan like a timepiece. Wasilla Bill had turned in the doorway. While Ransom was chanting, the storm's black medusa had embraced the sun. Inside those fierce arms, the molten orb blazed red, its escaping breath staining the sky peach and orange.

"Mt. Wrangell is a temple for him," Katherine said. She watched Ransom's eyes shift beneath his lids.

Wasilla Bill faced them, a paunchy herald silhouetted against the apocalyptic sky. "The elders believed spirits danced in that crater."

———•———

Ahead, the icefall looms. I'm springing through the seracs, kicking up loose powder, the way softening in the afternoon sun. Light blazes over the perilous course, bridging the fissures with white flame. I'm determined to be careful, but I don't see the holes until I'm directly over them. Is my god with me? My leap dislodges a snowbridge. I vault from the far side's sagging lip, dizzy from the heat and faint of heart. Fearful the snow won't hold, fearful I'm on my own.

Without his roar, this sacred place daunts me. What am I doing here, so small and alone? Animus—do you see me? I remember his voice booming up from the crevasse, that terrible longing now hard to believe. What could the god who lives here want with a grub like me?

My stride is fouling, snow turning to fluff. Legs knee deep, now hugged to the thighs. I'm bogged, plowing through uncompacted snow. Beneath me, hidden, a chaos of holes.

Sudden shadows paint the blocks. Between two seracs the

pack lunges—Lead in front, Wise at his shoulder, the Younger, the Ruff, the Dangler and Scout trailing behind. I glance at my wound. The enameled seal gleams in the sun, rimmed by jagged edges and dusted with snow. If I call, will you answer? It's time to try.

I forge through the white mire as the wolves approach, reaching a slab plastered with frost, pressing my chest firmly to the ice. The raw cold pierces me. Your help, great god. I ask without knowing what you might do.

The Scout yowls, fearing my invocation. The Lead pays no mind, continuing toward me. The others follow, their confidence building as the calm draws out. Animus? The air hangs breathless, wolves circling.

Tremors! At a distance, my god trembles, approaching slowly, savoring the suspense. Now closer! He moans, immense and alive, playing the deep caverns like organ pipes, thrumming the dome, blurring it into the sky. My wound quivers at your kiss, tendering beneath the seal. Pounding! Declaring yourself! Bursts of powder erupt, drifts collapse leaving giant holes—the prints of a god invisibly advancing. Animus! I'm shaking, fearful and expectant as the snows give way, jolted by the boom of great drums as you hammer beneath. I cling here, trembling, my wound frozen to the ice.

The Wise lifts her head, nervous but eager. The Lead is surprised. The Younger is fearful and so is the Ruff. The Scout snaps and leaps back, glaring vindictively, blaming her sister. You hump the snow directly beneath me. Unfazed, the Lead takes another step. The ice around me bursts with turquoise cracks.

You roar, proclaiming "the Ram is mine," and your heaving redoubles, grottoes opening on all sides, gaping mouths gasping and shattering. A fierce jolt, I'm torn from the ice, feeling a sharp pain in my chest, fighting panic, firm to my faith. A thunderous grind and great beams of ice lift around me, waving and craning. Boom, they teeter. Boom, they swing. Boom, I jerk my trunk up, rearing on my hinds as the rafters come together with a crash directly above me. Dazzled, I hear you rejoicing, coveting me inside the blue ribs of your breathing tent.

The pack hems the pavilion, looking in. They've dodged death, barely. The Younger cries, but no one is listening. The Wise is enticing the Lead, looking from me to him, telling him I'm caged, knowing I'm not. Thinking the tables have turned, the Scout snarls at her, but the Wise pays no mind, wowing urgently to her mate, aiming her snout at my chest.

The Lead faces me, eyes flaming.

The enamel is cracked, torn open by the jolt. This is what my god wants! Heart's blood in the bright sun, trickling down my chest. A drop hits the snow and the dome is dashed. Another, another! You're lifting toward me with fierce intent, entering my hooves with great strokes and surging up! A deep grumble from the icefall. Between the rafters, I see puffs rising, giant cakes breaking loose, shuddering against each other as the stair pulls apart. Your booms infuse me, loads of ice plunge down, bursting, birthing swirling clouds.

The roar mounts, ranks of white scallops crossing the icefall. Beneath, rain falls with a fearful hiss, an enormous cataract, crashing down. Avalanches boil at the bottom and rumble to-

ward me, a multitude of cymbals played over the beats of a gong, till there's nothing but an explosion unceasing, possessing me completely. A wild flood, a blaze of suns, a blizzard wind, glowing with desire!

The avalanche reaches the base of the pavilion, strikes it and shoots into the air, rising before me like a white wall. Then the spatter descends, echoes rumbling, fading. My god withdraws. In his wake, my limbs jerk, my spine writhes, dancing till the convulsions pass.

Powder is everywhere, in my nose and throat, in my lashes and ears. The pavilion returns, and through the white rain, I see the pack. Dangler in a crouch, Scout on her side. The Younger half-buried, digging herself frantically out. The Ruff eyes the pavilion with fear, for good reason. They mean little to him. His love is for me. The Lead, despite everything, is fixed on the puddle of blood between my fores. Only the Wise understands, eyeing me with reverence. The spindrift makes her fur glitter, her ears keyed to the rustling, knowing what Animus has done, hearing his long sigh.

I turn. Through the whirling veil, I see the serac field. The avalanche has passed over it like a transforming cloud. The blocks and drifts are gone, leveled with pulverized ice. A courtyard, smooth and hard, paved by Animus to permit my ascent. He erected this tent to protect me while he brought the heights tumbling down. I shake myself, and an icicle slides off my shoulder into the puddle of blood. I pull my shanks from the pits they've trembled in the snow, set my hooves on the surface and step forward.

At the pavilion's curb, I glance back. The Wise licks the

Lead's muzzle, eyes darting at me. *See how tired he is? We'll have him at the next crossing. The Ruff is fearful, the Scout and the Dangler unwilling, the Younger trying to be brave. The Lead grunts, tail rising, and jostles among them, stirring their hunger with his own. Then he sets off at a lope, and as the wolves disappear through the settling powder, I see them with fresh eyes. They've lost their dam, their den and their pups. The chain of life is broken. All they have now is me. And I belong to him.*

I step over the broken plinth and leap to the courtyard below. Then into a trot, hooves barely pitting the compacted ice.

My path is before me. I'm grateful but tired, breathing deeply, my wound stanching in the cool air. The blinking particles sprinkle down, whispering sweet secrets. Can you be this kind? It's hard to believe. Gentle, unhurried and smiling. Come along, my child. I remember that tenderness. The world was full of it not long after I sprang from you, when life was beginning, joyful and new. Dear god, I feel that sweetness again, here inside me, unembarrassed, flowing from my heart without hesitation or remorse.

Of all those who have issued from you, one has come back. So small, crazed by dreams of glory, but precious for that. The spindrift is settling, the sun shines through. The scoured cliffs of the icefall are no longer threatening. You are with me, even when I can't see or hear you. You'll be with me all the way.

I hear burbling. I see silver trees. Fountains are spouting around me, rising from the court. Would you honor me? For what? That I've come this far? For my feeble belief? That's laughter I hear! You're pleased to tears, crying for joy— Your quakes have crushed the deep mains, your hidden rivers are overflowing.

Beneath your love everything melts: the ice, my fur, my flesh, my heart.

Puddles flash, thin pipes spreading out. I kick into a lope, splashing among them, seeing where the courtyard ends and the icefall rises into the sky. A turquoise chasm crosses my way, overflowing in pulsing disks. Melt surges within, blue bands undulating, detached icicles darting like translucent fish. I see, I believe, I hear you calling from the depths. If I could dive to the bottom of this chasm, I'd be with you, I know.

I leap the gap and land with new strength, pounding to the court's edge, catching sight of an icy ravine with dusted treads. The sweet moment is ending. I'm as reluctant to leave it as you are to release me. The way steepens abruptly. I'm gaining height again, starting up the icefall, feeling the thirst for still higher snows. Gusts comb my coat. Behind me, the fountains are subsiding, the wild god Animus sinking back into his dome.

—◆—

The sky above Tolsona Lake was serene, the lavender night marbled with steel blue. Swallows skimmed the silver, scribing it with their breasts and the tips of their wings. The Hurley home was lit, but quiet. In the guest house at the end of the path, a strange liturgy was in progress.

> *Across the court,*
> *Grateful but beat.*
> *Particles sprinkling,*
> *Secrets sweet.*

Ransom's wound had been tended by the doctor, and after two days' rest, his strength had returned. He was sitting up in bed, wearing a flannel shirt without headdress or regalia, chanting with his eyes closed, swaying in time. People were seated and standing around him, silent and listening.

> *I remember that voice*
> *From before I was tossed*
> *Into the world.*
> *It's not lost.*

Doug Hurley stood close, gripping the bedpost. He too had his eyes closed. Skimmer was by the foot of the bed, mirroring Ransom's movements. Calvin Bauer was there out of concern for Ransom. The intimate setting made him uncomfortable, and he leaned forward in his chair, frowning. Beside him, Katherine sat with a troubled face. Ida was by the door, nervous, watching the room. Her gaze paused on Vince, who stood behind Katherine, gazing unabashedly down her blouse front.

Lindy stood at the rear, stiff with resentment. Only strangers could be entertained by this. Her resentment mounted as she glanced around the room. Even those who knew Ransom had the luxury of indulging him. She was the crutch he'd fall back on once they were gone. Hank Papadakis noticed and edged toward her.

> *Of all you've hurled,*
> *One has come back.*
> *Crazed by dreams of glory.*
> *Precious for that.*

Ransom, still chanting, peered through half-closed lids, saw Wasilla Bill's grin and smiled self-consciously, admitting he was reveling in the attention without missing a beat.

The melt is piping,
Guiding skeins shimmer by.
The icefall rises
Into the sky.

His voice faded and silence filled the room. No one spoke. Doug opened his eyes and glanced at Ida. Ransom stared at his lap, too nervous to face them.

"You sing from your heart," Doug said. The compliment sounded forced. He gave Ransom an appreciative look.

Ransom didn't respond.

"I could imagine him trotting," Katherine said.

"The rhythm of the ram," Hank agreed. He glanced at Lindy. She was stony-faced. He put his hand on the small of her back to comfort her.

Ransom raised his head. "He's the yearning inside us." He gazed at them, recognizing the distance in their eyes, but unafraid, baring the emotions that had brought him bliss. "His wild eyes light the way out of bondage."

"My wife did that for me." Wasilla Bill touched the glove folded over his belt.

Ransom nodded. "But she's gone," he said sadly. "We open our hearts, we give ourselves away, we feel love. But we are not the source. That's the mistake."

Calvin's face creased.

"We are mortal. We die," Ransom glanced from Bill to Calvin, "or grow weary. We offer our love and take another's, then find we've only traded stones." He eyed Katherine. "We carry love like a bird carries gravel in its crop."

She blinked and gazed at her knees.

"Love the source of love," Ransom said, "and your heart will be forever renewed."

"The source?" Calvin shook his head.

"You know his voice," Ransom said slowly. "You heard it in the womb, in a lover's whisper, in the wind on a stormy mountain."

Silence filled the room.

"Animus," Skimmer told the group.

Vince laughed.

"We dwell," Ransom glanced at the window, "in the shadow of volcanoes. Mountains that welled molten out of the earth. You can see where the crimson swirled and seethed, crumbling, popping with gas. You can envision the glowing front rumbling toward you, rippling the air with impossible heat. The shells of crust swelling and cracking while the rivers raged red beneath. It's all frozen now, motionless. The stuff fortresses are made of. Rock, the material of defense." His eyes misted with feeling. "I'm talking about our lives."

Ida's face was pitying, shaken by what Ransom had done even as his words reached her.

"We're no different than the mountains." Ransom lifted his hand from his lap. "Made of fire." He touched his chest. "We come from a place that's hot and flowing. We grow swaddled in a cloak of blood and the first sound we hear is its pulsing. We remember that throb, that warmth, and we're inspired by it, we seek it in others. That's the power and the joy we feel passing through us: our wonder, our love, our passion for life, our sorrow in leaving it all behind."

Wasilla Bill's eyes were full of longing, as if he saw his wife sitting on the bed beside Ransom.

"And the source?" Calvin said.

"Our colder parts, hair and teeth and bones—they huddle around the heart like a hearth." Ransom raised his brows. "We are teeth and bones in this world we live in."

"Teeth and bones?" Vince smiled.

"We're dollops and embers, cast off and cooling." Ransom eyed

253

each in turn. "We come from the headwaters of the molten heart. A glowing god set us loose on this world wrapped like a husk around a piece of himself."

Lindy scowled. Ransom gave her a tender look.

"Oh my," Ida sighed. Despite everything, his words seemed joyous.

"But the longer we are gone from him, the colder and harder we grow." Ransom was somber. "That's our sin. Our shame. To feel that iron chill enclosing us, remembering how gloriously our hearts once glowed."

In the quiet, Katherine looked glum. Hank fooled with his cuff. Vince cleared his throat.

Ransom made a simple face. "We must get back to him."

"Animus," Skimmer said.

Ransom smiled. "Yes, Animus. We want to be wild again. And he is why."

Through Wasilla Bill's pain, something dawned in his face.

" 'Get back to him?' " Calvin's consternation seamed his features. "What does that mean?"

"Shake with his throb," Ransom said. "Bathe in his blood. Melt in his heat." He clenched his fist over his pectoral. "Circulate through him like the blood in any heart. Let him take us and return us. Cherish us and nourish us. Own us and give us back, or not, as he may decide. We have no reason to live if we cannot be renewed."

Ida bit her lip and turned away. Hank shook his head. Ransom saw the group disengaging, and he challenged them, peering into their faces one by one. "The mind says *I*." He clutched his shirt over his bandaged wound. "The heart says *die*." He twisted the cloth as if he would wring it so they could drink what he felt.

"We aren't all chased by wolves," Katherine said.

Ransom glanced from her to Vince. "Look behind you."

Hank laughed.

Katherine turned with a puzzled face, and Vince raised his hands and took a step back.

"Human love teaches us surrender," Ida said, forcing herself to face Ransom, trying to find some common ground. "Is that what you mean?"

Ransom nodded. "Too often, it barely scratches. The sweetest kiss leaves a chest wound."

"I'll take your word for it," Vince joked.

"Surrender's an emotion," Calvin said. "You keep talking about physical violence. We can't find joy by harming ourselves."

Ida looked for Ransom's response. She was shocked when he peered back at her, as if sharing a secret.

"What if pain is the only thing that makes you feel alive?" Wasilla Bill spoke in a low voice.

Katherine glanced at him. "We all have dark moments," she muttered.

"Ransom—" Ida gave Doug a fearful glance. "The doctor said—" She saw Lindy's face and cut herself short. Ransom acted as if he hadn't heard.

Lindy was twisting, barely able to look at him.

"I want life," Ransom told them. "Not death. But the heart only lives in the act of renewal. And once that is over, it grows dark and hard. It turns cold and resisting. Past surrenders become present defenses. To preserve the joy it remembers, it walls itself up, protecting itself against fresh fits—the mad passions, black and despairing, that force the flowers of bliss to bloom. And because it's mortal—a product of something holy, not holiness itself—it erodes. The elements beat against it. It still eats. It sleeps. It thinks. It covets. It provides. It crumbles to dirt and becomes a generative place, a seedbed for offspring. Is that life?" Ransom regarded them. "Is it?"

Katherine nodded numbly, understanding.

Calvin watched her with a sinking look, seeing his own unhappiness.

"Do you mean people shouldn't have children?" Hank wondered.

"That's when we gave up," Calvin acceded with a sigh. "Stopped chasing our dreams and started nurturing theirs."

"I get what you're saying." Wasilla Bill spoke to Ransom with his head bowed. "My heart's cold as stone. Only whiskey warms me. When I'm drunk, I remember."

"This is sad." Doug's gaze darted among them, anxious and uncertain. His comment seemed to include both their malaise and Ransom's unthinkable remedy. "I can't believe having children is the end." He glanced at Skimmer with humor in his eyes.

Skimmer looked from his father to Ransom.

Doug sighed. "It's the sky for me," he said. "I can see it flowing, its currents dividing, where it races and pools. Not just around the plane, but everywhere, up the valleys and through the peaks. That was my picture of the heart flowing through things," his gaze narrowed as if peering through a fog, "when I was young and afraid, and didn't care what kind of risks I took because there was nothing to lose." He was speaking to his wife now. "When I was in love, and what I felt for Ida and the rivers and mountains was all mixed together."

Ida caught her breath. She moved around the room toward him.

"Alaska's a place where people come to let the wildness in them run free." Doug gazed at the others. "That's why I'm here, and you Vince, and you Hank. What happened to us?"

Almost inaudibly, Katherine began to weep. Calvin put his arm around her, unsure what was happening.

"Would you like to speak?" Ransom asked softly.

Katherine shook her head.

Skimmer's eyes gleamed at Ransom, seeing his triumph, polishing every angle of it.

Hank glanced at Lindy. She was regarding Ransom coldly.

Ransom read the message in her eyes. "I think you should leave," he told the group.

As those seated started to rise, he did as well, his eyes flickering from face to face. "What a moment this was." He touched Katherine's shoulder. "A little of the molten heart flowed here."

Vince drew beside Katherine and tried to put his arm around her, but she shrugged it off.

Ida leaned toward Ransom as the group filed out. "You're melting that hardness in us." Her voice begged him to take care for himself, and she cast a worried glance at Lindy.

Lindy turned away, gazing out the window toward the lake. Ransom closed the door and they were alone.

"Please," he said.

She remained with her back to him, slowly shaking her head. Her eyes were closed, and she stooped as if the world of *Wild Animus* —mountains and rivers and flowing ice—was a burden she was carrying. He coaxed her around, seeing the defeat in her face.

"Lindy—"

"I mean nothing to you," she muttered.

"I love—"

"Animus," she burst out angrily. She gave a bleak laugh—not many lose their man to a god. "You've left me behind."

Ransom frowned. "You're right here with me."

"Your first disciple." She cast a caustic look toward the Hurley house.

"How can you say that?"

"Your heart's bleeding for everyone but us."

"They're desperate to find what we have," Ransom said. "It's strange, but I feel responsible. Their hope is so fragile, it's like handling a newborn child."

" 'What we have?' " Lindy eyed him despairingly.

Ransom gazed at her, his euphoria leaching away. "I'm sorry," he said softly. He turned his head, thoughts directed inward. "Do you think I'm a sham, telling them how to live their lives?"

Lindy sighed. "Let's think about ours."

He shook his head. "It's ridiculous. All that talk about families." He gave her a helpless look. "Animus is the only father I've ever had."

She softened. "I know." Her eyes were understanding. "He's given you more than any human father could." She saw the innocent child in him, begging for forgiveness, and she touched his shoulder, drawing against him for an embrace.

Ransom flinched. She saw the pain in his face and was instantly fearful. He tried to turn away, but she grasped his shirt and opened it, gasping at the sight of his bandages hanging loose and bloody. "What have you done?"

He made a perturbed face, acknowledging her upset, as if he too was troubled by the discovery.

"The stitches are cut." She peered at him with horror.

He looked confused.

Lindy gazed around the room, at the bed and the desk, and his parka on the chair. She stepped over to it and pulled the willow knife out of the pocket. Its blade was streaked with blood. "You've opened yourself up again," she whispered.

"Not deeply," he assured her.

"You're insane."

"Am I?" Again he seemed to search himself. "The most glorious aspirations of man have been called that." He frowned. "Are there any spiritual leaders who weren't mad? To the everyday world, seeking things sacred is lunacy."

Lindy stared speechless at his wound. He closed the shirt like a woman realizing her nakedness was an immodesty.

"Men with great missions disregard their bodies." He spoke tentatively, half to himself, as if testing how the words might sound. "The weakness of the flesh doesn't get in their way." His hand slid over his scarification, caressing it. "Holy men go farther, confirming a transcendent self by giving up the temporal one. It's the ultimate expression of faith. It will wake those who can be woken. That's why they must be sacrificed."

"If this is where *Wild Animus* is leading, there can't be any good in it."

Ransom's face fell. "Don't—"

"I can't take anymore," she said, breaking down.

The severity of her distress triggered his worst fear. "You're not thinking of—"

"I'm frightened," she muttered through her tears. "I feel so alone. We were going to be together. The two of us. Remember?"

He nodded, imagining his quest without her. Lindy had made it all possible. "That's what I want." He embraced her despite the pain. "You. No one else."

She clung to him.

"That's my dream," Ransom said. "That I've reached the high place and you're with me. I'm naked, feeling your kisses, surrendering."

Her hope welled, uncertain what he meant, but swayed by his romanticism, at the center of his world again, if only briefly.

"The first time, there wasn't any choice," he said. "It had to be with someone like Harvey."

"What do you mean?"

He held her close. "The dome."

She drew back far enough to see into his eyes.

"Wasilla Bill's going to let us move into his cabin," Ransom said. "I'll be there full time, close to the mountain, to finish the manuscript and record my chants. You'll stay here during the week." He indicated the guest house. "Ida said she'd help you find work in Glennallen. Doug will fly you out on weekends."

Lindy was stunned. None of Ransom's leaps had prepared her for this. Her features worked as if she had something important to say, but her voice wouldn't come. Her rage was exhausted. Only weariness and sorrow remained.

Ransom put his cheek to her temple and held her close. "I know my pack. You can't abandon me. You're coming with me. I meant what I said."

Lindy closed her eyes, her mouth sagging miserably. She was unable to resist or control him. She was even losing the power to drain his doubt away. Animus was his source of confidence now.

"You've missed me, haven't you?" Ransom whispered. His voice was thin and frail, like a little boy's. He touched his groin to hers, aroused.

Lindy gasped, suddenly faint, clutching him. Out of the devastation inside her, the innocent child rose, blind to every sign their love had gone wrong. Hope, that was all it was—a hope devoid of any foundation. Was she so starved and needy that an hour of love would smother all this pain? The thought mortified her, then faded beneath her sighs. She could feel Ransom's heart opening to her, pure and freely given, and nothing else mattered.

The following afternoon, the two of them stood outside the Hurley hangar while Doug loaded the Cub.

"Take care of yourself." Lindy kissed him. Her smile had a sheltering fondness. Somehow she had come to accept their situation.

"Don't worry." His eyes searched hers.

As he climbed into the plane, Ida moved beside Lindy. The Cub taxied up the slope toward the strip. Lindy took a couple of steps, as if to follow it.

"Let's watch from the aspens." Ida pointed to a stand of trees.

They walked together up the incline as the Cub circled for take-off.

"Men are always seeking," Ida said. "When a man stops seeking, he's an empty man."

Lindy glanced at the older woman, seeing her strength, her firm smile and bright eyes, the hangar and home behind her. Ida didn't understand. How could she?

"That business with the knife," Ida shook her head. "He told Doug he was done with it." She waited for Lindy to confirm this, but the younger woman remained silent. "Doctor Jim said the cut wasn't deep enough to be dangerous."

They stepped beneath the aspens. The Cub's engine revved and Lindy felt a rush of dread. Ida was smiling at the plane. Above, the leaves were rustling and flashing. Something dire was happening and the world was cheerful and heedless.

"He's a rare creature," Ida said. All her fears about what Ransom was doing to himself seemed buried beneath the joy she felt.

Lindy glared at her, seeing how little Ransom's destruction would affect her. "Will you leave me alone?"

Ida lowered her arm, regarded Lindy sadly, then turned and headed back.

Doug opened the throttle and the red foxtail grass thrashed in the prop wash. The Cub sniffed at the air and leaped forward, and the foxtails became a shimmering path, flashing and fluid in Ransom's wake. The plane rose and dwindled in the sky, smaller and smaller. It was invisible, the hum barely audible, and then even that was gone. There was nothing to hear but the lapping of the lake and the leaves in the trees.

Twelve

*I*t was late afternoon and the sun was shining on the Cheshnina. The Cub glided above the winding skeins of the river, dipped beneath the spruce tops, tilted toward the strip and touched down. It bounced and bumped to a halt, the prop chugged and froze. Doug unclipped his shoulder harness, opened the clamshells and helped Lindy out.

It had been a month since Ransom had taken up residence in Wasilla Bill's cabin. The growth was yellowing, summer approaching its end. Tiny plovers darted up and down the river bar. Doug glanced around. There was no one to meet them.

Lindy caught the look in his eyes. She took a deep breath and scanned the spurs as he unloaded her things. This was her fourth visit, but the place still seemed like a fabled realm. The wind whispered secrets—there were secrets in the peaks, and in the hearts of the creatures hidden there.

He lifted the duffels and they started along the path toward the cabin. As they left the hum of the river, another rose to their ears.

"The generator," Doug said.

Lindy sighed. Ransom was alive.

"This can't go on," Doug muttered.

Lindy didn't reply. The path was hemmed with white parnassia. Violet monkshood nodded in the breeze. A tawny waxwing perched on a snag, watching her through its black mask as she passed.

The cabin appeared through the trees, surrounded by a scud of smoke. Over the drone of the generator they could hear Ransom chanting. They halted before the door. Lindy collected herself. Doug knocked. The chanting stopped.

The door opened and Ransom stood before them in full regalia, white fur and golden horns flashing, beads glittering in the cords of his ropy mask, eyes glinting behind the black screens. They waited for him to speak, but he just stood there. Doug eyed him with concern. Lindy's smile withered. She drew beside him and hugged his arm.

Ransom wobbled. "What is today?" he rasped.

"Friday," Lindy said. A sulphur butterfly settled on his horn. It turned on scarlet legs, and stared at her with lime green eyes, looking to her like an emissary of powers who knew him better than she.

"I'll turn the generator off," Ransom said, moving past them.

Doug carried the duffels inside, setting one by the bed and the other below the shelving. He opened it and removed the groceries. Lindy looked around. Socks and a tee shirt lay on the woodpile beside the stove. The chair was angled out from the table where a notepad lay beside sheaves of manuscript. On the other side of the cabin were the tape recorder, his instruments, and the mic stand. She imagined him tensed and jerking before it. The generator's drone died.

As Ransom stepped back through the doorway, Doug gazed at Lindy with foreboding. Ransom still had his mask and furs on. She noticed a black stripe up the side of his legging.

"What's that?" she said, rigid with alarm.

"Some of his heat," Ransom replied. The fur was scorched to his hip.

Doug regarded him with disbelief. "What are you doing?"

Ransom turned slowly. "I've been on the dome." His voice was tentative.

"Flirting with fumaroles," Doug scowled.

"He protects me."

"This is too far," Doug said. With each trip, his upset had mounted. The time for gentle concern was past. "You're climbing alone. You're not carrying a shovel or any emergency gear. The snow's soft. The bridges are rotten this time of year. You know how dangerous those hot spots are—"

Ransom didn't respond. Outside a gray jay squawked. Through the smoky window, aspen leaves fluttered like paper suns.

"Every week you're worse," Doug shook his head. "More fogged in. More disconnected."

Ransom stepped toward him, stopping a couple of feet away. "I can see the reflection of the ram in your eyes," he murmured softly.

"He means a lot to me," Doug said. "If you die, he dies with you."

Ransom just stared at him.

Lindy moved toward the shelves, then stopped and stood beside them.

"You should think about what all of this is doing to her," Doug said.

Ransom didn't react. He was waiting for Doug to leave.

Doug laughed dryly. "Here." He pulled an oblong yellow object from his pocket. "Keep this in your pack. It's for downed planes." He pointed at a lever. "If something happens, you trip this."

Ransom's silence persisted.

There was nothing more Doug could do. "See you Sunday." He

set the locator on the table beside the manuscript and departed.

When the door had closed, Lindy retrieved an armful of items from the shelves and carried them to the table. She motioned to Ransom as she spread them out. He stepped toward her. A package of swabs, gauze and tape, Bill's wormwood infusion and a tube of antibiotic ointment. She unbuttoned his shirt and slid it off. Her hands were steady, but there was dread in her face. The bandage over his left pectoral was soaked with blood.

"Is it painful?"

"Warm."

She lifted the bandage in a couple of places, then peeled it away. The sight made her catch her breath. "It doesn't look good." Studying it seemed to calm her. Nodding to herself that she could manage, she reached for the swabs and the infusion and began to clean the wound. She had kept Ransom's continuing self-mutilation a secret. No one could do anything to allay her fear, and talking about it would only make the two of them look more desperate. Ransom's survival depended on her. If she betrayed his confidence or gave up hope, she might lose him forever.

As she cleaned the wound, a deep sigh escaped him. Instead of recoiling from her strokes, he moved with them gently and with feeling, as if relishing the contact. Beneath the blood and crusts, the pink welt appeared, freshly cut down the center.

"I can't keep doing this. We need a doctor."

He didn't hear her. Her attentions to his wound drew the yearning from him, and it filled the space around them. She found it difficult to look at him, and her hand grew heavy.

"You were above the icefall again?" she asked.

"Yes." His voice was intimate and aware.

"You camped there?"

"No. I didn't take the tent. I climbed straight through." In order to ascend the mountain quickly, he had removed one essential after another.

"Where did you sleep?"

"In crevasses."

"Wasn't it cold?"

"I spent a night in the labyrinth." His voice trembled at the memory of things startling and arcane.

Lindy uncapped the ointment and dabbed the wound.

"He was with me," Ransom whispered. "Teaching me the discipline of sacrifice."

She peered up at him.

He began to chant.

> *Beneath the lace, glyphs rising.*
> *His nature they impart.*
> *Torn by violent dividings.*
> *I read them with my heart.*

The verse enlivened him, and the sight of his energy coming back was a relief to her. "You'd better hold still," she said, unwrapping the gauze pads. His movements ceased, but he continued to mumble. She taped the fresh bandage over his wound. His words were inaudible, but she heard the adoration in his voice and knew it was for Animus.

"Take your headdress off."

He seemed not to hear.

She reached to undo the clasps. He flinched. She raised her hands again. He grabbed her wrist.

"Let me do it," she said gently.

His arms fell.

She unfastened the clasps, puzzling at his reluctance, wondering what she might see when the headdress came off. He tipped his head forward, and she lifted the headdress by its horns and set it down. The face that raised itself to regard her was a frightening one, crossed with scores and cuts. It was all she could do to keep from crying out.

"How did this happen?" She put her fingers to his face.

"I've been the ram since you left," he muttered weakly, like a child confessing to his mother.

"You haven't taken it off?" She eyed his haggard features with distress. His hair was damp and matted. His mouth was slack, his eyes unfocused.

Ransom frowned and glanced at the bed. When he turned back, he seemed to see her for the first time. "There's not much air up there," he said, trying to explain what had happened since her last visit. Then, with a troubled expression, "Another wolf is dead."

"Which one?" she asked, then thought better and stopped him before he could respond. "That didn't really happen," she said gently.

He didn't challenge her, but his eyes hooded as if he suspected some betrayal.

"Ransom—" She shook her head, trying to keep him from slipping back.

"You've angered him," he warned her. "Your fear. Your doubt."

She nodded. "I'm afraid."

The sight of her quailing turned his upset inward. His eyes begged forgiveness for accusing her, then grew troubled. He was more fearful than she about what the fate of the ram and wolves meant.

She shivered and drew against him.

"I've missed you," Ransom muttered. He was miserable with despair.

She clung to him, her desire still strong and alive.

268

"I don't want to hurt you," he said abjectly. "I don't want you to die."

"Who said anything about dying?" She kissed him.

"Animus gives me no peace."

As distraught as he was, she could see the light of the tireless seeker still shining within him. "Your quest is not for peace."

"I know what he wants of me." His eyes searched hers. "Only the Wise understands."

"I love you."

"The Lead still hungers for me."

She shuddered. "Don't—"

"The Younger's trembling with fear."

"We'll get through this."

"The Ruff preaches false hope."

"No, no—" He was terrifying her. "No, no, no—" She burst into tears, her face twisting like a child's.

"Lindy," he sobbed, trying to blot out the wolf images. "Lindy—" He was pleading with a memory of her, trying to dredge it from his heart. Their days of joy seemed impossibly distant.

"I'm here," she said helplessly.

Her voice seemed to soothe him, but his gaze fell on the wormwood infusion and he saw her print on the bottle—the smudge of a palm and four stubby pads, the start of the fingers—and imagined his pursuers had again caught up to him. He was straying and they were recalling him to his purpose. "Higher," he whispered, nodding.

Lindy grabbed his shoulders and shook him. "I'm here now." She fought to control her emotions. "You're alright." She turned and put his guitar back in its case. "You're going to feel a lot better, once—"

His eyes grew wild as she boxed his manuscript. He moved to stop her, fearful of losing touch with his vision for even a moment.

"The labyrinth," he said, taking the sheaf from her. She didn't resist. "That part's done." In his eyes, exultation mingled with some appalling recollection.

"Come back with me on Sunday," she said.

He shook his head.

"*Wild Animus* is nearly finished," she said. "We'll make copies, let them read it."

"I can't leave."

"People want to see you."

He shook his head.

"We'll go to Fairbanks, visit Hank and the others. For a few days—"

"No."

"Someone has to look at that cut—"

"No."

"Please," Lindy whimpered.

He embraced her.

"How could this happen?" she moaned, rocking her head on his chest. "Just a few days—"

He turned his head away.

"If you don't—" The ultimatum died in her throat.

When he looked back she was limp with defeat. "A few days at the lake," he agreed. "Then you'll come back with me and we'll climb the dome."

She laughed at the idea.

"Together," he said.

She stared at him.

"Remember Mt. Rainier. It's the fulfillment of our vows."

"I can't do it."

"I know the way." He spoke to her fear.

"Let's talk about it at Tolsona."

"I'm only leaving if you promise to come back with me."

"Please—"

"You're going to be there." He spoke calmly of something pre-ordained. "To disrobe me, to help me bare myself." He touched his chest.

She regarded his hand with a glazed look. This same hand put on the headdress and wielded the willow knife, and now it was playing with her life. Lindy nodded slowly, accepting the compact. What choice was there? On Sunday, when Doug returned, they'd leave the Wrangells. A lot could happen in a few days.

"The labyrinth." Ransom spoke in a low register, reverting to his chanting voice. He turned, separated some of the pages from his manuscript, and motioned her toward the chair.

The icefall's behind me, the backs of blue waves descending a vertical sea. I'm loping over white swales, buoyant but tense, knowing a test lies ahead, hooves crunching the crust, heat blazing up. Forward, a great dicing of ice. A turquoise corridor, its threshold rippled with wind scour, leads into the heart of the labyrinth.

I hurtle toward it, the cool walls rising up, my legs tamping into the soft snow. As I drop to a trot, the corridor narrows and the floor descends. The labyrinth creaks, white drapes falling on my right, the banked floor trembling, gaps deep and dark blue. Floor, what floor? How brave are you really? All the floors here are false. How deep is your desire? As deep as these grottoes? His temple's body, these quivering halls—do you see, can you hear? The crystal walls cry, echoes of torment and release ghosting through the icicle rain. Cornices connect overhead, vaulting the corridor. The way grows dim, lit by frozen candles, their sharp tips flaming. In the spectral glow, the walls shimmer, laces shifting, glyphs of rime rising, revealing the nature of the god. I read them with my heart.

Born in fire from the void, rent by violent dividings. The creation of the many, the return of the few. Those who yearn, who understand. And the fewer still who are received. Others have threaded these frozen catacombs, thinking to meet him face to face. Their hierurgies, their disciplines unscroll before me. Their renunciations, their offerings. Their days of bliss and tragic nights. Boundless ecstasy, raving remorse. Lives cut short.

A marbled transept opens through gauzy drapes. Deep in the mountain, Animus moans and the passage shudders. Sections of floor sink around me. Only a ledge remains, leading into the transept. This is the way. The walls grow colder and closer. Animus echoes softly, and I see my own future in the storied frostworks. Will the ram surrender? Can he put fear away? He's a strand of myself. He longs. But not as I. Child of my depths— you've returned. But how much of yourself are you willing to give? Everything? This is the devotion your god will demand.

A cracking and crashing! White eaves fall behind me. The vault is collapsing! Is this your will—to bury me alive? What's that noise? I hold my breath. Hoarse panting, a yelp. The pack. They've plunged through the roof. I hear the Wise wowing, urging them on, and the Younger squealing, playing her game. The fast crunch of paws, approaching. There's no turning back, the wolves bar the way.

A zag in the channel, a gap in the floor. I leap, punching through as I land, pitching sideways, shoulder scraping the wall, pivoting and springing into a narrow slit. A terrifying place, two lengths wide, banded walls like purple marble, roofed and freezing cold, the floor nothing but moldings suspended over the void. Another zag and the passage dead-ends, pinching to a crack. Behind me, I hear the Lead panting and the wowing of the Wise. I face the slit, full of dread, realizing what I'm to do. Turn to the freezing wall. Press my wound against it. I shiver, feeling the contact in every nerve, flowing myself to him, fearful and expectant.

Animus roars.

My chest spasms. A chip of ice, cold and sharp, pierces me. You rise into the narrow cut, deafening, filling me with your power while my heat bleeds into the wall.

The labyrinth heaves, jerking wildly, shelves crashing down. Yelps thread the cacophony—the Dangler's gargle. Then everything is drowned by a horrific shrieking as the slit cocks and cracks open. Here's your way! Beneath the torn floor, bordered by shreds of trembling lace, I hear you melting a thousand blue grottoes. The quakes have opened the slit to the sky!

I pull my chest from the ice, feeling a sharp pain as the beams play over it. My wound is bright red, open and bleeding. I see its steam and feel its heat, a profound odor rising from my deepest part. You sigh and tremble, celebrating the letting. The scent fires the pack. Behind, the Lead bounds along the blue wall, his sulphur eyes glowing.

The passage dips. I spring down a ramp, wanting you near.

You're shaking the walls, throbbing with feeling, dark pits yawn-
ing, skylights opening while the wolves bay and yap, following
fast. What separates us? Nothing, great god. Nothing at all!
Another aisle angles to the left. I leap into it, vaulting a rift, rime
scales grooming my flanks. Will you give me your power? Let me
grow with your quakes? The high lancets shudder—giant icicles
fall, plunging through the floor like spears while your roar fills
and empties me. You're trying to decide. An aisle shrieks open to
the right, gates of glass swinging. What will I give? You want to
know.

Everything? I hurtle through the havoc, pulse booming in the
catacombs. Everything? Sections of vault fall, bursting against
the walls. Everything? White silks shear, opening fathomless
bays, midnight blue. You must give everything—that is the cov-
enant. Cold death surrounds me. The Lead turns the corner, the
pack's at my rear, kicking up snow. Dear god, what does every-
thing mean?

Animus hurls me through a curtain of ice into a hidden
sacrum, his triumph mounting in my ears. The enclosing walls
are puzzles of broken panels, flexing hypnotically. Clerestories
open, eyeless sockets with rivers of snow pouring down. Look
where you are! I give myself over, he takes my legs. Nothing is
solid—the sacrum bends, a thousand ribs flashing. Overhead, a
blue river with silver rungs glides, and the clouds' shadowed
bars bring the corridor to life. Everything flows to him and
through him, like blood from my furious heart. My precious
blood, my life— I can't. I can't!

The flux halts abruptly, walls shriek loose, and with a wave
of freezing air the roof descends. Animus withdraws, heedless,

uncaring as jagged blue panes and pieces of arch crash around me. *You're dead. You're frozen. You're not the one.* I shrink under a shelf, chill invading me, collapse clogging the sacrum, imprisoning me while Animus sulks at a distance.

The havoc abates. The god calms himself, his disappointment betrayed by stray jolts. Between the rumbles, I hear a grinding—the fevered snuffling of the Lead where my heart's blood splashed. Plaintive squeals from the Younger, hoarse pants from the Ruff. The pack is digging through the blockage to finish me. I turn in the cramped space, heart racing. The loosened ice moves and paws appear, scrabbling. Then the black face of the Lead punches through, sulphur eyes feasting on the blood streaming down my front. *Animus, please!*

The god returns grudgingly, fretful, making the chamber hum. The Wise's ears perk, she glances behind. The Lead moves closer, muzzle wrinkling. *Animus! Everything. I understand. You waver, doubting. Your power hedges, then enters me tentatively. I'm flesh, I'm despair. I remember. The scaffold of snow— I'm nothing without you. My blood, it's yours, every drop.* You quake inside me, hearing my plea. The Wise yowls. The Lead sidles, brow furrowed. The Dangler retreats, barking with alarm.

I move my hooves and the pack cringes back. *I can, I will.* Your tremors mount. *I'll leave this world, for you. At the summit, not here in this maze. Embrace me there. Let me escape.* You shake wildly, within me and without, jubilant, crazed! *Everything, I swear!* Great booms, and you're roaring back into my heart. Quivering, I step through the pack. The Wise stands rigid, sensing my possession. The Scout cringes, unwilling to let me come too close.

I leap into the corridor, Animus heaving within me as I bound through it. I must find a way out. Find? Animus roars. Gods don't find. My heart responds, unafraid, speaking with a voice like his own. Change the maze! Lift me out!

An enormous rending, the wall jolts on my left, sheets of rime sliding as it keels back! A blue vee is opening, wolf breath behind me, long tongues in panting throats. I spring into the ravine as it tears, pummeling chips and loose powder, sun and blue sky pouring over me. The ice lips part like casement doors and I burst into a blast of chill wind, blinded by glare. Behind me, the pack bounds one after another from the gap. I cock my hocks, but the snow bucks wildly, wrenching my spine and hurling me down. The wolves wheel quickly around me. My god, what are you doing?

The Lead's fangs rake my ham. The Scout nips my front. I jerk and writhe, infused with your quakes, trying to get my legs beneath me, jaws inches away. But they don't close. You won't let them. I rear now, confident. See me, my god? Fores shaking, head snapping on my neck, hinds trembling holes in the snow, not fighting or fearing.

Panicked yelps from the ravine. The Dangler has lagged. She appears in the gap now as the gleaming doors slam. A scream of agony, lost amid the grinding, returning as a groan. The pack whirls to see her crawling toward them, features twisted, spine broken. A violent jolt—I'm thrown to the snow and the shaking ceases.

The Dangler whimpers. The Ruff steps toward her. The others stand off, listening to Animus rumble. The Lead turns to the

Wise for guidance. She dips to gnaw a splash of my blood from the snow, murmuring beneath her breath at him.

I dig in my hooves and rise, beads of ice stuck to my wound. The Dangler relaxes abruptly—dead. Animus is done with her, and so am I. The Lead noses the Wise, lapping my blood from her lips, nostrils flaring. The Younger whines excitedly, smelling the game. Their lust is returning. I back through the snow, feeling you in my hooves. The Dangler, no higher. But the others must come.

The Ruff grunts, questioning the Lead, ready to abandon the pursuit. The Wise grumbles at the Dangler, calling her death just, wowing at the others, challenging them to continue. She swings her head past me, points her muzzle at the heights, and starts off at a trot. The Lead eyes me hungrily, licks his jowls and stirs himself after her, moving toward the next stage in the rite. The Younger follows quickly. Then the Ruff, obliging as always. And at the rear, the Scout, frozen and shivering, but coming along.

I pivot, feeling light-headed and bleary. The summit. How much blood have I lost? How much more can I lose? Everything. I know. To the left, the pack raises a wake of loose powder. I tighten my haunches, the urge to leap gathering in my hocks. My hinds fire, sending me forward, my heart crying "higher." Beneath me, Animus barely tickles my hooves, his attention ahead.

The weekend on the Cheshnina was more harmonious than Lindy would ever have imagined. After reading the manuscript passage, she coaxed Ransom to bed. They fell asleep on the small mattress, limbs tangled, hugging each other close. The next day, she forced him on an aimless walk along the river, and she made currant tarts with the berries they gathered. Gradually, the ram and the wolves and the wild god Animus retreated from Ransom's thoughts.

Doug returned in the late afternoon. He was surprised to find a lucid and attentive Ransom waiting with Lindy by the strip, and overjoyed when Ransom asked to be flown out. They returned to the lake, and on Monday and Tuesday Ransom and Lindy lazed, strolling the shore and floating in a borrowed dinghy with a lightness they hadn't felt for a long while. People responded to Lindy's calls, Ida proposed bringing them together, and it turned into a party to celebrate the completion of Ransom's manuscript.

On Wednesday evening, the drive of the Hurley house was lined with cars. Inside, a crowd was gathered in the living room, festive and chattering. A number of locals showed up at Ida's invitation to meet Ransom and see what the stir was about. Those who knew him were more subdued, some willing to share Lindy's optimism, others nervous about what they'd heard. Katherine Getz and Hank Papadakis stood listening to Wasilla Bill.

"That's how it was back then," Bill nodded.

Vince Silvano loomed up behind Hank. "Till the fruits and nuts arrived." His speech was slurred, and he swung toward Katherine as he spoke, eyeing her narrowly.

Katherine looked away. The Fish and Game officer was drunk.

"Easy," Bill laughed at Vince. "You're making a bad impression." Too late he saw Hank's warning look.

"She figured out I was a Neanderthal," Vince grumbled, "during the seance."

"Seance?" Katherine faced him.

Vince smirked. "You don't buy that horseshit, do you?"

Katherine glanced at Hank and pardoned herself, working her way through the crowd into the dining room. Platters loaded with food circled the dining room table. Lindy stood beside Ransom, her arm linked to his, smile a bit forced, but radiant withal.

Ransom wore jeans and a tee shirt and was clean-shaven and freshly groomed. The seams and scores in his face had disappeared, and the cut left by the headband was hidden beneath a flesh-colored bandage. Initially distant, he'd quickly warmed to the gathering and was talking to Calvin now, smiling, his expression wistful.

"So it's finally done," Calvin said, relief showing in his eyes.

Ransom nodded. "Not quite."

Lindy noticed Katherine halt a couple of yards from them. The professor fluffed her brown curls and stood there by herself, watching Ransom. Her short red skirt showed off her trim frame, and her low-cut blouse revealed the tops of her breasts. She looked discomfited and self-conscious, and when she realized Lindy was staring at her, she wrapped her arms about her middle.

Ida made her way among the guests carrying a slab cake, and set it down in the center of the dining room table. The cake was covered with powdered sugar and *Wild Animus* was written in red script across it. Ida turned at the compliments, sharing her new grace and dignity, showing them a woman whom love hadn't abandoned with age. She stepped beside Doug with a girlish grin. Doug's hand slid behind her and she gave him a scolding look. "You're like an eighteen-year-old." Then, tenderly, "I pray it will last."

He kissed her on the lips.

As they parted, Ida caught Lindy's glance. The women traded purposeful looks, then Ida put her hands on her hips and called for the group's attention. People moved from the living room, crowding into the small space.

"Something special has happened here," Ida told them. Her gaze took in her home and her life. "It couldn't have happened without you." She turned to Ransom.

He flushed.

"Those of you who know Ransom understand what I mean." She lifted the manuscript, raising her brows at its weighty matter. "Those who don't, I want you to hear the message from his own lips."

Ransom gave Lindy a bewildered look. Her smile betrayed her complicity.

"Will you tell them about yourself and *Wild Animus*?" Ida asked.

He took a breath and gazed at the curious faces. Then he looked down, bashful, collecting his thoughts. Doug watched him, nervous but hopeful. When Ransom lifted his face, it was creased with intensity. His hands trembled. For a moment, it looked like he might bolt, then he cleared his throat, closed his eyes and began to chant.

> *Shrinking loose, the walls.*
> *The roof falls.*
> *Animus withdraws.*
>
> *You're dead, you're done.*
> *You're not the one.*
> *Digging paws.*

Even those who'd heard him before were taken by surprise. His voice was choked. His arms twitched to either side while his legs remained rigid. His features were so strained and his movements so arrhythmic, it was painful to watch. The gathering became instantly uncomfortable. Lindy's spirits sank, and she forced a smile to hide her fear. Ida was transfixed, frowning as Ransom's movements grew more erratic. It was like witnessing a seizure. Doug looked ill. Skimmer slid through the crowd and knelt by Ransom's feet.

> *Through the lurching aisle.*
> *To find the hatch, my trial.*
> *Never doubt.*
>
> *A roar divine.*
> *Gods don't find.*
> *Lift me out!*

Ransom's frame jerked to the breaking point, and then the struggle was suddenly over. Whatever warred within him was overcome like an obstacle damming a river. His movements became fluid, his words deeply felt and personal, rolling with a steady pulse. Hank smiled, relieved. Wasilla Bill closed his eyes. Katherine still held herself stiffly, but her eyes grew misty, as if she could see his spirit soaring and longed to go with him. Lindy's distress only increased. The ram was alive again.

"He's going to be alright," Ida whispered.

Doug saw the love in her smile. He was doubtful, but he'd seen Ransom at his worst. Maybe she knew better.

Skimmer was swaying, his hand on the Jumar rope around his thigh, fingers stroking the feathers knotted in it.

"What's with the kid?" someone muttered to Vince.

"Been like that since he fell in the crevasse."

> *In the open,*
> *Blast of chill air.*
> *Dunes shaking, blinded by glare.*
>
> *Behind me, the pack bounds*
> *Through the breach.*
>
> *Cocking my hocks,*
> *Jolts hurl me down.*
> *Wolves wheeling around.*

Ransom pitched himself into the finale, then his voice cut off, his body went slack, and the energy drained out of him. After a moment, he opened his eyes. He raised his head and looked around the room, regarding the silent faces with a puzzled expression. Some were impressed, others unsettled. All were relieved it was over, even those who were caught up, as if a disease had passed among them without claiming anyone.

Ida started to applaud. "Extraordinary," she said. "Isn't he?"

Doug joined in. Then Hank and others followed suit.

"He's found a precious truth," Katherine muttered to Calvin.

"From what Doug says," Calvin replied, "he's paying a heavy price for it."

Skimmer stood, eyeing Ransom knowingly. "It's better with the headdress."

The locals were mumbling, guessing what it meant.

Ida reached Lindy and hugged her. "He's wonderful."

"Wonderful," Lindy echoed, glancing at Ransom. "Wasn't that great, Bill?"

Wasilla Bill nodded. "Write that one in the cabin?" He put his arm around Ransom's shoulders.

Ransom smiled.

People were milling, talking again, getting drinks. Doug emerged from the kitchen with a pair of large platters. "Give me a hand with this," he motioned to Wasilla Bill.

"Come on," Bill urged Ransom, and they followed Doug through the living room and out the front door.

Salmon steaks were cooking over a pit fire. Doug and Bill peeled them off with grill forks. Beyond, the lake was sinuous, waves crawling its surface like silver eels.

"My how things change," Bill laughed. "I'm the only one here who isn't drinking."

Doug was silent.

"Credit goes to you," Bill nodded to Ransom. "I wouldn't let her go. You made me understand that."

Ransom frowned, uncomfortable with Bill's solicitude. Doug was staring at him with a look that said, *See the power you have.* Then he turned and carried the steaks inside.

Bill faced him, the pit fire flickering in his eyes. "I didn't know where she came from." He fingered the glove folded over his belt. "I didn't think she had anywhere to return to." He removed the glove with a sigh. "I thought if I let go of her, she'd be gone forever."

Ransom watched him eye the glove adoringly.

"All that sweetness—" Bill was having trouble speaking. "I couldn't keep it alive, no matter how much I drank." A tear started down his weathered cheek. "I didn't need to. It has its own life, its own home, its own source." His eyes seemed to clear. He gave the glove a dubious look and dropped it onto the coals. As the flames flared around it, he leaned close and rubbed his stubble against Ransom's cheek.

Ransom put his arm about the older man.

"How are things out at the cabin?" Bill asked. "Taking care of yourself?" His eyes were tender as a child's.

Ransom felt Bill's love for his wife flowing through him. He laughed softly. There was collusion here, but it was so caring, he couldn't object.

"How old are you, Ransom?"

"Twenty-four."

"Life's a long road," Bill said. "I don't want to lose you."

Ransom nodded.

As they stepped back into the dining room, Lindy was waiting for him. She looked desperate.

"—like they say. The loons love it here." A man with no chin turned, his eyes rolling.

A hush fell over the gathering.

"What's wrong?" Ransom murmured.

Lindy smiled and shook her head. He could see the descending spiral in her eyes.

As if to correct the chinless man's slight, Katherine stepped forward. "Thank you," she said to Ransom. "Since that day we heard your ideas in the guest house, my life's changed." She laughed. "It's a mess now— Do you think something good will come of that?" Her tone was confiding, but the whole room was listening. "This grief—" The admission blackened her smile. "It's in the open now. My skin is gone. I'm raw. Things reach me. I'm happy sometimes, but it's terrible too. I'm so vulnerable. Every word, every sight and sound goes flying through me." She raised her hand to her left breast. It was instinctive, a shielding motion, but as Ransom watched, she succumbed to a deeper instinct, reaching out to stroke his cheek. "I'm afraid I'm in love with you."

Ransom froze. Calvin's jaw dropped. Lindy reached out as if the ground was shifting beneath her. The crowd was speechless.

"A toast," Ida said, waving her glass at Doug with a panicked look.

Doug raised his to Ransom. "For putting the fever back in our hearts."

"It's contagious as the clap," Vince said sourly.

A few laughs surfaced, but most were mortified. Katherine turned crimson and the drink slipped from her hand, shattering on the floor.

Ransom faced Vince. "Why did you say that?"

Vince gave him a scathing look. "Once in a while wolves pass by Chitina," he observed wryly. "Night falls and the pack starts howling,

284

and every terrier and spaniel in town jumps to the door, yapping and yowling."

Out of the corner of his eye, Ransom caught Lindy's flinch. He turned to face her and saw all of the group's pity and repulsion reflected in her eyes. Her cheer was a facade covering shame and remorse. She no longer understood him. For her, his sacrifice was a misguided fantasy.

He glanced at the cake, then gazed around the room, seeing the party's real purpose. Lindy was trying to dissuade him from his goal by pretending he had already achieved it. They humored him for her sake. They were wretched creatures, hopelessly frozen. What was he doing here? It was a gathering of ghosts. He turned, stepped through the living room and out the door.

Lindy hurried after him with Hank at her heels. They caught up to him halfway to the guest house.

"Come back," she demanded. "You have to come back." Fear made her strident.

"What are you doing?" Hank moved in front of him.

"The party's over," Ransom said.

"She did this for you," Hank protested. "Everyone's gone to a lot of effort—"

"What business is it of yours?"

"There's someone in Anchorage who can help find you a publisher. He'll be here," Hank looked at his watch, "any moment." He scowled. "It was supposed to be a surprise."

"Why bother?"

Hank glanced at Lindy. She was mute with chagrin. "What the fuck is wrong with you? You can't change the world by jumping off its edge."

"I'm flying back out, first thing tomorrow." Ransom saw Lindy clutch her pendant as if she meant to tear it loose. It didn't matter. Her love was a way station. "They don't understand," he said.

"When someone spends all his time talking to god," Hank replied, "he can become hard for people to understand."

Ransom seemed to relent. "I'm in a corner, Hank. I've lost touch. No one takes me seriously anymore. I've made a fool of myself."

Hank laughed, kindly and sympathetic. "We all make mistakes. You're too young to—" He saw Ransom snarl and realized too late that he'd fallen into a trap.

"I don't need your pity," Ransom turned on Lindy, "or your shame. I should have known to expect this." He continued along the path.

Lindy hurried after him, breaking down, sobbing hysterically. "I'm sorry— It's true— I just wanted to— Please, please—" She grabbed his shirtfront, hanging her weight on his chest. He kept moving, dragging her with him. "Please. Please—"

Hank watched them struggle along the path, baffled by their perverse interaction. It was beyond his understanding. Ransom was too self-absorbed to realize what was happening. Only Lindy, through her hysteria, had the vaguest inkling. In her effort to protect him, she had again drawn off Ransom's doubt. Weeping and convulsing like someone who'd swallowed poison, she freed him to continue with purity of purpose and an undivided heart. Perhaps he used her instinctively, or perhaps there was a wisdom in her that offered herself for that end.

The poplars clapped in the breeze. The fireweed verging the lake was smoking with seed. A shorebird followed the water's edge, but no matter how he cut and zagged, his shadow stayed right behind him.

Thirteen

arly the next morning, Doug flew the two of them to the Cheshnina, Ransom first. During the turn-around, Ransom gathered his equipment and provisions, and when the Cub descended toward the strip with Lindy, he stood waiting beside two large packs. The headdress surmounted one of them, horns coiling to either side.

The plane taxied to a halt. Doug killed the prop, popped the clamshell doors and climbed out. "What's this?" he nodded at the packs as he helped Lindy down.

Ransom didn't answer.

Lindy looked bleak. She steadied herself on Doug's arm and smiled her thanks, venturing a glance at Ransom. He was contained for Doug's benefit, but she could see the excitement in his eyes. "He's taking me to the top," she said softly.

Doug looked from her to Ransom. "You're not serious."

She stepped toward Ransom and put her arm through his. Ransom made an impatient face.

"When's the pickup?" Doug was disbelieving.

"Check back in a week," Ransom said.

Doug saw the dread in Lindy's eyes and his ire rose. "Toss your life away," he told Ransom. "But don't do this to her."

Lindy gazed to the east. The overcast was brightening, and she seemed to find something cheerful in that. Ransom stared at Doug without responding.

"I'm sorry I encouraged you," Doug said. "You don't belong out here."

"Your job's done," Ransom told him.

Doug shook his head and grabbed Lindy's arm. "She's coming back with me."

Ransom slid the willow knife from his parka. The short blade, now nicked and scarred, flashed as he raised it beneath Doug's chin. "Let go."

Doug glanced at Lindy with masterly calm. He could manage this.

Lindy put her cheek to Ransom's chest. "You'd better leave," she told Doug.

Ransom turned. "Come on." He lifted Lindy's backpack so she could slide her arms through the straps. Then he shouldered his own, and the two of them started through the brush.

They reached the heights of the greenstone stream by nightfall and crossed the saddle the next morning. The land tended up over rolling tundra, across inclines of broken rock, building toward the dome. The loads were heavy and they spoke only at intervals. By midday, Lindy's cheer was forced. The closer they got to Mt. Wrangell, the more its dazzling bulk threatened her. She was relieved when clouds obscured it. They moved onto a moraine beside the glacier. Not long after, the sky grew murky.

Ransom stopped and set his pack down. The moraine was smudged by darkness, only the swathes of snow were sharply defined.

Veils of mist slipped off the glacier, gliding toward them. "We'll camp here," Ransom said. Then he tipped his head back, closed his eyes and moaned like a wolf.

Lindy shrugged her pack off, relieved that the day's trek was over. Ransom unlashed the headdress, carried it a dozen feet and set it down facing the decline. Then he hunched and opened his parka. He flinched and she saw his hand emerge, cupped before him, ladling blood from his wound onto the rock around the headdress. Lindy's lips parted, her eyes dark, realizing how little she knew of the life Ransom had been leading on the dome.

He rose and came toward her. "Let's set up the tent."

When the tent was pitched and their sleeping bags unrolled, he howled again. And again before they began to eat. It was only a few minutes later that he grew still, his gaze fixed on something down the slope.

At first Lindy saw nothing. She was about to speak when her eye caught a movement. An animal was approaching, large as she, with long quick legs and a pointed face, its tail sweeping behind. "My god," she whispered.

"Sh-sh-sh."

The lithe form drew nearer, winding silently among the rocks. It stopped beside the headdress. The barest snuffle reached them, then its muzzle dipped and the wolf was lapping. Lindy glanced at Ransom with horror. He pointed to left and right at the others circling their camp. The pack. The dimness hid their identities. They were silhouettes except for the animal by the headdress. As it raised its muzzle, Lindy could see its black face and sulphur eyes.

"Can you make them leave?" she wondered.

"Nothing's going to happen tonight."

And nothing did happen. The air grew darker and the mist thickened, and the wolves vanished. Sleep didn't come easily to Lindy, but when it did, it was long and deep. The following morning was a beautiful one, and the dome was in all its glory. They started up it.

Two days later, they were approaching 13,000 feet. The surface was finally firm enough to shed their snowshoes and they walked in close file, Lindy behind Ransom, following in his bootsteps, unroped.

He stopped, planted his ice axe and gazed up. She drew beside him, nose burnt, eyes watering beneath her glare glasses. They were both breathing deeply.

"This is the spot." He glanced back. The line of their ascent was scribed down the glacier. Sprays of cracks crossed their path, the checked ice of the labyrinth just below.

"Unbelievable," Lindy murmured. The image of Mt. Wrangell had lived inside her for a long while. Hour by hour, ascending beneath a bright sun and blue sky, her fears had subsided. Now, as she scanned the heights of the dome, she saw the temple Ransom had described, wild and inspiring in a way that man's works would never be. She kissed his cheek.

"You see," he smiled. "We made it here together." He took her pendant and raised it to his lips.

"Ransom—" Her voice was choked. The truth was so fearful, it was hard to speak. "My heart is still yours." She lifted her glasses. "If this day was my last, it would be the life I'd choose."

He kissed her tenderly and lowered his pack. He removed the headdress and set it before him, then took out his regalia, arranging each item on the snow.

Lindy knew what to expect, but despite her agreement with him, she felt a moment of panic when the willow knife and the blue jar emerged.

"Animus is waiting," Ransom said.

He removed his outer garments and pulled the furs over his long underwear. Then he secured the knife to his forearm and slid on the sheep cuffs. "Here." He handed Lindy the headdress and flexed his knees. She lifted it by its horns.

"Golden eyes, know," he pronounced. "Golden horns, grow."

As it settled on his head, there was a crump. Lindy sank and cried out, and Ransom turned to see her knee-deep in sintered ice, suspended over the remains of a snow bridge. He grabbed her and wrenched her toward him, landing in a drift with her shuddering in his arms.

"It's nothing," he muttered. But as he stood, he wondered. Clouds were forming around the summit, veiling the sanctum. He drove the shank of his axe into the ice and clipped it to his pack. "We'll leave the packs here."

Lindy watched him anchor hers in the same way, grateful she wouldn't have to carry it, but conscious of the danger. They would be without a stove or food, without tent and sleeping bags.

Ransom wanded the spot, then retrieved the blue jar, opened it and spilled two quarter tabs into his palm. "Together," he said. He swallowed one and handed her the other.

Lindy took a breath and tried to smile. It had been a long time since she'd done this with him. "Together." She put the tab on her tongue.

It took them an hour to gain five hundred feet elevation. Despite his furs and headdress, and the mounting effects of the drug, Ransom maintained a steady pace. Lindy struggled to keep up, hyperventilating in the thin air, the acid scattering her thoughts. The glare was intense, and the midday heat seemed to pull at her, urging her to abandon her legs. She fought the temptation, and then succumbed, letting herself be borne aloft. When she returned, her sluggish body was still putting one foot ahead of the other, filling her with dismay that she should be burdened by it.

The slope beveled over and Ransom halted, pointing.

Ahead, a thicket of ice spires rose through the heat haze. Looking freshly cleaved and gleaming with turquoise bands, they were crowded within a giant rip, like gothic towers shepherded toward heaven by the converging white walls.

> *You rumble, you rise.*
> *Your deep voice calls and I hear.*
> *Wolves stopped, facing this shrine,*
> *While you shake, pushing me clear.*

Ransom assumed his ram stoop, knees flexed, and at the phrase "pushing me clear," he staggered to the side as if something had struck him. His features were masked by the headdress, but his quavering voice revealed his state. He started toward the shrine in a spastic crouch. Lindy moved alongside, watching, feeling the distance between them.

> *Up a funnel I spring,*
> *Dimpled walls buzzing like hives.*
> *A dream of sweetness. Your longing—*
> *What happens when the ram arrives?*

He was gasping as he sang. The ropy locks jounced on his back. Suddenly the air around them seemed charged with filaments of light, as if a current had been set loose from the sun. The spires rose from the drifts like icebergs surfacing from a milky sea. They were covered with hieroglyphs, a myriad ridges and dimples in the same script—an ancient ritual recorded in the secret language of the dome. She felt the magic powerfully, what dazzled Ransom and drew him, and made him mad to be a ram.

They entered the shrine. It was like no place she had ever seen. Around the top of the rip, white vapors twisted. She gazed up the tapering channel, feeling her body borne along by Ransom's chant, his rhetoric echoing through her mind. *A great mystery beyond a region of danger. Fear spurred me on when desire could not.* They were her torments, as well as his. And they were her rewards now that she had braved the dome.

She saw him through the heat haze, bucking and shaking, jagged pinnacles framing his crazy dance. He was as she imagined when she first met him—the one who would spirit her away. But not in human form. Even as she watched, his arms thinned and whitened, descending to the snow. His back assumed the horizontal, his mimicked leaping suddenly real. He sprang between these towers leaning against the sky, a beast with golden horns, a white ram with a bleeding wound. A moment of horror—she was losing her sanity. Then he turned and fathomed her with his golden eyes, and she surrendered and passed into his madness with him.

Her real love. Here in the shelter of mystical spires, under these graven rafters, between these weaving shapes, in this secret shrine of white snow and sun, blue ice and sky, they would be joined. He would know her and she would know him. She would cast off her struggle with Ransom and marry the ram.

At the top of the shrine, where the walls came together, was a place specially consecrated, fringed and dripping to receive them. An altar where she would offer herself in some violent ceremony. She could feel the desire for it growling inside her, imagine its wild rhythm raging, hooves pounding her chest, his muscled trunk writhing as she clawed his white fur.

In the midst of this abandon, something stopped her. She sensed a greater will, frightening in its profligacy. The shattered spires were the ruined playthings of a god. The ram sprang into view against the shrine, with the fumaroles twisting from his head, and in an instant she understood his quest for Animus. It was the god inside Ransom that the ram was seeking on this island in the sky. Not some foreign or distant deity, but Ransom's essence, that which was most sacred in him and which she most treasured. She had always loved Animus. It was to him she was being conducted, to him she would offer herself.

Feverish, imagining her submission in a bath of heat, she closed her eyes as Ransom had instructed, and the sun blazed red through her lids. It was a canyon of blood opening in Ransom's chest. Fear tried to freeze her, but she was heedless, charging toward him, imagining the molten god rising from the wound to meet her.

———•———

I hear padding behind me, paws kissing the snow. I scan the pylons. Shadows shift in the blue niches, then the Wise leaps through a gap and lands on the drifts below. The Lead follows, charging after her, then the others. Their ministry seems needless. Desire drives me now, not fear. And to remind me, Animus, you have split the cloud blanket and scrolled it aside, opening a portal to the past. I see the thread of my trail entering the labyrinth, crossing the court of fountains, down the wandering nave of the glacier, winding invisibly through rocky peaks and disappearing in the rolling lowlands where I first felt your fire.

You drew me, under your power and protection, through the tabernacles along that hidden path. Now I stand here, so high, so close, turning my amulet to this pane of ice, its annealed ciphers glittering in the sun. The promise of my heart sings to you. Listen—I'm pressing it to your ear, offering myself—

You rumble! You rise! My god, my joy. My beginning and end. Your deep voice calls, and I hear. The high sanctum—it's all I live for. So insistent! I'm nearly there. And the pack? Stopped in their tracks, listening, the Wise watching my chest where it touches the ice, knowing what's to come. The Lead nuzzles her for assurance, the Scout cowers. You shake impatiently, pushing me clear.

Up a funnel I spring, driving into dry powder, icicles raining from the pylons on either side. The dimpled walls jitter like buzzing hives, a myriad reflectors holding the sun's honeyed image—a dream of sweetness in mosaic eyes. More than your power, I feel your expectancy. I'm so close— But what could a mortal know or suspect? You are the father of longing. Longing itself.

Ahead, a shaking tower creaks and tilts, landing with a crash, raising a swirling cloud. I spring through it as another spire sways and swoons, shearing one near it like crossed swords. Your quaking mounts, tassels of ice dust pulsing from the pinnacles, icicle combs shattering like silver chimes. You make a way for me and I follow, leaping into the wreckage, breathing minced crystal. More, more! Judder my limbs, jar my bones! The air hisses with chips, spans of blue ice bounding down, scarred with your shock marks, crashing and shivering apart, echoes booming up and down the shrine.

The wolves' frosted backs zag among the breakings. I lunge at a cornice, horns smashing through, and a fierce jolt scatters the fragments around them. The Scout jerks to a halt. The Younger whimpers, her spirit gone. The Lead looks up. When I prance like this, do your juices stir? His sulphur eyes flare—to him, I'm still mutton.

I wheel and leap for the shrine's height, where the loving heat coils. The quakes redouble and I hear your voice, uncertain, tentative—not through caverns and chasms, but directly ahead! Down the steep incline streams are flowing, hot springs released like overturned vats, hissing, turning the ice to slush. It's you, seething up out of the abyss! You're melting the shrine, drawing hot knives along the base of the spires. Cascades dash through a gap above and swirl past.

You savor my surprise, then your quake renews and more gushets descend. I leap onto a jetty of ice, over broken planks, a steeple canted and swiveling. The pack traverses higher up, avoiding the melt. Your cock's tails scald my legs. I hear you hissing, feel you tonguing into me as I leap, dissolving me like the banks of ice. My god, how you gush! Where is your scorn, your proud reserve? Your love is a torrent, unthinking, unreined.

The chain unlinks. I'm near the shrine's top, reeling through a pool and vaulting up, blue ice slick to my hooves, breathless, weightless, my insides hollowing. The dome is convulsing, roaring at the sky. Where the shrine walls converge, a giant cake of ice perches, layered with blue and white. Around it, steam jets wriggle in time to the quakes. The pack is still with me, crossing the snows, headed for the base of the cake.

I spring forward, driving deep in the mash, the fumes from the heat holes gusting over me. Beneath the ice, the sun catches red in their depths, wraiths twisting in caves of dried blood. A god's desire, perceived by a mortal—caustic and sickening, heedless of life.

Shocks close by. The shrine walls are tearing. The apex cake shudders and pulls away. I vault headlong and hurtle the gap, ice screeching beneath me, eyes lacquered with white flame. Animus jolts madly, tilting the cake, pitching me down it. My hooves swipe the powder, scrabbling then catching at the very edge. My god dances me on the brink, dark and abandoning, teasing himself with my fate.

Below, the wolves approach the cake, Lead pulling hard, Scout puzzling the way up, the Wise wondering at my precarious stance.

Animus heaves me onto my hinds. I whirl for balance, seeing white waves sweeping the dome's flanks. Slopes are exploding, rent by blue lightning and sliding, clouds billowing above. Dark peaks spew rock across the glaciers, rivers jittering like shook threads, every leaf, every reed, every pebble joining the chorus, celebrating my ascent. These are a god's movements—I've lost control. This is you inside me, twisting my limbs, making me jerk and writhe! Your rage is mine. I am the wild god Animus—I create and destroy. My cannonades turn the tabernacles to smoke. Child of my heart, I'm casting them down, dashing the intricate stage to powder, obliterating the return. Animus surrenders everything to the ram.

Below, the wolves bunch at the prow of the cake. The Younger is panicked and so is the Scout. The Wise fixes on me, entreating.

Animus roars, insensate, and the jolts intensify, avalanche breakers crashing into each other, forming giant white rotors, the dome and the world around it dissolving, disappearing in the smoke. I feel a surging within me, outward and upward, pressure building in my head. A great bell curves over me, the sun swinging across it, a golden clapper jarring the blue, the echoing sky quivering to receive me.

The wild god catches himself. The cake cracks.

I hurl myself back. A giant slab keels out, descending on the wolves. Cries—they're crushed, two leaping clear. Cruelty, contempt? A god's indifference? I understand. They're no longer needed. Only the Lead remains, still hungering, and the Wise, who knew this would be their fate.

The cake wobbles beneath me. This isn't the end. I turn and spring, breathing white smoke and fighting the wind, vaulting to the edge and over the gap. Landing on the summit snows, I kick into a lope, crazy to reach you.

———◆———

Inexhaustible.
Vaulting— You rage— Slope's blurred—
Above, the blue canopy rocks.
Below—

Something grappled Ransom's back. At first he thought it was the wind, but when he turned, he saw Lindy, her features frosted, shouting to be heard over the moan. All that reached him was "storm." He drew himself out of his trance enough to absorb the situation. The glint of Animus was still in her eyes, but her mind was clouded with confusion. The way forward was dim and without relief, gray granite flecked white. Ice prickled his chin beneath the facepiece of the headdress.

"Just a little snow," he said, starting forward again.

Lindy hooked his arm and pulled him around. The wind grew

stronger, weighing over them with a steady drone.

"Tired?" he shouted.

She regarded him numbly. "Why is he doing this?" Her eyes were fearful, immersed in his vision of Animus, but on the verge of abandoning it.

"The crater." Ransom motioned into the blast. "We're not far." He was as surprised by this turn as she, but he was committed.

Lindy shook her head. "It's getting worse."

He saw the fear in her eyes. "Don't worry," he shouted, grabbing her parka. He pulled her forward and she didn't resist.

The blast dwindled and they moved a few steps. Then Lindy came to a stiff halt. "No," she shook her head angrily.

The wind returned, lurching around them.

"Please," Ransom glanced at the glove clenching his arm. "Let go." Through the eye screens, he could see she was already out of reach, plummeting from the current of faith that molten hearts know.

"Our packs," she insisted. "The sleeping bags are in them. The tent. The stove and food. We don't have any way to protect ourselves. I'll freeze if I get any colder."

"We're headed toward the heat," Ransom smiled. "This won't last long." The image of the glowing god was still with her, and he could see her waver as he spoke. Then her eyes grew hard, the corner of her mouth snagged, and she turned away.

The blast beat alternately weak and strong, threshing the air. Ransom imagined Animus hovering over him, watching.

"It's a test," he said. "He's showing us his violence to see if we have the courage to continue. That's his way."

"If we continue," Lindy was emphatic, "we're going to die."

"That's our weakness," he begged her to understand. "He has so little cause to believe in us. But he wants to."

Lindy's eyes grew wide, recognizing what he was prepared to do.

"It's nothing," Ransom said, glancing into the blast. "If we turn back—" He realized she couldn't see his face. His headdress must look frightful. He touched the ropy cheek. It was lumpy and slick with rime. Animus was roaring. The window to his own fear opened inside him. How long would the god let him coddle doubt so close to his throne? Had Animus already turned against him? Ransom had entered a sacred world, woven with interdictions. He imagined himself tangled there, far from the world of man, unable to persuade Animus of his devotion and unable to find his way back.

Lindy grabbed a horn tip and shook it. "Take that thing off."

He unfastened the headdress with her help. As he lifted it, the wind swooped powerfully. It had been approaching, and now it had arrived.

She kissed him with marble lips. "What are we going to do?" Her eyes were desperate.

His sigh was like a sob. The dream, his triumph—it was all dissolving.

"I wish we weren't high," she said.

He regarded her sorrowfully, cradling the headdress in his arms, gave her a look that begged forgiveness, and began to chant.

> *Will you show yourself—*

"No," she moaned.

He hurried his words, fear whispering half-thoughts in his ears.

> *My weakness— You tire.*
> *Impatient, galled—*

"You can't do this!" she screamed. Her eyes flared like a wounded beast and she threw herself at him, flailing his face and chest until he stopped.

He embraced her, feeling the wolves in his arms, all seven of them. It was the Dangler who'd screamed. The Ruff was ready to retreat, with the Younger beside him, whimpering and scared. The Scout measured the cold, gauging how far they could travel before they froze. The Wise was quiet, eyes to the ground, knowing they wouldn't listen. And the Lead just watched uncertainly, abnegating command to his squint-eyed mate. Ransom peered at the Hangbelly.

"Those ruled by fear can never surrender," he said. "Who are you?" He tried to face her into the blast. "Animus wants to know."

She pulled away, enraged that her destruction mattered so little to him, his piety making her hateful. A sneer broke the frost on her cheeks, dismissing everything but the insentient mountain and the freezing storm.

"There is no Animus," she said.

The drone swelled powerfully, diving toward them out of the sky. Vicious snaps exploded against Ransom's front, the wind-stropped cold cutting through cloth and skin. The blast struck Lindy in the face and hurled her aside. He staggered after her, seeing the spicules flack her back, tear her cap off with icy claws and rake her cheeks. Animus was trying to divide them. Ransom clasped his arms around her, sheltering her hunched body with his own while she recovered, heaving to catch her breath. She was a pitiable sight. Her fear pierced him. White snow devils were spinning madly around them. He was shaking with cold. She was right. They wouldn't survive.

Then a strange sound reached him—real or a product of his mind, he couldn't tell. In the drone and whirl he heard the rhythm of his summit chant, as if Animus was singing it back to him. As Lindy straightened beside him, he turned and gazed up the slope. There was a choice. A terrible one, but still a choice. Animus was daring him to abandon her. He stood motionless, facing the storm, wondering which of his loves to cleave to, and in that moment Lindy read his mind.

She clung to him with a heartrending sob.

Ransom held her, kissing her frosted brow, full of sorrow and despair. This was no test. Animus had gone mad and Lindy was paying.

"We need to find the packs," he said, putting his headdress on. She sobbed again, hugging him desperately, and they started back down.

The storm got worse. First it was a windward wall, then a tumbling morass that brawled them this way and that, then lashes cracking over them, whistling insanely. Lindy punched through, sinking to her thighs, and when Ransom pulled her out, the view into that bottomless hole terrified them both. He continued down, muttering to Animus, telling him he hadn't given up. He would return. But the god was all contempt and rage.

Night closed in with the storm beating furiously. Ransom could see fifty feet ahead, sometimes twenty, sometimes not at all. Was the slope steep or shallow? Were they in a trough or on a ridge? He couldn't tell. Even with Lindy a few feet away, there were times he feared he'd lost her. Hours passed. Then he thought he saw the wands. He turned back, shouting. Lindy drifted toward him through the snow, plastered white and breathing hard. By the time they reached the spot, it was roiling with fog. Ransom circled, waving his arms to snag a wand, then gave up and started back to her. Before he could reach her, the wind hooked him.

An invisible clutch crushed the air from his trunk and sent him reeling. He felt a blow on his side, lost his balance and tumbled into a trench. His shoulder dashed against solid ice and the wind came screeching to find him, scraping him along a wall and over an edge. He fell a short distance, landing on his side in soft powder. Squinting and blinking, he got his legs beneath him. Moaning blasts filled the air just above. He was in a crevasse. He could see Lindy clinging to the corner of its mouth, head bowed, shoulders shuddering. He gathered his strength, climbed up to her, circled her with one arm and guided her back down.

It was dim as a cave and freezing cold, but they were out of the storm. He removed his headdress and took a couple of steps, testing the snow. "False floor," he muttered. Pits were visible where it met the crevasse walls. He could see the blue darkness below. Lindy wouldn't look. The storm clawed at the cornices, sending spindrift down. Just the two of them, Ransom thought, suspended over the void.

He crept along the wall, steadying himself with his hand, crusts of ice coming loose. The walls converged, forming a thin pocket, roofed over and protected on three sides. He motioned to Lindy and together they shuffled in.

"Don't sit on the ice." Ransom put his headdress on the floor and seated her on it. Then he crouched down on his boot heels, his breath steaming.

"If we only had one of the sleeping bags," she lamented.

"He'll understand," Ransom murmured, "once he calms down."

Their clothes were soaked with sweat. They started to shiver.

"My feet are numb," she said.

Ransom could feel her anger. In his manuscript, the Wise and the Lead survived, but in the real world, it was the Hangbelly and the Dangler that prevailed. He realized Lindy was abandoning him, and his confidence went. The storm was a test and he'd failed.

"We should have gone on," he said.

"Are you crazy?" Her voice was low and emotionless. "We'd be dead."

"We would have passed through the storm. He was waiting beyond it. To fear is to be cast down, and we've been cast down."

She shook her head, eyes burning with injury.

"Animus cared for you," he said, thinking of the Lead and the Wise.

Night turned their flesh to ice. They couldn't lie down. They took turns rising and tromping around to loosen cramped muscles and move blood into numbed parts.

Three hours after entering the refuge, Ransom was on his feet, clenching his hands before his face, listening to the storm. Everything was oblivion and dimness. The fire in his heart was dying. Did Animus wish him dead, or was he waiting in the storm, ready to lay his fury aside and pour gold from the skies if only his ram would return?

"What are you doing?" Lindy's voice sounded in his ear.

He was at the mouth of the crevasse, gazing blindly out. He regarded her uncertainly.

She led him back to the pocket.

"Ransom—" Her voice was a whisper. They moved slowly, huddled close. "There's no god here." She spoke with compassion, but firmly. "Just the storm and the cold."

He nodded to show he heard her.

"We're human," she said. "The miracle we discovered was a human miracle."

He sensed the jealousy beneath her words.

"Our surrender fed a human joy," Lindy said. "Nourished human lives."

Outside, the storm swelled. Ransom heard Animus protesting.

Lindy saw her words meant nothing to him. They reached the pocket and sat down, and she folded her arms and closed her eyes.

Wisps of steam trailed from her lips and vanished in the dimness. Silence filled the space.

"Don't leave me," Ransom said.

For a long moment, she didn't respond. Then she opened her eyes. They were as cold as the ice. There wasn't anger or despair or regret in them. She was staring at him as if he was a stranger.

Ransom saw her shudder and realized her lips were turning blue. He put his arm around her and drew his face close, searching her. She was sorry, but he was not the man she knew. She was no longer fighting with him, no longer trying to pull him back. She was letting him go.

Panic choked his heart.

Lindy shuddered again, and this time it didn't stop.

"You're freezing," he muttered, embracing her. Heat was flowing out of her, her cold eyes grew colder every moment. Was it really Animus he heard in the storm? The wind droned like an engine, mindless and merciless. He might have imagined it all. "On your feet!" He pulled her up and started stamping. Her legs barely lifted. He was losing her. He pulled off his mitts, using his bare fingers to undo his furs, then wrapped her middle with them. She watched, squinting against the spindrift. Then, in nothing but his long underwear, Ransom turned his back to the storm, using his thin body to shelter her, breathing his warmth into her nose and mouth.

Her decline seemed to abate. After a while she dozed off. Ransom didn't let her sleep long. Fearful she was turning to stone, he forced her up and they tramped the tiny space again and again while the wind droned.

It was the longest night on earth for both of them, but when the darkness finally began to pale, a lull in the fury drew out. The buffets faltered and the violence died into the ice.

Hearing the calm, Ransom stirred himself. He was no longer high. His body shivered uncontrollably and his movements were painfully slow. He left Lindy in the pocket and shifted along the false floor. Through the lips of the crack above, he could see blue sky. The clink of falling icicles presaged a warm dawn. He returned and they clambered out of the rift together. Then, taking the horn of his headdress in one hand and Lindy's sleeve in the other, he started down.

The mists swirled purple and blue over the glacier. Ransom stared at his boots.

"The packs." Lindy pointed.

It was true. Everything they had needed to warm themselves had been a short walk from the crevasse. They retrieved them. Ransom stowed the headdress and they continued down.

The mist dissolved. Beyond the glacier, the Cheshnina spurs came into view. The air grew warmer and the snow softened. Lindy was quiet. Ransom was sunk in defeat. His steps pitted the perfect surface. The crystals cried, the sastrugi hissed. Every voice of the temple rebuffed him as he passed.

"I can't believe it's over," Lindy murmured. She turned to him, relief lighting her face.

Ransom was silent.

"You saved us." Lindy embraced him, kissing his cheek.

He shook his head.

Her heart went out to him. "Remember that afternoon in the garden? We can share that miracle again. We're alive."

He didn't respond.

"Love is a strange thing for us," she muttered. "*Wild Animus* is a true picture of it."

He scanned the lowlands, the distant rivers like aimless scribblings. "I was seeking more."

She regarded him sadly. "Why isn't it enough?"

The question rang inside him. He pondered it while his gaze wandered. "Maybe it was never human love I wanted."

306

Just then, the dawn glowed in the east, washing the glacier with soft pastels, turning everything around them pink and mauve and baby blue. It was a moment of infinite delicacy, and Ransom felt in those colors a presence, generous and understanding. His spirits soared—he felt Animus with all his heart. The god heard his lost child and was whispering to cheer him, loving him still.

As the heat touched his brow, Ransom wheeled with the sun glowing over him, gazing at the great dome. Below its summit, the fumaroles were coiling up. The storm was a test not for Lindy, but for him. Animus knew her fear and called it forth for a reason. Could Ransom let her go? Animus wanted to know. That was the covenant. He would lay bare his power and take Ransom in. Ransom had to give up his humanity, even the one closest to him.

Lindy observed his silent joy with dread. He turned without saying a word, and when he resumed the descent, she avoided his gaze, too weak to challenge him.

By midday they reached the moraine, and as they moved among the scattered boulders, a pipit found them. Within seconds, a small tribe came weaving through the sky. Ever Ransom's friends, they peeped and circled, cheerful and curious, eager to play. But the playing was over.

They made it to the head of the greenstone stream by dusk and slept on the tundra. The next morning, they followed the stream to the Cheshnina, reaching Wasilla Bill's cabin around noon. The poplars had turned gold while they were gone and the leaves hung calmly, waiting for the frost. By the time Ransom had started a fire in the stove and Lindy had prepared a hot meal, a light rain was tapping on the roof. They didn't speak until they'd finished eating.

Lindy steeled herself. "This is it," she said. "I'm not coming back."

Ransom nodded. "You've helped enough." He spoke with the resignation of an older man.

"Helped?"

"Your love led me here."

The thought horrified her.

"It was you who taught me surrender," Ransom said. "No one in the world would have given so much, or come with me so far. But now we're here. I have to cross the threshold on my own."

She regarded him mournfully. "Where's Sam?"

He made a curious face. "Sam doesn't exist." He saw how deeply this was hurting her. "There's another kind of love," he said softly. "To reach it, you have to let go of human love."

She shook her head. "What about the manuscript, the chants?"

"I'll finish them for you. All that remains is the last scene."

"For me? I don't want that. All I care about is us."

"They're meaningless," he agreed darkly. "If you can't understand what I'm doing, who will? It was all just wishful thinking. How I wished it could be. Not how it was."

She frowned.

"What the wolves do for my ram," he explained. "The Lead and the Wise."

She thought she had cried herself dry, but tears came again. He was renouncing everything.

"Lindy," he said gently. "What is this?" His arms spread. "A speck sprayed out of some galaxy. A mote of dust, covered with moss. If a god lives here now, he'll move on. The dome will crumble, and all its bright flowers and struggling creatures—" He regarded her sorrowfully. "Which is more precious, a person's life or his vision? Should we whittle every moment time allows us, learn every dull lesson, jade every sensation? Is coveting and scavenging the way to life's gold? If life's glory rises blinding before me, should I say, 'no, not so soon,' and turn away to hoard sparks and embers till darkness falls?" He reached to caress her forehead and the red star that flamed there. "The solitude you felt in that icy hole? It will come. Sooner than you think. That hour when everyone's a stranger, when there's no Sam or Ransom, and never has been. I can't save you from that. And you can't save me." He smiled at her. "We know each other. Don't we? I will meet my Animus." He glanced at the sheaves of paper and the recorder. "And you will keep that in your heart, because you love me, and because I imagined it was our story."

The drone of the Cub intruded.

It seemed so abrupt. Lindy glanced at her pack, uncertain what to do.

Ransom rose, stepped over to it and swung it onto his back.

There were no more words. Lindy looked in his eyes. It was really goodbye. She listened to the drone mount, Doug Hurley coming to bear her back from the dead. Then hopeless and drained, she followed Ransom through the doorway and along the footpath.

It was an aisle of color, the dwarf birch blazing orange, the potentilla iridescent peach and carmine, with scarlet dogwood studding cushions of burgundy moss. When they arrived at the strip, Doug was cutting the engine and climbing out. He seemed relieved to see them, but his attention was mostly downriver. Clouds were massing there, leaden mushrooms with steely caps. His lips moved silently, like a schoolboy doing math in his head.

Ransom set Lindy's pack down, his face tense and determined. "Doug's in a hurry." He kissed her quickly.

She looked confused.

He put his fingers over her heart. "In the silence, I'll be there." Then he turned and started back down the path.

309

Doug was striding toward them. "You want a pickup?" he shouted. Ransom didn't turn. Doug faced Lindy with a mystified look. "What was that about?"

As soon as he was out of their sight, Ransom began to run. When he reached the cabin, he went straight to his pack and unloaded his regalia with shaking hands. He set his cuffs and headdress on the floor beside the furs, with the willow knife and blue jar directly before him, and began to chant. His voice froze as the Cub's engine fired to life. For a long moment, he held himself perfectly still. Then he burst into tears and ran back outside.

The small plane was dragging itself over the bumpy strip like a lame bird. He ran to the edge of the brush as it climbed, waving both arms, whether to halt their departure or in anguished farewell, he didn't know. The plane had already passed. It followed the river without lifting, flying just above the treetops. The steely caps had merged and were creeping up the drainage. It seemed like the Cub would have to turn back, but at the last moment, it slipped beneath them and disappeared.

Fourteen

It rained on the Cheshnina for five days. Just before dawn on the morning of the sixth, the sky turned apocalyptic. Arrows of diaphanous cloud lined either side of the valley and moved toward each other, engaging over the river bar, the serried ranks clashing with dizzying effect. It would have been a sign of great moment, but no human observed it and the juncos pecking at the border of the landing strip didn't notice.

At the end of the trail through the dwarf birch, Wasilla Bill's cabin stood quiet in the dimness, with the door open. No one was inside, but a few things had changed. Ransom's possessions were gathered by the table, clothes folded, equipment and instruments covered with a shirt. The place had been left clean, but mice, always quick to sense a vacancy, had savaged the food shelf. The remains lay scattered across the floor. On the tabletop was a loose-leaf manuscript and a reel of recording tape.

That same morning, bare feet hurried down the gravel path from the Hurley's guest house. The sallowing willows were motionless in the mist, leaf sprays frozen like fossils in stone. "Ransom," Lindy whispered. "Ransom." Above, a magpie glided silently through the trees.

Inside the Hurley bedroom, the noise penetrated Ida's sleep. She rolled onto her hip and reached for her husband, finding his shoulder, drawing herself closer. He turned instinctively, burrowing in her embrace like a bear in a cave.

"Ransom," Lindy's voice sobbed.

Ida drew herself up with her hand on Doug's chest as if to prevent the disturbance from reaching him. He frowned, turned his ear and opened his eyes. The sobbing grew louder. He sat up.

"The storm's close." He shook his head sadly.

She touched her breast to his arm and stroked his cheek. He sighed and faced her, finding relief in her eyes.

"What time is it?"

She stood and clicked on the dresser lamp. "Six-thirty."

"It's supposed to hit by noon."

She nodded.

Lindy knocked on the front door.

Doug stood and drew his pants on. Ida handed him his shirt.

"What can I do?" he said, bereft.

Lindy was pounding on the door now, sobbing hysterically.

"Poor girl," Ida murmured. Tragedy hovered over them, but she smiled at her husband, unwilling to deny the joy and desire she felt. She faced the Bible on the dresser, then set her trembling hand on it.

Doug gave her a wondering look.

Ida's lips crinkled, succumbing to tears. "Death will be a triumph for him."

———◆———

My legs are inexhaustible. I vault over the crusted snow, the slopes around me blurred by jolts, feeling you heaving beneath me, raging and impatient. Above, the sky's canopy rocks. Below, everything is obscured by smoke. The pack is nowhere in sight.

The moment approaches. Will you show yourself? I confess, I'm afraid. Is my weakness galling? Is your rage rooted in desire? My hooves crash through the sastrugi. Ahead, a dark pyramid of rock rises, veils streaming from its face. Then the crater rim lifts—the sanctum, your throne! I'm galloping to meet you, powdered and glittering, hooves and horns polished, white fur woven with crystal thread.

Dear god, don't deny me!

The dome jerks and grinds, whipping my spine and wrenching my stride. A sharp pain and the wound splits, scarlet within, dripping pearls of fresh blood.

Appear! I won't slow and I'm not turning back!

Cracks ray from the crater, fences of fire rising between blue walls—three molten arteries, glowing red. Feverish groans, throaty salvos! Magma lands on the snows with steaming gasps. Is this really you? Let your dam burst! Drown me with your flowing heart! Ahead, the red fences converge at the place we are to meet, high on the rim.

But you're shuddering back, doubts surfacing, tentative with injury and regrets. I spur my hinds, thrusting hard where snow meets rock, fores reaching high, feeling a pulling in my chest. I know, I don't have to look. The wind chants, the crater is hot to my hooves! My confidence soars as the dome quakes! I'm lunging mightily, steam eeling from a hundred holes, blood ribbons trailing back. My left pectoral is gaping, the wound gushing, heart beating madly, straining to push through its broken bars. The blood pulses from my chest in time to the quakes! The dome—it's

my own white body. And the god pounding is pounding within—
the throb of my own molten heart.

I breathe sulphur, throat searing, eyes crying, senses swimming as the quaking tears my hoofbeats apart. Louder, faster! The tremors take me over, driving my thrusts, fears conquered, hurtling me forward with all my heart. The god is here, in my shaking frame! I feel you, Animus, mad with my offering, frantic, lurching me fiercely, wind huffing giantly, my blood-soaked fores raking the rock as I lunge onto the crest.

Pieces of the crater appear through the steam, dark crescents connecting, linked together in a black ring. I'm on an overhanging jut, rearing on my hinds, gazing into a seething cauldron a hundred lengths deep. Within, congeries of pillars coiled in fumes, obelisks and meltpits, half-eaten slabs swimming in haze. Vapors perforate the snow, chugging furiously, vents sleeving up and down their jets as the crater heaves. Where the rifts have torn the ring, lava spews onto the ice, hissing and meeting in a heaving place webbed with cracks.

On my left, dark shapes bounding! The Lead charges around the crater rim with long strides and fierce eyes, the Wise right behind, her sharp face aimed, gaze unflinching. Brave creatures, still with me, together to the end— A mammoth lurch, the crater tips toward me like a circle of fate, rending screams rising from the cracks below. A bass groan and the snow-covered plates open like giant doors. I leap as the crater explodes, seeing the red nose, hot and gushing beneath me.

A pillar of glowing magma catches me on its spout. For an instant, I'm juggled, feeling the liquid boiling against my belly and sides. I writhe, limbs smoking, flesh bubbling and sliding, *a fluttering sound as my ears clog and melt. Through blazing eyes, I see the wolves lunge, reaching me as the fountain pulses higher, jaws biting from either side, fangs driving in. With a thunderous snarl, they tear the ram from me like a robe, revealing the naked god beneath, flowing and molten.*

I'm the one roaring, it's my power letting loose! The violence is mine! I am this fountain, this torrent jetting skyward, this tower of blood reaching heaven high! Another pulse inside the first, and another still. My glory reigns, and I never come down. My sweet child, you've surrendered. You see I am here, melting you into me, taking you back. You drown in my roar, screaming and weeping, laughing inside me as you bobble and melt. All of you, down to that wriggling little heart, that glowing worm. I gave you life. I am the blood of the cosmos, the boost everything craves. Mounting detonations, wild exclamations, my deafening roar! I'm the center of your being, your deepest feeling, the headwaters of your heart. I am Animus, fresh and glowing, foaming and flaming, dissolving and growing, fire to matter, the batter of bliss. What mortal dream—stranded, winking its last, arcing and coasting down and down—could be more than this?